R. GUALTIERI

MIDNITE'S DAUGHTER

Edited by Megan Harris at
WWW.MHARRISEDITOR.COM

Cover by Orina Kafe at
ORINAKAFEDIGITALART.WIXSITE.COM

Proofread by BZ Hercules at
WWW.BZHERCULES.COM

Published by Westmarch Publishing
WWW.WESTMARCHPUB.COM

ISBN: 978-1975941031

Special thanks to Annette Marie for tolerating my constant questions, and providing so much helpful feedback. And, as always, a big thanks to my awesome beta and ARC crew.

AUTHOR'S NOTE

Welcome to a story that's a bit of a departure for me. Even when writing humor, I typically like to dwell in dark places where terrible things happen to undeserving people … and sometimes to those who very much deserve it.

But for this tale you are about to read, I have stepped firmly into the realm of fantasy. Now, this doesn't mean horrible things won't happen, or that there won't be those who meet it with some catchy snark escaping their lips. Quite the contrary. However, rather than draw from western horror, I instead took inspiration from the Japanese art of manga, as well as its cartoon counterpart – anime.

What can I say? I've always had a soft spot for larger-than-life heroes and villains, especially those who like to scream out the names of their attacks before letting loose with an energy blast powerful enough to shatter a mountain. But it's not just the fantastic aspect of it. Quirky and likeable characters abound in this medium. And ultimately the deciding factor almost always comes down to their friendships and strong relationships to one another.

My hope was to take that inspiration, mash it up with a bit of urban fantasy, and come up with mythology and characters that are both fantastical and lots of fun.

I sincerely hope I have succeeded.

PROLOGUE

THE ORDER OF the heavens is a known quantity. Established when the elder gods defeated the entropic chaos that threatened to destroy this nascent universe, the cycle has stood for as long as the stars have shined down upon us and, if dictated, will continue until those very stars burn out.

At the very bottom of the order, non-divine beings such as humans scurry about, living their short lives. They create but the barest blip upon the face of the universe and then they are gone, their energy dissipating until they are reborn to do so again.

Youkai, the least of the divine, walk among these lesser races, sometimes preying upon them, sometimes being preyed upon. They represent balance – order versus the chaos that forever threatens to return – sometimes serving their masters' whims, sometimes serving their own. Many imagine themselves to be powerful, but then so, too, does a mouse alone in a field of grain until a wolf catches its scent.

The mazoku and oni stand above them in the celestial order, tasked with the upkeep of the heavens, the casting of judgment, and delivering boon and bane alike against mankind whenever such is needed – a flood to punish an arrogant warlord, a tornado as warning against insufficient tribute, a field of flowers for a pious child with an appreciation for beauty.

Strongest among demonkind are the daimao. We are the custodians of the multiverse, serving in the stead of the gods, who now slumber within the confines of the celestial palace, deep within the vast island in the sky upon which it rests.

The gods are cared for meticulously, so their rest remains undisturbed for all of eternity. It has been a necessity since the order of the heavens was established. Their power is such that even the barest of coughs from one is enough to snuff out an entire civilization. Whole worlds have perished from something as seemingly insignificant as an elder god doing little more than the equivalent of stretching their limbs.

It is said their dreams influence the palace, sending it to new worlds as their whims demand.

So it was that we came to Earth, hovering far above this world, yet always a moment out of sync so as to remain unseen. And here we have stayed, for over five thousand of its inhabitants' years, sometimes interacting, sometimes influencing, but always watching ... eternally wondering why the elder gods have brought us here, what they see in this otherwise unremarkable world.

Though beneath our masters, my people often sleep alongside them. Our power makes us dangerous to lesser beings, such as mankind. My brothers have been known to wipe out cities for the most minor of slights and raze villages for little more than base amusement.

Though lesser demons are openly envious of our power, it is only because of their own ignorance. If they knew better, they would cease their petty jealousy, for we long ago grew bored with this world much as a child quickly tires of watching an anthill.

Those who have seen what we can do call us uncaring, but that is not so. Though we would not wish it known among lesser beings, we are susceptible to the same whims as they are: anger, envy, boredom, happiness, and even love.

It is that latter which caused me to stray from the path of my people, to betray their covenant, and protect my child.

But that very act also opened my eyes. For where once I thought the ability to shape worlds to be the ultimate power, I now know better. Indeed, I once thought the elder gods slept because, like us, they were bored. But I now believe that they do so out of that simplest of emotions – love. They love this universe but realize they also have the power to destroy it. As such, they have locked themselves away in a living death rather than betray that which they love.

It is a lesson I wish I had learned sooner. If so, perhaps I would not have allowed my curiosity to get the better of me. I would not have given in to the base desires that commanded me. And I would not have borne the child whose very existence came to threaten the eternal cycle of the heavens.

1945

ONE

THE DAIMAO WERE revered as war gods. This was not without merit for, in the early days of the universe, they had acted as the enforcers of the elder gods, their foot soldiers in the crusade to bring order from the entropic chaos that existed before.

Though that was untold ages past and many generations removed, the instinct for battle still remained in their blood, much how a domesticated dog might still howl at the moon, even if it can't remember why it is doing so.

So it was that Midnite awoke for the first time in three hundred years, drawn out of her slumber by a deep resonance within her bones that told her battle was afoot. It had been some time since anything of note had happened. The constant warring of the humans who lived upon the islands blessed by her kind had been amusing for a time, but soon grew tiresome. Mankind was a dedicated race when it came to slaughtering one another, but they seemingly lacked the creativity to be more clever about it.

Watching the same battle unfold time and again under different warlords quickly became uninteresting and, when it did, Midnite pulled back from the world so as to sleep, much like her brothers. In doing so, they dreamt, allowing their astral forms to visit myriad worlds and races, many of whom were far more interesting than those of Earth.

Something had changed, however. Midnite's servants had noted that her sleep had been fitful this past century, but there had been no occurrences significant enough to wake her … until now.

One such servant raced to his mistress's side, wanting to be there when she rose so as to ensure her needs were tended to and her mood was pleasant.

Though Midnite was perhaps the most even-tempered of her siblings, it was well known among the many denizens of the celestial palace that it was never a good idea to allow a daimao to remain in an ill mood for long.

"Mmm," Midnite purred as she stretched. The sheets of mist and flame that covered her slid down her body, revealing her flawless alabaster skin. "Shitoro, is my…"

"I am here, my mistress," the diminutive youkai replied eagerly, his head barely visible above the clouds that made up the mattress of Midnite's bed. "I have your robe, and a bath has been drawn and is awaiting you."

Midnite smiled and sat up. Shitoro had always done his best to make her happy, ever since she'd rescued him from a band of human hunters some fourteen hundred years earlier. The truth of the matter was, she found him to be adorably cute, but being that he was a tiger demon, albeit of much smaller stature than normal, she would never have insulted him by saying so. "I see my mighty guardian has been watching over me."

"Now and always," he replied proudly.

Midnite stretched again and yawned. "How long?"

"The barest of moments in the cosmos. One such as you would barely have time to blink in the…"

"How long, Shitoro?" Midnite asked impatiently. Though she was dearly fond of him, he could get caught up in the pomp and circumstance of his station from time to time.

"Three hundred and twenty-four years, by human standards."

Midnite nodded absentmindedly. The daimao were a timeless race, the birth and death of stars barely a heartbeat for them. So there was some irony in relying upon the methods of such a low species to delineate its passage.

"Hmm," she grunted, swinging her long legs out from under the sheets. It was, she noted, just barely a long enough nap for her to feel refreshed, but refreshed she was.

That wasn't all, though. Along with a sense of being fully awake, there was something else, something deeper – an anxiousness in her bones that she hadn't felt in a long time. Had something at long last changed in the world of man?

She reached out with her senses, probing. Yes, they were still near Earth. She'd have sensed the residual energy had the palace moved elsewhere in the universe.

Pity. It would be a welcome change.

Mankind had long since grown repetitively dull, so she wasn't certain exactly what kind of disturbance from below could have possibly awoken her so abruptly.

"The planet hasn't exploded, has it, Shitoro?"

Her servant raised one eyebrow. "Not to the best of my knowledge, mistress."

Midnite stood, excess divine energy crackling off her body. Whatever it was she felt, she doubted it couldn't wait for a steaming hot bath. Shitoro, ever vigilant, could fill her in while she enjoyed the feel of the boiling spring against her skin.

She allowed him to lead her to the bath, all while reaching out with her senses to the endless corridors of the palace. It didn't take her long to realize she wasn't alone. A few of her siblings were awake, too. Most were still slumbering, but even they were beginning to stir. Curious indeed. Had she alone woken up, she would have dismissed it as a quirk, bathed, and then perhaps returned to her bed.

If the others were waking up, though, then something was indeed happening. Midnite allowed herself a small grin at the thought. It had been dreadfully dull for so long. Perhaps the humans had finally become clever enough to catch their attention again.

Once she was nestled in her bath, she lay back and enjoyed herself, closing her eyes and slipping beneath the holy waters of the palace, enjoying the feel as it reinvigorated her senses and made the tiny horns on her head tingle.

After a time, when she felt she had soaked long enough, she turned to Shitoro. "Do you know the cause of our awakening, my friend?"

"Oh, that?" he asked dismissively. "Just another war between the humans. Nothing more. You know their kind. Can't even go a decade without slaughtering each other for sport."

"Nothing more? Are you certain? I sincerely doubt some petty feud over water rights or arable land would have caused me to stir." After a moment, she added, "Nor would it have awoken my siblings."

Rather than answer, Shitoro did his best to look busy straightening towels, making sure the right amount of candles were lit, ensuring that the scalding water was the proper temperature – anything to seemingly avoid meeting his mistress's gaze.

Midnite smiled at his backside. He truly was the most loyal of servants, but he was easily the poorest liar in the palace.

"What about the world of man bothers you?" she asked.

This seemed to catch the diminutive demon by surprise. "The outside world, my lady? Oh, that?" Midnite raised an eyebrow. Before she could prod him, he continued. "You may be surprised by the humans, mistress. They have … changed. Their methods of waging war have evolved significantly, especially in the last half century."

"Oh?" she replied lazily, her attention once more focusing on the soothing way the roiling water lapped against her skin. It was almost enough to make her want to doze off again. "Tell me, do they no longer use ships?"

"Yes, but they…"

"What about chariots? Have those, too, been discarded?"

"They have changed a bit, but…"

"Have the humans perhaps sprouted wings to take to the air?"

"Not exactly."

"Then I do not see how different it could possibly be." She closed her eyes and tried to lose herself in the comforting feel of the water against her body.

Despite her dismissive attitude, though, she couldn't quite shake the feeling that something had indeed changed. Perhaps she'd been too quick to scoff at Shitoro. Alas, it would be beneath her station to apologize to a servant.

Some things simply were not done.

Once Midnite had bathed, she made her way back so as to dress. Despite her boredom with mankind, it had been too long since she'd felt grass beneath her feet, enjoyed the smell of the wind as it carried through the fields. Her intent was to visit the blessed islands of the small world far below. Certainly a little time away from the palace would ease the odd calling inside of her.

She entered her audience chamber, planning on passing straight through, then stopped short as her breath caught. The entire room was filled with wind lilies, all of them in hand-carved vases of the finest jade. They were her favorite because, when in bloom, their scent was that of the night sky right after a storm. They were very rare, only growing in a small corner of a distant world at the far reaches of the stars. Only a few knew of their existence, and fewer still knew of her love for them.

Still, she repressed the whoop of delight she wanted to let loose. If these were here, then that meant someone had invaded her private chambers while she slept. It couldn't have been Shitoro or any of her other servants. Though they could have used the crystals to travel such a distance, they would not have done so without her permission, even knowing it would please their mistress.

"Shitoro!"

She waited patiently for him to answer, her annoyance warring with a desire to breathe in the clean scent of the flowers. She was just about to call for him again, something that would certainly ignite her ire, when he answered sheepishly from behind her. "Yes ... m-my lady?"

From the way he stuttered, she immediately realized her mistake from earlier. Shitoro hadn't been nervous about her questioning the state of the outside world. There had been something else bothering him. Midnite suspected what it was, but she wanted to hear it from him. "Who?"

"Who?" he repeated, drawing an annoyed sigh from her.

"Who placed these here? Was it you?"

"I ... helped arrange them, my lady."

"If I wished to know that, I would have asked." She put just enough steel into her voice to break the little tiger youkai's nerve.

Almost as if on cue, he blurted out, "It was Ichitiro! He brought the flowers."

Midnite closed her eyes and silently cursed in annoyance. Of course it was him. Who else would be so bold? Which of her other brothers would be so bull-headed as to refuse to take no for an answer? "And you let him in?" She turned to find the small demon sweating profusely. "Well?"

"After some … *persuasion* on his part, mistress."

Midnite didn't need to ask what that meant. Ichitiro was another of the daimao. Her older brother, as a matter of fact. He was perhaps the most fearsome warrior to ever grace the multiverse, living to fight, excelling at battle. He was also a petty bully, prone to tantrums when he didn't get his way, and not afraid to use violence as a means to an end.

Her heart immediately went out to Shitoro. She had little doubt he did his utmost best to bar the way, but it was a battle he'd never stood a chance at winning. Ichitiro outranked and outclassed him in every aspect imaginable.

No, that wasn't quite true. Shitoro was kind where her brother was cruel. He was considerate where the ancient demon was selfish. Also, Midnite much preferred the visage of her little servant to that of her sibling. Ichitiro may have been powerful, but she found him repulsive to look at.

Nevertheless, that hadn't stopped him from taking a shine to her. At some point in the last millennia, he'd decided they should be mated. It wasn't unheard of among the daimao, and a pairing of powerful demons made for powerful offspring.

"Think of our future children," he had once told her, lust in his greedy eyes. "They will be an unstoppable army, pouring forth across this world. We will enact the will of our masters through them, forcing any who oppose us to their knees."

Love, tenderness, even base compatibility; these things meant nothing to Ichitiro. He had his own twisted interpretation of the will of the elder gods and was not to be dissuaded – not by his siblings, and certainly not by lesser beings.

No matter what empty flatteries he told her, she knew what he really wanted. Had she consented, he might've enjoyed her body, but she had no doubt it was a secondary prize to him compared to the Taiyosori – the blade of heaven, the sword of a thousand deadly cuts.

She let her eyes rise above the flowers to where the sword hung in midair above her throne, seeming to guard the way to her bedchamber beyond. If one were to study the weapon, one would quickly notice the notched blade, perhaps the sharpest edge in the entire universe, was semi-transparent. Inside appeared to be a universe of its own, full of swirling galaxies and twinkling stars. It truly was a marvel to behold, even among beings who had seen the births and deaths of worlds.

Midnite had purposely placed it there to vex her would-be suitor, both as a reminder of what he could not have, as well as knowing it angered him to see such a formidable weapon relegated to a mere decoration.

However, it was hers and hers alone to do with as she pleased. The Taiyosori had been gifted to her by the elder gods themselves. She thought back to the day it was first given to her, so many eons ago. Such a strange moment, cloaked in more questions than she had answers to. It was an experience she had never forgotten, one which was impossible to fully explain to her siblings, save for the knowledge that one of the gods had reached out and bequeathed it to her.

She found herself wondering how long Ichitiro had stood here, after forcing his way in, staring at the sword, debating whether to try and take it.

Midnite barked out a chord of laughter at the thought.

The elder daimao was a bully, but he was no fool. As much as he lusted after the weapon, he knew it would reject him as surely as she had. The blade would not acknowledge a thief as its master. It could be inherited, gifted, or won in honorable combat, but not stolen. Unfortunately, it could also be claimed through the union of two beings, their souls forged as one. Therein lay Ichitiro's hope, a hope that she had no inclination to ever grace with anything remotely resembling serious consideration.

Continued thoughts of her brother angered Midnite, stealing from her the sense of ease she'd gotten from her long bath. These flowers, beautiful as they might be, were tainted. They would bring her no enjoyment, so she saw no need for them to remind her of the lout. With a wave of her hand, the wind lilies all burst into blue flame, burning nearly as hot as a star for a scant second, until not even ashes remained.

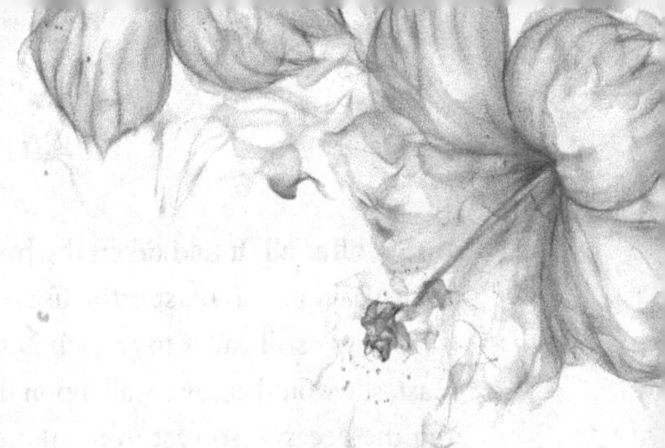

TWO

"HOW DO I look, Shitoro?"

"As exquisite as the full moon on a clear night. As majestic as all the stars that have ever shined in the sky. As…"

She silenced him with a wave of her hand, suppressing the grin that threatened to blunt her bad mood. She hadn't been going for regal. If anything, she had been hoping for plain, nondescript.

Partially to help erase the shadow that Ichitiro had cast upon her day, but mostly out of curiosity as to the cause of her awakening, she decided to pay a visit to the planet below. Even if there was a petty war afoot, it might serve as a temporary distraction.

Her people were attuned to war, having once – long ago – served as the generals and taskmasters of the elder gods. Though those days were long past, her people could still sense upheaval. Oftentimes, it was minor, barely a blip in their subconscious. On rare occasion, however, something occurred that was significant enough to wake the great demons from their slumber.

Nevertheless, Midnite found it hard to believe that anything of true importance had occurred. It had barely been three centuries, after all. It had taken the humans a good thousand of their years just to master the use of fire alone.

She was still eager to stretch her legs, though. At the very least, she would enjoy a walk upon the white beaches overlooking the ocean – so vast to mankind, yet so small to her own perception. Perhaps a stroll through the waist-high grass of a field as well, enjoying the feel of the sun on her skin. Yes, that would please her.

Though in the past, the daimao had appeared to mankind in all their glory – inspiring fear, awe, and worship – it was occasionally desired to put forth a less intimidating presence so as to more closely observe them scurrying about in their short lives. Some daimao, such as Ichitiro, would never deem to lower themselves that way, considering themselves above such folly, but Midnite and her less warlike siblings occasionally enjoyed such forays.

She opted for such today, donning the clothing of a simple peasant girl and willing all of her divine markings hidden. To the uninitiated, she would appear as nothing more than a simple, if stunningly beautiful, woman in her mid-twenties.

"When shall I expect your return, mistress?" Shitoro asked.

"Why, whenever it pleases me to return, my servant."

Shitoro turned a shade whiter and added, "I do not wish to pry, my lady. It is simply so that I may have another bath waiting for you. The world of man is so … dirty at times."

This time, Midnite allowed herself to laugh. The little tiger demon was always masking his concern for her with some mundane task. Fine. If it would keep him from pulling the hair from his paws with worry. "A day at most, I should think. I wish to enjoy the sun, but I have always enjoyed gazing at the stars, too. Draw a bath for me come the morning." Time passed differently on Earth than in the celestial realm, but it would still afford her a goodly visit before he began to fret.

"It shall be done," the little demon replied, visibly mollified.

Midnite smiled, then eyed the rows of shimmering crystals along the wall of the summoning chamber. A tiny bit of daimao life force filled each. Though youkai such as Shitoro could not make the journey under their own power, the crystals allowed them to do so. A little bit of their master's power, so that they might venture out as needed or directed.

Despite his fear of displeasing her and his perhaps even greater fear of the world below, Midnite had little doubt that, should she be late in returning, Shitoro would come looking for her. Others of her kind might have found such a thing to be tiresome, but she considered it an endearing trait.

Good intentions aside, though, if that happened, he was bound to end up in some trouble or another. A full-sized tiger was something most humans avoided. A tiny one, somewhat less so. She made it a point to mind the hours so as to spare either of them such an ordeal.

With that, Midnite raised her hand and began to summon the cosmic energies needed to make the journey, preparing to transfer her essence to the small blue world below and the islands her people favored above all others.

"Be careful, my mistress," Shitoro said.

And then she was gone.

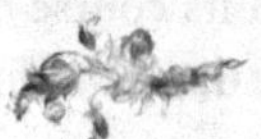

Midnite expected to appear upon a calm beach on her favorite of the blessed isles. Though she knew the inhabitants had a name for this land, she had never bothered to learn it. It was simply her preferred spot upon the Earth, a place where she could enjoy the wind in her hair and the fresh smell of the salty sea air.

What she did not expect was to arrive in the middle of Hell. Wind and rain pummeled her, but despite the weather, smoke hung thick in the air. Though she had no need to, she took a breath and coughed, the odor of sulfur heavy upon it. She knew that scent. It was the smell of war itself.

As she took in her surroundings, she noticed the bodies lying upon the scarred and pitted remains of what was once a place of serenity. Scorched and blackened, some of them lay in pieces, and many had strange wounds upon them.

Though a part of her was aghast at what she saw, excitement quickly overcame it. She was no stranger to the battlefield, having looked down upon the dead and dying many a time, but this was new. Though some of the fallen had obviously taken their own lives via ceremonial blades, many more had not. Yet there were no signs of arrow or sword wounds upon those who hadn't. It was as if the fires of heaven itself had descended and wrought its vengeance upon them. But that was silly. She would have known had that happened.

Strange, she thought. *Strange, yet exhilarating.* Perhaps there was a reason she and her siblings had been roused after all.

An unfamiliar noise came from overhead, a bizarre whistling roar. She glanced up to see the oddest bird she had ever seen swoop past overhead. Some kind of oni, perhaps – one with strange metallic skin and bright red markings on its wings.

No. It didn't move like anything natural, at least that she'd ever seen. She followed its course out over the ocean and her breath caught in her throat. At first, she thought she was looking at whole islands made of iron just off the shore, but then she realized her mistake. She'd seen human ships before, feeble fragile things that they used to cross the seas, explore, and – of course – wage war on one another, but never anything like this.

They were like mountains of steel upon the water, mountains from which thunder now sounded. Smoke and fire came from the top of the ships, and a sense of familiarity hit home. She remembered seeing cannon fire, primitive and cumbersome weapons, but curious as they brought a new element to the battlefield. This reminded her of it, but many times more devastating.

She watched as the strange metallic creature in the sky caught fire. Bits and pieces of it were blown off until finally it slammed into the ocean at tremendous speed, exploding upon contact.

It seemed impossible, but her senses told her the flying creature wasn't alive. It wasn't anything natural to this world, even with all its wonders. Could it be? Yes. It had to be some kind of craft, a ship of the air.

Unbelievable.

After countless centuries of the same thing, over and over again, this was all new. How had the humans come so far in so little time? Had something helped them? Had some divine force gifted them with this knowledge?

She initially suspected Ichitiro's hand in this. If there was one daimao who would wish to see the art of war increased to such a level among the humans, it was he, but she quickly dismissed it. No. Her brother was far too stupid and self-absorbed. This was beyond him.

A chill ran through her as she continued to watch, slowly realizing these vehicles of war were potentially beyond what any of her siblings might be capable of building.

The weaponry on display was awe-inspiring. It almost brought a tear of joy to her eye to behold. Such might wielded by such small, insignificant beings. They were still nothing individually, but housed in such iron titans as now rode the rough waves before her, they could potentially overcome that weakness. Though she still hadn't seen anything on par with the worst a daimao such as herself could wrought, surely even a mazoku would have to give pause before such a sight.

The wind buffeted her as she watched, but she paid it no mind. The storm was nothing to her. She felt no chill beneath the rain, nor discomfort as her simple dress billowed around her like a flag in a breeze.

She might have stood there for the entire day, staring at the spectacle unfolding before her, drinking it in as one who has been parched for too long might guzzle water. But then she was roused by a loud noise – another roar of thunder like that which came from the ships, but smaller and much closer.

Her keen senses picked up the whine of something small cutting through the air as it raced toward her, quick as a lightning bolt. Time slowed around her as she focused on the source, a small capsule of metal flying in her direction. Curious. Again she was reminded of cannon fire, but this time it was much smaller.

The bullet – although she didn't know it was called that – slammed into her midsection, barely an insect sting to the ancient creature. The hole it created in her flesh sealed itself almost immediately, although, she rued, it did leave an unfortunate tear in her dress.

"What in holy hell?"

"Hah, you missed."

"Fuck you."

She turned toward the sound of the voices. Two humans wearing uniforms of drab green were advancing upon her, pointing what looked to be hollow sticks in her direction. Though their words were alien to her at first, her advanced mind quickly made sense of the chattering that was their primitive tongue. Though a human would most likely drown in its own blood before mastering the celestial tongue, their many languages – crude as they were – were easily learned by her.

Though she didn't quite understand what she was being called, she perfectly grasped the meaning when one of them stepped forward and said, "Move a muscle and I'll blow your Jap face clean off."

THREE

"ITHOUGHT THE captain said the beach was clear."

"That stupid son of a bitch wouldn't know if his nose was clear."

"Don't let him hear you say that."

"Do I look stupid?"

"You want an answer to that?" The human male glanced back toward Midnite. "Hey! I said don't move!"

Midnite found their banter amusing as she did their hostile, if ignorant, intentions toward her. Her guise had worked. These humans had no idea as to whom they were speaking so impudently.

"What do you think?" the second asked the first.

"I don't know. Most of the locals have been committing that hari kari bullshit. Maybe she was too chicken."

"Understand what he's saying?" the second asked her with a laugh. "Of course you don't, you stupid Nip." He began flapping his arms up and down, making "buck buck buck" sounds.

Midnite raised an eyebrow. Curious, indeed.

"Hey, hold on," the first said. "A buddy of mine in the 6th said he'd heard they're using women and children as kamikazes now."

"She ain't in a Zero."

"I know that, stupid. They're strapping bombs to them and using them to blow up tanks."

"Son of a bitch, really?"

"Yeah. I don't know about you, but I ain't taking her back to camp until I know for certain." He focused on Midnite again and raised the hollow stick he'd been pointing at her. "Strip."

Strip? Certainly he doesn't mean...

"She doesn't understand you."

The first narrowed his gaze. "Well, she'd better learn to understand real quick. Otherwise, I'm putting a bullet in one of her slant eyes. Besides, look at her. I ain't ever seen Jap tits before. What do you think they look like?"

The second grinned even wider. "I don't know, but I wouldn't mind finding out." He turned back toward Midnite and mimed taking off his shirt. "Come on, let's go! Move it!"

Midnite felt a sting of irritation beginning to worm through her gut. These men, it would seem, might dress differently than the humans she remembered, but at their core, they were the same as always, driven by base urges. How disappointingly dull.

"Hey," the second asked his friend, "are you thinking what I am?"

He laughed. "That we might have to *thoroughly* search her for weapons?"

"Yeah. Who knows where she's got it stuffed?"

"What do you think about that?" the first asked her, moving a hand to his crotch. "I lost buddies at Pearl. Thinking we might be due some payback."

Midnite was rapidly tiring of their threats. She cracked the knuckles of her right hand, preparing to remind them of their station in the grand scheme of the cosmos, when a different voice spoke up.

"Hey! What are you two doing?"

Another man, dressed similarly but slightly different to the first two, came marching over.

"Huh?" the first grunted, then turned. For a moment, he kept his weapon – or at least that was what Midnite presumed it to be – trained, then he quickly lowered it. "Oh, sorry … lieutenant. Didn't see you there, sir."

He and his friend both raised their hands to their heads in some sort of salute.

"I asked a question," the newcomer said.

"We were just taking this woman prisoner, sir," the second replied.

"Didn't sound like that to me."

"We wanted to check to make sure she wasn't armed. My buddy…"

"Your buddy ain't here," the third man snapped. "I am, and I don't like what I was hearing."

"C'mon, sir. It's not like it would matter. You know how these Nips are. I'd sooner kick one than a dog."

Midnite stayed her hand. The once boring discourse had become interesting again.

The third man, obviously some sort of superior, stepped up and glared at the first two. "It matters because we're better than that."

"You know they'd do it to one of ours."

"So you're saying you're not any better than they are? Get your asses back to your squad before I have them handed to you."

The second saluted, but the first looked reluctant to do so. He said, "With all due respect, sir, you army grunts can't just…"

"Do you want to test that, soldier? Because, if so, I will look forward to seeing your ass in irons before the day is out."

The threat was enough to cause the first to back down. He lowered his gaze and shook his head.

"What was that?" the newcomer asked.

"I said no, sir."

"That's what I thought. Now double time it and maybe I'll forget what you two look like."

The two men immediately broke off and ran back in the direction they'd come from. Once they were gone, the third turned to her. When he spoke, it was in a different dialect ... somewhat similar to the language she had heard the local population use in centuries past. "My apologies if those men frightened you."

His voice was choppy, broken. Obviously, he was attempting to speak in a tongue not entirely familiar to him. Midnite was not surprised. She knew the humans possessed myriad dialects even within the blessed isles. Outside, the differences only grew, and his look told her he was definitely from elsewhere. Nevertheless, she was impressed. She was familiar with the concept of chivalry, although many humans ignored it – even those who professed to be champions of it. For a human warrior, for that was what this man obviously was, to rise above his base impulses was rare indeed.

She decided to honor him by answering in the language he had originally used. "My thanks to you."

The man's eyes opened wide. "Wait, you speak English?"

So that was what they called it. Such an odd name. Regardless, it was an uncomplicated tongue for one such as her to master. "Yes." His surprise was evident, so Midnite thought it best to keep up her guise with a simple lie. "I speak many languages. My ... father was a learned man. A scholar." Hopefully, the humans still had such a concept after all this time.

The man's eyes grew suspicious. "Could be. Or could be you're a spy."

Midnite repressed a chuckle. This human was far less brutish than his peers had been, but he was still a warrior. If pushed the wrong way, he would certainly revert to his baser instincts. It normally wouldn't matter to her. It wasn't like he could even hope to harm her. Yet, oddly enough, she found him intriguing. Perhaps it was his behavior. Or maybe it was his appearance, with hair and eyes much lighter in appearance than those native to this blessed land.

Whatever the cause, she attempted to diffuse the situation. Looking around at the bodies lying all about, she said, "Were I a spy, who would be left to report my findings to?"

"Fair enough. But then, what are you doing here?"

An apt question. This human had the spark of intelligence about him. Midnite found herself growing more intrigued by the moment.

The rain had started to slacken, so she turned to the ocean, again marveling at the armada before her, like nothing she had ever seen before. "I used to come here during more peaceful times. It was a place of comfort for me."

The man raised an eyebrow questioningly but nodded all the same. "I can understand better times. There's a lake back where I live. The fishing is lousy, but there's nothing like casting a line and letting the current take it while you relax under a tree." He shook his head, as if not wishing to succumb to the memory. "That's far away, though, and nobody ever took a shot at me there. You're taking a hell of a risk just for a view."

"Some things are worth the risk."

"I have to ask, are you with the Jap … imperial army?"

Midnite turned to face him, locking her eyes with his. They were the windows to one's soul and she could see a strong spirit in his – brave and bold, yet lacking the petty brutishness of Ichitiro. "I serve no army and I acknowledge no emperor upon this plane."

"Do you live here, have family close by?"

Midnite contemplated telling the truth or a form of it that this human might understand, but she didn't want to arouse his suspicions more than they already were. However, in the back of her mind, that word *arouse* stuck for a moment longer than it should have. How odd. She normally considered humans to be sub-creatures. Despite it being common for youkai or mazoku to take human lovers, and even her siblings occasionally doing so, she'd never found them more interesting than perhaps as pets.

After a moment, she realized he was staring hard at her, so she answered a half truth. "I live in a village not too far from here, but I have no family left there."

"Are they dead?" he asked. "Or conscripted?"

Midnite simply stared, allowing him to form his own conclusion lest she say too much. The longer she spoke to this man, the more she found herself losing her calm demeanor. How very unbecoming of her.

"I'm sorry," he finally said. "My name is Steve … err … lieutenant Stephen Fuller. I'm with the 77th."

"Stephen Fuller," she said, tasting the words on her tongue. "My name is … it translates to Midnite in your language."

"Midnight? Like the time of day?"

"So I have heard."

"That's very unusual. Not particularly Japanese."

"Japanese?" she asked softly. She couldn't recall hearing that word before. Perhaps it was one of the many names the humans used for these islands. "No," she replied, hoping her lie was adequate, "as I mentioned, my father was a scholar. He was a man of … unusual tastes."

"So it would seem," he replied, staring intently into Midnite's eyes as if he were as transfixed by her, as she by him. "Err, listen. I'm sorry about this, but I need you to come with me back to camp. Standing orders are to detain all non-hostile locals."

She raised an eyebrow.

"Don't worry," he added. "Those jackasses back there won't try anything. I promise you'll be fine. Don't believe everything you've been told about us. You'll be fed and well cared for."

"Detained," she repeated. Was this human actually suggesting she accompany him as his prisoner? It would seem so. But it was being done in a way unlike what she had come to expect from humans. Prisoners of war were typically the lowest of the low, their lives only allowed to continue at the grace of whatever general was in charge. Typically, if one did not have a wealthy family to pay ransom, the best one could hope for was to be worked to death. The lives of their females were worth even less.

Stephen's promise, however, caught her attention. An offer to be treated fairly. That was not often heard from captors because it was not something they needed to care about offering. To have it put out there as an enticement against fighting or fleeing was unusual.

Midnite considered things. She had nothing to fear from this or any other human. They could only imprison her for so long as she allowed. Compared to them, she was as the wind, the sky, the sea. Such things could not be contained or mastered. Had she wished, she could have walked away, and there was nothing this man could do to stop her.

However, she found herself oddly loath to leave his company so soon. Shitoro wouldn't start fretting over her absence for some time, thus she was free to do as she pleased without interruption.

Midnite smiled at the man before her. "I will offer you no resistance."

She was surprised to realize she was only partially talking about being taken prisoner.

Though many of the soldiers in the vast encampment looked upon her with a mix of emotions ranging from raw hatred to lust, Stephen Fuller kept them at bay, barking orders for them to return to their posts.

Despite being told his presence was no longer needed, he stayed with her as she suffered the indignity of being searched. True to his word, her treatment was fair, if not entirely kind. Finally, as she was led away to join the other prisoners, he left her. She reached out and touched his hand before he walked away, earning a sad smile from him. By then, Midnite had made up her mind.

She waited until the fall of darkness to act. It gave her time to observe, not only the forlorn faces of the others held prisoner, but also the new art of war that seemed to have blossomed while she and her siblings slept. Explosions rang out constantly – some from the ships at sea, others from giant metal carriages that moved on their own with no horses or oxen to pull them. She spied many more of those strange flying objects she had originally mistaken as a form of oni. They were impressive. No wonder she and the others were roused.

Finally, when she had observed her fill, she closed her eyes and summoned a small fragment of her power, allowing it to coalesce around her. She had marked Stephen Fuller with her touch and now was reaching out, past the guard towers into the camp beyond, searching for his essence.

There! She felt him, the troubles of the day seemingly gone from his spirit, a sense of temporary serenity about him. He was asleep.

Midnite slipped mostly unseen from the prison camp. A small, wide-eyed boy spied her as she gathered her power and turned translucent. She smiled at him but was otherwise unconcerned. Let the child have some hope that greater forces than himself were at play in this world.

Neither the barbed wire fence nor the many guards manning it proved to be an obstacle. Midnite moved past them all as if she were one with the very wind itself. A sharp-eyed human might have sensed her passing as a minor disturbance, but these men were all exhausted from days of battle.

She followed her senses while, at the same time, reaching out to the sea and drawing upon the cold waters within it.

As she neared where Stephen Fuller lay sleeping, she drew those energies around her, causing a thick ground fog to rise up. A few guards noted the odd change in weather but laughed it off, making comments about what a godforsaken land this was. They couldn't have been more wrong.

There. She glided into the flimsy structure – a tent, if she recalled the human name for such things. It couldn't have been more different from the celestial palace had they tried. Such a covering might keep out the rain, but that was all. A strong wind, a fierce predator, an enemy, the walls would stop none of it. She marveled at the humans' ability to sleep in such a weak structure. Considering how frail they were, Midnite would have thought them incapable of rest knowing that only the barest of fabrics stood between them and the harsh world beyond.

She pushed that thought aside for now. It, along with nearly everything else the humans worried about, were of no matter to a being such as her.

The irony was not lost upon Midnite, that she found herself looking down upon the sleeping form of Stephen Fuller. He wasn't alone. Many others shared this structure with him, all of them asleep on uncomfortable-looking cots, but she wasn't worried about rousing them. She could make it so that he and he alone heard her voice. To the others, it would be nothing more than a whisper upon the wind.

Never before had a human intrigued her as he had. So different from the others, so … handsome, too. *Yes*, she thought, *he is indeed handsome.* Considering the reason for her visit, it was foolish to deny such base thoughts. Her heart fluttered as she watched the peaceful look upon his face. After a few moments, she reached out and caressed his cheek.

He stirred, breathed deep, then opened his eyes wide as she allowed herself to become visible to him. He opened his mouth, seemingly to cry out in surprise, but she placed a finger against his lips to silence him. "Shhhh."

She smiled down upon him, hoping to ease his alarm, although she could understand his confusion. There she was, standing in his tent, glowing in a cool divine light while fog rolled in through the opening and seemed to coalesce around them.

He turned and looked around, noting his sleeping fellows. "Is this a dream?" he whispered.

"The dreams of men are but another state of what you call reality."

"I don't understand."

She smiled again and placed her hand upon his, gently taking it and guiding him to his feet. "You need not understand. Merely follow."

"Follow?"

"I wish to show you something."

"What?"

"Follow and learn."

The mist from the ocean swallowed them up as they walked out. None were aware of their passage as she led him away from the camp. His eventual return might cause a stir among his fellows, but that was a concern for later.

The ground fog followed, growing thick a few steps before them, then thinning out following their passage. To anyone observing, it would have seemed as if a cloud had descended from the sky to take a leisurely stroll before assuming its proper place high in the heavens once again.

She led him away, to a place she used to know well. Once, tall grass had grown there. It would move with the wind as the crickets serenaded her, but now there was nothing but desolation. Blackened and pitted by the war that had descended upon this land, this place of peace was now a field of death.

For one such as Midnite, though, the ravages of both time and men were but minor inconveniences.

"It's just an empty battlefield," Stephen said once she stopped moving.

"Now. But once, it was so much more. Allow me to show you."

"I don't understand."

"You will."

Midnite gathered the energy of the ocean and added to it that of the earth and sky. It required an effort even from one such as she, but it was worth it.

The mist which had concealed them now spread out, encircling them in what looked to be a wall of fog fifty feet in diameter.

Midnite noted the incredulous stare from Stephen Fuller. If he thought this was impressive, he would certainly enjoy what happened next.

A light shone down upon them from above. He looked up and shielded his eyes, perhaps wary of an attack, but then he relaxed when he realized it was the clouds above parting to reveal the moon, full and strong. A shaft of light seemed to reach down from it, illuminating them and the area around.

Midnite willed the moonlight to show them not the present, but things as they once were, during the more peaceful times when she would visit these lands.

He let out a gasp as the light revealed not the dead earth they'd been standing upon, but tall green grass. The sound of crickets chirping suddenly filled the air. Where death once held sway, life again reigned supreme.

"This is how this place used to be in days past."

"It's beautiful."

"It was," she replied, a touch of sadness in her voice.

"It will be again." He approached her from behind and put his hands upon her shoulders. "Once we win."

She had to stifle a laugh. Special he might be, but he was still a warrior. Likewise, as much as she enjoyed peace and beauty, she also couldn't deny what she was at her core.

Even so, now, in a place like this, one could be allowed their illusions. For a time, one could pretend to be someone or something else, a whole other life.

She turned and put her arms around him. "Let us speak no more of war. This is a place of life."

"Life," he repeated as if in a dream.

"Yes," she said, drawing him down with her to the soft grass. "And we should celebrate that life in the short time we have."

He made to say something in response, but it was lost as she pulled him into her embrace.

PRESENT
DAY

FOUR

"**K**ISAKI! LADY KISAKI, where are you?"

Shitoro stopped in the hall, feeling quite exasperated. Where in heaven's name was that ungrateful whelp of a child? She was late for her lessons *again* and if her mother found out, he would share in the scolding.

Late, that one. Always late and always up to no good. Why, if he had his way, he would have long ago taken a switch to her backside. He would have taught her the true meaning of resp…

The diminutive tiger demon sniffed the air and sensed something behind him a moment too late.

The attack came without warning. He was thrown off his feet and went sliding across the exquisitely carved but damnably slippery floor. Before he could push himself up, he was pinned as a weight fell upon his back.

"Gotcha!" a cheerful voice said into his ear. His attacker reached down and pinched his cheek playfully.

Shitoro's teeth were as small as he, but they were sharp. He turned his head and bit the hand of his harasser before he could think better of it.

"Ouch!" Kisaki cried, jumping away. "You bit me."

Shitoro pulled himself to his feet and dusted off the regal red of his robe. He rounded on the girl, his teeth bared. He'd hoped to teach her a lesson, but upon looking up at her face, he saw only mischievous good cheer. "Impudent whelp!"

"You're just mad because you're getting slow in your old age," she chided.

"Old age is meaningless to ones such as us. We're immortal."

She bent down and poked him in the stomach. "Too much good food, then."

Shitoro swatted her hand away. *Yes*, he thought, *definitely in need of a switch to the backside.* "I'll have you know I have fit into these same robes for at least five centuries, long before I was charged with dealing with your childish antics."

"Oh, don't be grumpy, Shitoro," Kisaki said, her face turning serious. "I was just having some fun. I'm bored."

"Then you should study more so as to keep your simple mind occupied. In fact, that's why I was calling for you. It's time to…"

"Not more lessons!" She leaned back against the wall and sulked, for a moment appearing much younger than her age – making a face one might more expect from a toddler being denied a toy. "All I ever do is study."

"Of course you do. Your mother has high expectations for you. A lady of your standing should be knowledgeable in the ways of the multiverse."

"I've been studying that stuff for years."

Shitoro crossed his tiny arms and stared up at the much taller girl – almost the same height as her mother, he noted. Kisaki had inherited her mother's flawless skin and exquisite looks, but her hair and eyes were both several shades lighter. Ironic, Shitoro often considered, that the daughter of Lady Midnite should possess features more closely related to the morning sun.

In human terms, Kisaki appeared to be a girl in her late teens, but appearances had nothing to do with one's true age in the celestial palace, something Shitoro had to constantly remind her of.

"One does not learn the intricacies of billions of years of rich history in the span of barely six decades. It is doubly impossible when one spends so much of that time whining about it."

Kisaki's face fell and Shitoro knew he'd won, for now. With each passing year, she'd grown more willful. Despite his official status as her mentor and guardian, he knew his job would only continue to become more difficult.

That was a worry for another day, though.

"Come along, child," Shitoro said, leading the way to Kisaki's study chambers. Her steps were light, but his hearing was excellent and he heard her falling in line behind him.

"Maybe we can study somewhere else today," she suggested hopefully after a few moments of walking.

"If you wish," he replied. "Your bedroom, or perhaps the walled garden."

Kisaki's steps fell silent behind him and he turned to find her again pouting. "That's not what I meant. I've studied there hundreds of times."

"Yes, and they have somehow managed to survive your tantrums."

"I'm not having a tantrum," she replied before sticking her tongue out at the little tiger demon. "I'm just bored. Maybe someplace new will, I don't know, stimulate my mind."

"I sincerely doubt that," Shitoro muttered. "Besides, you know the rules."

"The rules are stupid."

"The rules were put in place by your mother. Perhaps you would prefer an audience with her to let her know how *stupid* you find her judgment."

That finally gave Kisaki pause. Shitoro knew the girl wasn't afraid of him by any stretch of the imagination, but she knew better than to risk a tongue-lashing by her mother. He almost wished she'd push the point. Watching Lady Midnite at work was pure pleasure, something he would never grow tired of despite his relatively new station as the girl's guardian. "I thought not," he said. "Now come along."

Kisaki paused for a few moments longer, stopping and staring at the door leading to her mother's audience chamber. Beyond it lay the exit to other wings of the celestial palace, places Kisaki had never been.

Sadly, he mused, noting the heavy reinforced bars sealing the door from the inside – bars he himself oversaw the construction of over seventy years ago – despite her inclinations to the contrary, Kisaki would never be permitted to explore the rest of the palace.

It was for her own well-being.

Kisaki fumed at being rebuked yet again. All she wanted was a change of pace. Ever since she could remember, she'd seen the same walls, the same floors, the same faces. True, she had servants, and yes, she lived in finery – never being hungry, never feeling threatened – but it felt to her like a prison nevertheless. She'd read about them in her seemingly endless studies, knew they were where those who broke the law were put to serve their sentences. She also knew they were designed to break the spirits of those trapped within.

Why couldn't Shitoro, or her mother, for that matter, understand that her spirit would eventually break, too, despite everything that was provided to her?

Her mother was free to walk the halls, or so Kisaki believed. At the very least, she spent a great deal of time in her audience chamber – a place Kisaki had briefly seen a few times, before having the doors slammed in her face and subsequently locked. Even one new room would be a breath of fresh air to her stagnant life.

Nevertheless, she considered as she pretended to read the scroll in front of her, it wasn't like she would be given much chance to enjoy any new surroundings, not with Shitoro's seemingly endless litany of lessons. History, in particular, irked her. Not because she found it unpleasant. It was quite the opposite. Learning of the grand adventures others embarked upon, while she was kept cooped up like a pet, was maddening.

Today's lesson was a prime example. She was reading about Yamato Takeru and his victory against an army of youkai. The scrolls in front of her discounted him as a mere human, their tone dismissive, but she could imagine the battle in her mind. Everything she read about humans had pegged them as lesser beings but, despite their frailty, time and again they were victorious over creatures much greater than themselves. In fact, despite the arrogant assumptions Shitoro made about them being a barbaric species, it instead appeared they excelled at being underdogs.

Kisaki could relate. She certainly felt like an underdog most days. Despite Shitoro and the others ostensibly being labeled as her servants, oftentimes she felt far beneath them, especially since they weren't bound to the same rules she was. She'd seen them come and go, unlocking the barriers that kept her in, before quickly shutting them up again before she could even take a peek through.

She'd once, about thirty years earlier, tried to bully her way past one of her more easily browbeaten servants, only to find her mother's stern gaze waiting on the other side of the door, cutting her adventure short before it could even begin.

Since then, she'd been given very strict orders to not interfere with the comings and goings of the youkai who served them. As usual, her protests to the contrary had borne no fruit.

"And what does Yamato's victory teach us?" Shitoro asked.

"Huh?" She looked up to find the little tiger demon staring at her expectantly. He was obviously waiting for an answer, and she was in no mood for another lecture from him this day. Besides, if he thought she wasn't paying attention, he would just make her start over again. His lessons were already painfully long as it was.

"That…" she hesitated, trying to think of an answer that would make it seem as if she had been engrossed in the story before her. "That, no matter the odds, victory is never assured. The proclamations of others that something is impossible doesn't mean that it is."

"Nonsense," Shitoro replied dismissively, a look of annoyance crossing his face. "It simply means that anyone can get lucky." He leaned over Kisaki and pointed out several sections of the scroll. "Look at this, here, here, and here. Yamato had no real strategy. It was little more than a stroke of…"

The rest of his words were lost to her as she spied the golden key dangling from the chain around his neck. It unlocked the door to her mother's audience chamber. He was never without it, and now it was mere inches from her face.

As she stared at it, she began to consider that perhaps the little tiger youkai, despite his smug demeanor, was wrong after all. Just because something was deemed impossible, didn't mean she couldn't succeed. Even if it was, she should at least try.

Days passed while Kisaki planned her escape. The truth of the matter was, it wasn't really much of a plan. Sadly, she had little idea what lay inside her mother's chambers, much less beyond. She would have to play it by ear once she was out.

Kisaki wasn't stupid. In truth, she expected to be caught quickly. But she felt the risk was worth it. Even a glimpse of something new, something different, could sustain her for years after the malaise of confinement she'd been feeling.

In order to make it work, though, she needed two things – Shitoro to drop his guard, and for her mother to be elsewhere. Without both, she would fail and, knowing her luck, the barricades on the doors would be doubled or tripled to dissuade further attempts.

The first of those was easy enough. She fell into her studies, making it a point to be on time and pay attention. It was painfully dull, especially during Shitoro's nearly endless lectures on mathematics and conjuration, two subjects which Kisaki seemed to have no aptitude for. She only perked up during her history lessons, becoming lost in the tales of humans – seemingly so small and insignificant compared to their divine betters – overcoming insurmountable odds and pushing their domain ever further.

Yes. If they could do it, then so could she.

It was the second part that would be tricky. Her mother was far more cunning than Shitoro. She would see through a simple ploy almost instantly.

Her mother was also quite busy, often dealing with matters of court or with the other daimao, who Kisaki assumed lived elsewhere in the palace but had never actually met. Most often this was done in her chambers, but on rare occasion, matters would draw her away. That was what she kept watch for.

She waited for the days when her mother did not summon her for tea or to discuss her lessons. On those days, she purposely pestered the little tiger demon for an audience. She wasn't particularly intent on being granted one. In fact, she knew Shitoro would, in most cases, dismiss her with replies of how her mother couldn't be disturbed. It was actually his answers she was most interested in.

She hoped to come off as merely a needy child. Thus, his refusals were often met with sullen responses of "Why?" At first, Shitoro stuck to his mainstays, that it was time for her to study and it wasn't her place to question. However, she was persistent and, no doubt hoping to quiet her *tantrums,* as he liked to call them, Shitoro began to give more detailed answers.

"No, you cannot see your mother because she is discussing matters of importance in her audience chamber."

"No. You cannot see your mother because she is busy entertaining today."

"No. I am afraid that is impossible for, you see, your mother has been summoned to an important gathering and, before you ask, it is not something I can discuss with you."

It was that last one she was truly waiting for.

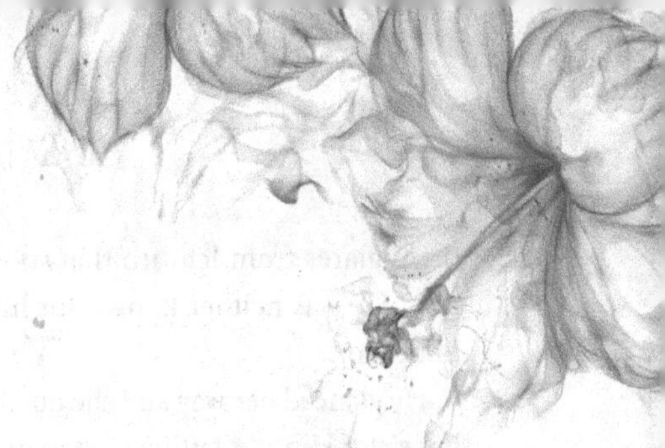

FIVE

"**S**OMETHING MUST BE done!"

"And what do you propose, brother?" Rokusan asked from his usual seat in the assembly chamber. Ichitiro slammed a black gauntleted fist onto the table, the sound echoing through the room. "Action. Anything. More than we have done the last seventy of their years, hiding here while the humans grow stronger by the day. The power they have harnessed, it is an insult to us and to the elder gods."

"I am not certain I agree," Reiden commented from the head of the table. "For thousands of years, Ichitiro, have we not had to listen to you bemoaning the humans' stupidity, their lack of progress in the art of war? Now they have finally made the progress you claim to have hoped for, and yet you are the first to complain that it is too much."

Midnite stifled the smile that threatened to escape her lips at watching her would-be suitor knocked down a peg. Ichitiro might be unstoppable on the battlefield, but waging a war of words was an entirely different matter altogether.

Others in the room were not so generous toward the war demon, agreeing with Reiden, eldest of the daimao, and earning them glares from Ichitiro that spoke of promises of retribution. He was neither known for his eloquence nor his sense of humor.

He glanced her way and she quickly averted her eyes toward her sister Hinode, sitting next to her. Midnite was fond of her, but not so much that she didn't occasionally wish Ichitiro would turn his advances her way.

Alas, so long as she possessed the Taiyosori, that wasn't likely to happen.

It was almost as if Ichitiro read her mind, because he bellowed, "I say we flood their cities. We rain fire from the sky upon their fields. We unleash the Taiyosori upon them, show them that no matter how far they believe they have progressed, their power is nothing compared to the gods."

"The blade of heaven is not yours to unleash upon anyone," Midnite replied. "And what makes you think they would cower before your so-called show of strength?"

"What else could they do?" he asked arrogantly, his eyes drinking her in.

"Match your force with equal or greater," she stated.

That had been the argument which had kept them deadlocked for over half a century. Once again, it served to silence all discussion in the chamber.

Midnite considered this. The battle she had witnessed all those years ago, it had been but a small part of a much larger conflict. In retrospect, it was no wonder she and her brethren had awoken from their slumber. When last they'd walked amongst mankind, their world had been a large and daunting place. Only the bravest of humans would dare to venture out on rickety ships bound for new lands, knowing the odds were against them ever returning. In those days, most wars were petty affairs. True, there had been some visionaries, but they were few and far between.

However, the world had apparently become a much smaller place in the time since they last strode upon it. Midnite had been impressed with the ships she'd seen – those in the air as well as upon the sea. What she hadn't realized during that fateful night was the conflict spanned nearly the breadth of the entire planet.

At first, upon her return to the palace the next day, she'd found her drowsy siblings as excited as she was. Ichitiro had been singing a different tune then, crowing about how mankind had finally managed to overcome their many limitations. They now sailed in mighty ships made of iron that could spew death in many directions at once. They now crossed the land in metal chariots that didn't rely upon beasts of burden. They had even conquered the sky itself.

In those early days, a sense of anticipation flowed from this chamber. Several of her brothers and sisters made similar sojourns to the planet below, marveling in the new sights and sounds. Many talked about openly presenting themselves upon the battlefield so as to test the mettle of this new level of warfare the humans had developed. Soon, they had shed the malaise that had led them to slumber and the halls of the celestial palace had become busy with activity again.

It was perfect timing, for it meant they were too busy to notice her and how her body was changing.

Then *it* happened.

An entire city destroyed in one fell swoop. A burst of energy upon one of the blessed isles, so powerful and devastating that all of her kind felt it in their very bones. Though none dared admit it afterward, they trembled – for what the humans had unleashed felt akin to the power of the elder gods themselves.

Disbelief spread through the halls of the celestial palace. It was a fluke, Reiden declared in this very chamber. It had to have been some accidental magic, perhaps another dimension brushing against this one too brusquely. As far as they had come, surely what had happened was impossible for such lowly beings as humans.

Then, a few days later, it happened again, this time even more powerful.

Another city was felled within minutes.

This time, there was no denying the truth: the humans, for so long pathetic beings barely worthy of recognition, had harnessed a power far greater than any of her kind thought them ever capable.

In the past, humans had been able to defeat various youkai, through strength of numbers or cunning. A few of the mazoku had even fallen to their more exceptional members. But a daimao? Such a thought was laughable at best.

In a flash, that had all changed. As powerful as they were, as much divine energy they had at their command, they were forced to admit this new power the humans had harnessed was capable of killing even their kind. The humans – lowest of the low – now possessed a capability that none save the gods themselves wielded.

Following this realization, something new happened within the ever-turning celestial cycle, for perhaps the first time in forever – the daimao retreated from the Earth, not out of boredom, but out of fear.

The ways were shut and locked. The gates sealed. None of the daimao dared visit the planet below. Likewise, access to the crystals that allowed servants to venture forth between the two realms was forbidden. Many of their cousins, both youkai and mazoku, were trapped on Earth, left to fend for themselves. Those who survived retreated to the forests or mountains to live like dogs, lest they find themselves hunted.

At the time, Reiden claimed it all to be temporary. The ways would be opened again as soon as the daimao reached a conclusion as to what needed to be done.

Yet decades had passed, and they continued to do nothing but argue. All the while, mankind continued to march forward at a pace undreamt of, building ever more powerful weapons of war. They'd even gone so far as to touch the face of the moon orbiting their planet. Some began to speak in hushed tones that soon the humans would possess the ability to detect the celestial palace itself. If so, what then? What if they invaded? What if they accidentally woke the elder gods?

Barely contained panic had taken hold.

Not all of it was bad, though, Midnite considered.

The chaos that had been borne of this had benefited her, given her an opportunity to fortify her chambers without question.

It had allowed her to keep safe the very special secret that none of her kind could ever know about.

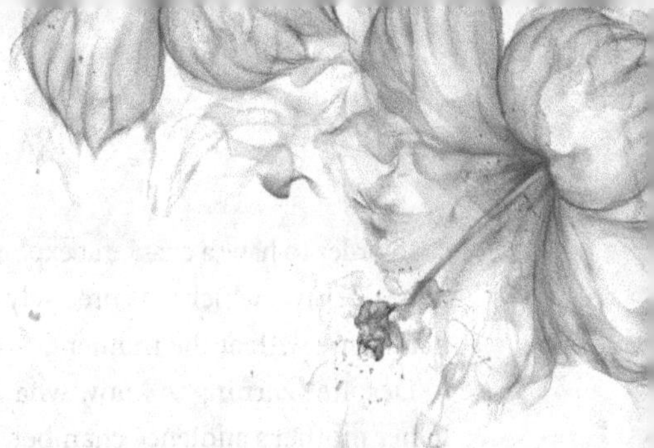

SIX

KISAKI'S WINDOW OF opportunity was short. There was no time to dawdle or have second thoughts.

Shitoro might not have been as clever as he thought, but he wasn't stupid by any means. He was also a stickler for detail and routine. It wouldn't be long before he realized she had swiped the key from around his neck.

It had been a particularly dull session, focusing on the politics of various interdimensional species – comparing and contrasting them – but that had been perfect. At one point, Kisaki had pretended to nod off, something very believable considering the topic. When Shitoro had walked over to wake her, she'd toppled over, forcing him to catch her.

In the fumbling that ensued, she managed to grab the key unnoticed.

Even more fortuitous had been when he, in a snit at her inattentiveness, declared she should take a short break so as to compose herself – after which they would dive back in for several more hours. Pity for him, he would return to an empty lecture hall.

In order to have a chance at exploration, however, she needed to be decisive, which was precisely what she was having a difficult time with at the moment.

Despite yearning to know what lay past the doors leading to her mother's audience chamber, she found herself hesitant. After all this time, she was holding the means to explore a place she'd only glimpsed. But it was what lay beyond that paused her steps – the rest of the palace she called home. To venture further was forbidden, almost unthinkable, not to mention certain to incite her mother's wrath.

What would she find there? More servants, more finery? Perhaps someone else like her?

That was the thought that finally got her moving again.

It wasn't so much meeting others as much as the thought of making a new friend. Sure, Shitoro could be considered that, but he was also her guardian, not to mention her school master. To meet someone new and just talk with them without minding her tongue; it was a concept she wasn't sure she was ready for. But she realized she was willing to try.

The impasse broken, she unlocked the heavy bars standing in her way, pushed them to the side, and, with a deep breath, opened the door beyond.

She'd caught fleeting glimpses of her mother's audience chamber before, barely enough to leave her with half-formed images for her mind to fill in. Now she was able to drink in what she saw to her heart's content.

The multi-hued chandeliers that hung from the ceiling, the smooth stone of the walls – polished to an almost mirror-like sheen – and the thick red carpet on the floor. All of it was magnificent. Near the back stood the ebony throne from which her mother entertained visitors – or so she'd been told. She'd never actually seen it happen. So dark was the material from which it had been carved that it was as if a chair-shaped hole had been cut into the very air, leaving behind nothing but a void.

It was what hung in midair above the throne, though, that really caught her eye.

The weapon glimmered with a light seemingly all its own, tiny pinpricks of brilliance shining from a blade that seemed to be made of some type of smoky glass that – despite the richness of the rooms she lived in – she'd never seen before.

Remembering her limited time, she tore her gaze from the sword and shut the door behind her. She had no way of reengaging the complex locks from this side, but hopefully, the sight of it shut would afford her a few extra moments.

Kisaki knew she should be testing the key upon the door at the far end of the chamber, the one that led to areas unknown. Yet, instead of heading that way, she found herself turning back to the sword that hung above her mother's throne.

She stood staring at it for several long seconds, almost mesmerized by the multiple lights glinting from the blade.

It was strange, hard to explain, but somehow it seemed as if the sword was calling to her. It made no sense. After all, she knew what it was, having seen depictions of many such weapons in her studies, albeit never one quite like this. Regardless, Kisaki had never actually handled anything like it. The sharpest thing she'd ever touched had been the quills with which she'd written out her endless lessons, having worn out many over the years.

That had to be it. The sword was something new, something she'd never experienced firsthand. That was why she found herself still staring at it, long after logic dictated she should continue with her exploration.

The pinpricks of light on the fragile-looking blade appeared to grow brighter as her eyes continued to focus on it, until it seemed as if they might be miniature stars somehow trapped in the strange glasslike material from which it was forged.

That was silly, though. Even sillier was the concept of a glass sword. Such a thing would be useless in combat, a mere decoration – which was what it seemed to be.

Yet she couldn't help the yearning to hold it.

Kisaki let out a deep sigh, her mind made up. She was already in trouble for her transgressions, that much she knew. What would one more matter? Besides, it's not like Shitoro couldn't just hang it up again once she'd been caught and sent back to her room.

That spurred her to action, and she crossed the room to her mother's throne. The material of the chair was truly dark, seeming to drink in the light around it, and for one quick moment, Kisaki was certain that she'd fall into it.

But then her foot touched the seat and found it to be solid. Laughing at her own foolishness, she stood upon it and lifted herself up. The sword was still out of her reach, so she was forced to climb upon the heavy arm rests and then finally the back, balancing herself precariously as she reached for the weapon.

Despite it looking like nothing more than a fragile decoration, she strove to be careful. Something deep inside warned her to steer clear of the edge of the blade. It did appear sharp and glass, fragile or not, could slice skin just as easily as steel.

She stood on her tiptoes upon the back of the throne and reached up. Inch by inch she stretched, trying to reach the grip of the weapon, a brilliant white material – almost porcelain in appearance – in contrast to the blade itself.

Almost...

There! She grabbed hold and smiled triumphantly, right before a shock of energy jolted down her arm. It was as if she'd grabbed hold of something burning hot. For a moment, she was glued to her spot, unable to let go. Then, just as abruptly, she pulled back, freeing the weapon from the invisible bonds that held it aloft.

The movement caused her to lose her balance. She teetered atop the back of the chair for a moment, pinwheeling her arms before she overbalanced, losing her grip on the sword in the process.

Kisaki fell, landing upon her backside on the rich carpet in front of the throne.

She winced, both from the impact as well as the embarrassment of having fallen, then looked up. Her eyes widened as she beheld the sword, sticking out of the seat of her mother's chair where it had landed point down, sinking itself deep into the ebony material.

Yet one more crime to add to her growing list of infractions this day.

Shitoro was going to be mad, but her mother would be furious.

Kisaki pulled herself to her feet and brushed herself off, despite the room being so immaculate that one would have thought dust was outlawed.

What's done is done.

She'd gone too far to explain this as a simple accident. At the same time, she hadn't gone far at all. If she were to be caught now, her punishment was likely to be harsh. And for what? All she'd managed to do was open one door, knock over a sword, and cut a gouge in her mother's chair. If she was going to be given a tongue-lashing, followed by confinement in her room until the stars burned out, she might as well earn it.

Yes, she'd tarried long enough. It was time to see what lay beyond this place. That was, assuming her stolen key could unlock the door beyond. There was only one way to find out.

She turned toward it, took a single step, then hesitated again.

Grr! What is it with that stupid thing anyway?

Kisaki spun back and, without knowing why, she stepped up and grabbed the sword by the hilt again. That same fire she'd felt before seemed to radiate from the blade for a scant moment, but then it was gone, leaving the weapon cool to the touch. Odd. Perhaps she'd imagined it, a side effect of her nervous state of mind.

Yes, that had to be it.

She lifted the blade easily, sliding it out with little effort from the groove it had cut. Despite its size, it was ridiculously light in her hand. *No more than a fragile decoration.* It would be foolish to take it with her. One good bump would surely shatter it into a thousand pieces.

Yet, still she found herself mesmerized by the weapon. She glanced at the point, then again at the cut in her mother's throne.

Hmm, she thought, *maybe sharper than those silly quills after all, but a bit less inconspicuous, too.*

Before she could turn back to the door, the sword began to glow in her hands. It was as if the miniature stars shining inside the blade had decided to go supernova, filling the weapon with a brilliant white light.

Kisaki cried out in surprise before closing her eyes against the glare of the weapon, almost blinding in its intensity.

What now?!

She expected to feel that burning sensation in her hands again, for surely the weapon would soon become too hot to hold, but it remained cool in her grasp.

Cool and ... *smaller?*

Though she couldn't look directly at the sword, she could have sworn she felt the grip of the weapon shrinking, becoming much more familiar, more like a...

All at once, the glow abated. Kisaki blinked several times to clear the spots from her eyes. Then she blinked again at what she saw in her hands.

Impossible! The sword was gone and in its place was a simple quill, like those she wrote her lessons with.

Upon closer inspection, though, she realized it was different after all. It was far finer in appearance than those she normally used, and the white of the feather turned to a deep black near the top. She stared at it, realizing she could see tiny lights twinkling in that blackness.

Somehow the sword had turned into this. No, that wasn't right. Somehow the weapon had *read her thoughts* and acted upon them.

She wasn't sure whether to laugh or scream. It was a good thing she hadn't been thinking of dragons or the six-legged war gryphons she'd been reading about a few days prior. That decided it for her and she began to giggle.

Still, strange or not, she had to admit carrying around a quill was liable to be slightly more convenient than a sword. She stuffed it into a pocket inside her kimono, then took a deep breath and turned to the outer doors.

If there were so many new and strange things to experience in her mother's antechamber alone, then what did that bode for beyond?

Kisaki wasn't sure, but it was time she found out.

SEVEN

HALLWAYS, HALLWAYS, AND more hallways.

Kisaki had been expecting the wonders of the universe to lay beyond her mother's chambers – enough so that a single step would have fueled her imagination for years to come.

The seemingly endless maze of corridors she found herself in wasn't exactly boring, but it was certainly a bit anticlimactic following her interactions with the quill-sword.

After a while, she began to suspect that would be the only memento of her trip. Yes, the passageways were quite opulent, lined with beautiful fineries such as vases, chalices, and suits of armor. There were massive, finely-detailed statues at some intersections, depicting beings she didn't recognize but suspected to be some of the great heroes she'd read about in her lessons.

Nevertheless, exquisite as everything was, it was nothing out of the ordinary compared to what she'd seen in her own chambers. If this was all that lay beyond her mother's abode, then she had surely risked a great deal of punishment for very little gain.

Soon, she began to consider returning. If she was back home when her transgressions were discovered, she could potentially minimize the damage, claim that she'd only visited her mother's chambers. But she quickly dismissed those thoughts. To return now would be cowardly, especially after all this time planning and dreaming of visiting the outside.

Besides, she realized with a laugh, she was no longer certain she could find her way back if she wanted to. This place was truly vast and, in her haste to explore, she'd turned down several corridors with abandon, never bothering to note the way she'd come.

She had little choice but to continue forward.

Now to only hope she found something interesting before Shitoro found her.

Kisaki let out a whoop of joy. She couldn't help it. The little youkai standing at the far end of the corridor and staring back at her had been the first sign of life she'd encountered since leaving. Best yet, it was someone she'd never seen before.

Movement had registered in her periphery upon turning the last corner. At first, she'd thought it was a trick of the light, for it seemed that she was staring at nothing more than a shadow.

But then it had turned toward her, its glowing blue eyes staring widely over a mouth full of needle-sharp teeth. It was some kind of animal demon, a ferret perhaps, and the darkness she'd mistaken for a shadow was some kind of miasma, perhaps meant to conceal it. It certainly couldn't have been an offensive weapon, for the creature inside the shadow was even smaller than Shitoro.

"Hello," she said, bending down so as to be closer to its level. "I'm Kisaki."

The youkai cocked its head to the side but said nothing.

"It's okay, I won't hurt you." She took a step forward, then realized she was being foolish. The youkai gave no indication he was afraid of her. Also, it was quite likely older and wiser than she, thus there was no reason for her to be talking to it like a child. Yet, it was so cute, despite the miasma, that she couldn't help herself.

The youkai muttered something, although she wasn't certain if it was to her or not.

"Do you live here, too?" Kisaki asked, continuing to approach. How wonderful would it be if she could make a new friend. Even if nothing else came of her journey, it would be marvelous to know there was someone beyond her mother's doors that was thinking about her … who could potentially visit her and relay stories of what lay in other parts of the palace.

"I live in…" She paused as she realized she had no idea what directions to give. Instead, she simply hooked a thumb over her shoulder. "I live back that way somewhere."

Again the ferret demon opened its mouth, this time seeming to ask a question. Kisaki was close enough to hear it utter a single word. "Who?"

"Like I said, my name is Kisaki. I live with my mother. Maybe you know her. Her name is Lady Midnite. There's also Shitoro and…"

"Midnite?" it chirped in response.

"Yes. You know her?" Excitement started to build in Kisaki. If this creature knew her mother, then that made it all the more likely it could maybe pay her a visit from time to time.

"Mother?" the ferret asked.

"Yes. She's my mother."

The ferret demon lifted its head, the miasma dispersing around it. Kisaki's heart soared as it took a sniff of the air, then abruptly crashed back down as the creature bared its teeth in a snarl and backed up a step.

"Wait, did I say something wrong?"

"Hanyou," it snarled.

"What…?" But Kisaki was too late. The ferret youkai hissed at her, then turned and took off running down the hall. "Come back! I didn't mean … whatever I did."

Kisaki chased after the ferret, but it was quick and apparently knew these halls much better than she. Several minutes and many more corridors later, she realized she'd lost it.

With a heavy heart, she stopped and wondered what she'd done wrong. The little demon hadn't seemed overly friendly at any point during their brief interlude, but he'd only turned hostile at the mention of Kisaki's mother.

Was it possible the little youkai was less than a friend to her mother? But why would an enemy share the same palace? Surely that made no sense.

But then, neither did a sword that turned into a feather quill.

The truth was, Kisaki was in uncharted waters. That she expected anything to make sense, based on her sheltered existence alone, was the height of naivety. Assuming she knew anything about this place or its inhabitants was foolish, something likely to only result in disappointment or worse.

She resolved herself to stop assuming and to start listening. If only Shitoro was here, he'd surely appreciate the irony that she'd finally accepted it was time to study and learn.

"What is this place?" she asked herself.

Whatever it was, it more than made up for the endless corridors she'd walked down, doubled back on, and gotten hopelessly lost in.

This was more like what she'd hoped to find, something new amid all the sameness.

The octagonal room was large, bigger than her mother's audience chamber, with expanding circles of polished metal inlaid into the floor. They started in the middle and grew larger as they moved further away from it.

The floor was certainly interesting, but it was the walls that caught her attention or, more specifically, what was in them. Multiple recessed shelves ran the length of each wall at varying heights. These shelves were filled with crystals of different hues, spaced a few inches apart, encircling the entire room.

Each seemed to shimmer with its own power, illuminating the room with myriad colors that seemed to be ever-changing as they danced on the walls and reflected off the circles in the floor. It was the most beautiful thing Kisaki had ever seen.

Despite her earlier despair at the botched attempt at befriending the ferret demon, Kisaki found herself glad this room was currently unoccupied. Something about this place made her want her first experience within it to be all her own.

She gingerly stepped inside, laughing as the lights danced against her skin.

Within moments, she found herself in the center of the room, standing within the smallest of the circles. It seemed as if the power of this chamber were converging upon her. She held her hands out to her sides and began to slowly turn in place, drinking it all in, marveling at what she'd found.

She would need to ask her mother about this room. What purpose it served. What the crystals were made of.

But perhaps that would best wait until after whatever punishment was in store for her came to pass. Kisaki's mother wasn't cruel, but it was wise to know one's boundaries around her. Angering her further when she was already incensed seemed a poor idea.

That was for later, though. For now, this place was all hers.

After a time, she stepped away from the center and approached the walls and the prizes contained within. She walked along, following the outline of the room, her eyes drawn to the rows of crystals she passed. Soon she began to see a pattern, how the colors repeated themselves – thirteen crystals of unique hue, then they would start again, over and over. There had to be hundreds of them, maybe more.

Surely a few wouldn't be missed.

Though she didn't expect to get away with it, the thought of hiding them beneath her pillows, taking them out and marveling at them at night when the servants were either asleep or tending to other duties, was a compelling one for someone aching for new experiences in life.

Taking one of each seemed too risky to her. As many as were in the room, she felt that number might be too great to go unnoticed. But one or two … maybe three of them? Surely, she thought, that wouldn't seem out of place.

She spied one, black as night, the same color as her mother's throne, and decided to start with it. She reached out, preparing to grab it, but then remembered what had happened when she'd first touched the sword in her mother's chamber.

Kisaki hesitated for a moment, but then laughed at her own foolishness. This was nothing like that had been. A tiny pebble didn't compare to a weapon. Besides, she wasn't standing on top of a chair, practically begging to be overbalanced.

Nevertheless, it would be foolish to not exercise at least a little caution.

Finally, she agreed upon a compromise between the warring opinions in her mind. She reached out slowly to the black gem, holding her finger above it. Then, fast as she could, she placed it upon the crystal and just as quickly removed it.

Nothing.

She laughed at herself. Was this how it was going to be for every new experience she encountered? Some bold adventurer she was turning out to be. If the heroes from her scrolls were present, surely they would have laughed at her timidity.

That settled it.

She quickly snatched the black crystal from the shelf, braced herself, then laughed when again nothing happened. She opened her hand and found the gem sitting in it, looking no different.

A fitting souvenir of her adventure. She next decided on a greyish crystal. At first glance, it appeared drab and boring, but when she got closer, she could see it was multi-hued – the coloration more that of a stormy sky, or so she guessed. She'd never actually seen a storm in person, just through the imagery Shitoro sometimes conjured during their lessons. The thought fascinated her, though. Rain, wind, and lightning. Such an exhilarating change of pace from the normalcy of her life.

As those thoughts swirled through her mind, she felt the black crystal in her hand seemingly grow warm, but she dismissed it as nothing more than the gem taking on the warmth of her body.

She continued to stare at the grey crystal, letting her mind wander. Yes, this one reminded her of adventure, braving the high seas upon a ship, standing on a beach after a storm, battling enemies as lightning crashed overhead.

That one would do nicely for her new collection.

The crystal in her hand pulsed, shaking her from her reverie. For a moment, it had almost felt as if it had a heartbeat.

Kisaki shook her head. For all the wonders of this place, she wasn't quite ready to believe that a rock could be alive. It must have been her imagination.

That reminded her she'd probably tarried long enough. Certainly someone would be along soon and, while she loved the thought of meeting new faces and possibly making a friend, she didn't care to be caught in the act of selfishly purloining the contents of this place.

She grabbed the grey crystal she'd been eying and a red one sitting next to it, then quickly stuffed them into her pocket.

It was time to go.

But perhaps one more look at this wondrous place, so I can commit it to memory.

Glancing at the doorway to make sure no one else was in sight, she stepped to the center of the room again and slowly spun in place, taking it all in.

Marvelous as it was, though, her mind was still drawn back to the fantasies she'd conjured a few moments prior.

Yes, she thought, indulging herself. *I am a great general and this is my secret treasure room, won after many hard battles against mighty warriors.* She remembered the great celestial wars she'd read about, but it was the smaller, more intimate conflicts that truly fascinated her. The ones where victory was decided by the swing of a sword as kings battled each other one on one.

As she thought, she continued to turn in place, enjoying the multicolored hues of the many crystals. So caught up in her fantasy was she, that she didn't notice that the circle she stood within had started to glow.

Battles, storms, lightning, the high seas, Earth itself. Though Shitoro had dismissed them as a low people, the humans fascinated her. For some reason, she was drawn to them and their history.

Truly, she thought, *if there's only one place in all the multiverse I could visit, it would be Earth.*

The black crystal still in her hand pulsed again and then cracked open in her palm, releasing its energy.

Kisaki had only a moment to panic as a flare of white-hot light erupted from the circle on the floor and engulfed her.

And then she was gone.

EIGHT

ICHITIRO'S IMPOTENT PONTIFICATIONS of war against the humans was instantly forgotten once Midnite sensed the weak pulse of power, her own energy being released.

But that was impossible. Access to the crystals was currently forbidden. None dared venture forth from the palace until such time as it was allowed. True, some of the youkai could be rebellious at times, but they knew the limits of their impudence and that certain lines were not to be crossed without terrible retribution.

Besides, all who resided there were immortal, and if there was one thing immortals understood, it was patience. What was a decade, a century, or more of waiting to beings for whom the passage of time was meaningless?

Still, there was no denying what she felt. Someone had accessed a crystal, specifically one of the many she had imbued with her own life force. All within the daimao great court had done so, sharing a portion of their power so that servants and other lesser beings could venture forth as needed.

Though the transfer was harmless to her and her siblings, they still remained connected to the energy sealed away in the crystal matrix until such time as it was released to dissipate into the ether. Such an event could be sensed by the progenitor of each crystal.

Under normal circumstances, it was barely noticeable amid the normal traffic to and from the palace, but now, with passage forbidden, it stood out.

Who would have dared? Certainly not one of her servants. Though it was tradition that minions of the daimao used the crystals empowered by their own masters, it wasn't law. Had another youkai used hers so as to mask their passage from their respective lord?

If so, their transgression would be in vain. Midnite wasn't above keeping secrets, but she wasn't about to let something like this pass without mention. If the youkai in question had hoped she would let them get away with it, they were wrong.

She glanced up when Ichitiro slammed his massive fist onto the table again, no doubt trying to emphasize some tiresome point that the others would disagree with. Sadly, she made the mistake of making eye contact with him.

"And what do you think of my plan, fair Midnite?"

Yes, tiresome indeed. "I think that you will continue to believe what you will, despite the wise counsel of your peers, brother."

It was a routine answer, meant to mask that she'd been ignoring him. However, he narrowed his red eyes at her. "One day, you may find yourself wishing you had sided with me."

"Perhaps, but that day is not today, nor do I believe it shall be tomorrow."

Chuckles could be heard around the table, which Reiden quickly silenced with a crackle of red energy. He was not one to allow petty digs or squabbling at the council table ... unless, that is, he was the one to initiate it.

Nevertheless, it had served its purpose, turning Ichitiro's attention away from her so that she might once again concentrate upon this new development.

She reached out to the power that had once been a part of her before it could fully fade away. Her control wasn't so precise as to tell who had made the passage, but she could trace where her energy had taken them.

One of the blessed isles of Earth. Of all the places to venture forth to, why there? Surely whoever had done so knew it wasn't allowed.

Many youkai had been left abandoned on Earth when passage was forbidden, including mates, children, and cousins of the many servants within these vast halls. It was regrettable, but it was thought that all of those here now understood the sacrifice, the larger stakes at play. But perhaps not. Some of the lesser demons could be petty when it came to their emotions, letting them dictate their actions despite the wishes of their masters.

Had that been the case? Had a youkai's spirit become so broken and desperate that they decided to risk the wrath of the daimao?

Midnite considered this. Once upon a time, the concept of sacrifice for a loved one was alien to her. She understood her duty and what needed to be done during times of war, but there had always been cold, calculated methodology to it. Never had her heart ached at the thought of one of her siblings in danger.

But then she had made that fateful journey to those same blessed isles. Kisaki, her daughter, had been born of the forbidden union that resulted from that night. Since then, Midnite had done everything in her power to conceal her birth, her very existence from her siblings out of fear of what they would do.

She knew of the taboo imposed, one of the few that was honored from lesser youkai all the way up to even the daimao. Indeed, she had been one of those who had endorsed it so many centuries ago.

Hanyou, half-breeds, were tolerated if not particularly accepted among her kind. Of them, those of the highest station were offspring created between different castes of divine beings. If anything, the child of a mazoku and youkai union would not have faced much if any scrutiny.

Children born of one human parent were different, though. They were the lowest of the low, certainly never afforded quarter within the celestial palace. Oftentimes they found it hard to find a place in either world – too weak to survive among their demon brothers, but often too malformed to be accepted by humans.

There were exceptions, of course – hanyou who had persevered to become great warriors, heroes of legend, but they were the rarest of the rare.

Considered to be beneath the notice of the daimao, half-mortal hanyou were allowed to live, but only so long as they were the product of a human born of the blessed isles.

That had been her people's conceit. The islands, the place the daimao had first touched down upon arriving at this world, were considered blessed above all. The humans living there were thought to have been influenced by their divine presence, retaining a little of it within their souls. Though humanity as a whole was not held in high regard, those from the blessed isles were favored among them – considered of superior stock compared to the savages that roamed elsewhere.

As such, only unions with them were tolerated. Mating with humans from other lands was considered beneath contempt, a heresy. Though these other cultures had names for such bastard offspring – Nephilim, demigods, and the like – the daimao knew them only as abominations to be destroyed.

However, as much as Midnite once believed such things herself, she could not come to view her daughter that way. No matter his birthright, she had sensed a brave and noble soul in the human who had fathered Kisaki. On occasion, she found herself wondering what had become of him, but his ultimate fate remained a mystery to even her. Despite yearning to know what path his life had led, she'd opted for caution where her daughter was concerned. Regardless, the man she'd known, Stephen Fuller, had been worthy.

Midnite could see that worthiness in her daughter. Whereas many hanyou were born little more than deformed oddities, Kisaki was perfect in her eyes, beautiful as the sea after a storm.

Unfortunately, Midnite also knew that she couldn't hide Kisaki's heritage from her siblings. Her hair, her complexion, her facial features – all of it would make her brethren suspicious of her stock.

Then there was Ichitiro to deal with. Regardless of who Kisaki's father was, her very existence was liable to drive him into a murderous rage.

Though Midnite was secure in her power, even she had doubts as to whether she'd be able to stop him if he truly set his mind to it. If need be, she might have to do the unthinkable and turn on him with the Taiyosori to protect her daughter – even if doing so would render her an outcast, her life forfeit.

She quickly pushed those unpleasant thoughts to the side. Such concerns were unfounded. Kisaki was safe in her wing of the palace, sealed inside and with the very best guardian one could imagine, Shitoro.

Her daughter's safety aside, Midnite still needed to track down whoever the transgressor was. Such a crime could not be overlooked.

While Ichitiro and Reiden continued to argue some point or other, she reached out with her mind to Tanaki, her chief servant.

Tanaki was a dour badger youkai. All business, but exceptionally good at her job. Even so, Midnite frequently found herself missing Shitoro's fussing. However, he was busy elsewhere. She'd entrusted Kisaki to him, knowing he was worthy of such a task. She could count on him to safeguard her biggest secret. If doing so meant she had to deal with Tanaki's stern, humorless tone for all of eternity, so be it.

Yes, my mistress? Tanaki replied almost instantly.

There has been a breach of the crystal chamber. Someone has used one of my own to send themselves to Earth.

But that is forbidden, mistress.

As I am well aware. I need you to look into it. Speak to the other servants of the palace, find out who is missing so that I might inform their lord.

It shall be done, mistress. I will not rest until it is so.

Midnite cut off the conversation. If there was one thing she was certain of with Tanaki, it was that she could be counted on. Dour she might be, but she was dogged when it came to her duties.

She'd tirelessly pursue her task until the culprit was brought to light.

NINE

KISAKI WASN'T A girl easily given over to fear. Despite her sheltered existence, she'd seen a great many wondrous things, and her favorite part of her studies had always revolved around wars and battles.

Nevertheless, she cried out in shock as the room faded away in a flash of light, to be replaced by somewhere much larger. As her eyes adjusted, she realized the floor, the walls, everything that had been around her mere moments earlier, was gone.

The hard floor had been replaced by something white and with much more give to it. Off to one side she saw trees, but much larger and more numerous than in the two walled gardens she was allowed to visit.

In front of her was an impossible sight: water, sapphire blue, stretching as far as the eye could see.

Is that an ocean?

Kisaki's shock gave way to wonder as she took in the sights, but that wasn't all. The air was warm, and she could smell the clean scent of the salt water. She dared a glance up and saw a clear blue sky with a yellow sun smiling down at her.

It's an illusion. It has to be.

Surely that was the purpose of the room she'd stumbled upon. Though she didn't fully understand illusion magic, she'd learned the basics and could perform a few tricks. Nothing like this, though. If anything, this was the work of true masters of the craft.

A properly conjured illusion could fool the senses, but she'd never experienced anything on this level before. The few so-called advanced spells Shitoro had demonstrated to her in the past were child's play in comparison.

But how?

Then Kisaki remembered. She'd been daydreaming while in the center of the marvelous crystal room, thinking about the high seas, about Earth. That had to have been it. The view around her certainly resembled some of what she'd studied, if only vaguely. Her books were filled with stories of war, but this appeared to be a place of peace. Also, the weather was clear, whereas in many of the scrolls she'd read, there was always a storm taking place during a pivotal battle.

Perhaps if she concentrated harder, the magic of the room would show her something a bit more visceral.

She hesitated doing so, however, enjoying the tranquility of what was before her. What would it hurt to stay and enjoy this for a few minutes longer?

I could be caught, that's what could happen.

Any second now, the illusion could be dispersed and she'd turn to find the disapproving gaze of Shitoro or, worse, her mother glaring at her.

But so far, she'd gone undiscovered and, after a few moments, Kisaki found her feet moving, almost of their own accord, toward the water.

Further out, past the shallows, she could see waves breaking. Here, though, closer to the ... beach? Yes, that was what this place was called. And what she was walking on was sand.

Suddenly, Shitoro's never-ending lessons didn't seem so foolish, even if she'd never tell him that aloud.

She reached the very edge of the vast ocean and then kept going, curious to see what would happen. Her slippers, feet, and the bottom of her kimono all became wet as she stepped into the water. Despite this, she laughed. Truly a marvelous illusion! Oh, if only the demon who had conjured this was her teacher. If she could learn to do magic like this, then she might never need to leave her chambers again.

She might explore all manner of…

Kisaki stopped and turned around, noting her footsteps in the sand and how far she'd seemingly come. It wasn't a great distance, but unless she was mistaken – which she didn't believe to be the case – she'd walked further than the radius of the room should have allowed. As real as this illusion appeared, she should have bumped into the wall a good ten paces back.

She was contemplating what this all meant when she was startled from her reverie by sounds.

No, not just sounds … voices.

Despite the myriad creatures that served her mother in all of their different forms and visages, Kisaki was well aware that she looked different than most of them. She resembled her mother in some ways, although not nearly as stunningly beautiful, but in others did not. For instance, their hair and skin colors differed. In addition, Kisaki lacked the fine row of regal horns that rested upon her mother's head, something she always rued.

If anything, based on the many images she'd seen during her countless hours of study, she most closely resembled humans in appearance. Or at least she thought so. The truth was, most of the humans depicted in her lessons had been male warriors. Though their features were similar, their bodies were typically much broader and muscular than her lithe form.

The beings approaching her, chattering away in a strange language, looked vaguely like the humans she'd seen in her studies. However, these creatures were dressed very different from the armored forms she expected. Their body shapes varied, too. One of them was quite rotund, whereas three were thin, even thinner than she.

They noticed her and approached, pointing in her direction.

All at once, Kisaki grew fearful again. The distance she'd crossed, and now creatures – *humans* – approaching her, having apparently seen her?

This was like no illusion she'd ever heard of.

And then, in the back of her mind, she asked herself something she'd been subconsciously avoiding since arriving. *What if this isn't an illusion?*

The newcomers kept approaching, continuing to chatter away as they pointed at her. They stopped while still on the beach. Truly their dress was strange. Not regal finery by any means, and certainly not armor, but unlike any peasant garb Kisaki had ever seen – flimsy pants that stopped at their knees and simple but colorful tunics upon their upper bodies. One, with long black hair, wore slippers upon its feet similar to Kisaki's, but missing the front so that its toes showed through. This one was different from the others, more closely resembling Kisaki than them. *A human female, perhaps?*

The other three – males, she concluded – wore short, white boots upon their feet.

They continued to point and chatter at her. Kisaki briefly considered the quill within her robes. It was currently useless, but if it was once a sword, then perhaps it could become one again … if she could figure out how to do so. But then, quite suddenly, the humans' chatter changed to laughter, something she understood.

If they were laughing, then maybe they didn't mean her harm after all. If anything, they seemed to be enjoying themselves. After a few moments, Kisaki realized it was contagious and she joined in, which caused them to start talking among themselves again.

And that's when something strange happened. As she listened to their chatter, utterly unintelligible mere moments earlier, she began to understand them.

"… water…"

"Look … her…"

"Why is … laughing…?"

"… she's … stupid."

"She has to be."

"Yeah, look at her … standing there in the water like some dummy."

"Look at the way she's dressed."

"Is she getting married?"

"She probably escaped from a circus."

Kisaki couldn't believe her ears. Their tone aside, she understood what they were saying. One moment, their language had been utterly alien to her, the next she had near perfect clarity. She decided to test it out with her own tongue. "Can … you understand me?"

"Hey," the rotund one said. "The freak can speak!"

"Ask her if she ran out of detergent," another of the males said.

"You just did, stupid."

"Oh, yeah."

"Detergent?" Kisaki asked. Though she seemed to understand the basics of their language now, it appeared she didn't have perfect comprehension over the nuances.

"Yeah, it's what you use to do your laundry, freak, instead of wading into the ocean wearing it." That caused the humans to all start laughing again.

Kisaki wasn't stupid. She knew she was being made fun of for some reason. Still, unlike the ferret youkai she'd met before, at least these creatures weren't running from her.

"What, haven't you ever seen water before?" the girl asked.

"Water, yes, but not the ocean," Kisaki replied.

"She's a freak and a liar," the large one said, causing the other males to chuckle.

"I am no liar. My name is Kisaki. My mother is…"

"Awww, are you gonna cry for your mommy now?"

"Cry?" She was feeling a lot of emotions right at that moment, but the urge to weep wasn't one of them. Such strange creatures, these humans. Even stranger than Shitoro had made them out to be.

Kisaki began to walk back toward the beach, but the four humans moved to the edge of the water to block her. As she approached them, she realized they were all a good head shorter than she. Were these human cubs … children?

"Please allow me to pass, I…"

"You can't leave," the round one said. "You're not finished with your laundry yet." He stepped forward and gave Kisaki a shove. She hadn't been expecting it and, as a result, lost her balance and fell backward into the water.

More annoyed than hurt by this creature's impudence, she glared up at him from where she sat, the water drenching her robes.

"Let's dunk her!" one of the other males said, much to his friends' approval.

As the large one started forward again, another strange thing happened. For a brief moment, the world greyed out around her, and she saw someone else standing before her … a strange ghost-like image superimposed upon the reality in front of her. Another person, a much larger human male, was standing where the human boy was. All at once, she saw what appeared to be her own leg kick out, striking the ghost image in the side of the knee and knocking him down.

The odd vision ended just as quickly as it had appeared. Before Kisaki was even really aware what she was doing, she mimicked the move, kicking out from her prone position. She knocked the rotund boy's legs out from under him, causing him to topple into another of his friends. They both fell into the water beside her.

As they cried out with indignation, Kisaki felt a stab of heat at her side, as if something were jabbing her. It was coming from where she'd hidden the sword turned quill. Almost as if it were…

"Hey! What are you doing? Leave her alone!"

TEN

"LEAVE ME ALONE."

"But, master…"

Ichitiro glared down from the council table at the diminutive ferret demon, silencing him immediately.

Midnite felt pity for the little youkai. To be saddled with such a cruel master for eternity must've been a burden even for an untrustworthy thief such as Ito. He was well known among the denizens of the palace. She'd continually cautioned her own servants against fraternizing with him. Items went missing whenever he was around – never anything of great importance, but annoying nevertheless.

Of course, whenever confronted about his servant's sticky paws, Ichitiro would deny it all but vow to punish him nevertheless. Midnite had a feeling he was lying about the first, but feared he wasn't regarding the second.

Something must have gotten Ito into a tizzy if he was daring to interrupt the celestial court while it was in session. Though they weren't arguing about anything they hadn't already debated to death a hundred times before, there was still protocol to be maintained. Such an interruption was allowed, but it was understood it should be for matters of importance only.

She much preferred reaching out with her mind to her chief servant, often at regular intervals. It allowed Tanaki to convey to her any matters of interest while avoiding the annoyed stares of Midnite's brethren. However, such workings were subtle, requiring mental clarity. Such things were not Ichitiro's style, if indeed he was even capable of it. Matters of the mind were not his specialty.

Still, the interruption reminded her to check in. Not enough time had passed for Tanaki to report any results on her investigation – although listening to the other daimao drone on about the humans made it seem as if decades had gone by. However, the proceedings were currently halted as Ichitiro dealt with Ito.

She initiated contact. *How goes it, Tanaki?* she thought in a bored tone.

Mistress? Oh, thank goodness! I was just on my way to the council chamber to see you.

That caught Midnite's attention. As dogged as Tanaki's respect for protocol was, she had never once interrupted court in person. She was a smart youkai, preferring to solve problems rather than dumping them at her mistress's feet. It was a virtue that Midnite highly respected. For her to even consider changing tactics meant that something out of the ordinary had occurred, something that even the resourceful badger demon felt she could not handle alone.

What is wrong?

I don't know how, or who … it is impossible, unthinkable!

Slow down, Tanaki. Tell me what happened.

The Taiyosori, mistress! It's been stolen!

It was with supreme effort that Midnite did not launch herself out of her seat at the news. Tanaki had been right to panic. It *should* have been impossible. The Taiyosori would automatically protect itself, lethally if necessary, against transgressions by anyone it didn't acknowledge as master. A few had tried in the distant past, and the lessons of their demise served as a reminder to all others, even beings as powerful as Ichitiro.

Was her servant somehow mistaken?

No, that was unlikely. The Taiyosori, in its spot above her throne, was hard to miss.

That made two mysteries in the space of less than an hour, albeit this new one eclipsed the old many times over in importance. The Taiyosori was a weapon capable of incredible destruction. Worse, it had been bequeathed to her by the elder gods. Should they sense it missing and awaken, untold cataclysm could unfold.

"I call for a recess," she said in a voice far calmer than she felt.

"A recess?" Reiden asked from his spot at the head of the table.

"Yes. It would seem one of Ichitiro's servants has urgent business with his master." The war daimao shrugged as if to disagree, but she ignored him. "Surely he would not disturb us otherwise. Besides, I believe we can all agree that the matters before us will not be solved this day."

Most of those gathered, save Reiden, nodded in agreement. Though time meant nothing to those gifted with eternal life, that didn't mean they were immune to growing bored of the same tiresome discussion.

"Very well," Reiden proclaimed, his tone dispassionate. "These proceedings are hereby suspended."

Despite her near panic, Midnite allowed herself a smile. Regardless of his love of protocol, Reiden too had apparently grown weary, although he would never admit to any such thing.

If she was able to solve the mystery of the missing Taiyosori in short order, she might consider indulging in a long bath as reward for her troubles. Such a thing would do wonders for her rapidly fraying nerves.

Ichitiro approached her before she could leave, doubling her resolve to bathe as talking to him always left her feeling somewhat dirty.

"Dearest Midnite," he greeted with an exaggerated bow, his eyes drinking in her form as he did so.

"Brother." Her tone practically oozed disinterest. She needed to end this conversation quickly, return to her quarters, and see what had transpired. A long, drawn out session of him pathetically flirting with her was utterly revolting during the best of times, much less now.

"Thank you for your concern regarding my servant."

"I am sure Ito had news of great importance to dare interrupt his betters. Surely it is a matter to which you should attend," she replied, hoping he took the hint.

Ichitiro leaned against the wall, blocking her way forward. "Doubtful. His mind is as slow as his paws are quick. Chances are he merely lost some unimportant bauble somewhere and is now in a panic about it."

"If so, then I would hope you would explain to him the error of his ways."

"Have no doubt he will be dealt with accordingly."

Midnite's skin crawled at the insinuation. She knew Ichitiro to be a bully of the highest order. The lower the caste of his victims, the more cruel he became.

Even the least servants of the daimao were more durable than their earthbound cousins, thanks in part to the many enchantments upon the palace. That, combined with the potent healing waters that flowed through the palace springs, meant that Ichitiro could afford to indulge his twisted cravings without fear of having to replace a servant.

"I am certain that talking to him would be more than sufficient."

Ichitiro stepped in closer to Midnite, uncomfortably so. "Why waste words when actions are so much more satisfying?"

It took all of Midnite's willpower to not spit in the war demon's face, even more so to not unleash a hex upon him. But that would not do, especially not in the court chambers. Fortunately, salvation was near.

"Mistress, mistress!" Tanaki cried as she came racing up.

No matter what happened to the Taiyosori, Midnite owed her thanks for her timely arrival.

"Yes, actions are more satisfying," she replied to Ichitiro. "But, alas, mine are currently required elsewhere."

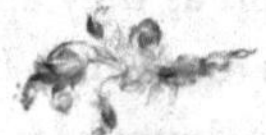

"Slow down, Tanaki, and explain it to me again."

The badger demon took a deep breath, despite her pace back toward their wing of the palace remaining frantic. "As you wish. I was preparing to…" She looked around, didn't see anyone within earshot, but still lowered her voice to the barest of whispers. "…conduct the other matter we discussed."

"Go on."

"My plan was to ask Shitoro to invite some of his associates over for tea."

Midnite smiled slightly. Though Tanaki had been around for a long time, she mostly chose to keep to herself. Shitoro, however, was on good terms with many other servants. That was an excellent place to start. Invite them over for some friendly conversation, then subtly discern if they had heard of anything strange going on.

"When I went to prepare your audience chamber to receive them, however, I found it in disarray."

"How so?" Midnite asked, curious to hear what her servant had to say. Tanaki's version of disarray often greatly differed from her own.

"The doors were unbarred and the Taiyosori was missing. There was a gouge in the seat of your throne. I fear it may have been a message meant for you." She lowered her voice even further. "You may have enemies about, mistress."

It seemed a very subtle message to her if indeed she had, as Tanaki put it, enemies. Still, the fact remained that the sword was missing. That was a difficult detail to ignore. The weapon wasn't something that could simply be misplaced.

Tanaki had sent word ahead of their return. The grand doors were opened from within as they approached. Midnite did not even need to step in to see that Tanaki had spoken true, not that she had cause to doubt her.

The Taiyosori had been strategically positioned to be as visible as Midnite herself to all who were allowed entrance to her domain. The combination was a formidable one – her atop her obsidian throne with one of the most powerful weapons in creation hanging above her head as if waiting for her command.

She had kept it that way for centuries. But now it was simply gone.

"Tanaki, I want this entire room torn apart and rebuilt from the ground up."

"Mistress?"

"We cannot afford to let anyone else know the Taiyosori is missing." She wasn't quite prepared to declare it stolen yet. As far as she was aware, such a thing simply wasn't possible. Though she would barely admit it to herself, she found it more than a little frightening to imagine that the unthinkable had occurred. "If any dare ask, tell them that I grew bored with the stagnant look of this room."

"How shall we rebuild it, Mistress?"

"You know my tastes. I trust you will come up with something suitable. The more important matter is that it will give us time should any of my siblings request an audience with me."

Left unsaid was that it was time that would be spent discovering the whereabouts of the sword, retrieving it, and punishing the transgressor, whoever they might be. Midnite silently vowed they would not escape her wrath. They…

The doors leading further into her wing of the palace burst open and Shitoro stepped through, looking a bit out of sorts. He saw her and immediately bowed deeply. "Ah, mistress! My apologies."

"Apologies?" Midnite asked, only partially paying attention.

"For my rude entrance. I was looking for Kisaki."

"Kisaki?"

"Yes. She is late for her studies and I have not seen her for some time."

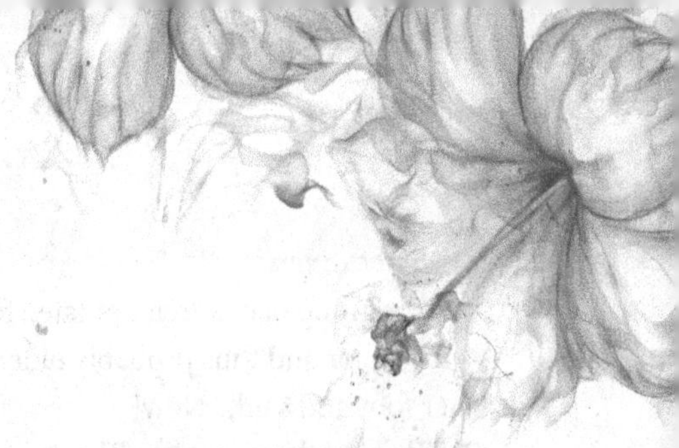

ELEVEN

"**S**HE PUSHED ME into the water!" the large child complained to the newcomer, a girl of roughly Kisaki's height.

"I saw what happened, Hojo. You started it. You'd better apologize."

"You're not my mom, Tamiko."

"No, but she works for my dad, so maybe I can tell him about it."

Kisaki had no idea what the two humans were talking about. She'd been distracted by the apparent activity from the quill in her robes. However, whatever it was, it appeared to have ceased with the appearance of this new girl.

She seemed to be talking down to the first group of humans, the ones who had dared to manhandle her. Perhaps they were servants. Though they were only children, maybe the girl intended for them to be whipped for their impudence.

Whatever the case, the large child – Hojo seemed to be his name – stopped arguing and looked uncertain.

"Take your friends and get out of here. I don't want to hear about you bullying anyone again, especially not the entertainers."

Entertainers?

The group of children hesitated for a moment, then the new girl, larger and thus probably older than the others, stamped her foot and said, "Now!"

That got them moving. The four ran off, back the way they'd originally come when Kisaki was still convinced this was some sort of illusion. Hojo stopped at the edge of the trees just long enough to turn around and stick out his tongue, but then he disappeared from her sight.

Kisaki suddenly felt foolish sitting there in the water. For all of her time spent reading about battles and warriors, she'd been bested by a group of mere children seconds after arriving.

"Are you okay?" the older girl, Tamiko, asked. She approached Kisaki, stepped into the water up to her ankles, and leaned down to offer a hand.

Kisaki hesitated to take it. She was quite embarrassed by what had just happened. That, and she'd also learned two harsh lessons this day about assuming everyone she met would want to be friends with her. She didn't care to learn it a third time.

Again, almost as if in response to her wary thoughts, she felt momentary heat at her side where the quill lay in her robes.

Tamiko smiled. "It's okay. They're gone." After Kisaki continued to hesitate, she added, "Do you understand me?" A moment later, she said something in a different dialect, one that Kisaki didn't know.

Kisaki wondered if perhaps she could pick up this new language the same way she'd apparently learned the first or whether that was merely some quirk of her appearing in this new land. However, her pride overcame her caution and she decided to answer. "I understand you."

"That's good," Tamiko replied with a grin. "English is the only other language I know well. If that didn't work, I would've had to start making hand gestures."

"English?"

"Yeah. That's what I just asked if you spoke." She straightened up and again held a hand toward Kisaki. "So … do you like sitting there, getting your uniform all soaking wet?"

"Uniform?" Kisaki asked, but before Tamiko could answer, she took the human girl's hand and pulled herself up. "No. It was not my intention to get wet. Those others…"

"They're jerks, but pretty harmless otherwise. Hojo is a real wimp to anyone who stands up to him. I saw the way you knocked him down. If I hadn't shown up when I did, he probably would have run home crying."

Kisaki wasn't entirely certain what this girl was talking about, but her tone seemed far friendlier than the others she'd met. Though Kisaki's instincts for others had atrophied due to her long isolation without any peers, she decided to take a chance with this girl. She desperately wanted to make at least one friend during her sojourn, even if that friend was a human who she would likely never be allowed to see again. "Thank you."

"Hey, it's no problem. Besides, wouldn't want your first day working here to be a bad one."

"Working here?"

"Yeah. Aren't you one of the performers for the Star Festival this weekend?"

"What is a Star Festival?"

Tamiko stepped from the water and Kisaki followed. When she turned back, she looked confused. "If you're not here to perform, then why are you wearing that?"

Kisaki looked down. "This? These are my robes. I am always dressed in such attire."

"Really? Are you from some rich girl boarding school I haven't heard of?"

Though she was still catching up to Tamiko's choice of words, Kisaki began to understand. Upon seeing the four children in need of discipline, she'd remarked to herself how strangely they'd been dressed. Now, she realized, here on Earth – however she had gotten here – maybe *she* was the one dressed strangely. Most of her studies of this planet had been of its history and how it intersected with that of demon-kind. Perhaps when not waging war this was how the humans chose to appear. It seemed a logical assumption. "This is how I often dress within the celestial palace. Obviously, servants dress in lesser garb."

"Servants, eh?" Tamiko replied. "Must be nice."

"Nice," Kisaki echoed. "It is comfortable ... if stagnant."

"You must be one of the guests here, then."

Kisaki looked away for a moment, embarrassed.

"So you're not a guest?" Tamiko asked.

"I do not even know where here is."

Tamiko laughed but then, after a few moments when she saw that Kisaki wasn't joining her, asked, "You're not serious, are you?"

"I know I am on Earth, but beyond that..."

"On Earth?" Tamiko replied, blowing out a huff of breath. "That's a start, I guess. Hold on. Do you have amnesia or some-thing? You know, lost your memory."

"I am well aware of who I am," Kisaki said. "It's just, I do not know how I got here. I..." She paused for a moment, debating how much she should say. It was possible Tamiko's kindness was a ruse, but she genuinely seemed both friendly and helpful. After a moment's debate, she decided to trust her. "I left the quarters of my mother, Lady Midnite, without her permission."

"Lady Midnight?"

"You have heard of her, yes?"

"Is that a stage name, like Lady Gaga?"

"I am not aware of any daimao of that name. Perhaps she inhabits a different wing of the palace."

"Daimao?" Tamiko asked with a laugh. "Is that her band name?"

Kisaki didn't quite understand, perhaps a quirk of the local dialect, but it sounded reasonable. "Yes, they are her brethren."

"Okay, I think I get it now," Tamiko said. "Your mom's a musician, probably on the road all the time, never home. So you ran away." Before Kisaki could say anything to the contrary, she continued. "Don't you think she'll be worried about you?"

"I am certain she will be quite angry. Shitoro, too. I have little doubt he will be in charge of my punishment."

"Shitoro? Who's that?"

"My guardian."

"Like your stepdad or something? Wow, is he that bad?"

Kisaki didn't know what a stepdad was, but again she assumed it was probably just another human colloquialism. "He is very strict and will be particularly cross when he discovers I stole his key."

"To his car?"

"To the doors that kept me inside."

"They kept you locked up?!" Tamiko looked shocked. "The hell with that. You're coming with me. We'll figure out what to do, but in the meantime, you can stay at my place."

"You are not going to tell my mother?"

"No way."

Kisaki smiled. Though she was still wary, she began to suspect she had just made her first new friend. "You are called Tamiko, correct?"

"Yes." She gave Kisaki a quick bow, then held out a hand. "Pleased to meet you."

They grasped hands. "I am pleased as well. I am Kisaki."

"That's a pretty name."

"Thank you. So is yours."

"It's okay, I guess." She turned and beckoned Kisaki onward. "Come on, let's go."

"Where?"

"My dad's the manager at the Kabira Beach resort. We're pretty full up right now, but I think I can find somewhere for you to stay. But first…"

"Yes?" Kisaki asked tentatively, falling into step with her new friend.

"First, we're going to find you some new clothes so you don't stick out like a sore thumb."

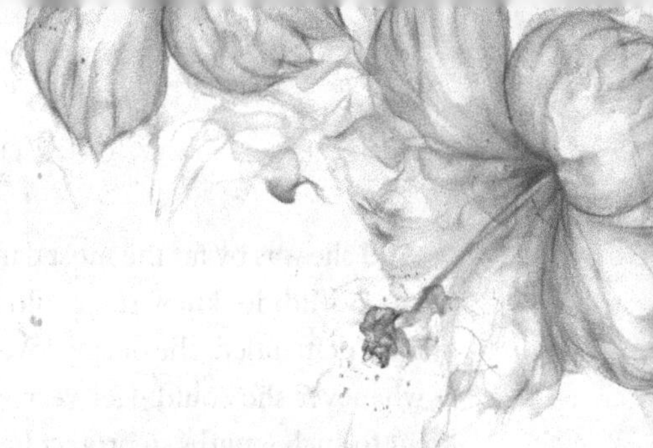

TWELVE

MIDNITE WASN'T OFTEN at odds about what to feel. Most of the decisions in her life were easy to judge.

This, however, was different. She was equal parts angry, impressed, and worried out of her mind. She was angry with Shitoro, that he had let his guard down knowing how mischievous and willful Kisaki could be. But she was more furious with her daughter, that she would steal his key and leave, despite doing so being expressly forbidden.

All the same, she felt a grudging respect that Kisaki had proven herself so resourceful. Shitoro was meticulous in his methods and not easily fooled. His early life, before she had rescued him, had taught him to be wary. That her daughter had gotten past him without his knowledge spoke of cunning on her part, a far cry from the complaining child who often whined about wanting to see what lay beyond her domain.

Cunning or not, though, Midnite knew she was ill-prepared for what awaited her outside her doors. The youkai who served the other daimao weren't of concern, but if they learned of her existence, then so would their masters. If that happened … she didn't care to think what would become of her darling daughter.

And she was by far the most darling thing in Midnite's life. Though Midnite knew she could be distant, something her station demanded, she deeply loved Kisaki and tried to show it whenever she could. Her very existence and that Midnite went to such lengths to protect her was evidence of that.

But now, she was gone. Her chambers had been thoroughly combed, both physically and magically, and there was no sign of her.

That in itself was bad enough, but what the girl had somehow done in the process of escaping was potentially catastrophic.

Midnite summoned both Tanaki and Shitoro to her audience chamber. She ordered all the others out and had the doors sealed so they might discuss matters privately.

Shitoro, in particular, seemed nervous about the meeting, probably rightfully so, but Midnite realized that nothing would be solved by unleashing her wrath upon him, even if he likely deserved it.

"We have a very grave issue at hand," she said from her place upon the throne. "One that needs to be solved post haste."

Shitoro bowed deeply, shaking ever so slightly. "Kisaki will be found, mistress. S-she cannot have gotten far."

"Farther than you may think," Midnite replied. "There have been three transgressions this day. I am not inclined to think they are unrelated."

"Three?"

"The unexplained sending and the theft," Tanaki said in a matter-of-fact tone.

"Yes," Midnite replied with a nod of her head. "First, there was an unauthorized sending to Earth, made with a crystal filled with my own power. Then we learned the Taiyosori had gone missing. Finally, there is the matter of my daughter. I would propose, that if one were to reverse the order in which I learned of these happenings, then one would have a very clear line of events which occurred."

Shitoro's eyes opened so wide, Midnite was certain they might come tumbling out of his head. "You don't think…? Surely the girl isn't nearly that clever."

Midnite allowed herself the ghost of a grin. "Are you saying my daughter isn't intelligent? She did outsmart you, after all."

"N-not at all," Shitoro sputtered. "But for her to sneak out and make her way to Earth is unlikely enough. But to steal the great blade, too? That's impossible. The sword cannot be stolen. She would have been utterly destroyed."

"Not necessarily," Midnite said. "The weapon can be gifted, won, or inherited."

"But…"

"Do I not considered Kisaki my heir?"

"An heir who can never claim her birthright, my lady."

"Yes." Midnite nodded. "But an heir nevertheless. My blood flows through her veins. Though even I cannot claim to fully understand the power of the blade of heaven, I propose the possibility that the Taiyosori may have sensed her connection to me."

"But why steal it?" Tanaki asked.

Shitoro nodded vigorously. "I have known the child ever since she was a babe. She is willful, stubborn, even infuriating at times, but evil? Never."

Midnite folded her hands and contemplated this. "Let us not forget perhaps the worst flaw she possesses, a flaw that I myself am guilty of having instilled in her. She is ignorant."

"But her studies…"

Midnite waved off the tiger demon's concerns. "Yes, yes. I am well aware you have been diligent in her teachings, but she is ignorant of nearly everything outside of those doors." She gestured toward the entrance to the inner chambers, locked up tight again. "Even her time in my audience chamber has been limited to moments out of the past several decades. The fault of this lies solely with me. In my desire to protect her,

I purposely refused to discuss matters that she should have known about, matters of importance."

"Then why take the sword?" Tanaki asked.

"Who can say? Curiosity, spite? It could have been any reason. Perhaps she simply wished to gaze upon the marvel of the blade, then panicked. All we know is that she somehow managed to grasp the sword without facing its wrath."

"The weapon found her worthy," Shitoro said in a voice barely a whisper.

"I would not go that far," Midnite chided. "My daughter is neither daimao or mazoku. She is not even particularly formidable for a hanyou. That is, assuming no transgressions in her studies occurred."

"Of course not, my lady," he replied indignantly. "She has never even touched a weapon so far as I know. She only barely understands the basics of magic."

Midnite raised a hand to quell her servant. "Be at peace, Shitoro. I know all of this. The Taiyosori is a mysterious object. There is no way of knowing why it allowed my daughter to handle it, save for us to know it did and she survived."

"And Earth?" Tanaki asked.

"That I cannot answer."

"The girl is fascinated by the humans," Shitoro said. "I don't know why. Perhaps she can sense her heritage."

Midnite narrowed her eyes.

"B-but, that is only a guess, because *I* certainly never told her anything about it. The fact remains that she is. How she managed to get there, though, is beyond me. We covered the basics of trans-dimensional passage in her lessons, but that is all. The girl knew nothing of the sending chamber. How she even found it is a mystery to me."

"As it is to me," Midnite said.

After a moment, Tanaki spoke up. "Perhaps she had help."

"One of our own?" Midnite asked, her tone growing dangerous.

"No, mistress. I would bet my life upon that. All of the servants within these walls are loyal to you and your wishes. But what if another…"

"That is a very serious accusation," Midnite warned, but it was halfhearted. It wasn't unknown for the daimao to plot against each other, whether to gain favor with the court or for other petty reasons. But that assumed her siblings were even aware of Kisaki's existence, something she had taken pains to prevent. Even if they were, then why work this way? Why not just confront her openly in front of the court and demand that her child be executed for the transgression of being born of an unworthy human?

Unless…

"The Taiyosori," Midnite said. "If one of my siblings is after it, then Kisaki would be the only way to accomplish their goal."

Much as she didn't want to admit it, that made sense. If Kisaki were killed trying to grasp the weapon, so be it in their eyes. One less half-breed to worry about. If not, then her daughter would be infinitely more easy to defeat in combat than she, one of the few other means of gaining the Taiyosori's favor. The sword would have a new master, and it would all be accomplished without the potential for causing all-out war among the daimao.

Left unsaid was the name she thought most likely behind this … Ichitiro.

THIRTEEN

ICHITIRO SAVORED THE shrill screams of his meal as he bathed in a mixture of its blood and the boiling mud he favored.

The more the tiny youkai begged for mercy, the more Ichitiro enjoyed the taste as he ripped chunk after chunk of still quivering meat from its body.

Had any of his brothers known of his tendency to devour the flesh of his own servants, leaving them just barely alive enough for the healing waters of the palace to restore, they would have been appalled. But restored they were, and in short order, too, only for him to do so again whenever the mood, and appetite, was upon him.

And why not? He was a daimao, a superior being on any world he deemed to set foot upon. However, as the eons passed, it became more and more clear to him that not all daimao were created equal.

Hah! The thought of his siblings, with their misguided sense of regality, left him equal parts amused and disgusted. They thought themselves enlightened beings. What they failed to realize was that they'd lost their way, forgotten themselves. The sounds of battle still called to them within their dreams, but it was no more than an empty shadow of the past, an echo of the days when they fought the entropic chaos at the bequest of their masters.

The daimao were originally born for battle, bred for it. Yet, what were they doing now? Endlessly debating how best to deal with the humans, a race of insignificant insects who arrogantly aspired to more than their lowly kind was fated.

His brothers, Reiden in particular, thought him stupid. They rolled their eyes, called him tiresome when he argued the same point again and again. Yet they failed to see the method behind his reasoning. Every time Ichitiro put forth his argument to invade Earth, to lay low the humans, there were fewer rolls of the eye, less sighs of boredom. Little by little, he was making his point known, worming his way into their thoughts. Soon enough, his wishes would be theirs, and they would never once suspect he had manipulated them.

No, they thought him dull-witted, a mere dog of war. Ichitiro knew that much. If anything, he encouraged that opinion. It ensured that even while they respected his strength of arms, they underestimated his cunning.

Ichitiro smiled to himself, taking one more bite from the nearly lifeless youkai before tossing it to the side like rubbish, where his other servants would tend to its wounds.

He swallowed, savoring the flesh nearly as much as his grand designs.

The others would never suspect that he, seemingly a proponent of the old ways – when he and his brothers rode forth into battle at the whims of the gods – aspired to greatness they dared not comprehend.

The elder gods. Such wasted potential. Powerful enough to bend creation to their own will, yet content to dream away the eons like tired children. If only they could be smothered in their sleep, Ichitiro would have done so untold millennia ago. But alas, such a thing was not so easy. Sleeping they might be, but vulnerable they were not. Unless one had the means.

Sadly, Ichitiro did not … at least for the moment.

The Taiyosori had been his goal for ages now. Supposedly forged during the heat death of the prior universe, its blade was said to be able to cut through anything if the one wielding it had a strong enough will. *Anything*, even the throat of a sleeping god.

That its incalculable power was wasted in the hands of his fool sister was maddening. It should be wielded by one who was both worthy and willing to use it. But instead, it hung impotently in her throne room, mocking any who dared look upon it and imagine its potential.

A part of him wondered if perhaps the elder gods had done so purposely, entrusting it to one too cowed to ever make use of it and far too frigid to ever let a worthy mate share her bedchamber and make claim to it. At times, he feared the gods had foreseen his treachery and prepared for it accordingly. The enchantments upon the weapon, rendering it virtually impossible to steal, seemed to suggest so. Ichitiro laughed it off as nothing but paranoia. The elder gods might be great, but so were the daimao.

Time and again he'd courted Midnite, seeking a union with her, only to be rebuffed. He had figured the same logic by which he was slowly wearing down the resolve of the council would work upon her. That, little by little, she might come to reconsider his request until such time as she was his and, by virtue of marriage, so was all she owned.

Infuriatingly, that had not come to pass, despite his best laid plans. Several times he had been almost tempted to challenge her to a duel, a battle for ownership of the sword, one of the few ways the weapon could be won. Ichitiro wasn't a coward, but he was no fool either. Midnite was formidable, as were all the daimao. However, if she decided to use the sword in such a battle, something that would be in her right to do, then she could very well destroy him.

Such thoughts had sent him into a rage in the past, requiring his servants to pick up the pieces and rebuild, both his chambers and their own broken bodies.

But things had changed in the last several decades. The Taiyosori was still his best hope for conquering the accursed gods dreaming their damnable dreams. But, as it turned out, it wasn't his *only* hope.

The humans. Who would have guessed that such a pathetic species would have discovered such incredible destructive potential? True, he had argued that they should be crushed, and he meant it. But where his brothers would seek to grind the humans beneath their heel and send their civilization tumbling back to a time when they knew their place in the cosmic order, Ichitiro wished to conquer them and take their power for his own.

Despite the edict against travel, he had kept close tabs on humanity these past decades. There were many demons still on Earth. In fact, some had been purposely sent there in the days before the restriction was imposed. They were loyal to him, willing to infiltrate human society and keep watch on it. Though they were foot soldiers at best, cannon fodder too stupid to properly understand the power the humans had harnessed, they had kept him informed over the years.

Ichitiro was well aware that the humans' technology, as they called it, had continued to advance in the decades since the daimao had retreated from their world. As awe-inspiring as their display of power had been at the time, they now possessed weapons hundreds of times more deadly.

The Taiyosori would be unnecessary if he could possess that power. He could lay low the elder gods once and for all in a fitting pyre worthy of them. It was possible the celestial palace itself would not survive such an attack, but so be it. With the elder gods dead, Ichitiro's ultimate plan would be set into motion. He would ascend. A new age would begin, led by a new god, one who would remake reality into his own image.

As for the other daimao, they would either acknowledge him as their superior and serve him, or they would be destroyed. He smiled as he considered the glorious destiny ahead of him, one that would soon be within his grasp.

"M … master?"

The rare smile fell from Ichitiro's lips as the sputtering voice interrupted his thoughts. He looked down and spied Ito, a wretched ferret youkai who served him in only the barest of sense. The useless little demon often seemed far more preoccupied with stealing baubles than doing anything of note.

Ichitiro only tolerated his existence because he was often a source of consternation for his brothers and sisters, something the great demon could appreciate. However, the youkai's actions had long since ceased to amuse him. The ferret was at least cunning enough to realize this and oftentimes stayed out of his master's sight.

So why now was he daring to ruin Ichitiro's musings on a future when he and he alone would reign supreme?

Wait. This wasn't a lone offense. Hadn't the insufferable little weasel likewise tried to get his attention during court earlier, nearly causing him embarrassment in front of the council? And for what? Probably to show him some earring or bracelet he'd swiped in a pathetic attempt to win his favor.

Ichitiro was having none of it. Though he was sated from his meal, that did not mean he wouldn't enjoy wringing the little beast's neck. And if he happened to kill the youkai in the process, what of it? He had plenty more servants who were of far more use to him. Ito would not be missed. Not by him, and certainly not by anyone else.

True, his appearance had been the catalyst that had broken up the meeting, ending Reiden's tireless pontification for the time being. However, Ichitiro was not one prone to showing gratitude toward those less than he.

Quick as a snake, he lashed out and grabbed the ferret youkai by the neck, eliciting a frightened squeak from him. He dragged him over until they were eye to eye, the youkai's tail landing in the boiling mud and causing it to squeal in pain.

"You have either become very bold this day, Ito, or even stupider than you normally are. I will give you one chance to convince me that I should not skin you alive for your earlier interruption of the council."

He switched his grip, holding the tiny demon by the scruff of his neck, just inches above the steaming mud.

"A hanyou!" the ferret squeaked.

"What of them?"

"I ... I saw one today."

Ichitiro's eyes narrowed. Was this Ito's new form of amusement? He'd grown bored of petty thievery and was now resorting to lies? If so, he'd picked the wrong audience for his idiocy. "Impossible. There aren't any of the disgusting little half-breeds in the palace."

"Untrue."

"You would call me a liar?"

"Never, master! Merely uninformed."

It was a poor choice of words. Ichitiro quickly dunked the ferret youkai in the boiling mud, causing him to scream in agony. He lifted the little demon up to eye level again. "I am Ichitiro of the daimao. You would dare think me ignorant of *anything* that occurs here?"

"No … m-master! Please. You are wise and see much. But not if something were purposely hidden from your eyes."

Ichitiro was growing tired with the ferret's ramblings, regardless of whether they were thinly veiled insults to his power or the truth. "And who would be able to keep something hidden from me?" He lowered the ferret again, this time intending to keep him submerged until he was properly cooked.

"Midnite!" Ito screeched just as his paws touched the viscous fluid.

"Midnite?" Ichitiro asked, suddenly intrigued. If the little demon was indeed lying, he had at least picked a topic of interest. He again lifted the ferret up until they were eye level. "And why would Midnite harbor a hanyou?"

"The hanyou," he squeaked in full panic. "It claimed that Midnite was its mother."

FOURTEEN

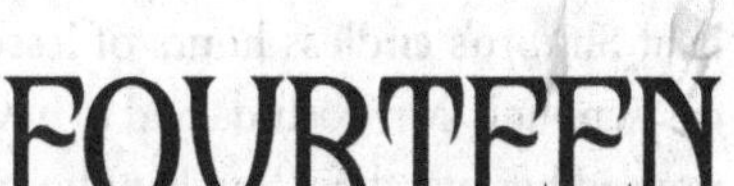

"**G**OOD WORK, KISAKI," the older man said, viewing the rows of empty tables and their shining tabletops.

"Thank you, Yoshida-san," Kisaki replied. "Is there anything else I can do?"

"Don't you ever get tired?" he asked with a laugh. He was a short, stern-faced man, but when he smiled, it lit up his whole face, making him seem much younger than he was. "I swear, my regular busboy asks for a break every time he lifts an empty glass. Thank you for filling in for him."

"I'm happy to be of assistance."

Mr. Yoshida nodded, seemingly impressed with the work accomplished. "I think that's all for today. Why don't you take the evening off? You have a whole lifetime of work ahead of you. You might as well enjoy yourself a little while you're still young. Besides, I believe my daughter was looking for you."

Kisaki smiled, bowed to him, then excused herself.

"Just don't spend your pay all at once," he called after her. "And be mindful of boys. Pretty girls like you two are going to have to beat them off with a stick, and not all of them are going to be worth the trouble."

She turned back, waved to her *boss*, then gave him a thumbs-up – a gesture Tamiko had taught her.

The concept of being the servant for a change was a novel idea, but one she hadn't found onerous in the least. It certainly beat Shitoro's endless hours of lessons. The work itself was easy enough. Mr. Yoshida had to have been teasing when he'd praised her just then. Surely nobody could get so easily tired doing what she had done for the past six hours.

Besides, she'd enjoyed it.

Her friend Tamiko – and Kisaki definitely considered her such, something that caused her heart to swell every time she thought of her – had spoken to Mr. Yoshida at length. He'd finally agreed to take her on for what he called odd jobs. She was intrigued by the concept, and rightfully so, it had turned out. What a wonderful thing these *odd jobs* were. Every morning for the past three days Kisaki had been given a different task to perform, which she dove into with great aplomb.

She'd found them simple enough, but what gave her true joy was all the humans she was able to interact with. She didn't understand all of their actions or customs. Indeed, there was much she didn't understand. However, so long as she accomplished what she was given to do, all seemed well, and she received praise at the end of the day.

Kisaki spent her nights with Tamiko, asking any questions she'd come up with during the day then listening to the answers her new friend gave her, learning what she could, much as she'd done during her studies. Shitoro may well have marveled at what a good student she was being. It would seem that his tireless work had not been in vain after all.

She slept in a small room with an uncomfortable bed, a mere closet compared to what she was used to, but she took it all with good cheer. That she would awake every morning to this invigorating new world, the seemingly endless ocean only minutes away, made her feel more free than she had in years.

If anything, it was only that concept – time – which confused her. Tamiko had told her that she was fifteen years of age and Mr. Yoshida was forty-five. It was that latter which worried her. His hair was thin and he appeared to tire easily. She had learned in the many hours spent studying at her desk that the lifespans of humans did not compare to that of youkai, but in practice, she found it hard to understand.

Apparently, humans had the same trouble understanding as she did, for Tamiko had laughed when Kisaki had told her that she was over seventy of her years in age. She'd thought Kisaki was joking.

"I'll just tell my dad you're sixteen," she'd said.

There were many visitors to this place – the resort, as others called it – and they were seemingly of all ages, young and old. Kisaki was only now beginning to understand that Shitoro had been right. It saddened her to think that in perhaps another thirty or forty years, Mr. Yoshida might be gone. It made her even sadder to think that one day the same would be true of Tamiko.

What a cruel planet this was, to create such wonderful beings but then to pluck them away so soon.

Speaking of which, despite the days which had passed, she was still certain that it was only a matter of time before her transgressions were discovered and she was plucked away, too, except it would be back to the living death that was her chambers in the palace. Time was short, no matter which way she viewed it, and that annoyed and even angered her. Fortunately, the wonders of her surroundings helped keep those feelings at bay.

Despite wearing new and strange clothes, ones that Tamiko had been good enough to lend her so that she blended in, she kept the prizes from the start of her journey with her at all times – the crystals and the quill, even if the quill in particular sometimes worried her.

It seemed that whenever her temper flared, so too would it. It would heat up and pulse, almost as if it felt the same emotions she did, as if it were a living thing. In truth, it frightened her a little. It still rightfully belonged to her mother, though, and that made her reluctant to part ways with it. It seemed an act of utmost disrespect to do so, and she had been raised better than that.

Besides, it reminded her to keep her emotions in check, and perhaps that wasn't a bad thing.

"Hey, Kisaki!"

All of those thoughts scattered to the wind as she looked up and saw her friend approaching from the direction of the office where Mr. Yoshida kept her busy during the day with what she called paperwork.

Kisaki bowed as her friend approached, but Tamiko laughed. "You don't have to be so formal."

"I enjoy being polite to my friend."

"Well, your friend is starving for some dinner. How about you?"

"Yes, I would like some dinner. Perhaps another of those hamburgers you showed to me the other day. They were quite delicious."

"I can't believe you've never had them before. I also can't believe you ate four. Where are you putting them all?"

Kisaki's understanding of Tamiko's language had come quickly, but she was only beginning to pick up on some of the idiosyncrasies. At least she understood her friend was joking and not being literal in her question.

"I have a better idea," Tamiko said. "Have you ever had taco rice?"

"I have had rice, but I don't know what a taco is."

"What did they feed you in that prison you were locked up in?"

"Many delectable dishes, but nothing like I have sampled these last few days."

Tamiko put her arm around Kisaki's shoulder. "Then I think you're in for a treat."

"Excellent," Kisaki replied, her heart warm from the glow of friendship.

Tamiko led the way. "Let's go!"

After a few minutes, Kisaki pulled out the strange papers covered in numbers and the faces of other humans from her pocket. "Yoshida-san gave these to me today. Said it was for a job well done. Is this normal?"

"Put those away. You don't want to lose your week's pay." She let out a sighing laugh. "You really are an odd duck, you know that?"

Kisaki was delighted. Not only was her friend right about dinner, but the dessert, a thick pastry called sata andagi, was equally marvelous. Best yet, when it came time to pay – for here, one seemingly paid the servants for preparing and bringing meals – Kisaki was delighted to see that the papers Mr. Yoshida had given her were able to be used for such.

This led to an after dinner walk along the beach back toward the resort, where Tamiko attempted to explain how commerce worked. It was so simple a concept, yet alien to one who had lived their entire life in a place where the lords – or lady, as in her case – of the palace commanded absolute loyalty by sheer virtue of their status. On Earth, humans worked for one another, not necessarily for a lord, but for a boss, much as she worked for Mr. Yoshida. In return for that labor, they were compensated. That compensation could then, in turn, be used to purchase the goods or services of another. So on and so on. In theory, as Tamiko explained, one could be a servant one moment but the boss the next.

Such a concept was mind-blowing, another colloquialism Kisaki had recently learned. But, as she considered it, she realized she had seen a form of that in action. Wasn't she her mother's heir? As such, she was ostensibly of higher social standing than her many servants. Yet Shitoro was also her guardian and tutor, which meant she was expected to obey his commands. All of this happened, of course, without the concept of pay. However, when Kisaki considered Tamiko's words in those terms, she found it more understandable.

"You really have led a sheltered life," Tamiko said as they walked along the beach, shoes in hand, feeling the sand between their toes. Just as quickly, she added, "I'm sorry. I forgot how things were for you. I didn't mean … It's just…"

"What?" Kisaki asked, curious.

"It's wrong to joke about leading a sheltered life to someone who was, in essence, kept as a prisoner."

"If it helps, it was a comfortable prison most days. There was no physical discomfort on my part, just a … longing to be free."

"I can't imagine it," Tamiko said. "My dad has always allowed me a lot of space. I mean, I practically have the full run of this beach whenever I want. He's never tried to keep me locked up anywhere, except maybe when I've been sick."

"How could he? You only work for him during the day. The nights are your own."

"Weekends too," Tamiko said with a smile. "But that's only because school is out. He's still my dad, though. He could ground me if he wanted to."

Kisaki found herself confused. Tamiko had called Mr. Yoshida her *dad* before, but she had assumed it meant the same thing as boss. She had simply thought it was a more formal title. Kisaki had tried to call him that two days ago, but he merely smiled awkwardly at her and walked away. Now she began to wonder if it was more than that. Perhaps Mr. Yoshida was not only Tamiko's boss, but something akin to her guardian as well. After all, Tamiko had referred to Shitoro as her stepdad at one point. Curious, she decided to ask, "What is a dad?"

"Excuse me?"

Kisaki stopped walking and turned to face the ocean, enjoying the sound of the waves lapping off shore. "What is a dad? You call Yoshida-san that. I'm somewhat embarrassed to admit, but I do not entirely understand."

"You're kidding, right?" After a few moments, however, she said, "You're not kidding. Wow. I have to say, of all the questions you've asked, that's maybe the strangest."

"This whole world is strange to me."

"Ishigachi can take some getting used to for outsiders, but it's not like this is Mars."

"I have not been there either."

Tamiko laughed again, but Kisaki found no rancor in her tone. She seemed to be genuinely amused. "I thought you said that Shi … whatever his name is was your stepdad."

"Shitoro. He is my guardian, assigned stewardship over me by my mother. I assumed perhaps Yoshida-san was yours."

"He is, but he's still my dad. Hold on. You know what a mother is, right?"

"Of course."

"But not a father?"

"Father? You mean a lord?"

"No. It's the same thing as a dad. Just a different name."

"I believe we have already established that."

Tamiko sat down in the sand and looked dumbfounded for a moment. She lay down, put her hands behind her head, and looked up at the stars. After a few moments, Kisaki joined her, enjoying the peaceful darkness despite knowing that somewhere up above were people likely quite angry with her.

"Where to begin?" Tamiko said at last. "A father is basically the other half of a mother."

"Other half?"

"Figuratively. I mean, it takes a mother and a father to create a child."

"Oh? How?"

"We are *not* having that talk, not tonight."

"I'm sorry. Did I offend?"

"No, it's just a bit of an awkward discussion." She glanced over at Kisaki. "You're serious, you never learned how babies get made?"

"My studies covered vast lessons on the multiverse – history, war, beings of power, even magic. There was mention of children, but they were always there. No discussion on how they got there, though."

"Fair enough. For now, let's just stick with the basics. Everyone has a mom and a dad, even if they aren't around physically, like my mom."

"Aren't around? Where is she?"

Tamiko sighed. "She died when I was a baby. Dad doesn't talk about it much, but she was sick for a long time."

"I'm sorry to hear that."

"It's okay. I never met her, so I don't really know what I was missing. Still, every so often, I'll go over to a friend's house and wonder if that's what it would have been like for me."

"So you say everyone has a father?"

"As far as I know. Heck, chickens come from eggs and even they have daddy roosters."

"Are they all like Yoshida-san?"

Tamiko laughed. "No. They're all different. Heck, not all of them are even men."

"Mothers can be fathers?" Kisaki asked, more confused than ever.

"Well, there's always got to be a … donor. But someone can be raised by a dad who's also a woman."

"I'm not sure I understand."

"Physically, a baby has to be made by a man and a woman. But they can be raised by anyone."

"Including a guardian?"

"Yes, although it sounds like that Shitoro creep was more a warden than stepdad. No offense, but I think your mom could have chosen someone better to marry."

"Marry?"

"Y'know, fall in love with. Kiss, all that stuff."

"Shitoro is loyal to my mother, but they are not married. He is her servant. Though I don't doubt he would gladly take a spear for her, I have never seen them kiss."

"Servant? You mean like butler?"

"He serves her, along with many other youkai."

Tamiko sat up and stared at Kisaki for a few moments in the dark. Finally, she laughed. "You really have some imagination. But I guess maybe you needed it. All I know is if I ever meet this Shitoro loser, I'm going to kick his ass."

"If he manages to find me, he will…"

"Oh my God, how cute!" Tamiko suddenly shouted, interrupting Kisaki. "Come on, boy. I won't hurt you."

Kisaki sat up and stretched, curious as to what had caught her friend's attention. She turned in the direction Tamiko was now facing and then froze as she caught sight of what was approaching them from the trees.

"I don't think I've ever seen such a big cat," Tamiko said, delight in her voice. "And white, too. Oh my gosh, he's so precious!"

Kisaki stared wide-eyed as the creature neared them.

It stopped a few feet away and looked at them both, but seemed intent on glaring at her.

"Awww!" Tamiko cried, getting to her feet. "I think he likes you."

"Quite the contrary. Right at this moment, I am most irate," Shitoro replied. "As for you, human, you would be well advised against kicking *any* part of me."

FIFTEEN

TAMIKO SCREAMED AND backed up several steps before falling down into the sand again.

"Such bothersome creatures," Shitoro commented before turning to face Kisaki again. "You are in a great deal of trouble, young mistress."

Kisaki sighed dejectedly. She'd known this would eventually happen, had been anticipating it ever since she'd stepped foot from her mother's chambers. Yet, following the last few wonderful days, she'd begun to entertain the fantasy that perhaps she'd be allowed to stay with Tamiko. She now saw what a fool she was to think that.

"Do not ignore me, young lady!"

"I wasn't ignoring you," Kisaki replied.

"Don't take that tone with me. A few days on Earth and the entire concept of respect is lost upon you, I see."

"I haven't lost my…"

Hands grabbed Kisaki beneath her shoulders and began dragging her away. When she looked up, she saw it was Tamiko.

Her friend's eyes were as wide as the full moon. Finally, after about ten feet, she stopped and then dropped to her knees in front of Kisaki, continually glancing back over her shoulder to where Shitoro sat looking quite annoyed. "How are you not freaked out by the fact that a cat is talking to us?!"

"I will have you know, human," Shitoro said with a sniff, "I am a tiger. I hunted prey before your kind had even discovered fire, which I might add was quite by accident."

"Tiger?" Tamiko cried, turning and facing him. "I hate to break it to you, but tigers are big and … and now I'm talking with the cat. I don't know what was in that taco rice, but we are never going there again."

"Tigers also have claws, which I will be happy to show you if…"

"That's enough, Shitoro." Kisaki stood up and brushed herself off. "Even you have to admit, you're somewhat … small for a tiger."

"Small in stature but large in spirit, as your mother would say. That is, if you ever stopped disrespecting her long enough to listen."

"*Shitoro?*" Tamiko asked. "This is Shitoro?!"

"Yes," Kisaki said calmly, not entirely sure why her friend was reacting this way. Certainly Shitoro was a bit on the diminutive side, but nothing that should have alarmed her to that degree.

"I thought you said Shitoro was your stepdad."

"I said he was my guardian, which he is."

"Your guardian is a cat?"

"Tiger!" Shitoro snarled.

Tamiko spun toward him again. "I've seen tigers in the zoo. They didn't talk."

"Of course not," Shitoro replied. "Regular tigers are dumb animals. Like present company, I might add. I am a tiger demon."

"Demons aren't real."

"How your species managed to survive the last ice age is beyond me."

"Enough!" Kisaki said, stepping between the two. "Shitoro, can you please assume your regular form?"

"I am in disguise, as per your mother's orders. Do you know what happens to youkai who disobey one such as she?"

"There's no one else here. It's just us."

"Fine," Shitoro replied. "If it will cease this human's prattling, so be it." His yellow eyes began to glow and, a moment later, so too did the rest of him. There came a flash of light, and then Shitoro adopted the bipedal form he most typically took in the celestial palace. "Better?"

"Not really," Tamiko replied, dumbfounded. She turned to Kisaki. "Now he's a two-foot-tall talking cat standing on his hind legs and wearing a kimono."

"How many times do I have to say it? I am a tiger."

"Should I get a ball of yarn so we can find out for sure?"

"Yarn? I don't understand what…"

"How did you find me?" Kisaki asked, tired of their bickering. She was relatively certain that if she tried, she would be able to get up in the morning, go to work, and then come back to find these two still arguing.

"Huh?" both of them asked.

"How did you find me, Shitoro?" Kisaki repeated.

"Find you? I have been searching this accursed island for two days now. You have no idea the indignities I have had to endure. Children throwing rocks at me. Mongrels chasing me. At one point, a fat human female grabbed hold of me while I was unawares and tried to put a collar around my neck."

"Seen many tigers wearing collars?" Tamiko asked. "Like I said, cat."

Before Shitoro could start in again with her friend, Kisaki asked, "But how did you even know to look here, on this island?"

"Perhaps if you had paid better attention to your studies, that would be self-evident," he chided. "You used your mother's crystal to come here. I don't know how you knew to do so, but you were a foolish child if you thought she couldn't trace her own power."

"My mother's crystal?"

"In the sending chamber."

Kisaki remembered what had happened, how she'd been standing in the middle of that room, thinking of Earth, then suddenly found herself on the beach. "The black crystal?"

"Of course. As if you did not know."

"What's he talking about?" Tamiko asked.

"I am not entirely certain myself."

Shitoro walked up to them, ignoring how Tamiko flinched away, then poked a clawed finger at Kisaki. "A likely story. I will warn you, child, that your lies will not get you out of this. Your mother will most likely order you chained to your study desk from here on out."

"Hey!" Tamiko cried. "She can't do that. It's illegal."

"You would presume to tell the great Lady Midnite what she can and cannot do?"

"Lady Midnite..." Tamiko turned to Kisaki. "Your mom. She's not like..." She inclined her head toward Shitoro.

"Lady Midnite is like nothing your feeble human mind could comprehend," Shitoro said. "And be thankful for that. Should you ever find yourself standing before her divine grace, you would do well to cut that tongue from your mouth before letting it flap incessantly."

"She sent you, didn't she?" Kisaki asked.

The little demon rounded on her. "Of course she sent me, and I was glad to heed her command. Unlike *some*, I am both loyal and respectful to my mistress, even willing to break our laws at her command ... at great personal risk to myself, I might add."

"What laws?" Tamiko asked.

"Such as the one forbidding passage to Earth."

"There's a law forbidding passage?" Kisaki asked.

"Yes. There is."

"How come I never heard you talk of it?"

"Because you were not meant to. You were never meant to venture forth from your chambers, as such there was no need for you to know of such matters."

Tamiko stepped in front of Kisaki, having seemingly gotten over her shock, and stared down at the tiger youkai. "Well, I hope there's a law against anyone leaving Earth, because she's not going back."

"What?"

"You heard me, cat."

"You won't find that so funny once I turn you into a mouse."

Kisaki slapped a hand against her forehead. These two couldn't seem to help themselves. Even so, she found her heart warmed that Tamiko, a mere human, would stand up to a youkai for her. Despite her first instinct to do as she was told, she began to realize she didn't want to give up her friend. And if Tamiko was that fierce of a friend, then perhaps she was worth fighting for. "What if I don't wish to leave?"

"Preposterous!" Shitoro cried. "You truly have been ruined by this savage place. Over sixty years of routine and discipline gone in the space of a few days. The great daimao should have put their edict in place for that reason alone."

"Sixty years?" Tamiko turned to Kisaki. "So you were telling the truth?"

"Yes."

"Whoa! You're like, old enough to be my grandmother."

Kisaki chuckled, not entirely certain what a grandmother was. "Perhaps…"

"I want to drink from whatever fountain of youth you have up there."

"Do not be foolish, human," Shitoro said.

"My name is Tamiko!"

"Oh, so you do not like it when the sandal is upon the other foot? Nevertheless, it is impossible. Your feeble human mind simply couldn't handle the glorious wonders of the celestial palace. And, even if you could, I dare say some of my less tolerant cousins would be more than happy to enjoy making a meal out of you."

"I ask again," Kisaki said, interrupting the bickering, "what if I do not wish to leave?"

"That is out of the question. Besides, why would you even want to stay in this barbaric land? The stench alone is enough to singe my whiskers."

"You're going to be smelling like wet cat in about three seconds," Tamiko warned.

"As I said, barbaric."

"I haven't found it to be that way," Kisaki said. "I've actually enjoyed staying here at the resort, working for Yoshida-san."

"Working?"

"Yes. I have been performing odd jobs and receiving payment for it."

"You, a daughter of the mighty Midnite, have been serving a human? What have they done to you? Is this Yoshida a wizard? Has he bewitched your mind?"

Kisaki laughed. "Of course not. He's Tamiko's ... father." She looked toward her friend questioningly. Tamiko gave her a small nod of approval, so she turned back, intent on continuing her argument, but then hesitated as a thought suddenly popped into her mind. "Shitoro?"

"Yes, Lady Kisaki? Have you come to your senses yet?"

"May I ask a question?"

"Very well."

"Are you my father?"

SIXTEEN

"**W**HAT?!"

"Tamiko thought you were my stepfather, but I told her she was incorrect. However, I then realized that the truth is I do not know."

"K-know that I love your mother, truly I do," Shitoro sputtered, "but not like *that*."

"Do I have a father?"

"Well … err … of course."

"Who is he?"

"Why would you even think to ask such a…" He paused, then pointed an accusing finger at Tamiko. "You! This is your doing."

"My doing? How?"

"You put these thoughts into her head."

"It's a simple question," she replied. "A fair one, too, I think."

"Some questions are not to be asked."

"So you do not know who my father is?" Kisaki replied, crestfallen.

"I never said that," Shitoro stated. "As the former chief servant to your mother, I was her trusted confidant. I know a great many secrets."

Kisaki immediately perked up. "So can you take me to him?"

Shitoro seemed to realize the error of what he'd said a moment too late. "Let us speak no more of this."

Tamiko stepped in and pointed a finger at his nose. "You can't just shut her down like that. It's not fair."

Shitoro rounded on her. "Oh? Is that so? Let me tell you something, child. The multiverse is vast and old, much older than a simple monkey such as yourself could possibly understand. There is a cycle in place, a grand scheme that defines all of creation. It would take years to even begin explaining it to someone like you, but I can give you this one nugget – nowhere is it written that life is fair."

"Oh yeah? Well, I think you're being a jerk."

"What?! You ... p-pea-brained..." Shitoro stammered, seemingly at a loss for words.

Kisaki let them argue while she considered things. Shitoro had revealed more to her in the past few minutes than he had since he'd been assigned as her guardian. She had a father. Who was he? She didn't know yet. Nor did she know why this information had been kept from her. Was he cruel or kind? Was he another daimao, or a mere servant? Had he abandoned her or did her mother spirit her away? Did he even know she existed?

She didn't have answers to any of this, had never even thought to ask these questions before today. But now that they were out in the open, she knew she couldn't rest until they were answered.

But how? Shitoro was obviously here to take her back. Once home again, she doubted her mother would tell her much beyond how badly punished she was. And she could only press the matter so far. Her mother was powerful and though her temper was even most of the time, that could change if Kisaki pushed too hard.

But why all these secrets? Why the isolation? She was fairly certain that the other youkai in the palace, even the lowest of servants, were free to do what she wasn't, explore as they pleased. So why was it different for her? So many questions, but along with that came realization, too. Now that she had gotten a small taste of freedom, she had no desire to go back to her old life, even at the risk of her mother's wrath.

And perhaps she had the means to escape at her fingertips.

She reached a hand into the pocket of her shorts and touched the two crystals she had left. She'd thought them keepsakes, a reminder of her adventure, nothing more. But Shitoro had said something about using one of them to come here.

It seemed crazy, but perhaps it wasn't. Hadn't she been fantasizing about Earth while holding one, only to find her wish granted a moment later? She'd had no thoughts on a specific place, aside from the sea, but what if she concentrated on someplace, or maybe *someone* specific?

Shitoro had also mentioned one other important tidbit. He'd said the black crystal had been attuned to her mother's power. That was how he'd been able to track her down. Though she didn't fully understand the workings of magic, she had a rudimentary knowledge of it. She also understood, via her studies of the ancient past, that there were others like her mother – the daimao. The black crystal had been her mother's, something she'd picked through little more than bad luck on her part. However, the other two were different in color. Perhaps that meant they'd been empowered by others.

If so, and she used them, then maybe Shitoro wouldn't be able to find her as easily. She'd never met another daimao, had no idea what they were like. But since – to the best of her knowledge, anyway – none had ever come calling, demanding to meet her, maybe that meant they either didn't know about her or, more importantly, didn't care. If so, then they would surely have little interest in her whereabouts.

Yes!

Kisaki was not a stupid girl by any means, and now a plan was beginning to form in her head.

"For the last time, I am not a cat."

"I know. Even cats aren't as big of jerks as you."

"You truly are insolent. Why, if I had my say in matters, I would have some manners whipped into you."

"I'd like to see you try, shorty."

Kisaki stepped back from where the two were arguing, her hand still in her pocket touching the two crystals. The problem was, she had no idea where to start or how the crystals even worked. Were they powerful enough to lock on to an unanswered question? Or did they require something specific? If she concentrated on her father, would it be enough to work?

There was only one way to find out. She randomly picked one of the two and closed her fist around it.

"And where do you think you're going?" Shitoro suddenly asked her.

"Um … back to my room. I … err … forgot something."

Tamiko turned to her, a look of confusion and outrage on her face. "You can't possibly be thinking of going with this mangy little feline?"

"Mangy?!" Shitoro looked like he was about to start in again with Tamiko, something Kisaki was hoping for, but he instead stalked toward her. "And what could be of such importance on this mudball of a…" He stopped mid-sentence, his eyes opening wide as if in realization. Kisaki had a moment of fear in which she thought he'd figured out her plan, but then he said, "You didn't dare, did you?"

"Dare what?"

"There's no point in lying. We don't know how you did it, but your mother knows you took the Taiyosori. You didn't just leave it lying around in some hovel on Earth, did you? If so, you are in such…"

"What's a Taiyosori?" Tamiko asked.

"Nothing you need concern yourself with."

"Fine," Kisaki said, "then I'll ask. What is it?"

Shitoro raised a hand to the bridge of his nose and sighed. "The Taiyosori is the blade of the heavens, a weapon of utmost power. In the hands of a master, it is invincible. In yours, though, I doubt it would even cut bread. You have no idea the power you are trifling with. Why, if it fell into the wrong hands … wait. How did you manage to take it anyway?"

"Take it? I…" It took Kisaki a moment, but then she realized what he was all in a huff about. "Are you talking about that silly ornamental sword?"

"Ornamental?" Shitoro's face flushed so deeply it was even visible beneath his fur. "We are talking about a weapon that could cut celestial armor in half like butter, and you dare think it a mere decoration."

"Well, who ever heard of a sword made of glass anyway? Doesn't sound too useful to me. Besides, it's not a sword anymore."

"What do you mean 'not a sword anymore'?"

Kisaki reluctantly let go of the crystal. She reached into the light jacket she wore and fished around in the inner pocket. There! For a moment, she felt a light heat from the quill, but then it was gone as her hand closed around it and pulled it out. "See? It turned into this."

"You stole a feather?" Tamiko asked.

"It wasn't a feather at the time."

Shitoro stepped over and glared up at her. "Are you seriously trying to tell me that the Taiyosori, one of the most potent weapons in all of creation, turned into *this*? Listen to me, young lady. I have heard a lot of lies in my time, but this is preposterous. You go and fetch the true sword right now, or I swear I will tell your mother about your impudent..." One second he was grabbing for the quill in Kisaki's hand, the next there came a bright blue flash of light from it, followed by a *crack* as if lightning had struck. Shitoro was sent flying back across the beach.

He slammed into a wooden bench, shattering it to pieces, then finally landed in the sand where he lay unmoving.

"Shitoro!"

"What the heck did you do?" Tamiko asked, her eyes wide.

"I ... don't know."

"C'mon, let's go help him."

That much they could agree on. Both of the girls took off down the beach to where Shitoro lay in a patch of scorched sand and smashed wood.

They knelt on either side of him. Kisaki was glad to see the little demon was still alive, albeit stunned by whatever had happened.

"Are you okay?" Tamiko asked as they helped him up.

After a moment, Shitoro shook his head and coughed up some dust and smoke. "Dearest gods." He turned toward Tamiko, noticing her hand on his arm. "Let go of me, human."

"I was just trying to help."

"By dirtying my fur with your monkey paws?"

"Fine." She released him and stood up. "Maybe next time you'll land on your head and knock some sense into that thick skull of yours."

"Are you all right, Shitoro?" Kisaki asked, helping him to his feet.

He nodded, still a little bit dazed, but then jerked his hand back when he saw she was still holding the quill. "Unbelievable."

"What happened?"

"The Taiyosori," he explained shakily. "It is capable of … defending itself. It's why none have dared to try and claim it from your mother. The sword will reject any who try to steal it."

"But I stole … err, borrowed it anyway."

"Yes, I can see that," the tiger demon replied in an annoyed tone. He began to dust himself off. "And you're telling me nothing like that happened to you?"

"No. I mean, it felt hot at first, but I thought it was my imagination. I was … a bit nervous after I unlocked the door and ventured into mother's audience chamber."

"With my key?"

Kisaki smiled sheepishly and nodded.

"Had I known I was helping to raise a thief, I might have taken greater precautions."

"I'm sorry, but it's just that…"

"You kept her locked up." Tamiko stepped back in and pointed an accusing finger at him. "What did you expect?"

"What did I expect? Perhaps a proper show of respect for her elders." He glanced back at Kisaki. "Kindly turn the Taiyosori back into a sword."

"I don't know how."

"How did you manage to turn it into a mere quill to begin with?"

"I … don't know."

He reached a paw toward the quill again, then apparently thought better of it. He pulled it back and began rubbing it over his ears. "Very well. Your mother will need to figure that out, although I dare say it will, in all likelihood, put her into an even fouler mood than she is already in."

"What are you doing?" Tamiko asked after another moment.

Shitoro stopped licking his paw. "Grooming, obviously. I have sand in my fur. I can't very well return to my mistress looking as if I were a ragamuffin such as yourself."

"You know what also does that? Cats."

Shitoro narrowed his eyes and glared daggers at her, but he held his tongue and addressed Kisaki instead. "Speaking of ragamuffins, why are you dressed like that? Where are your regal robes?"

"Back in my room. When I got here, some kids were making fun of me for them. One of them pushed me and…"

"They dared lay a finger on you? Tell me where they are and I shall make certain their homes are razed to the ground for such an insult."

"It's fine, Shitoro. Not a big deal. I just got a little wet."

"Well, those ruffians are lucky I wasn't around, otherwise I'd have…"

"Clawed their furniture?" Tamiko offered.

He refused to take the bait, although Kisaki could tell it took some effort. "Kindly put the Taiyosori away for now. I would wish to avoid further … incidents."

For a moment, Kisaki considered ignoring him. The quill, sword, whatever it was, had given her the means to make sure he couldn't come near her if she didn't want him to. But then she thought better of it.

Whatever it had done to him, it had looked painful. She couldn't be certain that next time it wouldn't actually hurt him, not to mention any humans who might be unfortunate enough to come into contact with it. Small as Shitoro was, he was likely far more durable than most of the inhabitants of this world. She would need to be more careful with it. For now, she did as told and placed the quill back inside of her jacket.

Shitoro nodded his approval, then stepped forward and took hold of her hand. "We're leaving now."

She panicked and tried to pull away, but he held her fast. "Err, what about my robes?"

"Leave them." He turned to Tamiko. "Consider them a souvenir of your time among superior beings. Try not to dirty them too badly with your stench."

"But … what about my father?" Kisaki asked. She reached into her pocket with her free hand and grabbed hold again of one of the crystals, pulling it out in her clenched fist. If she was going to make a run for it, it would have to be now. But first she needed to shake loose from the tenacious tiger's grasp.

"Your father?" he asked incredulously. "He has nothing to do with this. Forget him and any other humans you have met. They are nothing to us." Shitoro produced a black crystal from his robe and held it out. "Now, please silence yourself. The transference takes a bit of concentration to…"

Tamiko slapped it out of his hand.

"What the?! How dare you!"

"How dare I?" she replied, grabbing hold of Kisaki's other arm and trying to pull her free. "How dare *you*? You claim to be her friend, her guardian, but all you do is yell at her and keep her locked up. You're … you're … not a nice person."

"I am not a person, period," he said, refusing to let go. "What I am is a being far older and wiser than you could ever hope to…"

"Wait," Kisaki said. "Other humans?"

"What?" Shitoro asked.

"You said forget about my father and the other humans. Are you saying my father is a human, here on Earth?"

"No … I … suggested nothing of the sort. Now, if you will kindly…"

His sputtering answer, however, told Kisaki everything she needed to know. No wonder she'd always been so fascinated by Earth. Human blood ran through her veins, mixed with the divinity of her mother. It explained so much, including why she looked so human.

"I want to meet him," she said. "I want to meet my human father, wherever he is."

Shitoro started to say something, but she wasn't listening. The crystal in her fist had begun to pulse violently upon her voicing her stated desire, a desire which had filled her heart with sudden longing.

A moment later, a burst of dark grey energy, almost as if a storm cloud had descended to touch the ground, enveloped the group.

When it cleared, all three of them had vanished.

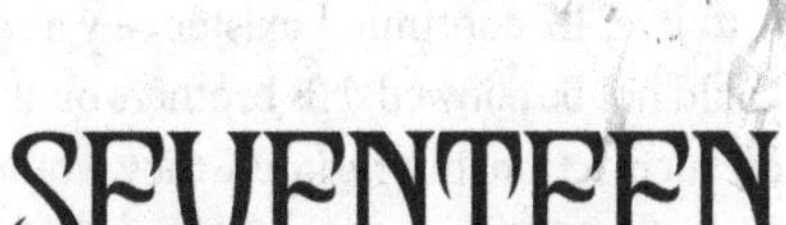

SEVENTEEN

ICHITIRO'S SERVANTS COWERED as he continued to rage, destroying everything he touched with violent finality.

How dare his sister allow herself to be dirtied, violated, by a lesser being, a human no less? True, bastard offspring weren't an issue unique to Midnite. Despite their fragile stupidity, some human women could be desirable. Even Ichitiro had taken a few in his time, although more to savor their screams than anything.

What angered Ichitiro more was that Ito claimed the child was of forbidden stock. The miserable youkai said he'd smelled it upon her. If his words were to be believed, a dubious proposition at best, then Midnite had sullied herself with little better than a pig.

Her worst transgression by far, though, was that she'd rejected Ichitiro to be with such a lowly creature. Such an insult was impossible to ignore. She could have consented to be his mate, borne warrior children of great power with him. Together they could have created an army that would have served none save him. With that and the Taiyosori in his possession, he would have been unstoppable.

Instead, her actions were the equivalent of spitting in his face. Even if the child had been born of the blessed isles, a union barely tolerated among his kind, he could not suffer it to live. Its continued existence was an affront to him that could not be allowed. His brothers on the council might frown on such action, but he knew they would do little to stop him.

As for Midnite, perhaps it would serve as a lesson to her. He was not one to be trifled with, no matter by who. Neither human, youkai, nor daimao were immune to his wrath. Even the elder gods would be wise to…

Ichitiro paused in his destruction. The barest tingle of power vibrated at the base of his skull. It was his own energy, calling out to him, letting him know it had been used.

Someone had used one of his crystals, and they had done so without his blessing. Though the crystals were supposed to be for any youkai's needs, there was an unspoken agreement amongst the many servants of the palace that those empowered by Ichitiro were to be avoided, unless told otherwise by him and him alone. He knew this agreement existed because he had fostered it, subtly encouraging the rumor that it would be wise to consider his wrath. Few had ever broken that pact, and none had openly complained about it. They knew better. Besides, there were plenty of others to choose from.

But even that fact was irrelevant. Permission to use *any* of the crystals had been rescinded. The ruling had stood for decades, ever since the daimao had witnessed mankind's destructive potential.

So, not only had someone broken that rule, they had done so with Ichitiro's power. *Interesting*, he considered. *Who would dare such a thing?*

His servants were all accounted for and none of them would dare make such a move without begging his favor first. Ito might have tried, coward that he was, but he was currently in no condition to do much of anything.

Ichitiro reached out to the errant strand of energy before it could dissipate, grabbing hold of it as if by the throat.

Incredible. Whoever had used it hadn't been in the sending chamber after all. Someone had dared to activate one of his crystals without permission, but they had done so from Earth. From one of the blessed isles, to be exact. How had they gotten hold of it, and why were they there?

He continued to trace the fragile thread of magic, following its strands to elsewhere upon that world, to a place far away from the isles favored by the daimao.

Though Ichitiro had little interest in the world of man, as a warrior he'd studied them much as a general studies an enemy army. Whoever the transgressor was, they'd used his power to send themselves to a land with the ridiculous name of America.

Ichitiro knew well the dictate Reiden had lain down regarding Earth. By all accounts, he should have reported this transgression to the court and then waited for them to contemplate an appropriate response. However, knowing about a dictate wasn't the same as respecting or even caring about one, and Ichitiro did neither.

Once upon a time, the court acted quickly. Those who were deemed criminals met swift justice, but the eons had slowly changed the daimao. Now the celestial court was less a military tribunal and more a home to bureaucrats and their endless pontification. The issue of what to do with the humans was a prime example – decades spent debating with no resolution. In the meantime, the humans had been allowed to continue to evolve their technology.

It was more than likely that the stars would burn out before any transgressors faced punishment from the council. That would not do. Ichitiro couldn't have cared less that they went to Earth. That was of no matter. He'd sent his servants there several times in the years since the edict was passed. He himself couldn't go, not without the rest of the daimao being made aware, but those under his rule, using crystals that only he was attuned to, had made the journey. That way, he'd been able to gather intelligence on the humans while also swaying many of the Youkai trapped on Earth to follow his rule.

Reiden and the council had abandoned them to their own fate, leaving them the choice of being hunted, assimilated like cattle, or hiding. Ichitiro saw opportunity in their misery. Though he cared for no one save himself, he'd sent supplies, aid, and advice wherever it benefited him. For over seventy of their years, he had been the only divine power that the youkai on Earth knew. As a result, he now had agents and assassins residing in all of the humans' many lands.

It was that latter he would call upon now. They would be tasked with hunting down the transgressor. It would be a simple matter to do so. Unlike the crystals of his siblings, Ichitiro poisoned his with his own personal miasma. Though it wouldn't kill the victim, it would stay with them for some time, allowing him to track them down long after the power of the crystal dissipated.

Yes. His minions would find the transgressor and make them aware that none could steal from Ichitiro without paying a dire price.

The thought pleased him, ending his rage and bringing with it cold and calculating logic. He still had another important issue to attend to, one that wouldn't be solved by destroying his own residence.

It was time he paid Midnite a visit. It had been far too long since he'd done so.

EIGHTEEN

THE FIRST TIME Kisaki had been transported by a crystal had been unsettling in the surprise it brought, but it hadn't been physically unpleasant.

A thick black smoke surrounded them upon their arrival, wherever that was. Rather than taking in their surroundings, she found herself and Tamiko doubled over, coughing out the foul stench that was trying to seep into their lungs.

Shitoro didn't appear to be affected the same way, although he was certainly not happy. "What have you done this time, Kisaki?"

"I … *cough* … didn't do this," she wheezed.

"What … is this stuff?" Tamiko choked out. "It smells like a sewer."

"It's a miasma," Shitoro explained. "I will admit, child, you surprise me. I didn't think you capable of conjuring one. But if you think this will give you cover to escape, then…"

"I said I didn't do this," Kisaki replied.

"Well, miasma certainly doesn't generate itself," the tiger demon said with a sniff.

"Could … ugh … we maybe move out of it?" Tamiko asked.

"Hold on for a moment." Shitoro reached for a small pouch at his side and then opened it. A moment later, a brisk breeze appeared around them, moving the miasma away and revealing that where once it had been night, it was now day – the early morning, it would seem. "Hmm. This is potentially troubling."

Kisaki stopped coughing as the air cleared, and took a look around. Gone was not only the night, but also the beach and ocean, too. They were standing along the side of a road, leading toward a collection of modest buildings far more reserved than the resort she had been staying at. There were trees everywhere, but they were different from the ones on the island – taller and with strange leaves.

"What just happened?" Tamiko asked, her voice rising in panic. "Where are we?!"

"I don't know," Kisaki said softly.

"You!" Shitoro pointed a finger. "Did you send us without my permission?"

"I…"

"You had another crystal, didn't you?"

Kisaki shrugged sheepishly but didn't say anything.

"And do you have another to get us back?"

Again, she didn't answer.

"Just wonderful!" Shitoro cried. "Now what do we do? That crystal you knocked out of my hand was my only spare. How do you suppose I am to return you home now?"

Kisaki still had another, one that she intended to use to ensure Tamiko got home, but not yet. She was too intrigued as to where they were and who might be waiting for them. For hadn't she wished to meet her father? There didn't appear to be anyone in sight at the moment, but that didn't mean he wasn't close by.

As unfair as it might be to her friend, Kisaki knew that if she sent them back now, Shitoro would retrieve his crystal and immediately transport them to the waiting punishment of her mother. She trusted that Tamiko would understand. In fact, she planned to tell her, as soon as they could find a moment alone without Shitoro to spy on them.

Speaking of the tiger demon, Shitoro's head turned toward the road. "What is that?"

"I don't hear..." Kisaki paused. After a moment, she did hear something – the hum of an engine. A car was approaching.

Wide-eyed as Tamiko was, she spun toward Shitoro. "Quick, before they see you!"

"See me? Who? What are you yammering on about?" the youkai asked irritably.

"Turn back into a cat."

"Did your evolutionary ancestors forget to develop a brain stem, human? I am a tiger!"

"Fine, whatever. But you're a tiger who's standing on two legs wearing a dress."

"This is not a dress, it is..."

Kisaki understood what Tamiko was saying. In her few days on Earth, she'd seen a lot, but there was one thing she hadn't ... youkai. Judging by the way her friend had acted upon first seeing Shitoro, she began to suspect the appearance of beings such as him weren't as commonplace here as they once were. "Tamiko is right, Shitoro. Change back. We don't want to draw undo attention."

He glared at her for a moment, but then finally sighed. "As you wish, Lady Kisaki. But know this conversation isn't over."

With that, he transformed back into his four-legged white tiger form, which Kisaki was forced to admit did actually look like nothing more than a large cat. He changed just in time, as the car they'd heard rounded a corner and came into view. "What are you doing?"

Tamiko had stepped to the edge of the road. "Stay back. I want to see if I can figure out where we are."

The vehicle was similar to those Kisaki had seen on the island, leading her to hope that perhaps they hadn't gone too far. If so, then it might not be necessary for her to use up her last crystal. She might even be able to save it for a later date … such as if she got lonely again and decided to visit her friend on Earth.

The car passed them and she watched as Tamiko's gazed followed. It turned down a side street a few moments later, but Tamiko continued to stare in that direction, her mouth agape.

"I think your pet human is broken," Shitoro commented.

Kisaki stepped forward and put a hand on her friend's shoulder. "Tamiko, are you okay?"

Tamiko turned back toward her, her face a shade paler than normal. "Did you see that?"

"Yes, it was a car. You showed them to me, remember? It was a pretty color."

"No. The license plate."

"License plate?"

"It's a tag on the front and back of cars. Tells you a few things about them, like where they're from."

"Oh, so what did this one tell you? What province are we in?"

"Not a province," Tamiko replied blankly. "Took me a moment, because the plate was in English."

"English? That other language you speak?"

"Yes," she said, sitting down hard on the curb. "Good thing, too, because according to that, we're in Pennsylvania."

Kisaki didn't like the way Tamiko looked. Her eyes were bulging and she was breathing hard. She thought maybe the best thing to do would be to keep her talking. "What is a Pennsylvania?"

"Not what," she replied. "Where. It's in the United States."

"United States. Is that far from where we started?"

"Over ten thousand kilometers," she said, wide-eyed.

"Approximately twelve thousand, to be precise," Shitoro casually added.

"This is … insane. How did we get here?"

"Simple," Shitoro replied. "Magic."

"But magic isn't…" Tamiko stopped mid-sentence. "Never mind. Arguing with a talking cat that magic isn't real is probably pointless." She held up a hand before he could reply. "Yes, I know. Tiger."

"The how is not nearly as important as the why." Shitoro glared up at Kisaki. "Well? This was your doing. Explain yourself."

"I … I wanted to meet my father."

"So you took me from mine to meet yours?" Tamiko asked accusingly.

"I'm sorry. I didn't mean to. It's just…"

"We were both touching Lady Kisaki when the crystal activated," Shitoro said. "They were designed that way for the purpose of transporting large numbers without the need for multiple charges."

"I didn't know," Kisaki pleaded.

"Obviously!"

"Wait," Tamiko said. "So your father is in Pennsylvania? I thought you said you didn't know him. How could you know where he lives?"

"I don't. All I know is that he's human, and I only just found that out a few minutes ago. I didn't even think it would work."

Shitoro let out a noise that was probably supposed to be a growl, but sounded more like an annoyed chuff.

"What is it?"

"It was me," he said, sounding quite put out. "Your desire to meet your father, yes, but you were touching me at the time and the thought must have still been fresh in my mind."

"Can it work that way?"

Despite being in his tiger form, he still managed to give Kisaki a look that conveyed how far from impressed he was with her. "Obviously. The crystals are empowered by the daimao, I might remind you."

"You've said that word before – daimao," Tamiko said. "You mean for real, as in demons of godlike power? I thought that was just mythology, a fairy tale."

"As I am certain you thought talking tigers a myth, too, up until recently."

"Point taken."

"The daimao are quite real, and they are potent indeed. Even a small fraction of their divine energy possesses more magic than even the most powerful human sorcerer could hope to harness."

"Sorcerers aren't ... never mind."

"Amazing," Shitoro replied. "You *are* capable of learning."

Tamiko stuck out her tongue at the tiny tiger.

"So you did know where my father lives," Kisaki said.

"I suppose the cat is out of the bag now," he replied before turning toward Tamiko's grinning face and adding, "Oh, do shut up."

"How?"

"Your mother," he explained. "As I said, I was once chief among her many servants. As such, it was my duty to know what she did, including about that particular human. She kept tabs on him for a time after your birth. I do not know many specifics of their relationship, but she seemed quite smitten with him, at least for a while."

"What happened?"

"Time. The daimao have pressing concerns that require their attention, such as maintaining the order of the heavens. Their duty does not allow them to devote more than a pittance to silly things such as human affairs."

"But you knew."

"Yes."

"And you kept it from me."

"Also yes."

"But why?" Kisaki asked, throwing her hands up in frustration.

Shitoro turned away from the girls, seeming to notice something else of interest.

"Find a mouse?" Tamiko asked idly, still appearing to process things.

Kisaki wasn't about to let him off so easily. "Don't do this now, Shitoro. You've told me this much. You might as well tell me the rest." The tiger youkai was still silent. "If you do, I might even forget to mention to Mother that we had this talk."

He spun back to her, panic in his eyes. "You wouldn't dare!"

"If I'm going to be punished, I might as well have company."

Again Shitoro made a growling sound in his throat. Finally, after several long seconds of pouting, he said, "Very well, but I want your word."

"You have my word as daughter of Midnite and heir to her throne."

Shitoro snorted laughter, but then replied, "Good enough, I suppose."

"So why didn't you tell me any of this?"

"Simple. It was for your own safety."

Shitoro considered how best to explain to Kisaki the circumstances of her birth and the taboo against what were considered to be hanyou of impure stock. He began by reiterating the daimao's overall disdain for humanity but mentioned that those on the blessed isles were considered of slightly higher stature.

"Blessed isles?" Tamiko asked, distracted from her own despair for the moment by his tale.

"Yes. It is where the daimao first touched down upon this planet. A series of islands they continue to favor. However, I must consider that perhaps they are misgiven about the so-called superior stock, since we somehow managed to pick you up."

"Ishigachi is one of them?"

"Is that what you humans call it these days?" he replied dismissively. "But yes, that and its much larger cousins to the north."

"The Japanese islands," Tamiko said. "I've read a bit about ancient mythology in school and..."

"Where do you think those myths come from?" Shitoro asked smugly. "Don't be embarrassed. It's not uncommon for lesser beings to base their entire belief system around creatures they cannot hope to fathom."

That seemed to answer Tamiko's question for the moment, but then she said, "So you think humans in general are inferior, but humans from outside Japan are somehow even more so? I mean, I'm from there and even I think that's pretty small-minded."

"A monkey such as yourself could not begin to comprehend the minds of the great daimao. You could only hope to ... Hey! Where are you going?"

Kisaki turned back toward them from several steps away. "You two can argue all you want, but we're here now. Inferior species or not, I'm going to find my father."

NINETEEN

"**D**AMNIT!"

Kisaki turned with a start toward her friend. "What's wrong?"

"My cell phone," Tamiko said. "I was trying to call my dad, but I don't have international minutes."

"I'm sorry if I scared you with … this." She waved her hands at the scenery around them. "It was not my intention."

Tamiko laughed. The initial shock had seemingly worn off, but she still looked a bit wide-eyed. "I'm more scared of what he'll do if he sees any roaming charges. Oh wait. I think someone has an open Wi-Fi connection nearby. Let me see if I can use that."

Kisaki stopped and put a hand on her shoulder. "I didn't mean for this to happen, but I promise I will get you home."

After a moment, Tamiko nodded. "I believe you. And, hey, magic crystals are bound to be cheaper than airfare." She looked down at her phone, smiled, and began to type on it.

"Wi-Fi?" Shitoro asked, still in his tiger form.

"Wireless internet. Not quite as good as magic, but it gets the job done."

"What are you doing?" Kisaki asked.

"Shooting my dad an email. I'm telling him we're going to be spending the weekend helping you with your sick grandmother, so he doesn't worry when we're not there in the morning." She looked around. "Or whatever time it is back home."

"I don't have a sick grandmother," Kisaki replied before turning to Shitoro. "Do I even have a…?"

"It doesn't matter." Tamiko pocketed her phone. "It's just to buy us some time." Kisaki inclined her head, not comprehending. "It's like you said. We're already here. We might as well make the most of it. I've never been to the United States before. So this is kind of like a vacation with friends … and their pets. It'll also give us time to try and find your father."

Kisaki didn't know how to express her gratitude in words. Instead, she flung herself at her friend and hugged her hard. After a moment, Tamiko returned it.

"Lady Kisaki," Shitoro chided, "let that human go. You don't know what kind of germs she has."

The girls disengaged, and then Tamiko got down on one knee before the little demon. "Don't make me buy a muzzle for you."

"You wouldn't dare."

"Try me. Oh, and from here on out, a word of advice: I've never been to America, but if it's anything at all like Kabira Bay, then the cats don't talk back."

"What does it say?" Kisaki asked. The words on the sign were a jumble to her, although she could have sworn they seemed to make more sense the longer she stared at them.

"We're in a town called Cartersville," Tamiko said. "Looks more like a dump to me."

"Amazingly enough, I believe we have found something we can agree on, human," Shitoro replied.

"What did I tell you about talking?"

"You do not *tell* me anything. I am a superior being."

"A superior being that needs a flea bath."

"How dare you…"

"That's enough, Shitoro," Kisaki said. Despite her far greater age, she had to admit her friend knew Earth much better than she could probably ever hope to. Shitoro would sooner combust than admit it, but it was painfully obvious the same could be said of him.

The town that lay before them was in stark contrast to the resort where she'd spent the last few days. The buildings were smaller and older looking. They were also further apart, with lots of trees taking up the excess space. She could neither see the ocean nor smell any hint of salt in the air, leaving her to conclude they were far from it.

There was, however, lots of life here. Birds, far different from those she saw at the resort, flew through the air and, every so often, she caught hints of movement in the trees – tiny furred creatures that scampered through the branches. They paid her and her companions not the slightest heed, leaving her to conclude they were merely animals, not youkai in disguise.

She found the lack of youkai to be curious. The histories she'd read of this planet had always included them, whether they were warring alongside mankind or against them. Yet, Shitoro aside, she hadn't seen any, nor had she been given any indication by the humans she'd met so far that they were even aware of them.

Kisaki wondered if something had happened, some event or plague that had either destroyed demonkind upon this world or sent them into hiding.

Before those thoughts could be allowed to wander very far, she was brought back to the here and now by a commotion from not too far away. Kisaki turned toward the source and saw a pack of humans, all males from the look of it, with a wide range of coloring and features. It appeared as if six of the males were harassing a seventh.

"What's going on over there?" Tamiko wondered aloud.

"It is of no concern to us," Shitoro said before being shushed by Tamiko.

Kisaki couldn't understand what the group was saying, but the voices of the six were rising in pitch. She didn't need to grasp their meaning to know that they sounded angry.

She remembered the group who had teased her upon her arrival on Earth, how they'd pushed her into the water. Those had been mere children, smaller than her, and easily chased off by a few words from Tamiko. These males were larger, older, and they seemed far more aggressive. It didn't appear to her as if mischief was all they had in mind. She watched as several balled their fists against the lone male. He had light brown hair, perhaps a shade darker than her own. Though as tall as the rest, he was lean where they were stocky. He held up his hands in a placating manner to the others, but Kisaki instinctively sensed that wouldn't do him any good.

The largest of the group, a pale, portly teen with hair as dark as Tamiko's but much shorter and greasier looking, stepped forward and grabbed him by the jacket. He dragged the lone male between two buildings, out of their line of sight. A moment later, the other five followed.

"Come on. We need to help him."

"Help him?" Tamiko asked. "How?"

"I don't know," Kisaki said, starting off in the direction she'd seen them go.

Behind her, she could hear Shitoro quietly pleading that they should leave well enough alone, but she ignored him. That boy appeared to be in trouble, far more than she had been. Though she doubted her harassers would have done much more than make fun of her, Tamiko had arrived and chased them off nevertheless. Though she wasn't a warrior, her actions had been those of a hero.

If her friend could do it, then so could Kisaki. She now knew she was half human, perhaps descended from the fine warriors of the past she'd read about. If so, then that same blood flowed through her veins. It was time to test her own mettle and do for this boy what her friend had done for her.

As Kisaki closed the distance to the alley, she heard the voices of the group again, still arguing angrily.

At first, it was just indistinct chatter, but then, as before, she was amazed to discover that the words quickly started to make sense.

"I … too. I … doing … job."

"… give a damn … teeth."

"Get him! … one for me."

"Come on, guys. I didn't…"

"Shut up, asshole. You … me out for shoplifting. Do you know what my old man did to me?"

"I work there. I can't just … *oof!*"

Kisaki sped up her pace, Tamiko and Shitoro still hot on her tail. Though she couldn't be certain, it had sounded like someone had been struck.

"Hold him up. Time to teach this loser that snitches really do get stitches."

Kisaki rounded the corner and saw she'd been right. The brown-haired male the others had been harassing was down on one knee, holding his stomach. Two others flanked him and were trying to drag him back up to his feet. Two more stood in front alongside the large male she assumed to be the one who'd made the attack.

A sixth, a young man with long hair pulled back into a ponytail, stood near the end of the alley she'd just turned down. When he saw her, he stepped forward angrily. "There ain't nothing to see here. Get moving!"

Kisaki decided to test whether her newfound understanding of this language affected her tongue as well as her ears. "Leave him alone."

"I said get out of here, unless you want some of the same."

"Kisaki," Tamiko warned from behind her.

"What's going on there?" the large one, perhaps their leader, asked from further in.

"We've got an audience."

"Get rid of them!"

"Help me!" the brown-haired boy pleaded. "Call the…"

He was again struck by the large one, a blow to his mid-section that put him back on the ground.

Kisaki had seen enough. She made to step past the one who was trying to block her, but he caught her by the arm and shoved her away.

"Lady Kisaki!" Shitoro cried from behind her.

Kisaki stumbled back a few steps before being caught by Tamiko. She quickly nodded thanks to her friend.

"We need to get out of here," Tamiko hissed. "We have to…"

"What the hell?" It was the boy who stood guard. He was staring down at Shitoro, his eyes wide.

Kisaki decided to use the distraction to her benefit. She pushed off Tamiko and raced forward, catching the guard with her shoulder and knocking him to the side.

She knew what she was doing was reckless, potentially dangerous, but she'd seen the good in these people through her friend. If there was one human like her friend, then there were others. Tamiko had taken a chance on her. Now it was her turn to even the scales by doing the same … or attempting to anyway.

One of the boys standing alongside the large male moved forward to intercept her, blocking her way with his superior size. "This isn't any of your business, bitch." He slapped a fist into his open palm. "I don't know you, so get lost before I'm forced to introduce myself."

"I am making it … my business."

"Yo, Robbie, you hear this? Egg Roll here is making it her business."

"Egg Roll?" Kisaki asked, confused.

"Hey!" a voice from behind her called, the ponytailed one. "I think this cat can talk."

Kisaki said a silent prayer that for once Shitoro let his ego go and remained silent. She had a feeling this group was going to be even worse trouble for them if they managed to stand out more than they already did.

"What?" the big one, Robbie, asked, ceasing his assault for the moment.

The one blocking Kisaki let out a laugh. "I think Jack's holding out. Been smoking some of the good shit without us."

"He better not be."

"Yeah, man. Say, what do you want me to do with Sum Dum Fuk here?"

"Do you really need me to tell you what to do with a woman?"

The comment caused the others to stop and laugh. Kisaki had just barely begun to understand some of Tamiko's colloquialisms, much less the ones from this new land. However, she wasn't a stupid girl by any means. It was painfully obvious that the boy named Robbie had just insulted the one trying to block her.

Perhaps it would cause him to rethink his allegiance.

He stepped forward and gave Kisaki a shove.

Perhaps not.

She landed on her backside on the hard ground, unhurt save for her pride.

"Kisaki!"

"Back off unless you want some, too," the pony-tailed one warned Tamiko from somewhere behind her. "And take your freak-ass cat with you."

Tamiko was putting herself in danger for her once again. This was not how Kisaki had envisioned things. She felt ashamed that in trying to help, all she'd managed to do was get knocked down again, same as the last time she'd faced a group of adversaries.

There came a stab of heat from her side. The quill again! It almost seemed to sense her mood when she was in trouble. She briefly wondered what would happen if she pulled it out. After all, Shitoro had claimed it was dangerous.

Kisaki didn't want to hurt anyone, but perhaps she could use it to scare them off. That seemed a viable strategy to her.

She reached into her jacket pocket and pulled it forth, imagining it as the sword she'd seen hanging over her mother's chair.

Climbing back to her feet, she held it out before her. "Behold, mortal, the power of..."

The sword was still merely a feathered quill in her hands. Nothing more.

"Hey, Robbie. Bitch thinks she's gonna fly away. Drop that thing!" he said, laughing as he slapped it from her hand. "Don't you know seagulls have germs?"

Kisaki watched in shock as it dropped lightly to the ground, landing in a puddle. Anger and outrage flooded her senses, and she stepped in close to the man. "That belongs to my mother."

"Oh? Your mama gave you a feather?" he replied. "Mine just gave me *this*." He backhanded Kisaki across the face with an audible *crack*.

TWENTY

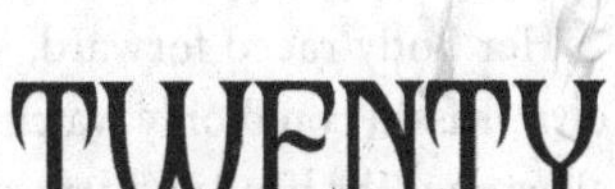

KISAKI'S HEAD ROCKED to the side from the blow and she tasted blood.

She staggered back several steps but managed not to fall.

All at once, the world seemed to be moving in slow motion. Pain from the hit, the coppery taste of her own blood, her friend screaming her name, and the huffing laughter of the human who had dared lay a hand upon her – all of it happening simultaneously.

It was the first time Kisaki had ever been struck. She'd often read about such punishments, and much worse, in her studies, but had never experienced it herself. She'd expected it to hurt, and it did. What she didn't expect, however, was the cold logic that descended upon her mind, nor how the world seemed to grey out around her.

He didn't hit me that hard, did he?

Before her eyes, the world seemed to change. The sounds around her faded away and she was suddenly no longer in an alleyway. Instead, she stood in a large room. A man was there with her. He was wearing drab green clothes and seemed to be yelling at her for some reason. For a moment, she feared that she'd somehow accidentally activated her last crystal, abandoning the brown-haired boy as well as Tamiko and Shitoro. But then she realized something was wrong about what she was seeing. The man's lips were moving, but she couldn't hear his words. In fact, she couldn't hear anything.

Her body raced forward, seemingly with a mind all its own. Kisaki could only watch as her fist shot out, but it was all wrong. The hand and arm attached to her was much larger and coarser than her own.

None of this mattered to the yelling man, though. He grabbed hold of her and then she was airborne, flying over his shoulder to land roughly on the wooden floor where she…

Just as quickly as the vision had come, it faded away and Kisaki was back where she'd been, tasting her own blood as color returned to the world and sounds started up again.

The world was still moving way too slowly, but that cold logic in her mind demanded that she use the time to study the foes around her. She became acutely aware of everything about them – their size, their weight, the way they moved, how quickly they did so. All of it registered in her senses within the space of a split second, locking itself into her memory with perfect clarity as if she'd spent months, maybe years, studying nothing but these humans.

With that clarity came understanding. She realized how sloppy the attack against her had been. It was a miracle she'd been struck at all, probably more a result of her outrage than any real attempt on his part. If anything, she didn't feel anger against him so much as embarrassment for herself. Such a blow was easily countered. Everything that these men…

No. Warriors were men. These were boys, peasants, children – warriors in their minds only.

It was time to teach them the error of their ways.

Time sped up again to its normal pace, but still that cold logic remained. She stepped forward again. The male who slapped her saw her coming. He looked surprised for a moment before covering it up with a veneer of arrogance.

"Want some more, bitch? Good, because I'm serving it up all day."

This time, he balled his fists, but it didn't matter. Kisaki somehow understood what he was going to do, perhaps even before he did.

She raised an arm and easily blocked the punch. Her attacker's eyes opened wide in surprise. Then, just as quickly, she threw a blow of her own, an open-handed shot to his throat. It caught him dead on, as she knew it would, and he doubled over, gasping for breath.

As he did, she brought a knee up into his jaw. She heard teeth crack and then he dropped to the ground. Unlike when he'd shoved her, though, it didn't appear he would be getting back to his feet nearly as quickly.

Kisaki had barely a moment to be amazed at what she'd done. She'd never been allowed to study fighting or weaponry, no matter how much she had begged. Her mother had forbidden it, and Shitoro wasn't the type to go against her wishes.

But then the moment was over, as the other boy next to Robbie rushed at her. This one was short, but thickly built. He moved as one who knew what he was doing. Not a warrior, but perhaps one in training.

None of that mattered. Kisaki analyzed his moves in the time it took him to pass Robbie and came up with a counter strategy.

She feinted to the right, but he seemed to anticipate that, which was precisely what she expected him to do. She cut hard left, sidestepping him. As he passed by, she shoved him from behind, using his own momentum to propel him into a pile of refuse along the side of the alleyway.

Rough hands grabbed her from behind in a bear hug, lifting her from the ground. Blast! She'd forgotten about the pony-tailed one, Jack. Perhaps sensing she was a greater threat than her friends, he'd come up from behind her unawares as she battled the other two.

"The hell?" he cried. "You some kind of ninja?"

Kisaki allowed herself the ghost of a smile. Ninja had been mentioned in her studies. They were said to be masters of stealth and combat arts. It was something she'd never considered herself to be, but she was currently too distracted to disagree with him at that moment. Instead, as way of response, she threw her head back, catching him on the nose with a satisfying *crunch*.

He screamed and let go, allowing her to throw a kick back into his leg, which dropped him to one knee.

She immediately realized that these three had been little more than the warmup. The real fight lay before her. Robbie and his two remaining friends had disengaged from the brown-haired boy. She now had their undivided attention. The first two, mere minions, wore uncertain looks upon their faces. Their leader Robbie, however, looked sure of himself, a fact attested to by his wide grin.

He had a confidence about him that suggested he didn't expect to lose. Robbie had the look of one who was used to having the advantage. Indeed, he was larger than most of the humans she'd met, including fully grown males such as Mr. Yoshida. For all intents and purposes, Kisaki should have been terrified of him. But she wasn't. She didn't know what was happening to her, but whatever it was, she reveled in it.

"Leave now and you may go unmolested," she said to the three still standing. She didn't expect them to heed her offer. Robbie in particular didn't appear inclined to parley. However, it gave Kisaki a moment to reach out with her senses, take stock of the situation.

Of the three she'd dealt with already, two appeared to have the fight taken out of them. The third, however, was stirring from the pile of trash she'd sent him into. He was likely to try his luck again.

Four against one. It seemed insurmountable odds, but at the same time did not. Something inside of her had changed. The question was: *what*?

Alas, it did not appear that answers were forthcoming at the moment.

"You may think you're hot shit with that karate crap," Robbie said, smiling a gap-toothed grin. He reminded her of the apes that Shitoro kept comparing Tamiko to. "If you'd walked away earlier, I'd have let you go. But then you had to go and rough up some of my boys. I can't let that stand." He turned to the two on either side of him. "What say we send her ass to the hospital with a side of rice?"

The uncertainty left their eyes, no doubt inspired by their leader's confidence.

"She's kinda cute," the one on the left said. He was second in size only to Robbie, with close-cropped light hair and a bent nose, as if it had been broken before and set badly. "I might want a piece of that."

"Help yourself," Robbie said. "I ain't never been one for Chinese takeout myself. I'm more of a meat and potatoes kind of man."

His friends chuckled and one cracked his knuckles, no doubt meant as a means of intimidation.

It didn't work.

Kisaki hadn't set out to hurt anyone this day. All she really wanted to do was make some new friends and create some good memories for when her unending confinement began again. The cold logic that still gripped her said otherwise, though. She now found herself eager for combat.

She recognized it for what it was: *bloodlust*, something she hadn't thought herself capable of.

It seemed this day was full of surprises.

Movement registered behind Kisaki – the one in the garbage pile. Even if it hadn't, she would have smelled him coming. Robbie's words had been a ploy, a means to ensure he had as much of an advantage as he could.

That's when she realized his confident smile was a sham. She was smaller and thinner than any of them. In human terms, she shouldn't have been considered a threat. But Robbie was a coward inside – someone who was only brave in the face of certain victory. He'd been attempting to gain an advantage over her but had instead given it away.

"Kisaki, look out!"

Tamiko's warning was welcome but unnecessary.

The two minions charged her from the front while the short, stocky one did the same from her rear, hoping to catch her in the middle and end this quickly.

Kisaki spared them a quick smile of her own before kicking off with her feet.

Barely believing what she was doing, she rolled backward over the one charging from her flank, his shoulder down as he tried to tackle her.

She landed nimbly behind him, the only discomfort being whatever garbage had rubbed off on her from the maneuver. Sadly, the same couldn't be said of him or his friends. Neither side could arrest their momentum in time and the three of them collided.

It was a solid hit, but not a battle-ending one. At best, the three were slightly staggered. So she stepped in to remedy that.

It was almost as if she were a voyeur inside of her own body – able to observe, think, and make suggestions while her limbs acted of their own accord. Somehow the blow to her face had woken something within her – a creature of instinct, *warrior instinct*.

She spun and kicked out low, taking the legs out from beneath the one who had tried to hit her from the rear. He went down with a whoop of surprise and Kisaki followed up by stomping down upon his midsection and knocking the wind completely out of him. He didn't even have enough left after that to cry out in pain.

The one with the crooked nose managed to grab hold of her arm when she spun his way. He twisted it, which she realized should have caused her pain, but didn't. If anything, it was like a small child, or youkai cub, doing little more than holding her hand. She flexed her muscles and saw the look of surprise in his eyes as she overpowered him. It almost mirrored the one on her own face at what she was doing.

His friend came in on the other side, grasping her free arm to stop her from driving it into her other opponent, or at least trying to.

She dragged him forward, slamming the two together with considerable force. Blood erupted from the already crooked nose of the first one.

Broken again, she mused before kicking out at the second.

She caught him dead-on in the midsection and sent him airborne, much to her surprise. He landed a good ten feet away, hitting the ground stunned.

Rather than admire her handiwork, she grabbed hold of the bleeding male's arm, spun, and forcefully flipped him onto his back where she drove the heel of her foot into his crotch.

He let out a high-pitched wheeze and began to actually cry as his hands moved to cradle the spot she'd struck. Kisaki wasn't quite certain what she'd done, but it appeared that he was likewise out of the fight.

That was five. Only their leader remained.

Interestingly enough, the smug look was gone from his face. He was their leader, their general, but he was also a sham. His expression told her he relied on his troops to do all the work for him. Without them, he was nothing.

Kisaki folded her arms and glared at him. Multiple history lessons played out in her mind, telling her that surrender was imminent. Then it would be up to her to decide how to proceed, to be wrathful or merciful.

She honestly wasn't sure which she wanted at that moment. It was as if her higher brain functions had been pushed to the side in favor of that cold logic, and that logic was apparently equally as fine with breaking this human's neck as it was with letting him go.

That sudden realization scared Kisaki – to think she might be capable of such violence when she'd never so much as hurt a fly before today.

"Listen, I was just kidding before about that side of rice crap," Robbie said, his hands up in supplication. "It was just a joke."

Kisaki struggled to push that coldness within her away, back down to whatever dungeon of her mind it had originated from. While it remained, she was uncertain what she might do. This man-child before her was a worm, unworthy of her consideration, but she had friends nearby. If she let the coldness stay, it might eventually begin to influence her with regard to them.

She didn't let the war raging inside of her show on her face, though. To do so might embolden her foe again. If that happened, she was almost certain whatever befell him would make the beating his friends had suffered look tame by comparison.

Instead, she reached up and touched her jaw where she'd been struck. "A joke, you say?" Kisaki took a step forward, enjoying the way he flinched at her approach.

"Please! I have money."

"I have no interest in your money. I…"

"Sure we do," Tamiko said in his language, running up to stand by her side. "How much?"

Kisaki fell silent. She wasn't certain what her friend was getting at, but was curious to see what would happen next.

Robbie pulled something from his pocket, some kind of folded pouch, then tossed it to the ground in front of him. "That's everything I've got."

"Good," Tamiko said. "Now get lost. Don't let my friend here see you again."

They stepped to the side to let him pass. He didn't even pause long enough to wait for his friends, who were just now struggling to get back up.

"Heed the human's words," Shitoro said as Robbie drew near him. "Pray we do not cross paths again."

Robbie's eyes opened wide as saucers as he looked down at the little tiger demon. He let out a screech of panic and ran.

Seeing their leader broken, the rest of his group pulled themselves to their feet and ran after him. Kisaki and Tamiko watched them wordlessly until they were gone from sight. Then Tamiko strolled over, picked up the pouch Robbie had dropped, and looked inside it.

"Why did you do that?" Kisaki asked. "We do not need anything of his."

"I beg to differ," Tamiko said, counting green-colored paper. "We're in a new land with no money. American money, anyway. I don't know about you, but I'm going to want lunch at some point."

Kisaki couldn't discount her logic even if it felt a bit petty to have done so. Still, she'd heard of warriors taking trophies from their defeated foes, so perhaps this was customary.

"Hey, um, thanks."

She spun as quickly as she could. In the heat of battle, she'd completely forgotten about the young man she'd been intent on saving. He was back on his feet, leaning on the wall of the alley for support. Though a bit disheveled, and with a bruise beginning to color his cheek, he seemed otherwise unhurt. "I am pleased you are okay."

"I wouldn't have been if you hadn't come along. That was ... incredible."

"I'll say," Tamiko added, stepping once again to Kisaki's side. "How come you didn't tell me you could do that?"

"I..."

"We should get out of here," the boy said. "I've known that dickhead for years and he doesn't give up easily. He's going to want some payback. He and his idiot friends are probably going to convince each other it was a fluke and then come back for round two."

Kisaki nodded. She wasn't particularly worried about a round two, whatever that was, but was curious about the person she'd just saved. It would be difficult to learn anything about who he was, where they were, and where they could find her father, if she was busy picking fights with the local populace.

"Agreed," Tamiko said, pocketing the money and discarding Robbie's pouch.

"Great," he replied. "Follow me. We can go back to my house. At the very least, I can offer you guys a place to clean up and maybe a glass of lemonade."

"One moment," Kisaki said, remembering she'd dropped something very important. Now where was … there! The Taiyosori was lying in the puddle where it had fallen, looking like nothing more than a simple feather quill.

Such ado about so simple of a thing. Whatever it was, though, it still belonged to her mother. She was in trouble enough already without having to confess she'd lost it.

Kisaki picked it up, gave it a quick shake to wring the water out, then stuffed it back into her jacket before turning to follow the young man, who seemed quite eager to leave this place.

He led the group out of the alley, stopping at the entrance and looking around, perhaps to make sure his tormenters were no longer in the area. After a moment, he waved them on. "The way you took care of those guys was seriously awesome."

"Thank you," Kisaki replied.

"By the way, how did you manage to throw your voice so it sounded like your cat was talking?"

TWENTY-ONE

THEY WERE MOSTLY quiet as the boy led them along. He seemed nervous, as if Robbie and his cohorts might be waiting around every tree.

Kisaki decided that further conversation could wait until he was in a place where he was more comfortable. She remembered her own embarrassment at being bullied and how she'd felt much better once she'd followed Tamiko home.

Through some minor miracle, Shitoro held his tongue as they walked, seemingly not in the mood to argue with the boy's earlier cat comment.

Kisaki tried to take in her new surroundings – Cartersville, Tamiko had called it – but instead found herself stealing glances at their new companion. He was a good head taller than she and appeared to be of comparable age – in appearance anyway. He was tall, thin, and with a strong chin. Kisaki had few reference points to judge attractiveness but decided he was pleasant to look at, certainly much more so than the brutes who'd accosted him.

"Where are we going?" Tamiko asked as he led them down a side street off of the main thoroughfare of the small town.

"Like I said, my place. Or my parents' place anyway. They're not home, though. They're gone for the week, visiting my grandparents. I had to work, so I stuck around. Trying to save up for a car. You know how it is."

Kisaki did not know how *it* was, but his answer seemed to satisfy Tamiko, so she decided to trust in her friend.

After about fifteen more minutes of walking, they came to a small dwelling. It was a drab beige in color and two stories in height. A portion of the street lay alongside it – a driveway, if Kisaki recalled correctly – and it was surrounded on all sides by a wooden fence that didn't look sturdy enough to keep out anything that truly wanted in.

"It's not much to look at, but it's home," the boy said brightly enough. "Come on in." He walked up a few steps to the door and opened it before frowning down at Shitoro. "Is he one of those hypoallergenic breeds, by any chance?"

Kisaki opened her eyes wide in confusion. She turned to Tamiko, who merely shrugged uncomfortably.

"It's just that my mom is allergic to cats. Nothing horrible, but she'll end up sneezing for a week if too much fur gets on things."

"Oh," Kisaki replied, not entirely comprehending. "He is…"

"Then it is a good thing I am not a cat," Shitoro said suddenly. "A fact that you humans seem to have some issue discerning."

The boy let out a laugh. "Which of you two is doing that? Because seriously, that is kick ass. We're talking Jeff Dunham level shit right there."

"Jeff Dunham?" Kisaki asked.

"It's her." Tamiko hooked a thumb over her shoulder. "She and her *cat* have a special bond."

"My claws are going to form a special bond with your leg, human, if you keep calling me that," Shitoro growled.

"Wow," their would-be host said. "That is wild. I can't see your lips moving or anything."

Shitoro let out a disgusted sigh. "Is the entirety of your species this dense? I swear, one would think opening that door would present a challenge to you. It's beyond me how primates such as yourself managed to spook the bulk of the celestial court."

"Shitoro," Kisaki warned.

"Is that his name?" the boy asked. "I had him pegged as more of a Fluffy."

That caused Tamiko to burst out laughing.

Shitoro, however, seemingly found the comment less than amusing. Before Kisaki could say anything to stop him, his eyes flashed and he transformed to his youkai form. He stood there glaring up at the wide-eyed boy. "I have had to endure a lot in my time, but I will warn you once and only once, that I am *not* fluffy!"

Anything further Shitoro might have had to say was drowned out.

"Holy shit! What the hell is that thing?!"

Though the nearby dwellings weren't nearly as close together as some Kisaki had seen on Tamiko's island, she suspected they were close enough to hear the panic coming out of her new friend's mouth.

Tamiko was apparently thinking the same thing. She whispered, "We need to get inside," then grabbed the boy from behind and dragged him through the door.

Kisaki glared down at Shitoro. "Go on."

"It would be rude of me to pass through first without holding the door for a lady such as…"

"In, *now!*"

Perhaps it was the tone in Kisaki's voice, but Shitoro hurried through the doorway as quickly as his little hind legs could carry him.

As soon as he was inside, she followed and closed the door behind them, hoping they hadn't attracted any undue attention.

If it hadn't been for the panic in the boy's voice, Kisaki would have found the interior charming. It was simple compared to the celestial palace, even compared to the resort she'd stayed at with Tamiko. If anything, it reminded Kisaki of a peasant dwelling, but that wasn't to say it was bad. What it lacked in finery and grandeur, it certainly made up for in comfort.

And then there was the smell. She couldn't put her finger upon it, as she'd never smelled anything like it before, but the dwelling had a pleasant, lazy odor about it. The brown-haired boy had called it home, and that struck a chord with her. Indeed, it smelled like what one might imagine a *home* should smell like.

Taking in the sights and scents would have to wait, however, for Tamiko had her hands full. She'd pulled the boy into a room off of the entranceway and was trying to get him to sit down.

"Get off me!" he protested. "What is that thing? Who are you people? And how hard did that blockhead hit me back there in the alley?"

"Calm down," Tamiko said. "This is all fairly new for me, too."

"I am not going to calm down. That … cat talked to me, and then it turned into a … I don't know, a freaking garden gnome or something."

Shitoro's fur ruffled at his words and he opened his mouth, but Kisaki pushed past, then turned and pointed a finger his way. "That will be enough."

"But…"

"I'm serious, Shitoro. It can wait for the moment. Just stand near the doorway for now until we calm him down."

The youkai made a sound of disgust. "Such insignificant creatures. Why I even bother trying…"

Kisaki stepped into the room slowly, attempting to appear as harmless as possible. She looked around and then took a seat on a comfortable, if worn-looking chair. "Your home is really nice."

"You're kidding me, right?" he asked. "That's the best you've got? You just kicked the crap out of six guys who've hounded me since the second grade, you have a talking gnome cat, and all you can say is 'your home is nice?'"

"It really is," Tamiko agreed before stepping back when he turned to glare at her. She turned to Kisaki and inclined her head before taking a seat of her own. The look on her face said it all. Scared and confused as he was, at least he was talking, which was infinitely better than screaming.

"I'm gonna call the cops," he said. "Tell them you forced your way inside and are holding me hostage."

"Cops?"

"Please don't do that," Tamiko replied, and then to Kisaki, she explained, "American slang. It means the police."

"Ah, the enforcers of your laws. Yes, as my friend just said, kindly do not do that. It is unnecessary."

The boy laughed, although there was a manic quality to it. "Not sure what I'd tell them anyway, at least that wouldn't get me locked up. They threw Mr. Dawkins, that's our neighbor three doors down, in the drunk tank for the weekend after he claimed to have seen Bigfoot out in the woods. Can only imagine what they'd do if I started yelling about talking gnomes."

"Shitoro is not a gnome," Kisaki said. "He is a youkai."

"A tiger youkai, if we are being specific," Shitoro added from the doorway to the room, where he looked to be busy pouting.

"Yes." Kisaki smiled at him. "He is a ferocious and loyal tiger youkai."

"Youkai?" the young man asked. "I've heard that before."

"It basically means demon," Tamiko explained.

"Oh yeah. From like manga, right?"

She nodded.

"My mom's into that and I've read a few." He turned toward Shitoro and blinked several times, as if not believing what he was seeing. "So you're actually telling me they're real?"

"Hopefully not all," Tamiko replied. "I've read a few stories that are a bit … disturbing. But trust me. I was just as surprised as you."

"Are there any others like him?"

Tamiko turned to Kisaki with an expectant look upon her face. Kisaki realized this was her friend's first chance to ask questions, too. She'd met Shitoro, only to be whisked away before she could properly process things. If anything, they were sharing the same surprised emotions. The boy's were just a bit fresher, that's all.

Speaking of which, she couldn't keep thinking of her host as "the boy." "My name is Kisaki. It is a pleasure to make your acquaintance. You've already met Shitoro, and this is Tamiko."

The boy nodded. "Are you two … y'know?"

"Y'know?"

"I think he's asking if we're youkai, too," Tamiko said. "I'm not. Just a fifteen-year-old girl from Kabira Beach. Heck, two hours ago, I was in your shoes."

"Kabira Beach? Is that in New Jersey?"

"Ishigachi … it's west of Okinawa."

"Okinawa?" The boy paused as if thinking. "As in Japan?"

Tamiko nodded.

"You're Japanese … I mean, obviously, you look like it. I mean, you look Asian, that is, not…"

"Oh great. Another broken human," Shitoro muttered.

"Sorry," he continued, throwing a quick glance the tiger youkai's way before turning back to Tamiko. "So you're really from Japan?"

"If you ask my father, he'd give you a long answer to that," she said with a smile, "but yes."

Their host didn't seem to know what to say to that. "Um … your English is really good."

"Thanks. My dad runs the resort there. I get a lot of practice with the tourists."

"I bet," he replied, still wide-eyed. "I'm sorry, maybe I'm thick, but I still don't get it. You said that two hours ago, this was all new to you. But you're here now?"

"Yes. A short while ago I, *we* were there standing on the beach back home. It was dark, and then poof, suddenly we were here and it was morning."

"It was my fault," Kisaki explained.

"I should say so," Shitoro snorted from the doorway.

"So what about you?" the boy asked Kisaki. "Are you … like her?"

She looked down at her lap and considered this. "The funny thing is, this is new for me, too, but to answer your question, I am … different. My mother is one of the daimao."

"Daimao? Is that like a shogun or something?"

"It's a greater demon of sorts," Tamiko replied. "Or maybe a lesser god. Depends on which myths you read. They're pretty high up the ladder, though. Like comparing a lizard to Gojira."

The boy nodded as if he understood, then turned back to Kisaki. "So you're … a goddess?"

"Lady Kisaki is a hanyou," Shitoro said with a pained sigh, stepping into the room. He stopped as the boy turned toward him. "Oh, calm down already, child. Had I wished you harm, we would not be having this discussion. She is a half demon."

Kisaki nodded. "I recently learned my father is a human. I'm here looking for him."

"In Cartersville?" the boy asked. "I think you're going to be disappointed. Not much happens here. At the very least, I'm pretty sure none of the townsfolk are married to a goddess."

Kisaki's face fell at the news, but Shitoro said, "He may not even be aware."

"What?" she asked. "How?"

"He … your father, that is … may … no, he is almost certainly not aware of his siring."

"Why?" Kisaki asked.

"It's difficult to explain."

The boy stood and stretched, seemingly more at ease following Shitoro's declaration of no ill intent. "If that's the case, then he's going to be a lot harder to find. But I'll tell you what. This is … I won't lie. This is really freaking weird. But it's kinda cool, too. Also, you helped me out earlier. I was sure that goon was going to feed me my teeth…"

"Why?" Kisaki interrupted. "What transgression occurred between you?"

"Life," he replied. "Robbie's had it out for me ever since we were kids. He's the closest thing this town has to an official jackass. Anyway, I've been mostly avoiding him since we started high school. He's not exactly in any honors classes, if you get my drift."

Tamiko laughed at this, although Kisaki didn't quite understand why.

"But last week, I was working at my new job, stocking shelves down at the Grub Stop. He and a few of his troglodyte buddies came in and started wandering the aisles. Next thing I knew, I saw him stuff a box of doughnuts in his jacket."

"Doughnuts?"

"You need to try them, trust me," Tamiko said before opening her eyes wide. "Hey, I just realized you've been speaking English, too."

"I am?" Kisaki asked.

"Yeah, remember? Three days ago, you told me you couldn't. What? Were you just being shy or something?"

Kisaki turned away, unsure of what to say. "I spoke the truth. I didn't speak it. I … only learned it a short while ago, listening to those boys argue."

"You're telling me that up until about an hour ago, you didn't speak English, but now, suddenly, you speak it better than me?"

"Yeah," the boy said. "I mean, I can't even hear an accent."

Shitoro cleared his throat, catching their attention. "Perhaps if you had paid better attention in your studies, such knowledge would be evident."

"How so?" Kisaki asked.

The tiger demon strolled further into the room, then hopped upon one of the many cushioned seats.

"Hey!" the boy said. "My mom is…"

"Allergic to cats," Shitoro replied. "Yes, I heard you. Fortunately for her, I am a tiger demon."

"Tigers *are* cats," Tamiko said triumphantly.

"Do you ever grow weary of being tiresome?"

"Not really."

"Eh hem," Kisaki interrupted. "You were saying?"

Shitoro crossed his arms and leaned back. "I was saying that this ability of yours is commonplace. The celestial tongue is far more complex than anything spoken by humans. Those who master it can often easily pick up other languages. They are child's play in comparison to the speech of the gods."

"In minutes?"

"No," he replied. "If you will allow me to finish. Your mother, like all daimao, possesses a mind more advanced than any human could even hope to understand." He paused to look condescendingly at the two others in the room. "It is my belief that you inherited this from her … a very small portion anyway, if your progress in your studies is to be believed."

Kisaki let the insult go for now. She'd always envied her mother – her power, her beauty, her regal bearing, everything. A part of her had always wondered if she was a disappointment, seemingly in possession of none of those traits. However, if what Shitoro said was true, then it had just been hidden until now. If she'd gotten that from her mother, then perhaps she'd also gotten… "Would it work the same way with combat skills?"

Shitoro's expression suddenly went from smug to unsure. "Err…"

"I was meaning to ask you about that," Tamiko said. "You kicked their butts pretty hard. You must have been studying martial arts for years."

Kisaki shook her head. "Before today, I have never had cause to raise my hand to another. When you met me, that boy Hojo, the one who pushed me into the water, was the first time any had ever accosted me."

"Really?"

"Yes. That is why I am asking. Shitoro?"

"I … do not know," he admitted. "I was actually just about to step in with my magic when you began doing whatever it is you did. It was most … unexpected."

Kisaki started to mention the vision she'd had, too, but then stopped herself. If her sudden skills made Shitoro nervous, what would that do?

"No matter the cause," he continued, "you must keep that to yourself. Do not even tell your mother about it."

"Why?"

"Because she would punish me, that's why! You were never supposed to be taught to fight. It was her wish."

"But you didn't."

"I know that, but she won't believe me. I'll be lucky to be demoted to the cleaning staff."

"Why didn't she want me to learn to fight?"

"A lady of your station needs it not. Also…"

"Also what?"

He shifted uncomfortably in his seat. "Those who learn how to fight often wish to test it out. Considering your heritage, it seemed a risk not worth taking."

"My heritage? What does that have to…" She stopped when she noticed the boy watching her intently. Feeling a strange heat rise to her cheeks, she quickly forgot everything they were discussing. "My apologies. I did not mean to interrupt your tale."

"That's okay," he said. "What you guys are talking about is far more fascinating than my day. I was just going to say, I told my boss about Robbie and he ended up calling the cops. End of story. That's pretty much the point where you guys stepped in, right when he was about to beat the snot out of me for ratting on him."

"He should thank you for forcing him to own up to his actions."

"I have a feeling he doesn't quite feel the same way on that subject. Personal responsibility isn't one of his better virtues."

"Perhaps he has learned some from today."

"I doubt it. Learning isn't his forte either."

Tamiko laughed at that, and soon Kisaki and the boy joined her. Only Shitoro remained silent, continuing to look put out.

After a few minutes of this, the boy looked up at them all. "Oh wow. I'm a terrible host. I got so caught up in…" He gestured toward Shitoro. "And all the rest of it, that I forgot I promised you all some lemonade."

"I'd love some," Tamiko said. Kisaki looked at her questioningly, to which she added, "Kisaki would love some, too. Trust me on this."

"I am quite fine as I am," Shitoro muttered.

"A warm bowl of … milk maybe?" the boy offered, to which the youkai narrowed his eyes. "Okay, nothing for you. Gotcha."

"Thank you," Kisaki said before adding, "I am sorry, but I do not know whom I am thanking for this hospitality."

The boy paused for a moment, then slapped his forehead. "Oh wow, I am such a moron. I'm sorry. I swear, that idiot must've beaten my manners out of me. It's just been a bit of a long day."

Kisaki smiled. "It is quite all right."

"I'm glad to hear that." He stepped forward and held his hand out to her. "Stephen Fuller at your service."

Kisaki was about to take his hand when suddenly Shitoro stood up from where he'd been sitting.

"*What?!*"

TWENTY-TWO

"OW! STOP THAT!"

"Shitoro, is this really necessary?"

The tiger demon continued to chase Stephen around the room, firing bolts of magical energy at his backside.

"That really stings!"

"I'm going to do more than sting you, foul deceiver!" Shitoro shouted, shooting out small flecks of yellow power from his extended claws.

"Did he say something wrong?" Tamiko asked, wide-eyed.

"I do not know," Kisaki replied, equally as confused.

"Call off your cat!" Stephen cried out as more of the tiny bolts hit him, leaving small crackling noises in its wake.

Shitoro leapt through the air and landed upon his back. "I … am … not … a … cat!"

"Is he playing?" Tamiko asked.

"I don't think so." Kisaki strode over to where Stephen was trying to pull the little youkai off of him. "Sorry. I've never seen him act like this. That's enough, Shitoro. I mean it!" She pulled him off the human, taking a few shreds of shirt with him. "What is the matter with you? All he did was offer you some milk."

"Not really a punishable offense," Tamiko agreed.

"It has nothing to do with milk," Shitoro said, his teeth bared. "Go on, tell them."

"Tell them what?" Stephen glared at him. "I have no idea what you're talking about, you pint-sized psycho."

"Tell them your name."

"I already did. It's Steve Fuller. My parents are Myra and…"

"I do not care about your parents," Shitoro hissed. "I care about you and the foul magic you are using to deceive Lady Kisaki, wizard!"

"Wizard?!"

Tamiko turned to Kisaki. "Are you following any of this?"

"No, I am not."

"Good. I hate being the only one left in the dark."

"You're not making any sense, Shitoro." Kisaki walked him back to his chair and placed him upon it. When he looked as if he were going to leap at Stephen again, she stepped in front of him and pointed her finger at the seat. After a moment, he acquiesced and sat, although his eyes never left their host.

"I swear I have no idea what I've done," Stephen said, rubbing his singed backside.

Tamiko looked between them all, then turned to Kisaki. "Do you two need a moment?"

Kisaki shrugged. "Perhaps that is not a bad idea."

Tamiko stepped up to Stephen and entwined her arm in his. "Come on. You promised us some lemonade. I'll help you get it. I've never seen an American kitchen before."

"Ouch!"

"Are you okay?"

"Yeah," he replied, leading her out of the room. "But first maybe we can stop so I can change my clothes and grab some Band-Aids."

Kisaki sat down opposite Shitoro. She stared at the tiger demon, who locked eyes with her for a moment before turning away. There was something in her gaze that was different, although he couldn't quite put his finger upon it.

"Explain yourself, Shitoro."

"There is nothing to explain, except to say that you should not trust that deceiver."

"*Explain yourself,*" Kisaki repeated, somehow doing a good enough impersonation of her mother that Shitoro's mouth dropped open in surprise.

"Yes, m-my lady," he quickly said. "Where to begin?"

"At the beginning, perhaps?" she replied with a smile.

Shitoro's eyes narrowed, but then he did as he was told. "Your mother met your father shortly after awakening from a three-hundred-year nap."

"Why had my mother been asleep?"

"Boredom," he replied. "The daimao often sleep for centuries at a stretch. It helps pass the time. Eternal life is a life often spent doing the same things while viewing the same sights over and over again. Even with the breadth of the multiverse at one's fingertips, it would be enough to drive one mad after several millennia. If anything, you were born into a unique age. I do not ever recall a time before now when all of the daimao were awake and active together for so long. Often a few or more will continue to slumber even when their brothers and sisters are up and about. It is all part of the celestial cycle."

"But you said something is different about now. What?"

"In the past, travel between Earth and the palace was commonplace. Nothing was thought of it. Mazoku and youkai alike would come and go. Even the daimao themselves frequently made the journey."

"But you said it was forbidden."

"It is now."

"Why?"

He waved a hand dismissively. "It is of no concern for what I am trying to tell you. What is, is that your mother was one of the last of the daimao to visit Earth. It wasn't a trip of any great importance. She merely wanted to stretch her legs after her slumber. But it was during that excursion that she met your father."

Kisaki smiled as if appreciating hearing this, which Shitoro imagined she did. Though loyal to his mistress, he was not without empathy for the girl's plight. Before coming here, she'd never been given reason to even consider the concept of a father. But now that it was out, he was certain it was like a growing seed inside of her. She'd always been a curious child, but now she had a focus for that curiosity: her own origin. He needed to tread carefully, but it was difficult to do when she was giving him orders in a tone that he instinctively wanted to obey.

"I'm still not following what this has to do with Stephen being a wizard," she said.

"It is simple," Shitoro replied, leaning forward. "The lying cur is not what he seems. He *is* your father!"

"What?!" Kisaki cried.

"Everything okay in there?" Tamiko called from elsewhere in the house.

"Yes, yes," Shitoro replied. "Stop eavesdropping!"

"No, it is not okay," Kisaki replied to him, but in a low voice. "What do you mean, he's my father?"

"Exactly as I have said." Shitoro hopped off the chair and walked over to stand next to Kisaki. He put his hand upon hers as if to be comforting. "Poor, ignorant child. I know this must be difficult to hear."

"It is more difficult to understand. Explain yourself."

"Have I not already?" When she didn't answer, he gave a pained sigh. "Very well. As I have told you, I was once your mother's chief servant. For nearly fourteen centuries, I served her faithfully. As a result, I gained her trust. Upon her return from Earth, she seemed different. I inquired as to this." Kisaki raised an eyebrow, to which he added, "Not to pry, but because I was concerned for her. Powerful as the daimao may be, I still worry about your mother's well-being."

"I would never question your loyalty, Shitoro. Don't worry."

"I am glad to hear that. Your mother told me about the human she met. According to her, he was different from the rest, obviously from elsewhere than the blessed isles yet sharing the same warrior spirit that the heroes of old possessed. Once she started talking, she could not stop speaking of him. She said he was kind, smart, exotically handsome. His touch was…" He stopped and looked at Kisaki, as if noticing her there for the first time. "Well, never you mind that. Suffice it to say, your mother was smitten with him and it sounded as if he felt the same, although in his case, I cannot say I find that surprising. Your mother is a divine beauty, unrivaled in all of the…"

"I get the point," Kisaki interrupted. "My father?"

"Your mother has never lacked for suitors within the celestial palace, including some who are clearly unworthy of her." His face clouded over for a moment as he seemingly became lost in the memory, but then he looked up and resumed. "But none caught her interest, at least until she met this human. They had one night together, just one, but in that time, she gave herself fully to him. You were the result of their short time together."

Kisaki smiled as she pictured it. Though she had no suitors herself, locked away as she'd been, she'd read a great deal. The stories of war and battle were the ones that caught her attention most, but many of those tales had undertones of romance, some of them epic in their scope. She would be lying if she claimed to have never fantasized about the doors to her mother's chamber being kicked open from the outside and in striding a great warrior come to claim her.

"But if they connected so deeply, why just one night?" she asked after a moment.

"The edict," Shitoro explained. "Travel to Earth was forbidden soon after she and your father met. It was only later that she realized she was with child."

"So what happened?"

"You were born and subsequently bequeathed the greatest of gifts," he said, grinning.

"Let me guess," Kisaki replied with a smile. "You as my guardian?"

"Precisely."

"But my father?"

"Your mother kept tabs on him for a time. Her powers are vast and she had touched him with them. Even years later, she was still able to reach out across the vast distance separating them and feel him."

"For how long?"

"A few decades. Over the years, your father moved on, chose a new mate, and had cubs of his own. Your mother didn't begrudge him his happiness, knowing that humans were as short lived as they are. After a time, though, her influence faded from him and she learned no more. This area of Earth was the last known place she was aware of him residing. It is why we came here."

"I don't understand."

"The crystal," he explained. "Because we were in contact, it reached into my mind, sensed I had knowledge related to your wish, and brought us."

"That still doesn't explain why you think Stephen…"

"I wasn't finished," Shitoro said, leaning forward and lowering his voice again. "For I now see that somehow he was able to fool your mother."

"Fool Mother? But how?"

"It would appear your father was seemingly more than either of us thought."

"But why…"

"I did not lie when I said your mother shared all of this with me. And what she shared included your father's name … and that name was Stephen Fuller."

TWENTY-THREE

CRAG THE HUNTER stood over the pile of exotic meats before him, drool dripping freely over his lips.

It had been so long since he'd seen such a bounty, too long since he'd feasted to the point where his belly nearly burst from being full. His servants stood around, staring greedily at the food before them, but none dared to make a move toward it. They knew that if they touched so much as a morsel before given the go-ahead, they'd end up in the pile themselves, and there were no healing waters in this wretched place to rely on.

Crag spat upon the ground at the thought, flexing the claws upon one hand. Once, the mighty mazoku had been feared and respected by both demons and mankind alike. He'd led youkai into battle and on raiding parties, nearly always coming back with the spoils of war.

Songs had been sung about him around human campfires by scared soldiers praying that this wasn't the night when he came prowling for them.

Only the daimao nestled within the celestial palace had ever looked down upon him, primarily because he preferred Earth to their coddled finery. Feh! Crag was no servant. He wasn't meant to draw baths or cook meals. The very thought brought a snarl to his lips. He was a warrior, bred to kill. It was what he knew, what he excelled at.

And now look at me. Mankind, for so long little more than prey, had risen up, grown strong. Their weapons, once mere insect stings against his flesh, were now much more powerful.

Then there were the daimao. For all their might, they'd abandoned Earth, hidden away in their palace – offering little in the way of succor save a warning that all earthbound youkai were now on their own. So it had been for over half a century.

At first, Crag hadn't believed what he'd heard. He knew the humans had come far in the prior century, developing weapons vastly superior to the crude arrows of their forefathers. Indeed, many of the youkai under his command had stupidly underestimated them and been laid low. Still, his was a superior race. He refused to retreat like the daimao had. He'd pushed back, sent those loyal to him to spy upon the humans, to prepare for war, a war that would remind those cowards in the celestial palace of their place in the grand order.

But he'd underestimated mankind and this new age of theirs. Wherever his forces struck, the humans pushed back harder. The wolf and ursine youkai under his command were decimated by human hunting parties seeking revenge for those taken. The smaller demons under his rule had mostly fled, becoming little more than the beasts whose shapes they assumed. The few others of Crag's people left on Earth were quickly cowed, advocating a peaceful existence, far away from the humans, in the woods and mountains where their encounters with man were few.

So it was for far too long. He'd all but given up hope, growing more bitter with every year, staring at the nearby human civilization in the dark of night and dreaming of a day when he could whet his teeth with their blood.

And now, it seemed he might finally have the chance to vent his wrath upon something.

He spied the small crystal that lay among the bounty of fresh meat, grey as a cloudy day right before a storm.

Ignoring the hungry mewling of those around him, he reached into the pile with both hands. With one, he pulled out a massive hunk of flesh. In the other, the crystal.

Crag took a large bite, easily parting the sinew with his teeth. He continued to work on his meal, determined to get his pound of flesh before even considering the duty being commanded of him.

No, not commanded, *asked*. The daimao had rejected Earth, fled from it. The best they could do now was hope that those left to answer the call were still willing.

At last, when he'd sated himself, he crushed the crystal between his thumb and forefinger. A small puff of miasma escaped from it, a scent trail. He didn't need to guess to know who it was from.

Ichitiro, of course.

So, the fool who fancied himself a war god had a job for him. Crag was tempted to ignore it, eat the food sent to them, and let Ichitiro go hang himself. It would serve him right for his arrogant presumption.

Only a few points kept Crag from outright dismissing him. It had been so long since he'd heard anything from the celestial palace, but now this. If they were reaching out, then perhaps that meant their cowardly edict was coming to an end.

Of far greater importance to Crag, though, was being both hungry and bored. The payment offered would satisfy the first. Perhaps whatever deed needed to be done would sate the other.

He lifted his head and sniffed the air through his voluminous nostrils while turning in a circle, continuing to ignore his minions. There! He caught wind of a distant scent that matched the miasma Ichitiro had sent, a foul odor that made even him want to retch.

Interestingly enough, it was coming from the direction of the nearby human habitation. Crag's level of interest immediately dropped. Whoever it was, it had to have been a weak youkai. Only those who could pass as either pets or pests dared venture to the human towns. Such youkai posed no threat to him. Sadly, they provided little sport either. Whoever they were, though, they must have angered Ichitiro greatly.

Crag eyed the bounty. It did not matter who satisfied the contract, so long as the deed was done. He could send his lesser minions to do this while he remained behind and filled his belly.

Yes. That seemed to be a grand idea. Ichitiro would only care about the end result, not how it was accomplished. And then, once done, perhaps more bounties would follow.

Crag bared his teeth in what passed for a smile, then turned and nodded to his followers, letting them know the feast was about to begin.

TWENTY-FOUR

ICHITIRO WOULD HAVE loved nothing better than to tear the badger youkai standing before him apart with his bare hands.

He did not like delays, being given excuses, and he especially despised being told no. He was a daimao, one of the princes of creation itself. All others were but puppets to him, and a puppet should know better than to do anything save what its master commanded.

Despite the overpowering urge, he restrained himself. It was frowned upon to dispatch those in the service of another of his siblings. This creature served Midnite and, though he had a great many things he wished to question her about, it would cause an uproar if he gained an audience through bloodshed.

One day perhaps, but not this day.

For now, it was enough to know that a bounty, however trifling, had been sent for the capture of whoever had dared use his crystal without permission. Crag was on the job, and mercy wasn't his style. The thought of what the mazoku would do to his prey was enough to keep Ichitiro from ripping the insolent creature before him in two.

"I apologize, my lord," the badger – Tanaki was her name – blubbered, "but Lady Midnite is busy. She…"

"Perhaps she is busy for *you*," he replied curtly, "but I am her brother and have matters of importance to discuss … matters which I prefer not to convey to her handmaiden."

"I am not a handmaiden."

"You will not be anything if you continue to stand in my way." Flames erupted from his body, blackening the white marble upon which he stood. Tanaki cowered before them, but still did not move aside.

What a stubborn creature, Ichitiro considered, not much different from Midnite's previous servant. He hadn't seen the diminutive pest in some time, or perhaps simply hadn't noticed him. He never could understand what his sister had seen in that flea speck of a youkai.

"It is okay, Tanaki," Midnite's voice called from inside, calm and almost musical in tone. How Ichitiro hated it. "You may let him pass."

Let him pass? Ichitiro fumed as the double doors before him opened. *As if anything in the multiverse could stop me.*

He stepped forward with a growl of impatience, but then slowed as he took in the sight before him. Midnite's audience chamber, unchanged in eons, was in disarray. The floor had been torn up and new stone was in the process of being laid. The walls had been stripped bare. Gone were the chandeliers, and in their place, a few temporary ghost lights helped illuminate the room.

Midnite herself sat in … a mere chair. Her throne was nowhere to be seen, replaced for the moment with a simple padded seat, functional but plain.

Of greatest concern to Ichitiro, though, was not the room, nor its mistress, but the Taiyosori, or lack thereof. It was no longer in its customary place hanging above Midnite's head, mocking all those who paid her a visit with both its untouchable power and its impudent use as a mere decoration.

As well versed in the art of deception as he was, even Ichitiro was unable to keep the shock of the weapon's absence from his face.

"You seem surprised, dear brother."

He quickly covered for his momentary lapse. "It is just … all this. I have never known you to be one for change, my dearest."

Midnite's smile faltered ever so slightly, but she replied, "It is no different than Earth once was for us. As fine as my chambers might be, I have grown dreadfully bored of them. Considering the current state of emergency, I thought it best to take advantage of the time."

"State of emergency," Ichitiro repeated. "Reiden so does enjoy his theater."

"In that we are agreed, brother," she replied. "I must apologize for the disrepair, but I find myself in a somewhat capricious mood. I have had my servants rebuild these chambers three times already, only to tear it down and start over. I fear that if I do not settle upon something soon, there will be open revolt among them." She laughed, expressing that she did not consider such a thing to be likely.

"If we cannot occasionally be capricious in our whims, then who in the multiverse can?" Ichitiro bowed in a feigned show of respect. Then he stepped forward and presented her with what he held in his hand. "Wind lilies. I believe they are your favorite."

"Indeed they are," she replied with a smile that he was certain did not reach her eyes. "How … sweet of you. But I again must apologize for the current state of my chambers. Tanaki, please find somewhere *appropriate* to place these."

The badger demon approached, glaring at Ichitiro out of the corner of her eye, and took the multihued flowers from her mistress.

"Be nice, Tanaki," she scolded mildly before turning back to him. "You must forgive her. She is a dutiful servant, but somewhat overprotective at times."

"Servants should know their place," he said, narrowing his eyes at the youkai.

"So they should," Midnite agreed. "But then, so should visitors. Speaking of which, what brings you here, brother?"

The veiled insult was not lost upon him, but he forced his demeanor to remain pleasant. "A small matter, perhaps nothing. You know of Ito, my servant?"

"The ferret youkai? Yes, I know of him and his fondness for, shall we say, acquisition."

"He is but a child at heart. A curious one, at that. His eyes continually spy items of interest to him."

"It is less his eyes I worry about than his hands."

Ichitiro balled his into fists. His sister appeared to be in the mood for idiotic banter this day, something he would certainly cure her of should she ever consent to be his wife. "Nevertheless, it is his eyes I wished to speak of. He came to me earlier, while we were in session."

"As I am aware," Midnite replied in a bored tone, her long fingernails beginning to tap on the edge of the seat upon which she sat. The repetitive *clack* sound they made was almost enough for Ichitiro to perform his own style of redecoration upon the chamber.

"Ah, but what neither you nor our brothers are aware of is the reason for his interruption. He claimed to see someone near the sending chamber, a figure he hadn't encountered before."

If Midnite was surprised to hear this, she did not show it. "The celestial palace and its lands are vast."

"True enough, but with the edict in place, it is not difficult for any here to notice that which is familiar versus that which is not."

"Oh? So you are saying that were I to march my servants out before you, one after the other, you would be able to name them all?"

Ichitiro narrowed his eyes at her. She was playing games with him, something which did nothing to improve his mood. "I, of course, meant the lesser youkai of our respective houses. They are our eyes and ears, are they not?"

"Of course, brother."

"Then believe me when I tell you that Ito's claims were a cause for interest. Of greater import is that when I myself visited the sending chamber, I discovered that some crystals – the same that Reiden had forbidden any from using – were missing."

It wasn't much, barely a twitch, but Midnite's eyes widened ever so slightly at his revelation. To him, that was proof enough that something was amiss.

"Missing? Are you certain?"

"I am. The crystal chamber has remained undisturbed for decades."

"Then why were you in it?"

Clever girl, but he was ready for her. "The same reason as you have for wanting to change your surroundings. I was bored." He could tell his answer annoyed her, which pleased him. Now was the time to strike, when her veneer of control was thinnest. "I came here to warn that you may wish to check on your servants, ensure none are missing … along with any items of importance."

"You think one of *my* servants would dare break Reiden's edict?"

"Of course not. They are loyal to you and you alone. Still, they are lesser beings, given to their primitive whims. It is not outside the realm of reason that one could decide to go rogue."

"I will … ask around," Midnite replied icily. "However, I believe all are accounted for. I've been keeping them quite busy with my changes."

"And, in the chaos of change, you are certain that nothing has been misplaced?" His eyes were rooted firmly in the spot above her head as he asked.

"All of my heirlooms and rightful belongings are here. They have simply been stored away until such time as my fancy settles upon something that delights me."

"Stored away?"

"Yes. Albeit a few of the more important trinkets have been moved to my bedchamber."

The taunting way she said it made Ichitiro want to leap upon her and wrap his hands around her regal throat, but he somehow held his ground.

"While I thank you for your concerns, dear brother," she continued, "I must ask why you have come to me with them before notifying the court as a whole?"

Ichitiro gritted his teeth. "It is because I hold you dear above all others. You are my sun and moon. The stars shall burn out before my desire for you does. Perhaps one day you will feel the same way, maybe even enough to show me some of the *trinkets* stored in your bedchamber."

Ichitiro fumed as he walked back to his own wing of the palace. Midnite and her word games. They never ceased to infuriate him. Several times, he stopped and destroyed the various wonders he came across: statues carved of the finest marble, suits of armor eons old. It did not matter their history or worth so long as red hot rage burned in him.

But that was not the only fire inside of him.

He'd meant to confront Midnite about her so-called daughter, threaten to kill her if she didn't cave to his demands. But her reaction to his mention of the sending chamber had given him pause. She was aware that something was amiss, aware but unwilling to discuss it. Then there was the disarray of her chambers. She claimed boredom, but why now?

Finally, there was the Taiyosori. No matter how much she claimed to be bored by her surroundings, the sword was the item that defined her power, made her stand out among her brethren. To pack it away like discarded garbage? Never. To even relocate it to another room, one which he knew none of the other daimao were given access to, was a lie. It had to be. The sword was an artifact of terrible power, not some vase to be moved to the side whenever there were no flowers to display in it.

An idea began to form in Ichitiro's mind. It painted a dire picture, but perhaps within it lay opportunity for one who was bold enough to seize it. One such as himself.

TWENTY-FIVE

"STOP FIDGETING, KISAKI. It isn't becoming to one of your station."

"I can't help it."

She was possibly more nervous than she'd been in her entire life. More nervous than when she'd faced down Robbie and his followers. Even more nervous than she'd been during the surprise oral exam Shitoro had once given her on the Fifth Age of the Ferzoe Empire, a dynasty that had ruled within the seven Hells for nearly fifteen thousand years.

Shitoro had insisted that Stephen Fuller was her father. But if so, how had he survived this long, especially when he'd seemed all but helpless in the face of a handful of human bullies?

The answer, if one were to believe the youkai, was obvious – magic.

Such things weren't only for the realm of the divine. Humans were a curious and adaptable race. When they saw something that was beyond their ken, they could be dogged in their persistence of conquering it. The only question now was whether the Stephen she'd met was an illusion covering an ancient body or if he truly was immortal.

Stephen and Tamiko returned to the living room carrying glasses of a semi-clear liquid. "Homemade and ice cold," he said. "You won't find better west of the Delaware River."

"Is everything okay?" Tamiko asked, seeming to take note of the silence.

"It's fine," Kisaki lied.

Stephen handed the glasses around, stopping last at Shitoro. "You aren't going to zap me again, are you?"

"That remains to be seen."

"Shitoro!" Kisaki hissed.

"Oh, very well. I shall endeavor to not do so, at least until such time as you upset my lady and cause her grief."

Kisaki let out a pained sigh but decided to let it go. That was probably the best she was going to get out of the overprotective little youkai. She took a tentative sip of the liquid. Not bad. Sweet, yet not overly so, with just a hint of tartness. Most agreeable.

Once they were all seated, Stephen asked, "So what did you two talk about while we were gone ... besides not zapping me?"

Tamiko laughed. "You have to admit, it was kinda funny."

"Easy for you to say. It was like being stung by a bee over and over again."

Shitoro, for his part, seemed pleased by Stephen's discomfort.

After a few more moments of awkward silence, Kisaki decided to get right to the point. "I have a question to ask you, Stephen Fuller."

"Shoot."

"I do not have a weapon."

"It means feel free to ask."

"Sorry. Language is one thing, but the colloquialisms take time."

He let out a chuckle. "I can only imagine. So what did you want to know?"

"I will be blunt. Are you my father?"

Stephen blinked a few times, then began to laugh. It wasn't quite the reaction she'd been expecting. He lowered his voice to a gruff whisper. "Yes, Luke, I am your father." Then he continued laughing.

He only stopped when he realized the rest of them were staring at him silently. "What? Don't you guys have *Star Wars* in your sky temple? You know, Darth Vader?"

"Celestial Palace," Shitoro corrected.

"Who is Darth Vader?" Kisaki asked. "Is that your true name?"

Stephen turned to Tamiko. "Help me out here."

"Sorry, you're on your own," she replied.

He picked up his glass and took a sip. "C'mon. You guys weren't serious, were you?"

Shitoro got to his feet and pointed a finger at him. "Enough with the games, wizard. Confess! Tell Lady Kisaki how you were able to fool her divine mother with your power and maybe I shall let you live."

Stephen spit out a mouthful of lemonade, dousing the tiger demon with it. "Are you for real?"

Shitoro backed up and raised his claws. "You all saw him. You saw the wizard attack me. For that I shall…"

"Settle down, Shitoro," Kisaki said. "I was not joking, Stephen Fuller, for that is your name, is it not?"

"Yeah. So?"

"Then please explain yourself, for that was also the name of my father." She glanced Shitoro's way as if to confirm this.

"Yes, my lady. Your father is Lieutenant Stephen Fuller."

"Now I know you're pulling my leg," Stephen said. "I'm sixteen years old, for Christ's sake. I'm not in the Army and

I don't have any kids. Hell, I've … never even had a real girl-friend."

"Really?" Tamiko asked with a grin.

"Don't rub it in."

"Besides, look at you," Stephen said to Kisaki. "We're, like, the same age."

Shitoro again pointed at him. "So you admit it?"

"Huh?"

"Kisaki isn't sixteen," Tamiko explained. "She's a bit older."

"Like how much?"

Shitoro folded his arms defiantly as he continued to glare at the boy. "Going by your primitive human calendar, Lady Kisaki was born in, I believe, the year nineteen forty-six."

"Nineteen forty…?! That's like," Stephen held up a hand and counted on his fingers. "A really long time ago."

"Feh," Shitoro spat. "A mere blink of the eye for those of the celestial palace."

"Unless you happen to be locked up studying all the time," Kisaki groused under her breath.

"What was that, young miss?"

"Nothing."

"Are you serious?" Stephen asked. "You're really that old?"

"You're talking to a girl who just beat up six guys and owns a talking cat," Tamiko pointed out, "and *that's* what you're hung up on?"

"Nobody owns me, and I AM NOT A CAT!"

"Okay, fine. I get it," Stephen said, setting his glass down and putting his head into his hands. "And you somehow think that I was around back then … err … dating your mother?"

"That is what we are asking," Kisaki said in a matter-of-fact tone.

"No offense, but this is sounding like the plot of a *Termi-nator* movie." When he saw their confused looks, he shook his head. "Never mind. Needless to say, it's weird. I mean, my parents weren't even born at that point. Heck, I don't know if my grandparents were."

"Kisaki," Tamiko said after a moment, "could you maybe have the wrong Stephen Fuller?"

"Wrong one? I do not understand."

"Yeah," Stephen said. "You do realize that more than one person can share the same name."

"They can?" Kisaki had never met two youkai with the same name. It was hard to even imagine. How could one tell one apart from the other when addressing them otherwise?

"He's not wrong," Tamiko said. "And, while I'm not really caught up on common American names, Fuller is pretty short. I have to guess it's not that rare."

"We're the only Fullers in town," Stephen said, "but we have family all over the country."

"That proves it!" Shitoro said.

"Proves what?"

"You just confessed it. This hamlet is the last known location of Kisaki's father. If you are the only Stephen Fuller here, then who else could you be?"

"I thought cats were supposed to have good hearing," Tamiko said.

"I will have you know my hearing is excellent."

"Then it's your listening that leaves something to be desired."

"I have listened to everything that has transpired in this house, including your somewhat sad flirtation with the wizard here when you two went to fetch our drinks."

"What?!"

Shitoro put his hands together over his head and leaned back. "Oh, Stephen. What a wonderful home you have," he said in a bad mockery of Tamiko's voice. "Why, I'm surprised you did not return already pregnant with his cubs."

Stephen spat out another mouthful of lemonade, which this time Shitoro was mindful to dodge.

Kisaki had never seen the tiger youkai act this way before. He was always so serious when it came to her studies. Though it was obvious he'd embarrassed her friends, she found it to be highly amusing nevertheless.

Tamiko, for her part, had turned several shades redder in the face, something Kisaki had experienced earlier when considering whether she found Stephen attractive. Although now a part of her was aghast at the thought, since they were trying to determine whether he was her father.

Kisaki had to admit to feeling an odd kinship with Stephen, but perhaps that emotion was best not trusted. If indeed her father had managed to seduce her mother, who she'd always seen as aloof and proud, in the space of a single night, then maybe he *was* a wizard.

Tamiko was the first to break the silence. "Are there any other Stephens in your family? Maybe an uncle or something? And just for the record, I wasn't flirting back there."

"Oh," Stephen replied. "I mean, yeah, that's cool." He too appeared flustered. "Anyway, no, not that I know of. I have one uncle, George. My father's name is Glen. His dad, my grandpa, was Jeremy, and he had two brothers … Christopher and, I think, William. So, no. There's nobody who fits … holy crap!"

"What is it?" Kisaki asked after a moment.

Shitoro leaned forward. "Finally coming to grips with your lies?"

"What? No," Stephen relied blankly. "I just remembered. My great-grandfather. I was named after him."

"Great-grandfather?"

"Yeah, my dad's grandfather." Stephen suddenly perked up as if remembering. "And he was in the military too. Retired as a major. Here, check this out." He stood and walked over to the fireplace. Above it was a shelf upon which stood many small objects. He picked one up. "This is his Purple Heart."

"He had a purple…"

"It's a medal," Stephen explained. "They give it out to those who are wounded in battle."

"He was wounded?" Kisaki asked.

"Yeah, took some shrapnel from a hand grenade, but he made it. Obviously, since I'm here."

Kisaki looked at Shitoro. "A warrior."

Shitoro nodded. "Yes, but we are seeking out a Lieutenant Stephen Fuller, not a…"

"You have to be a lieutenant before you can be a major," Tamiko explained.

Kisaki chuckled. "Yes, Shitoro. That was mentioned in my lessons. I would think you should know that."

The tiger demon appeared flustered. "If someone had been a more diligent pupil, than perhaps I wouldn't be constantly distracted. Besides, I am no warrior. I leave that to youkai more…"

"Capable?" Tamiko asked.

"Brutish," he finished.

"That must be it," Stephen said, sitting down and staring at the medal. "He fought in the Pacific theater during World War Two."

"Pacific theater? World War?" Kisaki asked. Though her studies had included a great deal of human history, these were two terms she was unfamiliar with.

"It was a massive war fought in the nineteen forties," Tamiko explained. "There were two main fronts, Europe and the Pacific. The Pacific one was mainly fought between the United States and Japan. My grandparents and I'm pretty sure their parents too, were conscripted. There was … a lot of bad blood on both sides of it."

"Pearl Harbor," Stephen said.

"The atomic bomb," Tamiko replied. "But that was all a long time ago."

"Well before my time," Stephen added, glaring at Shitoro.

"But not your great-grandfather's," Kisaki said, deep in thought. She turned to Shitoro. "What do you think?"

"I still think this wretch is a wizard, but his story is plausible, I suppose. Humans live such paltry lifespans."

"Hey, Great-grandpa lived a good long time," Stephen said. "He was almost ninety when he passed on."

"Passed on?"

"Yeah, he … oh shit, I'm sorry. I wasn't thinking. My great-grandfather, Stephen Fuller, he died about five years ago."

TWENTY-SIX

KISAKI WASN'T SURE what to feel. On the one hand, she'd gotten her hopes up of meeting the man who was the missing equation from her life. It was devastating to know that could never happen now.

But it was also difficult to work up emotion over someone she'd never met … someone she hadn't even considered barely a day ago.

Tamiko crossed the room and put a hand on her shoulder. "I'm so sorry."

Kisaki smiled up at her friend, feeling her warmth, and realizing something along with it. This was real, the here and now. Her father was but an illusion, a momentary ideal. Nevertheless, she felt her eyes filling with moisture at the thought of that which she would never know.

"Holy shit!" Stephen suddenly said.

"What is it?" Shitoro asked. "Did someone forget to walk you today?"

"Not that," he replied. He knelt down in front of Kisaki and looked her in the eye. "When I was a kid, my great-granddad used to sit me on his lap and tell me stories from his time in the service. It was mostly light stuff. I don't think my parents would have appreciated him telling gruesome war stories to a five year old. The thing is, a few of them were kind of out there. Tall tales, if you get my drift."

"He means exaggerated stories," Tamiko explained before she could ask.

Kisaki couldn't help but smile. If Tamiko could know what she was thinking before she could even voice it, then that made her a true friend indeed.

"Yeah, exactly," Stephen continued. "Like this time he claimed he and his buddies saw a mermaid and…"

"Mermaids are real," Shitoro said in a bored tone. "They are aquatic youkai who are not to be trifled with."

"Err, okay. Good to know for the next time I go fishing. Anyway, he had this one story that was really weird, but young me used to dig it. He told me of the night he met an angel."

"Go on," Kisaki said, intrigued.

"I never knew what to think of it. I mean, he never struck me as the religious type. More a no-nonsense kind of guy than anything. Nothing else he ever talked about was like it. I mean, he always said he didn't even want a pastor at his funeral. 'Just throw me in a ditch and get to shoveling, Stevie,' he used to say … uh, sorry. Not trying to bring you down or anything. It was just something that he found funny."

"It's okay," she replied. "I think it is … amusing."

"It always made me laugh as a kid. So, yeah, the angel. It was one of the few actual stories from the war he would tell me. He said she came one night, not long after his platoon had landed on one of the Japanese islands."

"Which one?" Tamiko asked.

"He probably said its name, but remember, I was barely in Kindergarten. I was a lot more interested in watching *Sesame Street* than being given a geography lesson. So they landed on the island, and there was a lot of fighting, bombs going off all around, overall chaos. It was a bad time, morale was low, and he was feeling particularly down. But in the middle of it all, he woke up one night to find an angel calling out to him. Said it was the strangest thing, this beautiful creature in the middle of all that ugliness."

"Did he say what happened?" Kisaki asked.

"He didn't really elaborate. Said she took him for a walk, but then he would always trail off when I asked where they went."

Kisaki glanced toward Shitoro and found his eyes to be wide with surprise.

"He said that was what changed it all for him. Afterwards, he just sorta knew that he would live to make it back home again. Which he obviously did."

"Shitoro?" Kisaki tentatively asked. "What is it?"

"Oh, it's nothing."

"I see the look on your face. Don't try playing games."

"Fine," he said. "It actually sounds very similar to what your mother once told me."

"How so?"

"She had wanted to visit Earth, stroll along the beach and enjoy the feel of the breeze in her hair, but when she arrived, she found herself in the middle of a great battle."

"Was she scared?" Tamiko asked.

"Do not be foolish. The daimao were born and bred for war. It is in their very blood. If anything, my mistress was intrigued and wished to learn more."

Kisaki leaned forward. "Where was this?"

"The very island upon which I found you loitering when I came looking for you."

"Ishigachi?" Tamiko replied. "This is starting to feel freakier by the moment."

"Our people call them the blessed isles, although I have a feeling that would change were they ever to meet a creature such as yourself." Tamiko stuck her tongue out at him, but he'd already started talking again. "She met your father upon that battlefield."

"As an angel?" Stephen asked.

"No. She was disguised as a peasant girl. She had wanted to visit without bringing too much attention to herself. It was only later, after having spent some time with her Stephen Fuller, that she decided to reveal herself to him. She called down the mists to conceal herself from the sleeping camp and sought him out."

"And then what?" Kisaki and Stephen both asked.

"Um, then they went … for their *walk*," Shitoro replied uncomfortably.

After a few moments, Stephen leaned back, recognition on his face. "Oh … I mean *oh*! I think I get it. No wonder he didn't want to share details with a five year old."

"That would have made a heck of a war story," Tamiko said.

"What would?" Kisaki asked, genuinely curious.

Shitoro coughed into his hand. "Needless to say, young lady, we have not reached that lesson in your studies yet."

"Learning the birds and the bees from a cat," Tamiko said, patting Kisaki on the arm. "That should be fun. Good luck with that."

"Birds and bees? But I am well versed in the many creatures of…"

Stephen abruptly stood up. "Hey! I think we have some pictures of him if you want to see what he looked like."

"My father?" Kisaki asked, brightening.

"Yeah. I mean, at this point, it kinda sounds like he's the culprit here. The stories match up. Might as well go with that." He turned, then stopped and glanced over his shoulder. "Weird."

"What is?"

"Well, I guess that sorta makes you my great-aunt."

"Auntie Kisaki?" Tamiko asked with a giggle.

"I suppose this means we should start inviting you to Thanksgiving dinner." He smirked at her. "Although, I have to warn you, some of my relatives make your background sound positively normal."

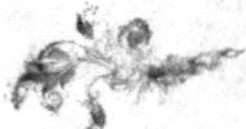

"This place is filthy," Shitoro said. "Completely unbecoming of creatures of our stature."

"It's an attic." Stephen pulled out another box. "They tend to collect dust. It's what they do."

"Dust and lots of boxes," Tamiko commented from her spot on an old chair, where she was busy looking at pictures from Stephen's past.

"What can I say?" he replied. "My parents are probably one step removed from being hoarders. The upside, though, is if we have any pictures of Great-grandpa Stephen, they'll be up here."

Neither the room, the dust, nor the searching bothered Kisaki. They'd been there for a few hours now, going through box after box. Though they continued to search for pictures of her father, what they had uncovered so far was fascinating by itself. Mementos of the past, of lives that had been led. She'd never seen anything like it in the palace, where everything was so pristine and ordered. She smiled as she imagined a vast attic within the celestial palace, full to the brim with objects dating back to the dawn of time. The dust alone would surely be ten feet deep.

Speaking of which, she sneezed as some got in her nose.

"Look at what this accursed place has done to my ward," Shitoro complained.

"I'm fine. You don't have to play nursemaid."

"Apparently I do. Since the moment I took my eyes off you, you decided to steal your mother's sword, somehow turn it into a feather, and go running off with it to a whole other planet."

Tamiko started playing with an old music box, adorned with a graceful white ballerina on top. "You have to give her credit for being ambitious."

"I dare say, her mother will be less than impressed with such ambition."

"What's she like?"

"Excuse me?"

"This Lady Midnite. What is she like?"

Shitoro puffed out his chest. "Like nothing your feeble mind could possibly imagine, human. She is power incarnate, one of the thirteen members of the celestial court who hold judgment over creation itself. She is…"

"I meant her personality. What's she like to be around?"

"Strong," Kisaki said, "and patient. Stern, but fair. Her many servants seem to adore her."

"What about you?"

Kisaki was silent for several moments. "I … honestly do not know. When she speaks to me, I can see her eyes light up, but there always seems to be an undertone of sadness about her. Perhaps I am a disappointment."

Several more seconds of silence passed until Shitoro finally let out a heavy sigh. "It is not disappointment she feels. You were right the first time. It is sadness."

"But why?"

The tiger youkai seemed to weigh his words. "What I am about to say, I do not say lightly, and I know your mother would not approve. So…"

"My lips are sealed, Shitoro. You have my word. Besides, as you said, any such transgression would simply put both of us in more trouble than we already are."

"She sent me to retrieve you, you realize, yes?"

"As I guessed."

"But do you know why?"

"Because I left without permission, because I took her sword."

"The sword that's a feather, right?" Stephen asked, digging through another box. "Pretty wild stuff."

"Wild and dangerous," Shitoro replied, for once not adding an insult directed at either him or Tamiko. "But the Taiyosori is only half of it. Should it fall into the wrong hands, it could be disastrous, and not just for you or the rest of the humans. It could very well bring ruin to demonkind all the way up to the daimao. But as I said, that is only part of the issue. In fact, I believe that to be the far less important part in your mother's eyes."

"How so?" Kisaki asked, her attention fully on the little demon despite the wonders of the past all around her.

"Your mother fears for your life. It was worry for you that drove her to break the edict against travel to Earth. She could not come herself, not without her brethren knowing, but she could send me to find and retrieve you … a task I have not executed to the best of my ability so far."

"You said it, not me," Tamiko commented.

"I think I have already proven I can take care of myself," Kisaki said, a touch of pride in her voice.

"She is not worried about humans, child. They are nothing." He turned to the others. "No offense intended."

"I sincerely doubt that," Tamiko replied.

"Amazing," Shitoro said with a grin. "You *are* capable of learning after all." He then turned to face Kisaki again. "It is other youkai she fears. And not just them, but her brothers and sisters as well."

"The other daimao?" Kisaki asked. "But why?"

"It is as I tried to explain earlier. Because they would kill you on sight if they knew of your existence."

"Why?" Tamiko cried. "What has Kisaki done to them?"

"It is not what she has done. It is what she is."

"You said before that she's a half demon. Is that it?"

"Partially." Shitoro sat down upon a box. "Hanyou are tolerated, if somewhat frowned upon, but the daimao are a proud race. Proud and, Lady Midnite forgive me, arrogant. They do not look upon humans as equals, not even remotely close."

Tamiko folded her arms. "You don't say."

"It is not an uncommon sentiment among our people," he said with an unconcerned shrug. "One might consider it not unwarranted either. Think of it. For how many countless centuries did your race live in caves, eating nothing but scraps? Then, how many more did they spend using crude weapons to wage petty wars? It is only now, recently, that your species has shown promise of being anything more than walking monkeys."

"Don't lump us all in as promising," Stephen said with a laugh. "You saw Robbie and his goons. Pretty sure they're only a few generations removed from sloped foreheads."

Shitoro ignored his comment. "The daimao originally landed upon this world on the blessed isles. It is there they made their presence first known, and it is there they first ... intermingled with your species."

"So they had a thing for us monkeys?" Stephen surmised. "Kinky."

Shitoro made a sound of disgust. "Because of that, they hold the residents of those islands in slightly higher regard than the rest of your species. Divine blood is mingled with their own." He glanced toward Tamiko. "In some instances, anyway. Hanyou born of the blessed isles are, as I said, tolerated. But those from elsewhere are not. I am sorry to say, Mistress Kisaki, but hanyou who are conceived of mortals from anywhere else are considered to be … abominations, automatically sentenced to death."

"That's pretty damned racist," Tamiko said.

"Perhaps," Shitoro replied. "But it is their way, their edict, their tradition. Such things are not so easily overcome."

All of this hit Kisaki like a kick to the gut. She sat down hard upon the floor, tears obscuring her vision. "So that's what I am? Merely an abomination in my mother's eyes?"

"No!" Shitoro knelt in front of her and took her hands. "Do you not see? Your mother hid you away because she saw you were anything but. She considered this Stephen Fuller to be a noble warrior, worthy of her love. And she considers her only child to be the same. She has kept you locked away all of these years because of her love for you, not shame. All she has done may seem cruel at times, but it has been to protect you, to allow you to live your life without fear. And it worked too until…"

"Until I escaped."

Shitoro lowered his gaze and nodded. "That is why I was sent. It wasn't so much the sword as you. Lady Midnite wishes you to return safely before the others learn of your existence. Powerful as she is, even she might not be able to protect you from her siblings if they discover what you are."

"You say this like her family are uncivilized animals," Tamiko pointed out.

"The daimao are ancient and powerful, true," Shitoro said in a soft voice, barely audible. "But some are not as civilized as others. They are the true threat. And there is one in particular, a loathsome creature that fancies himself a warrior god. It is heresy to even speak this way, but it is the truth. The celestial palace, indeed the multiverse itself, would be so much better off were Ichi…"

"Jackpot!" Stephen cried.

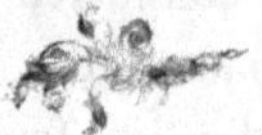

"What?" Kisaki asked. She'd been busy processing what Shitoro was saying. She always wondered why her mother had kept her confined for so long, especially when her servants were free to come and go as they pleased. She'd secretly feared that her mother's actions were the result of some shame she felt. But if what he said was true, then it was love, not shame, that drove her.

But if so, how had Kisaki repaid that love? By putting herself in the very danger her mother sought to protect her from. If anything, it was she who should be ashamed.

Kisaki had reached into her pocket – touching the last crystal she'd taken, the red one – and had been considering whether it was time to use it. Tamiko needed to go home, and it would give Shitoro a chance to find the crystal she'd knocked from his grasp. But then Stephen had spoken up.

"I found them, pictures of my great-grandfather." He paused for a moment, but then added, "Pictures of your dad."

All thoughts of shame were immediately forgotten as the group gathered around him. He was holding several black and white photographs, some of men in uniform, others of family life.

"There. That's him." He pointed to one. "If I recall correctly, that was taken right after he was promoted to captain. That one was taken right before the war ended, so it couldn't have been too long after he and your mother met."

"He was handsome," Tamiko said. "I can see what your mom saw in him."

She was right, Kisaki considered. The man in the picture – tall, muscular, and with short blond hair – painted an appealing picture. There was something in his face, the cut of his jawline, the brightness of his eyes, his smile, all of it. It was almost mesmerizing. It bespoke of strength, but strength tempered by kindness – a warrior who knew the value of both power and mercy. Kisaki couldn't help but smile.

"Shitoro?" she asked.

"It fits what I know of him. Quite the character … for a human."

"I'll say," Tamiko said. She elbowed Stephen playfully. "I can see where you get it from." Then, just as quickly, she added, "Not that I'm saying you're good looking. Anything but, really. It's just…"

Stephen's face was a mask of confusion at her sputtering, but he turned back to the album and flipped to another page. "This was an earlier picture of him at special forces training. I think he was an army ranger."

Again, her father was in uniform, albeit it appeared a more casual, more functional outfit than what he wore in the first. He…

Her eyes locked onto the photo, but not on him. One of the other men in it, a man standing next to her father, their arms around each other. He looked oddly familiar. Though she couldn't quite place where, she could have sworn she'd seen him somewhere.

Before she could dwell on it, though, Stephen handed her another. "Here he is after the war. That's my great-grandmother with him and she's holding my granddad."

"Your half-brother," Tamiko said.

"My…" Kisaki paused. She hadn't considered that. And hadn't Stephen mentioned additional brothers as well? Her father was beyond her reach, but what about the possibility of meeting siblings she never knew existed? "Is he…" She couldn't bring herself to finish the rest of the sentence.

"Alive? Grandad? Yeah. He retired down to Florida, but he comes up for the holidays. Doesn't stay long. Claims it's too cold."

"So, I could maybe meet him?"

Stephen seemed to consider this. "Yeah, I guess you could. Expect him to be a bit freaked out, though. Finding out you have an older sister who looks almost sixty years younger than you might be a bit weird for anyone."

Kisaki smiled. "Perhaps one day…"

Shitoro shook his head. "Out of the question. Were you not listening to what I just said? This is no mere outing for a picnic. We need to get you back home before…"

There came a hollow thud from somewhere above them.

"What was that?" Tamiko asked.

"I don't know," Stephen said. "Sounds like a bird hit the roof."

Shitoro coughed dismissively, then opened his mouth, no doubt to keep reminding Kisaki of what was expected of her, when there came another thud, this one louder.

"Okay, make that a really big bird."

A third impact hit the home, one which seemed to rattle the rafters around them. Then howls rose up from outside, as if coming from multiple beasts.

"What the hell?" Tamiko asked.

"Sounds like … wolves," Stephen said, "but that can't be."

Shitoro cocked his head to the side, his ears twitching as he listened. When he looked up again, his eyes were wide with panic. "Oh no."

"What is it?" Kisaki asked.

He grabbed hold of her by the arms. "Those are not mere wolves. I can hear their voices carrying in their cries. Those are youkai. Somehow they've found us!"

TWENTY-SEVEN

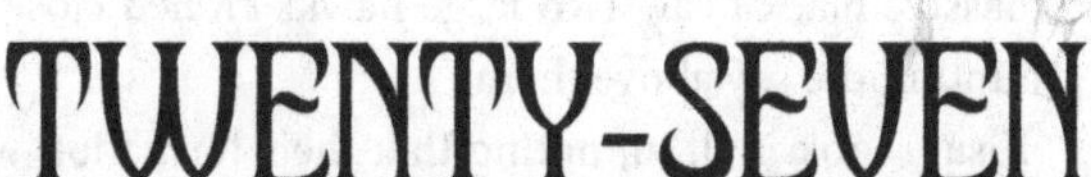

"ARE YOU SURE? Maybe something is just setting off the dogs in the neighborhood," Stephen said, as he followed Shitoro down the stairs.

"Dogs do not relay complex ambush strategies to one another," he replied over his shoulder.

"Strategies? I didn't hear anything except…"

"Nor would you," Shitoro snapped from the bottom of the stairs, "because you do not have these." He pointed to his ears. "I do, however, and they are telling me we are in grave danger. Follow me, before it's too late."

Shitoro ran for the front door, transforming into his tiger form as he did so. Kisaki was on his heels, followed by Tamiko and Stephen.

The little youkai abruptly skidded to a halt in front of the door, then looked back expectantly at the others.

"Let me guess," Tamiko said. "Forgot the value of opposable thumbs for a minute there?"

Shitoro fired back his best withering glare, but Kisaki was already pushing the door open.

"Quickly," Shitoro said, "before they have us…"

The words died in his throat as the group stepped onto the front porch.

Before them, standing in the street in front of the house, was a trio of large, muscular wolves. Just behind them stood a massive black bear. Two large hawks circled close to the ground in the sky above them.

Kisaki took it all in, noting that their formation was too deliberate to be the work of mere animals. The sound of doors being opened registered in her ears and she glanced around to see Stephen's neighbors peeking out of their doors.

"So much for this being a subtle getaway," Tamiko said from behind her.

"Stand back," Shitoro growled. "I'll carve a path through these mongrels for us to escape."

"Mongrels?" the largest of the wolves asked, erasing any doubt whatsoever of their demonic origin. "Big talk for such a small kitty."

"I'll help you," Kisaki said, worried for her diminutive guardian. Large in spirit he might be, but, tiger or not, she was doubtful he'd be a match for the youkai in front of them.

She realized she should have been scared, and for a moment she was, but in the back of her mind, that cold logic began to stir again. Besides, her mother was a daimao. She wouldn't be worthy of her lineage if all it took were a few mangy-looking youkai to send her running. "Tamiko, Stephen, get back. Lock the doors and stay inside until we say so."

"I … think that's a good idea," Tamiko replied uncertainly, backing up.

"Wait up," Stephen said. "My dad keeps a shotgun in his closet, and I know the combo for the safe where he keeps the ammo."

"Shotgun?" Kisaki asked idly, but he was already on the move.

"Come on, Kisaki!" Tamiko pleaded. "You get in here, too."

Kisaki was rooted to the spot, though, because Stephen wasn't the only one on the move. With a snarl of anger, Shitoro raced forward toward the wolves.

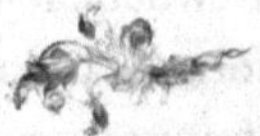

Shitoro leapt, claws bared, at the wolf who'd spoken … and was subsequently swatted aside like he was nothing.

"*This* is what we were paid for?" the wolf asked. "Pathetic. Easy prey."

"More meat for us," the bear said from behind him. "This just works up an appetite." It stood up on its hind legs and transformed. In its humanoid form, the ursine youkai stood over six feet tall. Though he retained a bear's head and claws, the rest of his body took on the appearance of a hairy, muscular human.

The large wolf, probably the pack leader, was next to change. He was more human in appearance than the bear, smaller and leaner – his extra-long canines and slightly pointed ears being the only indication of his inhuman nature.

He stepped up and sniffed the air. "A hanyou," he said after a moment, a slight twang to his voice. "Now this is interesting. Never ate one of those before."

"I hear they taste terrible," the bear said.

"Only one way to find out, Orsen good buddy," the wolf leader replied with a toothy grin. He raced forward, his hands clenched into fists. He was dreadfully fast, far faster than Kisaki expected, and for a moment, she felt fear welling up in the pit of her stomach.

But then, just before he reached the front porch, once more the world seemed to slow down around her.

Tamiko cried out from behind her, but her voice seemed to echo as if from afar. "Kiiiissssaaakkkkiiiiiiii!"

As before, Kisaki's vision blurred. It was as if a ghost image superimposed itself over the wolf racing toward her, then it solidified and she was elsewhere. Rather than a wolf youkai, she saw humans in uniform charging toward her. They had dark hair and their facial features vaguely resembled Mr. Yoshida's. They appeared to be screaming a battle cry, although she heard nothing. Her hands came up … again, larger than they should have been … holding a weapon of sorts. The object jerked in her hands and one of the enemy soldiers fell to the ground. Again, and another toppled over. There were too many of them, though, and they swarmed her.

Whoever's eyes she was seeing out of, for that seemed the only explanation that made sense, wasn't so easily defeated. There was a knife at the end of the weapon, and she used it to spear an enemy through the abdomen. She spun and brought the other end to bear, clubbing another enemy soldier across the jaw.

A hand fell upon her shoulder and she quickly turned to see a man fighting by her side. Kisaki immediately recognized him. He was the man she'd seen in the earlier vision, the one who had fended off her attack with ease. But that wasn't all. She now realized he was the same man from the photo Stephen had shown her, the one who had his arm around her father as if in friendship.

What is going on?

Whatever it was, figuring it out would have to wait. The vision faded as quickly as it came, leaving only that cold logic behind. Time, however, continued to move far too slowly – her friend's warning cry still escaping her lips and the wolf leader still closing in on her, albeit far slower than he should have been.

Amazingly enough, Kisaki felt the beginnings of a smile starting to work its way onto her face. Though much faster and obviously a lot more dangerous, the pack leader's attack was no less sloppy than that of Robbie or his followers.

He was moving as one who was sure of his power. He considered her weak, easy prey.

It was time to dissuade him of that notion.

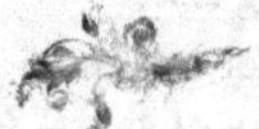

The pack leader leapt at her, a snarl of triumph upon his face, and time picked that moment to resume its normal pace. That was fine by Kisaki. She was already on the move, spinning and bringing her leg up. She caught the pack leader square on the side of the jaw with her heel. Teeth shattered and he let out a yip of pain before flying limply into a nearby bush.

The two wolves still in the street stared at her agape, as much shock showing on their canine faces as they could.

The bear, however, merely laughed. "Easy prey, eh? You must be getting complacent in your old age, Durgo." He turned to the other youkai. "What are you waiting for? Crag sent us to fight, so do it!"

Crag?

Who was that and what did they have against her? Questions for another time, Kisaki noted.

Two more of the youkai transformed. One of the hawks turned into a small, frail-looking humanoid with wicked talons on both his feet and at the end of his winged arms. Another of the wolves changed, too, becoming a fur-clad female with murder in her eyes.

"You hurt my mate. Now I'm gonna hurt you."

Mate? That explained why the female looked absolutely furious at what she'd done to the one called Durgo.

This time, all four of the smaller youkai charged forward, two from the ground and two from the air. With Shitoro still down and her not wishing to endanger her human friends, that left Kisaki alone to face them.

Her newfound fighting prowess had proven itself, but without knowing where it had come from or whether it would last, she realized it would be foolish to rely on it against these odds.

She needed something else.

The quill in her jacket began to heat up again, but she ignored it. The last time she'd drawn it had been almost disastrous. Not to mention it had remained a stupid quill. It was useless against the human bullies, and probably even more so against a pack of angry youkai seemingly bent on murder.

She quickly scanned the porch and the surrounding yard looking for something that could…

There!

The memory of her recent vision flashed again in her mind as she laid eyes on a promising-looking object. A length of wood was lying in the grass a few steps away. It had the words "Louisville Slugger" written on the side. She didn't know exactly what that meant, but the makeshift weapon looked sturdy enough to her.

First she would need to reach it, though, a challenging prospect, as the hawks were even faster than the wolves.

The one in humanoid form reached her before she barely had time to blink. Kisaki tried to sidestep, but was a hair too slow. Razor sharp claws raked against her, cutting through her shirt like it was paper.

Even as a bloom of heat and pain rose from her side, she was already analyzing the demon's movements and preparing a counterattack. As the youkai passed her, she swung and caught it in the back of its head with an elbow.

Kisaki heard a scream of fear and turned in time to see that her blow had driven the hawk youkai tumbling toward the house. It slammed into the wooden frame of the door, where it lay stunned.

Tamiko stood in the open doorway looking at it wide-eyed before turning to her friend.

"I did say to close and lock the door, did I not?" Kisaki commented.

Tamiko nodded blankly, then finally did as she was told.

Kisaki was already on the move again before she finished closing it. She instinctively leapt back, spinning to see the three other youkai converging on the spot she'd just been. The two wolves went tumbling onto the ground, but the hawk was much more graceful in adjusting its attack.

She was just barely aware of the sound of a door slamming shut when she was forced to throw herself into a dive roll to avoid the claws of the second hawk.

It wasn't a panicked move, though. Her aim had been purposeful and, when she came up again, she was holding the length of wood. She dared a quick glance down at her side, but fortunately the wounds from the first hawk were superficial, a couple of scratches at best.

When she looked up again, the wolf, still in its four-legged form, was nearly upon her. She brought the improvised weapon up in an arc and caught it under its jaw with a solid *crack*. The youkai went tumbling away where it landed in the grass unmoving.

She took a moment to look down upon the object in her hands, its weight comforting in her grasp. *A slugger*, she pondered. *Perhaps a fitting name after all.*

The female wolf was more wary than her companion. She began to circle Kisaki, looking for an opening to utilize her superior speed.

"I'm going to shove that bat down your throat," she snarled.

"I do not believe it would fit," Kisaki replied calmly.

"Let's see about that."

Kisaki raised the weapon, apparently called a bat. *An odd choice of names. I don't see wings upon it.*

Sadly for her, the wolf's banter had been a ruse, a distraction. There came a shriek from Kisaki's flank and she looked up to see one of the hawks descending upon her, claws outstretched and aimed right at her face.

Kisaki's eyes opened wide, but then something small and white hit the bird midair, driving it to the ground and pinning it. "Shitoro!"

He was back in the fight. A bit dirty but seemingly no worse for the wear.

There was no time to celebrate, however. Movement registered in Kisaki's periphery, but she'd been prepared for it. She spun, driving the wide end of the bat into the female wolf's midsection. The demoness let out a huff of breath and doubled over.

"I am sorry about your mate," Kisaki said, "but I cannot allow you to shove this down my throat." With a quick shift of her arms, she slammed the other end of the bat into the side of the she-wolf's face. Her eyes rolled into the back of her head and she dropped to the ground.

"Oh, stop squirming," Shitoro growled from where he had the second hawk pinned. "The day a bird can beat a tiger is the day I let that human put a collar around my neck and call me Fluffy."

Kisaki couldn't help but smile. All of the smaller youkai were either stunned or incapacitated, which left…

Strong arms wrapped themselves around her, pinning her own to her side and lifting her from the ground.

"Forget about me, little hanyou? That's okay. I didn't forget about you."

It was the bear, Orsen. Kisaki struggled against his grasp, but he was dreadfully strong and she had little leverage.

"Stop fighting," he snarled, "and I promise to make it quick." The snarl quickly turned into a laugh. "I do have to warn you, though, I am known to be quite the liar."

"Lady Kisaki!" Shitoro cried, but he had his hands full with the hawk demon, just barely keeping it in place.

"Don't worry about me," she called back.

"Like he would be much help anyway," the bear chuckled. "Where did you find such a midget tiger anyway? Munchkinland?"

"Your friend doesn't seem to find him so small," Kisaki replied, trying to find some purchase with which to escape.

"Friend?" the bear said with a cruel laugh. "These clowns? I'm glad you cleaned house. Less of the reward to share, I say."

"Reward?"

"Of course. We got paid handsomely to find you and teach you a lesson. Ichitiro sends his regards."

"Who?" *Ichitiro?* To the best of her knowledge, Kisaki had never met an Ichitiro. She couldn't imagine what she had done to offend him. Certainly she couldn't recall doing anything that would warrant sending youkai to kill her and her friends.

"It doesn't matter," Orsen replied. "Corpses don't need to ask questions. Now hold still. This will just take a minute."

Kisaki felt his hot breath against her cheek. She turned her head as far as she could and spied rows of teeth as he opened his mouth wide.

"Let her go, asshole!"

What?!

Stephen was standing just outside of his home, with Tamiko right behind him. In his hands he held something, a weapon not entirely dissimilar to what Kisaki had used in her vision. If that were indeed the case, perhaps it, too, was capable of spitting death from a distance.

"You've got to be kidding me," Orsen said.

"Human, look out!" Shitoro cried, still struggling with his opponent.

The other hawk youkai had pulled itself shakily to its feet and was approaching Stephen from his flank. He turned and shouted in surprise when he saw it closing in.

Kisaki wanted to cry out as well, to tell him to run back inside and bar the door, but whatever she was about to say was drowned out by a thunderous explosion of sound.

What in the name of the elder gods?

Despite what she'd seen in her vision, Kisaki hadn't expected such a loud noise. Whatever had just happened caused Stephen to stumble back a step. The hawk, however, was affected in a far more lethal manner.

It flew off its feet as the front of its chest exploded in a shower of blood and bone. When it landed, its body twitched for a few moments and then became still.

Though Kisaki had read countless tales of battles and knew that combatants on both sides died, it was the first time she'd seen something like it in person. Death had come to the hawk in an ugly, horrifying manner. Though she felt little sympathy for the creature, it gave her an idea of what the bear had planned for her, and that thought made her angry.

The bear spun, shifting Kisaki between itself and where Stephen still stood looking at the remains of the hawk. Shock was evident on the young man's face.

"You got it!" Tamiko cried.

"Yes," Shitoro said, sounding annoyed. "Now get the other one!"

Almost as if waking from a dream, Stephen shook his head, then turned toward where Orsen still held on to Kisaki. He pointed the weapon their way, but then uncertainty filled his eyes.

She realized what the bear youkai was doing. It was using her the same way a warrior might use a shield against an incoming sword blow. That made Kisaki even angrier. Where was the honor in this?

"That's it, human," Orsen said. "Put the peashooter down. Sorry to be the one to break it to you, but hunting season is over … for you anyway."

Stephen lowered the weapon, indecision etched upon his face.

"That's right. Now be a good meatsack and go back inside and maybe we'll forget this ever happened. I'm just being paid for the hanyou and her kitty cat. You're not worth the effort."

"No," Kisaki growled, "but I can assure you, I am."

Stephen had tried to save her, proving that he had her father's warrior spirit somewhere deep inside. Though he hadn't succeeded, he had given her something almost as good – hope, not to mention time enough to come up with a plan of action.

She kicked out, then brought her heel back into the bear's kneecap with a jarring blow.

Orsen cried out in anger, loosening his grip just enough for Kisaki to pull free. She spun, bringing up the Louisville Slugger, intent on making certain that this youkai had laughed his last for this day.

Much to her surprise, though, he caught the bat in his teeth. She tried to pull it free, but it held fast. Before she could counter him, he bit down with a crunch, snapping the end of the weapon and leaving her with the stump of its handle.

He spit out the wood, then bared his teeth at her. "Not really my idea of an appetizer. Think I'll wash it down with your blood."

Orsen took a step forward, but then paused as a sound began to fill the air. It was a wailing noise Kisaki had never heard before, almost as if screaming demons had been set loose and were heading their way, a prospect that didn't fill her with a great deal of optimism.

"Hah!" the bear snorted. "Guess someone called the cops. Go figure. Can't murder anyone these days without some asshole sticking their nose in your business."

Cops? The American police that Tamiko had mentioned. But who?

But then Kisaki remembered the curious faces who had been peering out of the neighboring homes when the youkai first attacked. Though she wasn't well versed with life on Earth, she'd come to at least understand that such an occurrence wasn't commonplace these days.

"Too bad for you," the bear continued. "They're still too far away to stop me from sending you to whatever hell awaits half-breeds."

The bear youkai opened its mouth and leapt, its large body momentarily blocking out the sky as it launched itself at her. Kisaki had only a moment to act. Remembering her vision again, she looked down upon the broken shaft of the bat. It ended in a point where Orsen had bitten through it.

With no time for thought, she lifted it up as the bear fell upon her.

TWENTY-EIGHT

"KISAKI!" SHITORO SHOUTED in a panic.

Kisaki, however, was in no position to respond, as all the air was knocked out of her from the impact. She lay with her back upon the cool grass, pinned down by the bear.

She waited for it to start pummeling her with its massive fists or maybe use its teeth against her, but it lay still. After a moment, she realized no attack was forthcoming. She still held the handle of the bat in her hands, but now it was slick and wet as something dripped down it and onto her.

Kisaki remembered what had happened in her vision and realized the same thing had just occurred. She'd impaled the bear demon through the chest with the wooden shaft. In the space of only a few moments she'd witnessed, not one, but two deaths, the latter by her own hand.

It was a sobering thought for one who had sought to do nothing more than make a few friends.

"Kisaki!" Shitoro cried again. "My lady!"

Tamiko and Stephen joined in, just barely audible over the sound of the keening wail, louder and closer now.

Though Kisaki didn't know what these cops would do once they arrived, Stephen had used them as a threat against her and Tamiko, making her suspect that perhaps it would be unwise to confront them.

She shifted, managed to get her hands up, and gave a shove with all her strength. Heavy as it was, she was amazed when she managed to roll the bear off of her with relative ease. Its body gave no resistance, being little more than dead meat.

"My lady," Shitoro cried out upon seeing her.

"Oh my God," Tamiko said, reaching her. She stared at Kisaki with a wide-eyed glare. "We need to get you some help."

"It is merely a scratch," Kisaki replied, but then looked down upon herself and realized the source of the confusion. She was soaked in the bear demon's blood.

"A scratch? You…"

"It's not mine." She gestured down at the corpse.

"Holy shit," Stephen said. "What the hell is that thing?"

"A youkai, obviously," Shitoro spat from where he still kept the hawk demon pinned to the ground. "Are you okay, Mistress Kisaki?" She nodded gratefully to him. "Good. Then let us dispatch this last one and we can…"

"No."

"What?"

"Let it go, Shitoro."

"I don't understand. These brutes came here to kill us … to kill *you*."

Kisaki was having trouble forming the words, or perhaps she just didn't want to say them aloud. That cold logic had dissipated as soon as the battle ended. Whatever bloodlust she had felt was gone along with it. Realization that at least two lives had been snuffed out as a result of their fight sank in.

When reading tales of war from a scroll, it was easy to dismiss such things. But experiencing it herself, *taking a life,* that was a far different thing. It was ... not something to be undertaken lightly, she now realized.

It had been an unfortunate necessity, though. She understood that the bear had every intention of doing the same to her, or worse. But necessary or not, this wasn't something she felt should be celebrated.

A hand fell on her shoulder. Stephen's. She reached up and took hold of it, grateful for his comfort.

"I must insist..."

"That's enough, Shitoro," Kisaki snapped, hearing an authority in her voice she hadn't known before. If anything, it sounded more like her mother's than her own. "I said let it go. This battle is over."

Shitoro looked at her askew for a moment, but then did as he was told. He backed off a step, allowing the hawk to regain its feet.

The smaller youkai, bloodied from his claws but alive, looked uncertainly between them all for a moment.

"Go," Kisaki said, "and tell whoever sent you that we aren't the easy prey it assumes we are. We have no quarrel with your master, but will give your people no quarter either."

The hawk squawked once, though whether in obedience or defiance, Kisaki didn't know. Then it took to the skies and flew off.

"What about the others?" Shitoro asked. "I think those wolves..."

"Are merely stunned," Kisaki said. "But I believe the fight has been taken out of them."

"I hate to break this up," Stephen interrupted, "but those sirens are getting awfully close and what happened here is ... kinda weird."

"Yeah." Tamiko nodded. "I don't know how the police in America handle these things but, well, look at you, Kisaki."

Stephen stepped back, noting all the blood. "Agreed. I just fired my dad's gun and you look like you stepped out of a slaughterhouse. This probably isn't the smartest course of action, but maybe we should be somewhere else when they get here."

"What will they do to those demons?" Tamiko asked after they'd put a few blocks between them and Stephen's house.

"I'm more worried about what my parents will do to me once they find out," he said.

Kisaki noted that he'd stuffed the weapon into his jacket as best he could, but it was a poor job at concealment. Regardless, it was still better than how she looked.

"Young mistress," Shitoro said, changing the topic. "Again you showed great prowess in battle, prowess that you should not have. The first time, against the humans, I thought it might be nothing more than dumb luck against an inferior species. But against youkai? Do you have an explanation?"

"I..."

"Spit it out, child." Whatever authority she'd wielded with him earlier was apparently forgotten. He was now firmly acting as her guardian again.

Kisaki wasn't sure how much she should say. Though Shitoro knew a great deal more than her, he'd been at a loss for her newfound abilities. She was afraid that anything more out of the ordinary would just double his resolve to lock her back up in her mother's chambers again. Then again, his current resolve on doing so was already pretty adamant.

She considered how he'd placed himself in harm's way for her. If anything, she owed him, all of them, an explanation. "It's hard to say, but before both fights, I ... I'm not sure ...

saw a vision of sorts. After that, it was like my body knew exactly what to do."

"A vision?" Shitoro asked. "Of what?"

"It was different both times, and I'm still not sure what it was about."

He glanced up at her, narrowing his eyes. "We need to discuss this."

"First we need to find a safe place, preferably somewhere I can wash off and find new garments to wear." He opened his mouth to respond, but she said, "I'm serious."

"Very well. But I believe I can help on that second issue." He began to glow, then changed back to his tiger-humanoid form.

"Isn't that a little dangerous out here in the open?" Stephen asked.

"You're carrying a big gun, Kisaki is drenched in blood, and the police are probably right now arresting a group of werewolves," Tamiko said. "At this point, I'm not too worried about the cat in a dress."

"Tiger," Shitoro muttered, gesturing with his hands. "And these are my royal robes."

"What are you doing?" Kisaki asked.

"You would know if you'd paid greater attention in your conjuring studies." Kisaki sighed painfully, to which he added, "Sorry, my lady, but merely stating the obvious. Stand back, humans."

"What are you going to do?" Tamiko asked.

"A subtle bit of magic, meant to make my mistress here stand out a bit less than she currently does. Are you ready, Lady Kisaki?"

She nodded, curious to see what Shitoro had in mind. Perhaps a glamour to disguise her until such time as…

A waterfall seemingly appeared above her. The heavens opened up and drenched her to the bone in the space of a second.

The water itself was freezing cold and hit her so hard that it drove her to her knees. She opened her mouth to protest and found it filled before she could say a word.

Just when she was certain she'd either drown or be crushed, it ended. She stood back up on rubbery legs, shivering from head to toe.

"Whoa. Instant Niagara Falls," Stephen said, letting out a whistle of appreciation.

Tamiko turned to the tiger demon. "I thought you said it was subtle."

"Subtlety is in the eye of the beholder," Shitoro replied smugly.

"What was that?!" Kisaki cried.

"As I said, a simple conjuring. You look much more inconspicuous now. You're welcome."

Kisaki looked down at herself. Soaked though she might be, he was right. The majority of the blood had been washed away. However, she couldn't help but think there were better workings of magic to accomplish the same thing. Considering the look upon his face, she thought it likely this was a form of not particularly subtle revenge for all the trouble she'd caused.

"Are you okay?" Stephen asked her.

"She'll be fine," Shitoro replied. "The sun is out and it's a warm day."

Kisaki glared sidelong down at the little demon. "Remind me to never let you draw me a bath."

"We have to think of something," Stephen said, stuffing the shotgun into the hastily dug hole and covering it with leaves. Kisaki had since learned its purpose. As she suspected, it was a weapon capable of spewing death from a distance, much like a bow and arrow, but with far more devastating results.

Tamiko turned and looked around. "I'm open to suggestion." Fortunately, the small park they'd retreated to on the outskirts of town was still empty.

"You guys have it easy," he replied. "Nobody knows who you are. I live here, though. People know my face. I mean, that's my house. They're going to have questions."

"Including how a girl kicked the butts of a bunch of werewolves?" Tamiko asked.

"Yeah, that might be one of them. But that's not the half of it. I mean, it's broad daylight. If this were a dark and stormy night, people could explain it away as a shared hallucination or maybe a drug trip. Heck, those wolf guys sorta looked like people. But the rest…"

"The bear and the hawk?" Kisaki offered.

"Yeah. No way is that not making the evening news. I have no flipping idea how we're going to explain how Cartersville suddenly became the X-Files." At the two girls' bewildered expressions, he added, "It's an old TV show, about some people who investigate strange happenings. Don't worry about it."

"Another of your American colloquialisms?"

"Exactly."

"I do not see why this is a bad thing," Shitoro said dismissively. "In the past, humans and youkai were well aware of each other. If anything, humans were once smart enough to know to respect their betters."

Tamiko folded her arms in front of her chest. "Betters?"

"Of course. No offense to you or your race, but you have to admit you would have been helpless against that group we faced, and they were little more than ragamuffins."

"I seem to have done all right against one of them," Stephen said.

"With my warning," Shitoro countered.

"We can argue who's the superior species at another time," Tamiko said. "The ones who rule this planet or the ones who need a flea bath, but the truth remains. Some strange stuff just happened, and I doubt the people who saw us are going to forget it easily."

Stephen nodded. "Agreed. This is a small town. People know each other and they talk. If it were one person, the police might just write it off as them being drunk, but I saw doors opening all up and down the block. That and it sounded like every cop in the county was responding to the war being waged on my front lawn."

"What are you implying?" Kisaki asked.

"I hate to say it, but I think the cat's out of the bag." He stopped as Shitoro glared up at him. "Not you, relax. What I mean is if we run, they're going to catch us. So maybe we don't even try."

"You think we should turn ourselves in?" Tamiko asked. "And do what? Confess?"

"Quite the opposite," Stephen said. "We're both human and Kisaki looks as human as either of us. If we walk in with a tiger demon by our side, it's going to look strange, but if we walk in with a *cat*." He held up the first two fingers on both of his hands in quotation marks. "Then maybe we can claim to have been as weirded out as everyone else. I don't think anyone will blame us for running from all of that."

"That sounds like it has potential," Tamiko said. "Basically, we play dumb." She turned to Shitoro after a moment of silence. "Come on, aren't you going to tell me that's something I excel at?"

"That goes without saying," he replied without any real aplomb, staring off into the distance as if looking for something.

"What is it, Shitoro?" Kisaki asked. "You're being unusually unopinionated."

"You're right, mistress," he replied, scratching his chin with one paw. "I've been thinking."

"About?"

He turned to Stephen. "You may wish to rethink hiding your weapon."

"I can't just walk into town, much less the police station, carrying it. I don't know if you get the news where you two are from, but people tend to get shot for much less."

"Getting shot is no worse than being mauled to death. I can assure you of that."

"What do you mean?" Kisaki asked.

"Think about it. Those youkai who attacked us. They did not do so of their own accord. They were sent."

"That bear guy seemed to be in charge," Stephen said.

Shitoro waved a hand at him dismissively. "I have known ursine youkai and they are little more than foot soldiers, brute force labor. He would have probably led those others to a mound of garbage if someone hadn't given him specific directions."

"So you're saying there's more of them?" Tamiko asked.

"More yes, but also worse. Ursine are not particularly intelligent, but they're strong and stubborn. They won't follow the commands of those they deem weaker than themselves. Thus, it stands to reason there is another demon out there, and I fear it is far more powerful. Worse, it knows what happened."

"How so?"

"It was me," Kisaki said. "The hawk. I let it go."

Shitoro nodded. "Alas, I am afraid that is true. There is no doubt that hawk fled back to its master." He reached up and took hold of one of Kisaki's hands. "Mercy is an admirable trait, my lady. It truly is. I know well the value of it. However, it is also a luxury and must be doled out accordingly. There are times when a leader wishes to give it, but cannot because their kindness would be returned with malice enough to bring them ruin. I am sorry to say, but I believe this is one such time."

Kisaki turned away and looked up at the sky. She hadn't wanted anyone else to die this day, but if what Shitoro said was true, then in doing so, she'd placed her friends in even greater danger.

She couldn't allow that.

"Tell me, Shitoro," she said, remembering what the bear had told her. "How long do we have until Ichitiro strikes?"

TWENTY-NINE

"**W**HAT?!" SHITORO CRIED.

"Ichitiro. Do you recognize that name?"

"Y-yes. But how do you know it, and how do you know that it was he who sent the youkai after us?"

"The bear," Kisaki replied. "He told me that Ichitiro sends his regards. I assumed that he is the earthbound demon you fear may be coming."

"No, not at all." Shitoro seemed to turn even paler than his already white fur. "Ichitiro is no mere demon."

"Oh, then is he a…"

"He is a daimao, like your mother."

Kisaki's mouth dropped open at the revelation and a cold chill began to spread down her spine. "But why? Why is he after us?"

"I do not know. We have been so careful. He could not know of your existence. It's impossible."

"I think all of us have had to redefine our definition of impossible today," Stephen said. "Welcome to the party."

"This is not a joking matter!" Shitoro snapped. "Do you not understand the power he has at his command?"

"Actually, no, I don't."

Shitoro ignored him and began to pace. "Why? As a hanyou, you should be beneath his contempt." At the look on Kisaki's face, he added, "Don't be insulted. It is merely the truth. The daimao are a proud and powerful race. Their station breeds arrogance, but Ichitiro's is legendary even amongst them. He treats his servants like playthings for his amusement. If he were to come across you in the palace, yes, he would kill you for what you are. But here, on Earth? Why go to the trouble? And how would he even know how to find…"

He spun toward Kisaki, grabbed both of her arms, and yanked her down to his level. "The crystal."

"Crystal?" she asked, certain he'd figured out she had another.

"Yes, the one you used to bring us here."

She almost let out a sigh of relief. "What of it? It's gone. Used up."

"I know that! What color was it?"

"I do not…"

"Your mother's are black as obsidian. Each daimao's crystals have a unique color according to their individual power. I had assumed the other you'd swiped was hers, too. Was it?"

After a moment passed, Kisaki shook her head.

"What color, then?"

She had snuck a glance earlier, when no one was looking, to see which of the two she'd used. "Grey, like a storm cloud."

Shitoro let go of her and backed away. "Oh, you stupid, stupid child."

"Let me guess," Tamiko said. "Grey belongs to that Ichi guy?"

"Precisely," he replied. "And worse. When a crystal is used, the owner can sense it. They do not necessarily know who did so, but they know it was used and where the user was sent. That is how I was able to find Kisaki in the first place."

"Yeah, but you said you were searching the island for two days."

"It gives a general location, nothing more. If the user moves, then the owner would still need to find them."

"But we did move," Tamiko pointed out. "We appeared at least a kilometer away from Stephen's house. So how did they track us so quickly when you only found us by accident?"

"I don't know. Wolves have good noses, even better than mine. Perhaps they got lucky and caught our scent."

"Could they find us again?"

"They will know of the human's house. We cannot return there. Aside from that..." He shrugged.

"So what do we do if this Ichi person does come looking..."

Shitoro took a deep breath, as if trying to calm himself. "He cannot. The edict. He can't come here himself. That is one plus on our side. But he can send his followers."

"Followers?" Kisaki asked.

"When the edict was laid down, many youkai were stranded on Earth, left to their own devices to either survive or die. We are speaking about thousands at the least, all across the planet."

"But if they were stranded, then..."

"Oh, do open your eyes, child. I am here, am I not? The daimao cannot go themselves, not without the others sensing it. They are simply too powerful. Their very passing leaves an absence of energy the others can feel. But a small sending, such as a youkai with his master's crystal, the others would not immediately know of it happening." He glanced up at Kisaki. "It is why I came alone at your mother's behest. If she could send me, then Ichitiro could send his servants as well. In fact, he certainly would. Your mother respects the edicts of the celestial court. She only sent me because she was in a dire panic over your safety. I sincerely doubt Ichitiro has any-where near that same respect."

"Sounds like a bit of an ass," Stephen said.

"I assume that is an insult," Shitoro replied. "If so, then yes. He is more than a bit of one. But still, many of the demons stranded here are bound to be desperate. I don't doubt they would rally to his flag upon receiving even the most minor of recompense."

"But why come after me here?" Kisaki asked.

"I do not know, but it may be little more than simple pettiness. The crystal chamber was established for us servants to use as needed. All of the daimao have contributed to it, but it was well known that Ichitiro despised anyone using his without express permission. Youkai who disregarded his warning were known to disappear. There were plenty of other crystals to use, so most of us took to avoiding his. It's possible he is simply acting out, trying to teach the offending party a lesson in respect."

"Add petulant to what I said."

Shitoro nodded toward Stephen. "Indeed. But nevertheless, if we have attracted his attention, then we should flee this place immediately. He cannot know of your existence."

"But you just said a hanyou like me was beneath his attention."

"In most cases, yes." Shitoro placed his hands behind his back and continued to pace. "Ichitiro's wrath is legendary, but he is neither known for his intelligence nor his attention span. The fact that you defeated some youkai mercenaries will intrigue him, but nothing more. But whoever sent those youkai, whoever commands them here on Earth, will most likely send more. Ichitiro is not tolerant of failure. Therein lies the problem. If more are sent and they find us, we cannot allow them to live."

"I know what you said about mercy..."

"It is more than that! It … is difficult to explain. Just know that it is something we must do. That is why I say we must flee this place at once."

"What aren't you telling me, Shitoro?" After another pause on his part, Kisaki reiterated herself, once more drawing upon that authority she'd discovered so recently. "Shitoro, *now*."

He looked up at her and smiled sadly before walking over to a nearby bench and sitting down. "Ichitiro is not merely another daimao. He is your mother's would-be suitor."

"Her what?!"

Shitoro shook his head. "Your mother has never expressed any interest in him. He is a brute, wishing to possess what he cannot. That she chose a human over him, though, is something that I doubt he could let go of if he ever found out."

"So that is the reason she hid me?"

"That is one of the reasons," he said. "Even so, with you here on Earth, his interest would likely eventually wane. The problem is only partially who you are. It is also about what you have taken."

"Taken?"

"The Taiyosori, child. You have stolen that which cannot be stolen and as such have put yourself in grave danger."

"Why? You said it was a secondary concern to my mother."

"It is, compared to you, but we are not talking about her now. It's Ichitiro. Your mother has long suspected that the reason he fancied her above their other siblings…"

"Siblings?" Stephen asked. "Is this heaven you're talking about or Arkansas?"

"The meanderings of the divine are beyond the understanding of one as primitive as yourself," Shitoro snapped before continuing. "Lady Midnite believes the only reason he wishes her as his consort is because of the Taiyosori."

"You said it was powerful," Kisaki said, subconsciously touching the spot in her jacket where it lay.

"Vastly so."

"So if this Ichitiro wanted it so badly, why didn't he just try to take it?" Tamiko asked.

"That would invite open conflict among the daimao," Shitoro explained, "conflict that the others would most likely not side with him on. Nevertheless, the heavens would burn before it was over and that destruction would spread to other worlds, such as this one. However, it would also be quite impossible, for, as I said, the Taiyosori cannot be stolen. It would defend itself against any who dared try, be they human, youkai, or daimao."

"It did kind of shock me when I first touched it," Kisaki admitted.

"Doesn't look like it did all that much," Stephen said, looking her over. "If that's the best antitheft device it has, then it's not all that impressive."

"Therein lies the conundrum," Shitoro replied, sounding exasperated. "The Taiyosori cannot be stolen, but I assure you it can and *has* done much worse to those who have tried. It can only be mastered in three ways. It can be gifted to one who is worthy, as it was passed from the elder gods to Kisaki's mother. It can be won in combat, something that even Ichitiro would not dare against Lady Midnite. Though he may be her match, with the sword she would prevail."

"What's the third?"

"The sword can be inherited, such as from parent to child."

"But her mother isn't dead," Tamiko said.

"As I am well aware, human. But her mother's blood flows through her veins. In a sense, she is her rightful heir. The sword must have sensed that when she touched it."

"But why did it turn into a quill?" Kisaki asked.

"How am I supposed to know? I've never been foolish enough to try stealing it. I can't even recall your mother touching it more than once or twice in the time I have served her. All I know of it are myth and legend."

"Okay. So this guy can't steal the sword and he definitely can't inherit it," Tamiko said. "So what if Kisaki just refused to fight him?"

"I'm afraid it is not that simple," Shitoro replied. "Lady Midnite is a daimao. Ichitiro risks much by goading her into combat. Such a thing is not undertaken lightly. Kisaki, however, is a hanyou. Her status as Lady Midnite's daughter will mean nothing to him. If he learns who she is, and what she has in her possession, then he will fall upon her without mercy."

"What if I don't use the sword? He won't have won it then."

"A mere technicality. If he kills you while you are in possession of it, that could very well count as a victory, or so your mother believes."

Kisaki repressed the shudder that threatened to escape. "But if he kills me, then he'll also risk angering her, won't he?"

"Yes. She would be heartbroken. Her fury would shake the celestial palace to its very foundation, but she would be in the same position that Ichitiro finds himself now. The other daimao would not rally to her cause to avenge a hanyou and, with the Taiyosori in Ichitiro's grasp, it is unlikely your mother could defeat him."

The truth finally out, it hit Kisaki like one of the cars she'd seen on the roads of this planet. She had truly messed up. All she'd wanted was an adventure, a chance to see what lay beyond her mother's doors, maybe the opportunity to meet someone new. She'd taken the sword as a curio, nothing more, but in doing so had set in motion a chain of events that threatened not only her, but her friends, too, and possibly much more if Shitoro's belief in the sword's power were true.

She still had one crystal, the red one. She could use that to send her and Shitoro back to the palace and return the sword to its rightful owner. But which daimao did the final crystal belong to? Who would be alerted to her passage? It sounded as if this Ichitiro was the worst of the lot, but that didn't mean the others would be as noble as her mother, or as willing to let her live.

Still, that seemed a small matter compared to her friends. Whatever was happening in this town, it sounded as if more youkai were coming to flush them out. She couldn't take Tamiko and Stephen with her to the palace. There was no telling what would happen to them as mere humans. But she also couldn't leave them here to fend for themselves. That would be no better than if she had killed them herself.

"We need to run," Kisaki said at last. "Leave this place, by foot or car. Go somewhere where Ichitiro's minions can't find us." She turned to Shitoro. "Will that work?"

"Perhaps. They will scour this place, but if they can't find you, then they will be forced to reconsider their options. I do not believe even Ichitiro has either the patience or resources for an extended search if he has no idea where we have gone."

"But what about the people here?" Stephen asked.

"Some may perish," Shitoro said. "But I do not think it will be many. The youkai of Earth have learned to be wary. They know better than to risk exposing themselves for long. That their existence seems to have been relegated to myth and legend tells me they have succeeded. Without Kisaki here, they will have no reason to tarry."

"What do you mean 'some?'"

"I wish I could give you assurances, human, I truly do, but the truth is that we do not know who is commanding them here. Youkai are as diverse as your people with regards to temper and power. If the one in charge is reasonable then casualties will be kept to a minimum, perhaps none at all. However, if that leader is…"

"*Bolder and stronger than the rest?*"

The group spun toward the tree line, where the deep voice had seemingly originated, but there was nothing there.

"*Perhaps one who is tired of hiding from the human vermin?*"

This time, the voice seemed to come from somewhere else entirely, but again they saw no one. Kisaki, however, noticed Shitoro sniff the air and the hackles of his fur raise.

"No," he whispered.

"*Yes, little youkai,*" the beast said, stepping from the tree line. It stood nearly nine feet tall, its form heavily muscled and covered in dark fur. And it wasn't alone. Wolves, bears, and more stepped from the forest alongside it.

"*Crag the hunter has come for you, and his sharp ears hear that you have a prize worth seeking. Give me the Taiyosori and I might allow your deaths to be quick.*"

THIRTY

"**A**M I LOSING my mind here?" Stephen asked, pointing at the demon who had threatened them. "Or did Bigfoot just walk out of the forest and start talking to us?"

"You're not crazy," Tamiko replied, fear etched onto her face. "But I kind of wish you were."

"Me too."

"Who are you and what do you want?" Kisaki asked before Shitoro could stop her.

"*You must be the hanyou who gave my followers so much trouble. To think such a tiny half-breed could defeat even that little mouse you have with you.*" The massive creature nodded toward Shitoro. "*Even more interesting that you would claim to have the blade of heaven. No wonder Ichitiro paid a bounty for your head. Mind you, I do not believe it. But if that fool does, then I suppose I will have to satisfy my curiosity and search your corpses for it.*"

"How did you find us, brute?" Shitoro growled.

"*Really, kitten? You can't possibly be that ignorant. The miasma, of course.*" Crag took a wet sniff through his nostrils. "*Seems to have finally worn off, but that doesn't matter. There is nowhere left to hide.*"

Kisaki wasn't sure what he meant, but then she remembered the smoke that had surrounded them when they'd used the second crystal. At the time, she'd thought it misfired, or perhaps overloaded due to the vagueness of her request, but now she realized it had been deliberate.

If what Shitoro had said about this Ichitiro was true, and she had to assume it was, then he was petty enough to do so.

A screech of sound caught her ear and she spun to find a hawk demon, perhaps the same one she'd spared, swooping down at them. No, not them ... Stephen. While the monstrous demon had been pontificating, her friend had reached beneath the covering of leaves and retrieved his gun. Unfortunately, it was for naught as the hawk tore it from his hands. It flew back toward its apparent leader where it dropped the weapon at his feet.

"*I am impressed that you even tried, human,*" Crag said, bending down to retrieve it. "*However futile it might be.*" With a squeal of metal, he bent the gun in half and tossed it away. "*Is there anything else we should be aware of, or can we proceed with your deaths?*"

"You can proceed to go hang yourself," Shitoro spat, "along with your foul master." He raised his arms and a cascade of water dropped down from the sky onto Crag and the youkai near him.

"You think a bath is going to stop that monster?" Stephen asked, wide-eyed.

"No, I don't." Shitoro held his hands out and yellow bolts of energy shot forth, similar to what he'd used on Stephen earlier.

Kisaki was about to remark that she was doubtful such an attack would do anything to their foes, but then the youkai started screaming and she realized Shitoro had used the water as a mere distraction.

"*ARGH!*" Crag cried out as a burst of yellow energy exploded in his face.

The same was happening to all of the larger predators. Hands, paws, and claws reached up to cover their eyes from the attack.

Shitoro finished his spell and turned back to the others. "That won't stop them for long."

"What do we do?" Tamiko asked.

Shitoro changed into his tiger form and bounded past her. "If I might be so bold to suggest it … run!"

Crag had to give credit to the diminutive tiger youkai for even trying. The useless little demon had been terrified, rightly so, at the sight of him. He knew Shitoro to be a servant to the daimao Midnite, but remembered him from much further back. The runt of the litter had escaped him so very long ago, somehow managing to subsequently secure a position that made him all but untouchable. But now, well, this had to be fate's way of repaying Crag for his time spent hiding in the woods like a dog while the daimao cowered from the comfort of their palace.

Finally, his vision cleared. A clever attack but utterly futile. When he looked up again, he saw the foursome was gone. No matter. He turned questioningly to one of the wolves at his side and the creature nodded once. Even with the miasma gone, his minions had their scent. Though the little tiger might lead them on a good chase, his two-legged companions couldn't hope to escape them for long.

And if they thought the human town would offer them sanctuary, then they were wrong. Had this been a mere contract, perhaps Crag would have been more cautious, heeded the wisdom of remaining hidden. But now, after overhearing his quarry talking, it all made sense to him. A bounty, from Ichitiro no less, and all for a measly hanyou? Somehow the daimao believed this pathetic creature was in possession of the Taiyosori.

It seemed impossible, insane.

He sincerely doubted the hanyou actually had it, but if there was even a small chance, then he would throw caution to the wind. The Taiyosori was prized by the daimao, but rumor was it was feared by them as well. With it in his possession, he could surely command a greater bounty than a mere pile of meat – passage off this world at a bare minimum, reinforcements, even respect. He could demand it all.

He paused, deep in thought, as the youkai around him waited for his orders. Crag was powerful, even among the mazoku, but he had no delusions about being a match for the daimao ... by himself anyway. But with the Taiyosori at his command, that could change.

The daimao, arrogant godlings. What he wouldn't give to be out from under their thumb. Sending Ichitiro's head flying from his shoulders would give him immense satisfaction. It would also rally other demons, both strong and weak, to his cause, making him unto a god himself.

Crag smiled and then simply pointed a finger toward the town.

The stakes had been raised, the rules of the game changed. There would be nowhere his prey could hide from him.

"Thank you, Shitoro. We definitely owe you one."

"Think nothing of it," he replied to Tamiko.

She turned to him, one eyebrow raised. "That's it? No insult?"

"Perhaps later," the little tiger said, panting hard. "Would I have been able to do more to that beast, I would have. Alas, I am no warrior."

"You could have fooled me," Stephen replied. "That was pretty awesome, what you did."

They'd run as quickly as they could. Cartersville wasn't a big town, but there were enough streets to hopefully lose their pursuers. Suddenly the idea of turning themselves in to the police didn't seem so farfetched. They could certainly use the extra manpower fighting at their side, Kisaki mused. Still, this Crag had ambushed them on the outskirts of town. That probably meant their current strategy had at least bought them some time.

Unfortunately, Shitoro brought that hope to a screeching halt. "We must keep going. He won't give up that easily."

"Are you sure?" Tamiko asked. "I thought you said they would be wary of humans."

"Exactly," Stephen added. "The cops are going to be on alert after earlier. It wouldn't be smart or subtle to…"

"Crag is neither smart nor subtle in his methods, human. He has never been. He is a brutal butcher, nearly as full of rage as he is of himself."

"You know this demon, Shitoro?" Kisaki asked.

"Unfortunately. His people declared war on my own almost eighteen hundred years ago. No, that is not entirely true. His forces attacked without provocation, ambushed my village and caught us unawares. It was a slaughter and Crag was the one leading their army, laughing as his troops slaughtered cubs and mothers alike." The anger in Shitoro's voice was evident as was the pain of the memory.

Kisaki knelt down next to him and began to stroke his fur. "What happened?"

"Only a handful of us escaped. Crag personally chased me down. He never was one to let the opportunity for an easy kill pass."

"How'd you get away?" Tamiko asked.

"By using the same trick I just did." Shitoro laughed bitterly. "As I said, that one is no thinker. He relies on brute force and breaking his enemies through savagery. But he won't give up. Not now."

"Why?"

"It was no secret that he was known to be jealous of the daimao. It's obvious he overheard us talking about the Taiyosori. That is a prize he won't so easily let slip between his fingers. If he thinks he can get revenge upon them…"

"Revenge?" Kisaki asked. "For what?"

"When the edict was passed and passage to Earth forbidden, Crag was one of those left behind. Word reached him too late and the ways were already shut. He tried to reach out to the daimao, demanding to be brought to the palace or at least sent to another world. The truth is, his station as one of their warlords might have swayed their judgment. But his message fell upon deaf ears. He feels they abandoned him, betrayed him."

"Did they?"

Shitoro looked up and smiled sheepishly. "As your mother's chief servant at the time, I might have played some small part in ensuring his pleas did not reach the proper channels."

Tamiko chuckled. "Does he know this?"

"I should hope not."

"Maybe that's news we should keep to ourselves, then," Stephen said.

Shitoro nodded. "I would appreciate that, although I doubt it will quell him much. Crag wasn't pleased that I escaped him all those years ago. Serving Lady Midnite put me beyond his grasp, but now…"

"I'll make sure he doesn't lay a finger on you," Kisaki said.

"I thank you, my lady, but you should know that Crag is far more powerful than the youkai who attacked us at Stephen Fuller's domicile."

Kisaki considered this, remembering how she'd pushed the dead ursine off of her as if it weighed little more than Tamiko. Whatever had awakened in her, it seemed to be evolving, growing stronger each time she used it. Unfortunately, she had no idea what her limit was. The bear had been big, but this Crag was enormous. There was no telling how strong he might be or what magic he had to use against them. "It sounds like we have two choices," she said. "We can fight or we can run."

"He had more wolves with him," Shitoro warned. "They will not be easy to evade. Crag may be an uncivilized brute, but he knows the ways of war and how to track an enemy."

Tamiko turned to Stephen. "I don't suppose you have a car we can borrow."

"My parents took ours with them. Besides, I only have my permit. I'm technically not supposed to be driving without an adult."

"A giant ape wants to kill us and you're worried about getting a ticket?"

"When you put it that way…"

"Where would we go?" Kisaki asked.

"No idea, but not here sounds like a good start."

Kisaki nodded, then glanced at Shitoro. "And this Crag will follow?"

"Almost surely."

A frown creased her face. "But before then?"

"As I said, my lady, he suspects you have the Taiyosori. I have little doubt he will throw caution to the wind to try to find you and take it. He will ravage this place looking for you or anyone who might know where you've gone."

"And by ravage, you mean?" Worry was beginning to creep into Stephen's voice.

"I think you know very well what I mean. He will tear this town apart, piece by piece, human by human."

"Damnit!" Stephen cried, slapping the side of the building they'd stopped near. "I have friends here. There's good people in this town. Hell, even Robbie doesn't deserve that ... mostly."

Kisaki approached and put a hand upon his shoulder. "I agree."

"But, Lady Kisaki..."

She silenced Shitoro with a look. "This is my fault. I should have heeded your wishes, Shitoro, stayed and studied, but I did not. And now all of this falls upon me. I won't allow innocent people to be slaughtered, not when there exists the possibility I can do something about it."

"We can't win this alone," Shitoro pleaded.

"Then we shall find allies to stand with us." She turned toward Stephen. "These police I have heard of. They are warriors, yes?"

"In a sense," he replied. "I mean, I think some of the cops in town are ex-military."

"Very well. We will reach out to them, have them warn the others."

"And then?" Shitoro asked.

"Simple, my friend. And then we shall fight."

THIRTY-ONE

"**L**ET ME GET this straight," the officer manning the front desk of the Cartersville police department said. "We need to evacuate the town because otherwise we'll be living out the plot to *Day of the Animals*, as led by *Mighty Joe Young*?"

"Well, when you put it that way, it does sound a bit far-fetched."

"Farfetched?" the desk sergeant, Ashby Coulson, replied. "You're that Fuller boy, right?"

"Yes, sir."

"Your mom works down at the Post Office."

"Uh huh."

"So, what, did you steal a box of stamps and try licking the glue to get high?"

"What?"

"Listen, kid," he said, his expression darkening, "it's been a busy day. We arrested a couple of weirdos earlier dressed like Tarzan and Jane and picked up some bodies that the coroner is losing his shit over. I don't have time to listen to your … come to think of it, didn't all of that crap happen near your home?"

"Um…"

"Yeah, it did. My buddies have been looking for you, wanted to know if you knew anything. But I see now that you were off getting stoned with your girlfriends here."

"I am not his girlfriend," Kisaki said. "I am his great-aunt."

Tamiko buried her face in her hands and simply shook her head.

"So what is it?" Sergeant Coulson asked. "Weed, meth, those new bath salts?"

"I'm not on drugs!" Stephen shouted, banging his hand against the desk. Judging by the look upon his face, Kisaki considered that it was an action he immediately regretted. "I'm sorry."

"Do that again and you're going to be," the sergeant warned. "Listen, I get it. I was young and stupid once, too. It's summer, you're bored, and you felt like experimenting. So I'm going to give you one chance. Go back to whatever basement you lit up in and sleep it off. Because otherwise, you're going to sleep it off in lockup while I phone your parents."

"That should be interesting," Tamiko commented under her breath.

Stephen seemed to be at a loss of what to say, so Kisaki pushed her way forward. "I am sorry, but we simply cannot leave. That would be the more prudent course of action for us, yes, but your town would suffer as a result. The creature who is looking for us will not give up easily. I fear many of your people would perish before his rage was sated."

The officer let out a pained sigh. "How about this? You either give me proof, or I put your butts in a cell. You have three seconds."

"Shitoro."

The tiger demon looked up from where he'd been lounging on the floor. "I was merely waiting for you to ask."

Sergeant Coulson stood up. "What the?! How did you do that?"

"With my mouth, human," Shitoro replied. Then, before the sergeant could say anything further, there came a flash of light as Shitoro transformed into his bipedal form. "Shall I offer anything else as way of proof?"

"Holy shit! What the hell is that?!" He began to fumble with the holster at his side.

"Whoa, hold on," Stephen cried. "It's okay. He's a friendly … err … demon."

Just then, another officer stuck his head in from an interior door. "Yo, Coulson, what's going on out there? We just got a bunch of 9-1-1 alerts about …" He trailed off as he caught sight of the youkai. "What the hell was in the coffee this morning?"

"Will someone please listen to us?" Stephen asked. "We need to talk to the captain, *now*. It's a matter of life or…"

The entire building seemed to rock as an explosion sounded from nearby. Tamiko and Shitoro were knocked to their knees, while Kisaki and Stephen just barely kept their feet as plaster dust fell from the ceiling around them.

Cries of disbelief and question rose up from elsewhere in the building.

If those inside were not aware that they were in danger before, Kisaki noted, then they surely were now.

Kisaki ordered her human friends to stay inside, hoping against hope they listened. She said the same to Shitoro, although she sincerely doubted he would follow her commands. He was loyal and brave to a fault, but he was in over his head on this one.

Deep down, she wondered if she was, too, but there was only one way to find out.

Before the police could organize themselves, but also before they could try to stop her, she raced out the front door.

When they'd gone in, just a few minutes earlier, the street had been quiet. Some townsfolk were milling about, enjoying the sunny day, but they were few and far between. Stephen had explained that a lot of people were out of town on summer vacation, which was fortunate. Sadly, Kisaki had a feeling there were still plenty left who would not live to see the end of this day if they weren't quick enough in their warning.

The scene before her now proved her deepest fears true.

Cars had been upended, one into the side of the building she'd just emerged from. She watched as wolves dragged a person from one and began savaging his body. Sadly, he was beyond saving. However, even had she tried to, it was doubtful she'd have been given the chance, for Crag stood in the middle of the street flanked by two bears.

He'd been in the process of tearing apart a traffic light when she'd exited. But now he dropped the twisted metal in his hands and smiled at her, revealing sharp teeth. "*See, little hanyou, there is no place to hide from Crag. For too long we have hidden from the humans, cowered in places they didn't deem worthy of venturing. It is time they once more learned who their masters are, and your death shall pave the way for that.*"

"You speak arrogantly, mazoku," Kisaki replied. "I am the daughter of Lady Midnite and I will not die so easily."

That revelation apparently caught the monster by surprise, judging by his almost comical expression. "*Midnite? Truly? It all makes sense then. So you do have the Taiyosori. Give it to me.*"

"It is not yours to take."

"*Tell me, child. What filthy human did your mother lay with to give birth to a bastard such as you? You don't have the look of one of the blessed isles.*" He flashed a predatory smile her way. "*I am right, am I not? If so, then your parentage means nothing to any of us. Your kind are forbidden. You were born already destined to die. I will be rewarded for erasing your stain from this world. That is, if I do not conquer it first myself. The sword, NOW!"*

Behind Kisaki, she could hear the sound of doors opening and men shouting orders. She risked a glance over her shoulder and saw weapons being brought to bear, aimed toward the creatures currently ravaging this once peaceful town.

"Take it if you can," she said a moment before multiple guns opened fire.

Time slowed once again as the first of the shots struck, hitting the ursine to Crag's right.

The sound of gunfire grew faint and then faded altogether as her vision clouded and she once more found herself in the body of another.

Strong arms were wrapped around her neck from behind, cutting off her air. She tried to pry them off, but they held her in a seemingly unbreakable grasp. Two more men rushed at her from the front, their hands balled into fists. Kisaki was in trouble but, oddly enough, felt no fear.

Instead of giving in to despair, the body she inhabited grabbed the arm holding her, bent slightly at the waist, and threw her attacker over her shoulder into the man attacking from the left.

They went down in a tumble of arms and legs and she saw that the one who'd been holding her was the same man from the photo again. There was no time to gawk, however, as she was already on the move, sidestepping the remaining attacker and delivering a blow to his back that sent him to his knees.

The man from the picture rose to his feet. Instead of attacking her again, though, he smiled and gave her a thumbs-up before starting to laugh.

She turned away from him and saw another man staring back at her. This one was very familiar, with blond hair and a strong build. After a moment, she realized she was looking into a mirror. The man staring back at her was the same that Stephen had identified in the photos as his namesake, Lieutenant Stephen Fuller – his great-grandfather, her father!

The vision faded away as the real world began to once more take precedence. Stephen's image blurred and merged with another for a moment, growing in size and stature, until it became that of Crag, charging her way, his massive arms raised above him.

Small blooms of blood erupted from his torso as several bullets struck him, but he seemingly ignored them as he reached her and brought his fists down, intent on ending this fight with one blow.

Kisaki was ready for him. The world was still moving as if in slow motion by the time he'd reached her, and that cold battle logic had already suffused her mind. Instinctively, she understood that Crag was yet another creature used to winning his battles by sheer virtue of his impressive physique.

He would need to do better.

She stepped nimbly aside as he brought his fists crashing into the ground, shattering the sidewalk, then brought her foot up in a kick that caught the brute straight in the mouth.

Sadly, it would seem she would need to do better as well.

Crag stood, a thin trickle of blood dripping down his jaw. He opened his mouth to laugh, revealing a few cracked teeth, but nothing more. "*Is that all the daughter of the great Midnite has to offer? You insult me with your weakness. Give me the Taiyosori and perhaps I shall snap your neck so that you will embarrass yourself no further.*"

"Listening to your voice is embarrassment enough," she replied, stepping out of his reach.

Movement registered in her periphery and she risked a look back to see two wolves racing toward her.

"Get out of there!" a voice shouted from somewhere nearby.

Kisaki wasn't sure if the warning was aimed at her or not, but more shots rang out and one of the wolves fell to the ground with several bloody wounds in its side.

Alas, that still left one. It closed on her position while Crag flanked her.

There was no way she could dodge both at the same time, but perhaps she didn't need to. Remembering how her father had used his opponents' strength against them, she stepped toward the wolf. It leapt for her throat, but she ducked down, catching it with her shoulder, and then flinging it into the arms of its commander.

Kisaki leapt away, aiming to put a little distance between her and her enemies, marveling at how she flipped through the air and then landed gracefully on her feet. That was new. She spun to see Crag angrily throw the wolf to the side. It hit the pavement with a yip of pain, bounced once, and then limply skidded to a stop.

As ancient and battle hardened as this mazoku was, he was an insult to the heroes from Kisaki's studies. Brave, noble, willing to do anything for the men under their command, Crag was none of these.

What he was, however, was large and strong, something she would do well not to forget.

Glass shattered and someone cried out, but Kisaki couldn't risk a look. She managed to just barely dodge another of Crag's blows as he raced toward her again. He outclassed her in raw physical power, by a considerable margin it would seem, but she had the edge in speed.

"Lady Kisaki, run!"

She froze in place, a stupidly dangerous thing to do, and stared wide-eyed as Shitoro raced up from behind Crag in his tiger form. The little youkai leapt upon Crag's back and sank his teeth into one of the brute's ears.

"Argh!"

Crag's cry of pain snapped Kisaki out of her shock and she used the distraction to step forward and deliver a punch to his midsection. It was like hitting solid rock. Though he let out a whoop of surprise from the impact, she was certain she'd done more damage to herself than to him.

Sadly for her, she had moved in too close for the hit, putting herself well within range of his superior reach. He lashed out sloppily, catching her with a backhand that sent her flying. She landed, tumbled a few times, and then came to a rest on her back, stunned.

Before she could recover, one of the ursines leapt upon her in its bear form – hundreds of pounds of muscle, claws, and flesh-rending teeth.

It used its size to pin her before driving forward again, intent on tearing out her throat. She grabbed its head by the ears, just barely holding its snapping jaws at bay.

That wouldn't help her for long, though. The bear had the advantage of superior leverage, using it along with its massive body to inch ever forward.

Kisaki turned her head to the side, sickened by its rancid breath, and saw a town in chaos. People, those foolish enough to step outside to see what was going on, were being pursued by youkai up and down the street. She watched as one woman ran blindly, flapping her arms in the air to try to ward off a hawk youkai harassing her. Elsewhere, a wolf tackled an older man from behind. He struggled feebly beneath it for a few seconds before falling limp.

All around her, the peace that had once reigned was being torn asunder and she was helpless to do anything about it, save keep this creature's teeth from clamping down on her windpipe.

No!

She remembered what Shitoro had said about mercy. How it was a luxury, one that sometimes came back to bite the hand that offered it. She understood that now, viewing the battle around her, especially in seeing Shitoro's brave stand against Crag.

It was only a matter of time before he pried the tiger youkai off his back and, once he did, she was certain mercy would be the last thing on his mind. It would have to be the last thing on hers, too, if she wanted to win this, if she wanted her friends to survive.

With a snarl of her own, she tightened her grip upon the ursine's head and then gave her hands a twist. There came a sickening *crunch*. The bear's eyes opened wide in surprise for a moment before glazing over as the life left them and its body fell slack upon hers.

She gave a heave, practically flinging the corpse off of her, and then stood, ready to give battle once more.

Kisaki wasn't the only one. The police continued to fire upon the youkai in the street, but soon even more gunfire erupted around them. She turned to find that some who'd managed to flee inside had returned carrying weapons of their own. It seemed that the citizens of this town were not willing to let it go so easily.

That was good, because it looked as if they were going to need every last bullet.

Let them deal with the smaller youkai, though. She set her eyes upon Crag just as he managed to reach behind him with one massive hand and grab Shitoro by the scruff of his neck. He gave a yank, but the loyal tiger's teeth held fast. He pried Shitoro loose, but at the cost of an ear.

With a roar of rage, he balled a fist and prepared to drive it into Shitoro's face.

Kisaki was on the move before she even realized she was doing so. Crag's body was built like a concrete wall. His face had proven to be almost as hard. But Kisaki was a smart girl. She'd been paying attention to the lessons shown her in her visions and listening to the cool logic in her mind when it dictated a course of action. And now it was telling her to go low and take this monster out at the legs.

She spun and drove the heel of her foot into Crag's shin. He cried out in rage, comically hopping on one foot for a moment. Pity for him, he'd forgotten the tiger demon still held in one hand. Shitoro, however, hadn't forgotten about Crag. He raked the claws of one paw down the side of the monstrous beast's face, drawing four deep lines that quickly filled up with blood.

The surprise of the attack caused Crag to let go and Shitoro fell into Kisaki's waiting arms. She immediately dove away from the brute, landing and rolling while cushioning her friend's body with her own.

"Are you okay?" she asked him.

He looked up and smiled as best as his feline face could. "I wasn't finished with him yet."

"You are as mighty a warrior, my brave Shitoro, as you are a wonderful tutor."

"Thank you, my lady." He paused, then raised one brow. "Wait, was that an insult?"

Fortunately, before she could answer, a cry rose from the nearby rooftop. "Get the big one! Now, before he can get away!"

Kisaki was certain the *big one* wasn't looking to get away from anywhere, especially not after what she and her friend had just done. If anything, he would be angrier than ever. But she was more than happy to accept the help.

A cacophony of shots rang out, near deafening as they echoed through the street. Crag was hit over and over again, the barrage finally driving him to his knees.

"They're doing it!" she cried, hugging Shitoro tightly.

"Let me go, child," he complained.

She did, giving him a chance to change back to his humanoid form. "Good idea," she said, getting back to her feet. "There's still plenty more to take care of."

"No!" he hissed. "You don't understand. We still have Crag to deal with."

"What do you…?"

But Kisaki's question was answered once Crag began to glow. A dark blue light suffused him even as he continued to be peppered by bullets.

"We need to grab hold of something, quick!" Shitoro cried.

"Why?"

The skies above them began to darken, clouds forming where there had been nothing but clear sky before. And then those clouds began to spin, slow at first, but rapidly picking up speed.

"Oh my!" Kisaki gasped as a funnel cloud began to form high in the sky, slowly reaching down to where the wounded mazoku now stood, his arms held out above him and a cackle of laughter upon his lips.

"What is he doing?" she shouted over the rising wind.

"His people," Shitoro replied, grabbing hold of her leg as a heavy gust almost took him off his feet. "They were known in the past as storm giants!"

THIRTY-TWO

For once, Kisaki wished she'd been a better student. She remembered seeing mention of such creatures in various scrolls but couldn't remember many details. She'd been fascinated by tales of Earth, so seemingly mundane lessons, such as youkai physiology, were often ignored in favor of daydreaming.

If we survive this, I'm going to re-read every single one of them all over again, she vowed to herself as the wind intensified. Kisaki found her newfound strength formidable, but she was still a relatively petite girl. The wind whipping around Crag, leaving him untouched in the center of it all, was already peeling pieces off the nearby buildings and sending garbage and debris flying all around. It was all she could do to hold her ground against it.

Worst of all, the gunshots had ceased, as those firing upon Crag no doubt took shelter from the rising winds.

Shitoro lost his grip and was swept away, his claws scraping ing uselessly against the ground as he futilely sought to find purchase.

"Shitor…" Her words were cut short as a garbage can flew into her, knocking her off balance. The wind did the rest. Kisaki went tumbling head over heels and still the wind continued to increase. She slammed into something, a tree … no, what Tamiko had called a telephone pole, knocking the breath from her. Nevertheless, she managed to wrap her arms around it before she could be torn away.

She and the townsfolk weren't the only ones being affected. A wolf went flying past her, only to slam into the side of a building. A hawk youkai in humanoid form had been caught in the swirling maelstrom surrounding Crag. Its attempts to escape were futile, as first its feathers were stripped from its body, then it was torn limb from limb by the onslaught.

Though it was impossible to tell, Kisaki could have sworn Crag's cruel laughter carried on the roaring wind.

I have to stop this!

Unfortunately, she had no idea how. Magic, offensive or otherwise, was something she had little talent at. She could barely conjure smoke, much less a gout of fire. She had no gun, not even a bow and arrow … not that any such weapon would be particularly effective at that moment. In fact, she could think of nothing that would help against…

What the?!

There came a throbbing of heat from her side. She looked down to find her jacket had flown open, revealing the quill that had once been a sword. As her eyes locked on it, it seemed to pulse again.

She didn't know what it meant. A quill was useless as a weapon, regardless of circumstance. In the face of this monsoon, it would do nothing. Neither would a sword, for that matter, Kisaki mused, feeling her grip start to slip. Soon enough, one of two things would happen: either she'd let go, or the pole would be ripped from the ground.

She realized that she had nothing to lose either way.

Fine, let's see what this thing can do!

She let go with one hand, barely holding on by her finger-nails with the other, then reached for the quill.

Almost...

The wind caught the plumes of the feather and ripped it from her grasp. Her cries of despair were lost in the fury of the storm. She watched, helpless, as the Taiyosori flew through the air. It did not tumble as she expected. Instead it flew straight, as if shot from a crossbow, to become embedded in the wood of a bench half a block away where it held true, despite the wind continuing to buffet it.

Sadly, there was no way for her to get to it, not without being swept away. All hope seemed lost as...

A horn blared from somewhere close by, followed by a siren, its sound distorted by the wind. Kisaki looked up to see a police car. No, something larger. Tamiko had called them SUVs. One was racing down the street toward Crag, its weight keeping it on the ground and its powerful engine driving it forward.

The storm giant turned and saw it coming a moment too late. He roared in defiance and the glow around him intensi-fied. The vehicle slowed in speed but did not stop.

It slammed into Crag at greater than running pace with an audible crunch of metal. Something white expanded in the cabin, obscuring the driver from view, while Crag was sent stumbling.

He went down to one knee, catching himself before he could fall, but the glow around him ceased. As if in response, the wind immediately began to die down. Within seconds, she no longer needed to grasp the telephone pole to hold her ground.

Kisaki didn't waste any time. She knew Crag couldn't be allowed to cast his spell again. She raced forward, pushing against the remnant wind with everything she had, fighting to gain speed and gradually winning the battle.

Crag looked up with a snarl just in time to catch her knee to his face. Powerful as he was, there came the crunch of bone breaking, and he fell onto his backside clutching his bloodied nose.

It was a good blow, but far from a fatal one. Kisaki would need to remedy that.

Before she could follow through, though, the doors to the crashed SUV opened and out stepped her friends – Tamiko from the passenger side and Stephen from the driver's seat.

"Oh, yeah! Bite me, bitch," Stephen said, pointing at the downed mazoku for a moment before rubbing his forehead. "Wow, those airbags really hurt."

"How?" Kisaki asked, stunned at their arrival.

"Someone left the keys," Tamiko said a bit shakily, her hair still whipping from the dying wind. "And he does have his permit, after all."

"You didn't really think we'd let you face this thing alone, did you?" Stephen replied with a laugh. He opened the back door of the vehicle and pulled out a weapon – another shotgun, from the looks of it. "Hope the boys in blue don't mind me borrowing this too."

They all turned at the sound of a low growl. Crag was already getting back to his feet.

Kisaki didn't relish fighting with her friends in the midst of potential jeopardy, but then she realized what they had just done for her. She didn't want them in danger, but neither did they want her to be in it. That's what friends did. They cared for one another like that.

Besides, she mused, it had been arrogant for her to presume she could win this fight alone. That was more the style of a beast such as Crag, who'd casually sacrificed his own troops as fodder. As much damage as had been wrought by his spell, the youkai bodies in the street greatly outnumbered the human casualties.

Speaking of which…

"Shitoro!" Kisaki shouted.

"*Dead like the rodent he is,*" Crag snarled, standing up. He was nearly covered head to toe in bullet wounds but was still very much alive.

"You lie."

"*Do I? Even if not, then he soon shall be, just like you, little hanyou.*"

Though his spell had savaged the youkai he'd brought with him, it had also served to scatter the human resistance. The gunfire had all but stopped save for stray shots here or there sounding out, no doubt against any youkai who'd survived the storm. That wasn't good. If the humans were scared, they were unlikely to distinguish friend from foe. Kisaki turned to Tamiko.

Her friend seemingly read her mind. "I'll find him. You take care of ugly here."

Kisaki flashed her a smile, then again faced Crag.

The beast had stumbled several steps to the side. He now stood between her and the Taiyosori, still firmly embedded in the wood of the now overturned bench several dozen yards behind him. She glanced past him, debating how best to reach it.

So far as she could tell, the best way to get it was to go through Crag.

So be it.

"Go. We'll hold him," Kisaki said to her friend.

Tamiko backed up, then turned and took off. Crag watched her go with mild disinterest in his eyes. "*You think she will survive? That any here will? Today is a glorious day, little hanyou, for we begin our march back to dominance on this world. And if the daimao do not agree, then perhaps it is time for them to be swept aside as well.*"

"By you?" Kisaki asked. "Do not make me laugh."

"*Very well. Then perhaps I shall make you scream instead.*" The wall of flesh and muscle that was Crag charged forward. Big as he was, he soon filled up most of her field of vision, and he had reach to match.

Kisaki shoved Stephen to the side, away from the mazoku's grasp, leaving her flank vulnerable to Crag for a second, but it was all he needed to fall upon her. One massive arm wrapped around her with frightening strength.

Kisaki had counted on that, though, remembering the lesson shown to her in the vision by her father. She bent and twisted, hoping she possessed enough strength to do what she'd planned.

For a moment, she feared she wasn't strong enough, but then Crag was pulled off his feet and sent flying over her shoulder. He landed on his back with a heavy grunt.

"Whoa. Remind me not to piss you off," Stephen said before breaking out in a trot toward Crag.

"What are you doing?" Kisaki called after him, but he was already outside of her reach.

"Repaying you for Robbie," he yelled back, lifting the gun to his shoulder.

Crag sat up and slammed a fist into the asphalt, obviously more angry than injured. He rose to one knee and turned, only to find himself face to face with the barrel of Stephen's gun.

"Smile for the birdie."

He pulled the trigger, emptying the weapon point blank in Crag's face.

After their previous battle, Kisaki thought she would never welcome the demise of another living being. But she hadn't counted on ever meeting a creature as reprehensible as the one they now fought. She cried out a cheer and raised her fist as Crag's face seemed to disappear in a mist of blood and smoke.

He fell back and lay unmoving as more voices rose to accompany hers.

She turned to find the police, some on the rooftop and others on the street, clapping. At the sound of celebration, other townsfolk came out from behind closed doors to do the same.

One of the police officers, a man with more authority about him than the sergeant, approached Stephen, who was still standing with the gun pointed, as if unsure that what he'd done had actually worked.

"Maybe you should give that to me, son," the officer said, resting a gentle hand on Stephen's shoulder.

That seemed to shake her friend from his daze. "Oh, um yeah. Sorry about … well, y'know."

"We can talk about it later, but considering the weird-ass circumstances, I think we'll write this one up as a wash." He turned toward Kisaki. "As for you. How in hell did you manage to…"

The sound of an approaching engine caught their attention and they turned to see another vehicle round a corner and approach them, swerving to avoid debris and unmoving youkai alike.

Kisaki was confused. Was someone else trying to help them? If so, they were a little late.

"Oh no, not now," the officer said. He grabbed hold of something by his side, a box of sorts. It was larger than Tamiko's phone, but he spoke into it much the same. "Coulson, you there?"

A voice spoke back, clearly audible. "*Yes, Captain.*"

"Get down here with Finchberg and cordon off this area ASAP. I want a blanket over everything weird, especially the big guy, and I want it done before our *guests* can start shooting."

"*Roger, Captain.*"

Shooting? Kisaki turned toward the vehicle, even larger than the SUV Stephen had driven. WGXP NEWS was printed on the side in large letters. Were these more enemies come to challenge them?

If so, the captain, as he was called, appeared to be far more annoyed than alarmed. He turned to Stephen. "Get your friend and find someplace out of sight. I don't want you talking to…"

He wasn't given a chance to finish as a snarl of pure rage rent the air.

Crag was still alive.

THIRTY-THREE

ONE MOMENT, THERE had been no sign of life from his body. The next, Crag sat up with a growl of anger. Half his face was in ruins from the shotgun blast. He was missing an eye, and parts of his skull could be seen.

Grievous as his injuries seemed to be, they didn't appear to slow him as he leapt to his feet and descended upon the unwary captain.

He pulled in the officer, still futilely trying to draw his own gun, and wrapped his massive hands around the man's head.

There came the sickening crunch of bone, and then Crag threw him to the side, discarding him as if he were one of the dolls Kisaki had once played with as a small child. The captain flew into the side of the battered SUV, then slid off onto the ground where he lay unmoving.

As this happened, the second vehicle's brakes screeched and it came to a halt not twenty feet away.

A door on the side flew open and two people, a man and a woman, came charging out. The man was holding something over his shoulder, a black device not quite as long as Stephen's gun, but bulkier.

Please be a weapon, Kisaki thought as she raced forward and grabbed hold of her friend's arm, dragging Stephen back as the man and woman approached them.

"Please tell me you're getting all of this," the woman said.

"Oh yeah. This is going to be the top headline for weeks."

The man pointed the device toward Kisaki. "Not us!" she cried to him. "Fire it at Crag!"

"Fire?"

"That's not a gun," Stephen said. "It's a camera."

"A camera? Why are they using that here?"

"Probably because they're insane."

Murder shone in Crag's remaining eye, but he seemed unfocused, as if he were still dazed from the blast. Kisaki realized she needed to get to the Taiyosori before he cleared his head and…

And then what? She and Stephen continued to back away from the furious mazoku, but the truth was, she had no idea what to do once she retrieved the quill.

Everyone seemed to think it was an all-powerful weapon, but she hadn't seen it do anything but turn into a feather and give out the occasional shock. It had stunned Shitoro when he'd touched it, but no more. What hope would it be against a monster like Crag?

"Get out of the way!"

The warning came from the police officers still on the rooftop of their building, again taking aim at the massive demon. However, the man with the camera and his female companion were too close, continuing on whatever mad quest possessed them.

"Run!" Kisaki screamed at them.

They only moved back once Crag got dangerously near, their only salvation being that the monster still appeared to be confused. He snarled at them as he passed, then charged the vehicle they'd come in.

With a roar of rage, he slammed into it, tipping it over onto its side. He drove his fists into it, denting the metal like it was paper, but then he abruptly stopped. He raised one hand to his injured head and gave it a shake.

When he looked up again, the grogginess was gone from his face. He turned, surveying the scene, and then saw Kisaki and her friend. "*You!*"

"Come with me!" Kisaki cried. She grabbed hold of Stephen's arm and pulled him in the direction where the Taiyosori lay. Unfortunately, his foot caught on a broken piece of asphalt and he stumbled into her, knocking her off balance.

"Sorry," he said, helping her back to her feet.

"Come on!"

He nodded. "Did you see what he did to that van?"

"Yes," Kisaki replied. "It's the same thing he will do to us if…" She trailed off. Crag was gone. He'd just been standing next to the van. But now, all she saw was the clearly insane human couple. The woman was speaking into a stubby black object while the man pointed the camera their way.

"*Going somewhere?*"

Kisaki spun to find Crag blocking her way again. For something so large, he moved disturbingly fast.

"*I am going to enjoy killing you. I will rip your screaming head from your body and throw it down at your mother's feet. She will know the pain of loss before I cut her down. Now where is…*"

Unfortunately for them, Crag was seemingly not as stupid as Shitoro had made him out to be. He inclined his head, then turned to follow her gaze.

"Something of interest behind me, little hanyou? Something you lost in the storm, perhaps." He smiled, showing cracked and bloodied teeth. *"Maybe a friend of yours … a certain tiger youkai who has been living on borrowed time for far too long? Or maybe a weapon."*

"It is not yours," she warned.

"Oh? And you claim it? You, a hanyou, lowest of the low. Bastard child of two worlds, yet belonging to neither. I think not. It is time the Taiyosori was possessed by one both worthy of its power and not afraid to use it."

He took a step back, the smile never leaving his ruined face.

Stephen grabbed her arm. "Kisaki, don't. He's goading you."

She knew that but realized she needed to act. The sword rightfully belonged to her mother. She'd already dishonored herself enough during this foray, being stupid and selfish at almost every turn. She wouldn't allow this beast to take what wasn't his.

Besides, Stephen had proven that Crag could be hurt. And what could be hurt could be killed.

With a battle cry of her own, she pulled free from her friend's grasp and charged. If she couldn't use the weapon against him, then she would be the weapon herself.

Again, though, Crag proved himself to be more intelligent than she gave him credit for. Her attack was rushed, sloppy. His was measured, backhanding her away almost contemptuously.

Kisaki flew backwards and barreled into Stephen, sending them both down in a tangle of arms and legs.

"Ooh, that had to have hurt," the man with the camera said from some distance away.

"Shut up and keep filming," his companion ordered.

Kisaki paid them no mind. She rolled off Stephen and turned to check on him. "Are you okay?"

"Nothing a couple weeks in traction won't fix," he wheezed. "You're heavier than you look."

She reached down to help him up, but he waved her off. "Go!"

"But…"

"I'm okay. Just be more careful this time."

She gave him a single nod, then turned to find Crag walking away from them, taking an almost leisurely pace toward where the Taiyosori still stood, sticking out of the ruined bench. He was almost there, just a few more steps.

Kisaki ran after him, moving quickly and with deliberation. She knew if she went high, he'd catch her again. She might be smaller and more agile, but he was far more seasoned than she. Injured or not, he had the advantage in raw power and durability. Truth be told, she had no real idea how to stop such a creature.

But maybe she didn't need to stop him.

Perhaps slowing him down would be enough.

She went low, diving at Crag's legs. Massive as he was, she was almost certain she'd bounce off, but she hit him solidly in the back of his knees and he tumbled forward.

There was no time for celebration, talking, or anything else. By the time he hit the ground, Kisaki was already back on her feet again. She raced past him, mindful of his long grasp.

She reached the Taiyosori and plucked it from its spot. Despite the wind, it was completely unruffled, in perfect condition, as if it hadn't been touched at all.

"Please become a sword again!" she pleaded with it.

A shadow fell over her and she spun toward it, only to be grabbed around the neck by a massive hand. Her air was immediately cut off and she was lifted from the ground as if she weighed nothing, which was probably not far from the truth for the mazoku.

"I knew if I let you, you would lead me right to it," Crag said with a laugh, spittle flying from his mouth. He glanced down at the quill in her hand. *"I must admit, I would never have considered this. Quite the disguise. Tell me, how did you do it? A glamour perhaps? Some other hanyou trick, maybe?"* He looked at Kisaki's rapidly reddening face. *"Oh, right. You can't answer. That's okay. There is really nothing left for you to say anyway."*

Kisaki tried to pry Crag's fingers loose with her free hand, but it was a losing battle. His strength was immense and she had little leverage dangling in midair as she was.

She thought she felt the Taiyosori throb hotly in her hand but realized she was probably imagining it. She was rapidly beginning to feel dizzy from the lack of air, and Crag didn't appear to be in the mood to let up anytime soon.

He drew her close, blowing his rancid breath in her face. *"And now, I think I shall claim my prize, insignificant as it might appear."*

He reached up to pluck the Taiyosori from her grasp.

The enchantments placed upon the great blade of heaven were many, but among them were three tenants which determined who the weapon would judge worthy to wield it.

The sword could be gifted from one rightful owner to another, assuming no trickery or deceit was used. Unbeknownst to most, the weapon possessed a rudimentary consciousness about it and could sense such duplicity.

It could be inherited. A rightful heir could attempt to lay claim to the weapon. If judged worthy, they would then become its rightful master. The blade could be a fickle thing if it so chose, however, and sometimes that judgment took time.

Finally, the sword could be won in fair combat. A worthy adversary, one who laid the sword's current owner low, could lay claim to it upon the owner's defeat. A duel of honor would satisfy these demands, if indeed the blade sensed such. However, most often, it was upon the previous owner's death.

If any other method were used to claim the blade, it would reject its would-be master, using force commensurate with the thief's power to *dissuade* them.

Such was Crag's folly. Had he kept his grip upon Kisaki for a few minutes longer, enough to assure her life force was snuffed out, then perhaps the fate of the heavens would have changed. Perhaps he would have laid claim to the blade and used it to set the celestial palace ablaze, proclaiming himself a god in the process.

But in his shortsighted greed, the mazoku warlord placed his hands upon the weapon while Kisaki was still conscious.

In short, he tried to steal it from her.

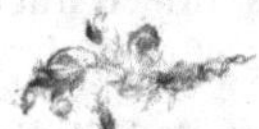

Crag's hand closed upon the blade turned quill.

Kisaki expected it to be plucked from her grasp with the barest of effort, but instead, the look of triumph on Crag's face turned to one of shock and then pain.

Glancing over as best she could, Kisaki saw the quill glowing, first red, then blue. She wasn't sure what it meant, but then Crag's hand, still grasping the top of the feather, burst aflame.

The fire, blue hot, traveled up his arm, igniting the fur as it went and leaving behind an acrid smell that burned Kisaki's nostrils.

Hold on, I can breathe!

Crag's grip upon her loosened as he screamed in pain, either unwilling to or, as seemed to be the case, unable to let go of the Taiyosori.

Finally, he dropped her. She fell to the ground, the quill pulled from his grasp by her weight. He beat at the flames with his uninjured hand, but the damage had been done. His right arm had been reduced to a charred mass of burnt flesh.

Crag reared back and screamed to the sky, the sound echoing around them, audible for perhaps miles. Kisaki coughed, trying to catch her breath. With every battle she'd fought, her body had proven far stronger than she'd imagined. Thankfully, it was more durable, too. Despite some lingering pain, she seemed to be otherwise okay.

However, she realized that might not be the case for long.

Crag looked down upon her, misery etched upon his face, which then gave way to pure unadulterated anger. "*You! Do you see what you have done to me?!*"

All at once, the doubt Kisaki had felt vanished. She hadn't known what to do with the Taiyosori once she retrieved it. If anything, she'd feared it might be useless to her. But she saw now that it wasn't. It was indeed filled with power and, if so, that meant she could use it.

"I do see now," Kisaki replied. She kicked out, catching Crag in the ankle with a forceful blow, strong enough to knock his leg out from under him and drive him to one knee before her. "But you do not."

With one fluid motion, she drove the tip of the quill through Crag's remaining eye, blinding him.

The demon screamed out and reached up to claw at his face, but Kisaki quickly backed up, still holding the now bloody quill.

Crag began to beat at the ground around him. "*I will kill you! I will find you and your friends and I will kill you all!*"

"No," Kisaki said, that cold logic seemingly filling all of the voids within her. "You will never kill another again. I will see to it."

The quill trembled in her grasp at her words. It heated up again, but not painfully so. Instead, it was a comfortable warmth, as if it were a living thing. It began to glow, growing brighter until it again reminded Kisaki of a supernova. She looked away but could still feel it in her hand, except now it was different. Gone was the softness of the feathered quill and in its place was a solid grip as if she were holding…

The light died down and Kisaki saw it was true. The Taiyosori was once again a gleaming translucent blade filled with an ocean of stars, but she knew now it wasn't glass. It was more, so much more.

But none of that would matter if Crag had his say. Blinded as he was, he'd heard her. He stumbled her way, reaching down to batter the ground as he went, no doubt hoping to crush her with a lucky blow.

She grasped the grip of the sword with both hands and waited for the right moment.

Crag's titanic fist momentarily blotted out the sun as he raised it above her and brought it down where she stood.

At the last possible second she sidestepped, and he again tore a gouge out of the concrete of the sidewalk, but it brought the rest of him level with her height.

Now!

Kisaki swung with all she had, expecting to meet resistance from the mazoku's massively muscled form, but the blade sliced through his neck as easily as if cutting through rice paper. Crag's head, a look of surprise upon its face, tumbled away from his body and came to rest several feet away as the rest of him crashed to the ground.

The hunter, so long the scourge of any who stood in his way, had been felled.

THIRTY-FOUR

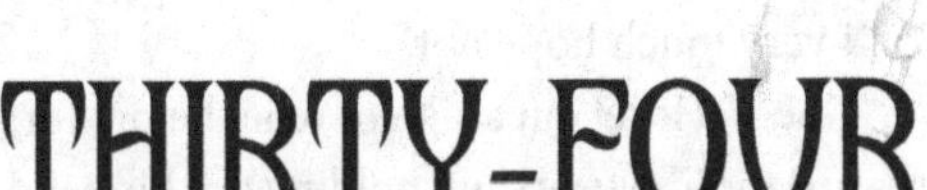

FOR A TIME, Kisaki simply stood peering down at Crag's body, as if unable to believe what she'd just done.

You have been judged worthy, my master.

At first, she was confused, wondering why someone had called her that, but then she realized she hadn't heard it with her ears, but in her mind.

She looked down at the sword, her eyes wide. "Did you just speak to me?"

If it had, it was now silent. The only thing Kisaki heard were the ambient sounds of the town around her, quiet now that the battle had ended.

"Holy crap, you did it!"

She looked up to find Stephen headed her way. He ran up and grabbed hold of her in a hug. Then, almost as if realizing what he was doing, he backed up a step, looking embarrassed for whatever reason.

"Heh," he said, looking down at the Taiyosori. "Is that a sword in your pocket or are you just glad to see me?"

She inclined her head at him, not understanding. "It's not in my pocket."

"I know, it's a … never mind. You were amazing."

"It wasn't me," she said softly. "It … the sword…"

"Yeah," he replied, looking it over. "Pretty wild. Although I'd be lying if I said that was the weirdest thing I've seen today." He gestured toward Crag's body. "By the way, he isn't going to get back up again, is he?"

"I very much hope not."

"Good." He let out a sigh of relief before turning once more toward the Taiyosori and holding out his hand. "Could I? Just for a second anyway. I mean, I haven't seen anything this cool since *Conan the Barbarian*. Heck, Frostmourne's got nothing on this bad boy."

She backed up a step. "I'm sorry, but touching it would likely destroy you."

"You're kidding, right?" He let out a laugh, but then noticed how she shook her head. "You're not kidding? Okay, I'll take your word for it then. It's still pretty darn cool."

Kisaki smiled. "I believe you are right. It is indeed cool."

"Although not even remotely inconspicuous."

"True, it is perhaps a bit overly..."

Kisaki trailed off as the sword began to glow again. The blood upon the blade instantly evaporated and then the glow intensified until it was once more painful to watch. When it cleared, she was once again holding a mere quill.

She and Stephen looked at each other in amazement, then back at the former weapon. "Better?" she asked after a moment.

"A cell phone would probably stand out less, but yeah. I'd say so," he replied with a laugh. "I guess in this case, the sword is actually mightier than the pen."

"Hey! How did you do that?"

Kisaki and Stephen turned to find the woman from the van approaching them, followed by the man with the camera. He aimed it at Crag's body for several seconds, then turned it toward Kisaki.

"You're certain that's not a weapon?" she whispered to Stephen.

"Depends on who you ask," he replied.

She looked at him sidelong for a few moments while the woman turned toward the camera and spoke. "Beth Billingsly here for Excitement News. Cartersville, a sleepy little town in the middle of nowhere. Normally a quiet place, one where you can safely leave your doors unlocked at night. But today, it's become a battleground in a war between monsters. Impossible to believe, but true. I can assure you, no camera tricks were used in the footage you just saw, nor now as we show you the aftermath of this battle in which the age-old words of King Kong were proven true. 'Twas beauty slayed the beast."

"Who is she talking to?" Kisaki asked. "Has she been driven mad by fear?"

"They're a local news affiliate out of Punxsutawney," Stephen explained in a hushed tone. "My mom sometimes watches them. They usually cover boring stuff: bake sales, pig roasts, crap like that."

"News?"

"You know, like gossip, except on TV."

"I do not know..."

Before Kisaki could say more, the woman stepped up and shoved something at her face, the cylindrical object she'd been wielding. Kisaki raised her hands in a defensive stance, but Stephen spoke up before she could throw a punch.

"Not a weapon," he whispered out of the corner of his mouth. "Just a microphone. It records your voice."

"Ah. Like a magic glyph."

"Excuse me?" the woman asked before turning back toward the man with the camera. "Keep rolling, we'll edit that out."

He gave her a thumbs up.

"I think I speak for the residents of this town, nay, perhaps the whole state when I ask how does it feel to have done what you have accomplished today?"

"Feel?" Kisaki replied. "I simply did what I had to. Many more would have suffered had I not."

"Tell me, do you have any regrets killing Sasquatch?"

"Sasquatch? You mean the storm giant? I regret the path he chose, that he attacked this town rather than leave peacefully. I regret that he slaughtered my friend's people a millennia ago. However, I do not regret ending the threat that Crag presented."

The woman raised a skeptical eyebrow toward Kisaki, but kept asking questions. "Crag? Was that its name?"

"Yes."

"And would you feel different knowing he might be an endangered species?"

"I believe I have already noted that he was a danger, to my friends as well as all those who walk upon this world. That danger would have been magnified a hundredfold had he managed to take possession of the Taiyosori."

"Oh boy," Stephen muttered by her side.

"Tie oh sore ee?" Beth asked, butchering the pronunciation.

"The blade of heaven," Kisaki explained. "A weapon of divine power."

"A weapon of … mass destruction, you might say?"

"No," Stephen said, jumping in front of Kisaki. "She did not say that. Nobody is saying that."

"Cut! Listen, kid, you can have your turn when I'm finished with her. But if this is something that people need to be aware of, then I'd suggest you get out of my way. My viewers have a right to know."

"All six of them?"

"Not after tonight's broadcast. Now kindly…"

"Oh great, the cops are headed this way," the man with the camera said.

"Quick, start rolling again." She pushed the microphone past Stephen. "Can we at least know your name?"

"I am Kisaki, daughter of Midnite…"

"Kisaki, Stephen!"

The pair immediately turned toward the sound of Tamiko's voice. She was waving to them from several buildings down. "Come quick! I need your help."

"People need to know if they're in any…"

Kisaki interrupted the reporter. "You must please pardon me, but my friend requires our assistance."

Stephen paused long enough to smirk in the news woman's direction, then they both turned toward Tamiko.

This didn't appear to discourage Beth in the least as she started talking again the second they stepped away. "You heard it here first on Excitement News. The impossible has come true. The world has its very first superhero and her name is … Midnight Girl."

Kisaki and Stephen ran to where Tamiko stood beckoning them on. As they neared their friend, she glanced over at him.

"Tell me. What is a superhero?"

Kisaki practically bowled over Tamiko, grabbing her in a hug and lifting her from her feet.

"Whoa!" she said. "Someone has been eating their vitamins."

"And then some," Stephen added.

"I'm so glad you're okay," Kisaki said at last, putting Tamiko down.

"Me too. I hated to leave you guys alone against that freak, but I didn't know what else I could do to help."

"You served an important purpose. It is far more honorable than perishing needlessly."

"I was hoping you'd say that. Speaking of which, that's why I was yelling for you."

"Not just saving us from the paparazzi?" Stephen asked with a grin.

"I found Shitoro," she said, "but I need your help with him."

"Is he ... hurt?" Kisaki asked hesitantly.

"I don't know," Tamiko admitted. "Best come see for yourself."

They followed her as she ran past another building, then turned behind it, where a large pile of trash stood heaped against the wall.

"Where?"

Kisaki's question was answered almost immediately by a small voice echoing from somewhere. "Human? Human, are you still there? I swear, if you have abandoned me, I shall call down a curse that will..."

"Shitoro?" Kisaki cried.

"Mistress Kisaki?" he replied from somewhere unseen. "Oh, thank the elder gods you're okay. I thought the worst when Crag unleashed his spell."

"Where are you?"

"That's what I wanted to show you," Tamiko said, leading the way.

On the far side of the trash pile lay a small metal canister, a waste basket if Kisaki remembered correctly. Shitoro's feet were sticking up out of it.

"See what I mean?" Tamiko gestured toward it. "I've been trying to get him out, but he's stuck."

"Does that sword of yours double as a can opener?" Stephen asked with a smirk.

"I do not know," Kisaki replied, grinning, understanding it was a joke. "But perhaps it wouldn't be wise to find out."

"Okay, then, let's do this the hard way. Tamiko, hold on to the pail with me. Kisaki, you grab his feet."

The next few minutes were spent alternately trying to force Shitoro free and gently trying to twist him out, all to his continued complaints about their ineptitude.

Finally, he came loose with an audible pop, sending both sides tumbling into the pile of trash.

"Well, this is gross," Tamiko complained.

"Oh, come on. I'm not that bad," Stephen said from beneath her.

"I … err … didn't mean it that way."

He laughed. "I know. Help me up. I'm sitting on something that's kind of sticky."

"I think we're back to gross again." She chuckled and offered him a hand.

Over on the other side, Shitoro stood and began to dust himself off. "Many thanks, my lady."

"Eh hem," Tamiko said.

"And you humans, too. I suppose you do have your uses at times. I…" He paused as he looked Kisaki over. "What happened to your neck?"

"This?" She reached up and touched her throat, still a bit tender from being manhandled. "Courtesy of Crag."

"That brute!" Shitoro cried. "Where is he? I shall teach him a lesson that one even as dense as he won't soon forget."

"Pushing up daisies," Stephen replied.

"Daisies? What do flowers have to do with…"

"I believe Stephen means he is no more." Kisaki glanced his way and he nodded. She then noticed Tamiko standing next to him, her cheeks bright pink. "Did the storm giant strike you, too?"

"Me?" Tamiko asked, quickly stepping away from Stephen. "No. It's just … kinda warm out, is all."

"Wait," Shitoro said, glancing between the trio. "You vanquished Crag?"

"Yes," Kisaki replied.

"With your bare hands?"

"No. He was too powerful for me to…"

Stephen clapped her on the back. "Don't sell yourself short. You knocked him on his butt more than once. And throwing him over your shoulder? That was freaking cool."

"Truly?" Shitoro asked. "Amazing. Crag was impressively strong, even for a mazoku. Yet you managed to hold your ground against him?"

"For a time," she replied.

"A mere second is more than most can lay claim to. Believe me, I know."

She bent down, put a hand on his shoulder, and looked him in the eye. "Know that your people are avenged, my friend. Crag died on his knees."

Shitoro nodded solemnly but still pressed on. "How?"

After a moment, she said, "The Taiyosori."

"Ah, I think I see. He tried to take it and it struck him down."

"He did, but it merely wounded him. I … it turned back to its true form for a time and I used it to behead him."

"*You* wielded the Taiyosori?"

"Yes. I have held it since leaving the…"

Shitoro waved a hand dismissively. "The Taiyosori allowed you to take it, yes, I already know that. It accepted your blood as that of your mother's line. But to allow you to wield it in battle, a thing which has not been done for several millennia at least, that means it has accepted you as its new master."

"But it's my mother's sword."

Shitoro placed a hand on his chin and thought about it for a moment. "Perhaps no longer."

Tamiko finally stepped between them. "Enough with the gloomy faces. Kisaki just kicked that monster's butt and saved the town. That calls for a celebration to me." She turned and began to lead them out of the alleyway.

"I'm not sure the town is in any condition to celebrate."

"Then we'll figure out something," she replied. "At the very least, let's find someplace to eat. I don't know about the rest of you, but fighting storm giants leaves me starving."

Unseen by Kisaki, her friends, or many others who were present to bear witness to the events of that day, another set of eyes watched it all from the shadows.

Small, black, and beady, they followed the battle with nervous anticipation.

A wolf spotted the interloper at one point and gave chase, but he managed to lose it by virtue of his small size and quickness.

Then, when Crag cast his spell, he had almost been swept away by the raging winds that followed, managing to barely find shelter in time.

All he truly wanted was to run and get as far away from this accursed place as he could. But he'd been given orders, and such matters weren't to be ignored lightly. He had already displeased his master once and suffered greatly for it, only surviving by his good graces. He wouldn't risk that again.

The girl had put up a surprisingly good fight. Even among his own people, Crag was considered a superior warrior, nearly unbeatable on the battlefield. Yet this girl and her pathetic human pets had managed to not only bloody the mazoku, but wound him grievously in the process.

However, in the end, it had all seemed for naught, and he'd been certain that the hanyou would die badly. But the girl had one more surprise in store for Crag – the very reason that he'd been sent to observe her – the Taiyosori.

At first, he'd been confused as to why she would attempt to use something as useless as a quill against a beast such as Crag. He'd stolen plenty of them in his time and never once found them to be of much use for anything. But then she'd proven him wrong by actually blinding the mazoku with it. It seemed impossible, but what happened next made that look mundane by comparison.

It wasn't a quill at all.

It was the Taiyosori, that which his master lusted endlessly for. Somehow, it was on this world and being wielded by the hands of a mere half-breed.

Within moments, the fight was over and Crag lay dead, vanquished by the most ignoble of foes.

He ignored the rest, as he processed that which had transpired. Besides, he had the information he needed.

Ito slipped away into a stand of trees, where he transformed back to his bipedal form. He pulled a crystal, grey as the sky during Crag's conjuring, from his robes and commanded it to take him back to the celestial palace.

THIRTY-FIVE

THOUGH NEITHER WAS aware of the other doing so, Ito was not the only youkai to visit Earth that day.

In a flash of light, bright but tinged on the edges with a deep blackness, Tanaki reappeared in Kisaki's study along with three of Midnite's other servants.

Though the sending chamber was the normal place of transport to other worlds – the spells woven into its framework specifically designed to aid in sending magic – it wasn't the only means of egress from the celestial palace. This was especially true where the daimao were concerned.

Midnite dismissed the spell, a concentration of energy in the form of a sending circle, once her servants returned. To keep it active was to risk it being sensed by her siblings, something she very much preferred not happen.

She immediately noted the lack of her daughter or Shitoro among them, worry continuing to etch her face. "Anything, Tanaki?"

The badger youkai averted her eyes and gave a single shake of her head. "No, mistress. We scoured the island where you sent Shitoro, but with little luck. We found residual traces of his scent along with that of your daughter, but there was no sign of them otherwise."

"First Kisaki and now Shitoro," Midnite said to herself. "What is afoot on that world?"

"Wherever they are, my lady, I believe they are together." She nodded to the canine youkai standing by her side. "Kita?"

The larger youkai nodded in deference to Tanaki. "If it pleases you, my lady, I believe that Shitoro was able to locate your daughter. I found his scent mingled with hers."

"That is no surprise," Midnite replied. "Shitoro was sent to the same spot Kisaki would have appeared."

"I beg pardon," the dog youkai said, "but I do not believe that is the case. The age of their lingering scents matched. They stood upon the beach together. I am certain of it. But they were not alone. I also detected the scent of a human there."

"The entire planet is full of humans, Kita."

"As I am aware, and indeed the sand reeked of them. But one in particular matched the age of Shitoro and Kisaki's scents."

"Are you certain?" Midnite asked.

"Yes, my lady."

"Where did they go?"

Kita glanced sidelong at Tanaki, who again nodded. "That is difficult to know. They did not appear to *go* anywhere. Kisaki's scent approached from the direction of a place of gathering for the humans. Shitoro's was from elsewhere. I believe he had been scouring the island for your daughter, and that is where he finally found her. Both scents lead to that same spot, but then go no further."

"Do you think this human is responsible for my daughter's disappearance?"

"No, I do not."

Midnite considered this. She debated arguing with the youkai, but then stopped herself. Kita was her best tracker. Her nose was exceptional even among her own kind. It was why Midnite had asked her to go on this risky mission after Shitoro failed to return. If she said something was so, then Midnite had no cause to doubt her. "Please continue."

"Thank you, mistress," Kita said with a deferential bow. "The scent was from a young human. Female, just entering the flower of womanhood but not fully grown. I very much doubt such a being could be responsible for abducting your daughter."

"I will remind you that my daughter is no warrior. She has lived her entire life between these walls, sheltered from those who would do her harm."

"I meant no disrespect, my lady," Kita quickly added, "but your blood flows in Kisaki's veins. Surely that makes her far more than a mere human."

Midnite's eyes narrowed. Worry was making her temper short. She was aware that some hanyou were born with powers. Occasionally, they mimicked that of their parents, but just as often, they were an odd quirk of the mixing of human and divine blood. But Kisaki had never shown any such talents. It was something Shitoro had been told to be mindful of. So far as she was aware, Kisaki was essentially human, albeit with a greatly exaggerated lifespan. Considering her sheltered upbringing, that made her vulnerable not only to youkai, but to other humans as well.

"There is also Shitoro to consider," Tanaki quickly added. "He is more than capable of dealing with a lone human."

Finally, Midnite's expression softened and she nodded for them to continue.

"There is also one additional oddity. The human's scent ended abruptly at the same time as Shitoro's and Kisaki's," Kita said. "Wherever they were sent, I believe the human accompanied them."

"Sent?" Midnite asked. "Why would you use that word?"

"I can find no other reason for their sudden disappearance," Kita explained. "There is also…" She trailed off as if uncertain how to continue.

"Kita?"

"I cannot be certain, my lady. There were many odors present, some quite alien to me. But I could have sworn that I caught the faintest trace of miasma there as well."

Ichitiro's bad mood had passed, but his good moods were often not much better. Indeed, he was sometimes crueler when his spirits were high. When he was in a foul temper, he often took it out upon his surroundings, creating a mess for his servants to clean up, but leaving them relatively intact. When he wasn't occupied with destroying his chambers, that meant he was more likely to do something that meant pain and suffering for those who lived to serve him.

He was a stark contrast to Midnite, who considered her youkai's loyalty to be something worth earning. Ichitiro thought nothing of the sort. Those who served him did so absolutely, out of fear or awe of his power. To show him anything less than the most groveling subservience was to invite disaster.

If anything, it had been even worse before Reiden had laid down his edict against travel. In the past, if a youkai displeased Ichitiro, he could kill them and have them replaced within the hour. Now, he was forced to be more mindful. His pool of servants was limited. He couldn't steal other youkai from his siblings and force them to do his bidding, not without being noticed. And, despite his lack of respect for Reiden's orders, any new youkai brought to the palace would be quickly noticed. As such, he was forced to curb his baser nature, but only by a bit. The healing properties available in the palace were more than enough to ensure that the only way one of Ichitiro's servants perished was if he truly wished it to happen.

As such, he took great satisfaction in his current meal – a small monkey youkai, normally tasked with cleaning the upper reaches of Ichitiro's domain that the other servants had trouble reaching.

Not today, though. The monkey's screams as Ichitiro ripped off an arm and began to strip the flesh from the appendage were music to his ears, a serenade to aid his digestion. He imagined the monkey was Crag, the overbearing mazoku he'd hired to track down Midnite's bastard offspring and, more importantly, the Taiyosori.

It still seemed such an absurd concept to him, that one so low could do such a thing. However, Ichitiro was not one to let the potential for opportunity pass. At the very least, it served as an amusing distraction from the normal boredom that the palace offered.

He could have conscripted some other demon to do his bidding, one that could have tracked the hanyou and reported back to him without bringing any undue attention to themselves. But that was precisely why he had paid Crag. The mazoku was battle hardened and experienced, but he was also known for being stupid and shortsighted when his dander was up. For over seventy years, Crag had stewed on Earth. Ichitiro was certain the fool was spoiling for a fight after all this time. He suspected that Crag would barrel ahead like a petulant child, causing chaos and death wherever he stepped.

Ichitiro wanted war with the humans. A brute like Crag was just the tool to make mankind once more painfully aware that they shared their puny world with superior beings. Even Reiden would be hard-pressed to ignore such an occurrence.

The only potential wildcard to his plan was the Taiyosori, if indeed it turned out to be in possession of the hanyou. It was well known that Crag was displeased with his place in the cosmic order. He resented the daimao, much as Ichitiro resented the elder gods.

In the hands of a weakling hanyou, the Taiyosori might as well be no better than a shard of worthless glass. But if Crag killed it and subsequently seized control of the weapon for himself, it could make him a potential threat.

Ichitiro did not think that scenario likely, but he was no fool. After Ito had healed sufficiently, he'd commanded the ferret to Earth to spy on Crag. If he was successful in his mission and somehow managed to attain the weapon, Ichitiro would be notified immediately so that he could take proper action against the mazoku – preferably before his siblings were able to mobilize.

A slight tingle in the back of his mind caused Ichitiro to pause before he could tear off the monkey's other arm. He smiled, revealing his sharp, blood-stained teeth. It was almost as if his very thoughts had summoned the little youkai.

The doors to Ichitiro's inner chamber opened and Ito scrambled in, practically tripping over himself in the process. The pathetic runt of a youkai dropped to his knees before the daimao and began prostrating himself. It was tiresome, but not entirely unexpected. Despite his recent healing bath, the scars from their last meeting were still visible beneath Ito's mangy coat.

His meal forgotten, he tossed the bleeding monkey to the side and turned to the ferret.

"My lord and master," Ito squeaked. "If it pleases you, I seek an audience."

"Yes, yes, on with it," Ichitiro said with an impatient wave of his hand.

"Thank you, my lord."

Ichitiro couldn't help but notice the little youkai seemed nervous, even more so than usual. He sincerely hoped the ferret wasn't here to report failure. Ichitiro could not let such incompetence stand. He would have the youkai flayed, and this time, no healing bath would be drawn. "Speak now or feel my wrath."

"Yes, my lord."

"What of the hanyou?"

"A female, my lord. I overheard her friends call her Kisaki."

"Kisaki?" Ichitiro rolled it over his tongue a few times. "A weak name for a pathetic creature. You are certain she is my sister's bastard offspring?"

"I have little doubt, my lord. She looks very much like Lady Midnite, save her hair and skin. It is as if your sister were reborn as a human."

Ichitiro bared his teeth. "Regardless of my disdain for my brethren, know that I will not tolerate any daimao being insulted as such by the likes of you. Tread lightly, Ito. I shall not warn you again."

"My apologies!" The ferret began to prostrate himself again, smacking his head against the floor each time he bowed.

Eventually, the daimao waved for him to stop. Much more and he'd knock himself senseless, which would do little to sate Ichitiro's curiosity.

"Thank you, my lord," he said groggily, blood dripping from the top of his head.

"Get back to it. The hanyou is dead, yes?"

"No, my lord."

Ichitiro sat up straight in his chair. "Are you telling me that Crag failed to find her?"

"No, master. He found her. Brought youkai with him and attacked a human settlement, just as you wisely foretold."

Ichitiro smiled. *Ah, Crag, so stupidly predictable.* If the hanyou was alive, that meant she escaped him somehow. Perhaps the storm giant was losing his touch. Too much time spent living in the trees, doing little more than picking gnats from his fur. "Did he destroy the human settlement?"

"He tried, my lord."

"*Tried?*"

"Indeed, he caused great damage with his powers, but it still stands."

Ichitiro began to grind his teeth. He was starting to get annoyed. Sadly, Crag wasn't here to vent that annoyance on. But Ito was. "So the hanyou escaped and Crag pursued her, leaving the town standing. So be it. Where is he now and is he still hunting her?"

"No, my lord. Crag lies dead in the human settlement. The hanyou vanquished him."

"*What?!*" Ichitiro slammed both fists down onto the arms of his throne, shattering the thick stony material, then stood up. Of all the scenarios he had planned for, this hadn't even remotely been a consideration. Crag the hunter laid low by a mongrel hanyou? "If you are making this up, Ito, I promise your suffering shall know no end."

"Never, my lord," the youkai screeched, glancing toward the door as if contemplating his chances for escape.

Ichitiro noted to himself that if his servant was in such a panic, then perhaps he was telling the truth. "How did this happen?"

"The Taiyosori, my lord," Ito replied. "The hanyou wielded it against Crag and laid him low by its blade."

Ichitiro commanded Ito to recount everything he saw, down to the minute detail. For a being who had witnessed the infancy of time, who had fought the entropic chaos, and who had battled myriad creatures on countless worlds, the daimao still found himself utterly stupefied by what he heard.

Much of the Taiyosori's history was shrouded in mystery, even to him, but so far as he was aware, nothing short of a god had ever wielded it in battle. Though Midnite was given possession of it, he had never actually seen her use it in anger. He had barely seen her wield it at all, aside from occasionally handling it to remind her siblings of its true ownership.

For a filthy half-demon to touch it and live was unthinkable, but for such a lowly creature to wield the weapon was almost beyond even his ability to grasp.

Wielding was not the same as mastering, though, he considered. Perhaps the girl's blood, some small morsel of divinity inside her that remained untainted, had somehow fooled the Taiyosori. Ito had said the girl resembled her mother. Was it possible this connection managed to temporarily confuse the legendary blade of a thousand cuts? According to Ito, the girl had not wielded it for long. She'd simply lopped Crag's head off, a relatively easy task for a weapon rumored to be the sharpest edge in all of creation. All it required was an arm to swing it.

Yes, that had to be it. The hanyou wielded the Taiyosori, but she was not its true master. A quirk of her loathsome birth, that was all.

Once again, Ichitiro sensed opportunity. Before him lay the chance he had waited eons for.

If the Taiyosori was confused, fooled into thinking the hanyou was Midnite, then if someone were to slay the hanyou and claim the blade, the right of transference would be fulfilled. He would be acknowledged as the sword's new master, and the blade of a thousand cuts would sit fallow no longer. It would taste blood, bathe in it, as it had not done in ages untold.

He looked down and smiled at where Ito continued to cower. The youkai had done well after all. Ichitiro would not compliment him for it, or even acknowledge such, but he would allow the pathetic beast to survive this day with no further suffering. If anything, he now had far more important matters to worry about than the thieving little rodent.

The time for inaction was over. It was now time for...

There came a booming knock from his outer chamber door.

Who?

For a moment, paranoia set in. Though he'd barely just made them, Ichitiro became certain that his plans had been found out, that the other daimao knew what he was plotting. But he quickly dismissed it as a mere side effect of his ultimate victory being so near. So what if the others had found out? He hadn't acted yet. And even if he had, none of them, not even Midnite herself, would choose an untouchable hanyou over him.

He gestured for Ito to answer the door and the little ferret youkai obeyed without hesitation. As he did so, Ichitiro spared a glance down at the floor. The monkey youkai had been removed by his other servants. Not so much as a drop of blood remained.

He smiled, but it quickly turned into a grimace as he spied a massive, red-skinned oni standing at the door.

Whereas most daimao used the small youkai of the castle as their heralds, Reiden insisted on keeping this loathsome troll in his employ. As strong as they were stupid, oni were often best put to use as shock troops in the field. Their massive forms and tendency to ignore pain until they were killed made them excellent cannon fodder.

Ichitiro often wondered if Reiden used it in a sad attempt to intimidate others. If so, this gambit failed where he was concerned. "What is it, Klortho?" he asked in a bored tone.

The towering oni entered and bowed its ungainly form before Ichitiro. "Lord Reiden requests your presence in the council chamber," he answered in a gruff voice. "He wishes to reconvene the court to continue discussing the matter of Earth."

"I am busy."

"Lord Reiden requests your presence in the council chamber," Klortho repeated.

Ichitiro's good mood evaporated in an instant. He knew the lumbering clod would keep at it no matter what he or the others said. Perhaps that was the true reason Reiden used him. Oni obeyed without question and were near impossible to bargain with. The brute would stand there until such time as his master's demands were acknowledged. As much as Ichitiro might want to reduce him to a pile of steaming guts, it would only incite Reiden's wrath.

He did not particularly fear his brother, but Reiden led the celestial court, and his edicts could serve to make Ichitiro's plans difficult.

Fortunately, he knew how his elder brother operated. Everything he did was dictated by procedure and debate. It was a wonder he ever left his chambers at all without first convening a caucus to discuss the matter.

"Very well," Ichitiro said. "Tell your master I will be there in short order. I have a small issue to attend to, though. Have him start without me."

Klortho appeared to ponder this in his mudball of a brain for a moment or two. Finally, he nodded. "I will tell my master." With no further business, the large oni bowed, turned, and left without so much as another word.

Excellent! It wasn't unheard of for members of the court to be late, or not show up at all, though they risked forfeiting their say in matters. At the very least, they would earn themselves a tiresome lecture on the need for keeping order in the multiverse and how that order stemmed from what they did.

He'd heard it all before but was beyond such concerns now.

By the time Reiden's impotent session got underway, Ichitiro would be paying a visit to Earth. He would not be able to mask his departure from his siblings. Even if he used one of his crystals to make the journey, the passage of his immense power signature would still be felt. He was connected to this place, as were all of his brethren. However, he could throw them off his scent by traveling to a different location immediately. His departure from the celestial palace could be sensed, but once on Earth, it would be far more difficult for them to track him, at least until he unleashed a significant portion of his power – something he sincerely doubted would be necessary.

Yes, that was the ticket. Even once they sensed he was gone, there would be plenty of time. Reiden would wish to discuss the matter rather than pursue him. That could take hours, days, perhaps even years.

It was quite possible that, in the time it took his brother to reach a consensus among the others, Ichitiro would have already retrieved the Taiyosori and returned to claim his rightful place as ruler of the universe.

THIRTY-SIX

THE HOURS FOLLOWING the battle were an exercise in chaos. There were deaths to be mourned, lives to be celebrated, and much cleanup that needed to be done. In the midst of it all, images from Beth Billingsly's news report had leaked to something Kisaki's friends called the internet. This resulted in multiple news teams converging upon the once quiet town, making the tasks which needed to be performed that much more difficult.

The police wanted to speak at length to the heroes of the Battle of the Beasts, as it was being touted. A strange name, Kisaki considered, as she was no beast. Neither were youkai, if one were to be truly honest about it.

The problem was the dozens of reporters who wanted to interview her and her friends.

The number of outsiders converging upon the tiny police station proved to be more than their remaining forces could handle. Outside help was being sought. In the meantime, the acting chief – taking pity on Kisaki and her friends – had sent them to Bob's, a small diner in the middle of town. The owner, a volunteer in the town's fire department, agreed to put out the closed sign to allow them a safe haven as well as fix them some lunch. In return, Stephen had pledged that none of them would try to leave town until such time as this matter was settled, something driven home by the acting captain reminding him that he knew his parents.

Stephen was currently in the bathroom. Shitoro had joined him, saying that he, too, needed a bath. Stephen had tried to dissuade him of that notion, but the little tiger demon dismissed his opinion on the subject as the ramblings of a foolish human.

"So what do you think of him?"

Kisaki looked up at Tamiko from where she'd been sipping her milkshake. Whatever the name, she found it delightful. If they had drinks such as these in the celestial palace, she might have never sought to leave. "Shitoro?"

"No," Tamiko said, lowering her voice. "Steve."

Kisaki picked up a French fry and dipped it in a sauce known as ketchup before taking a bite, savoring the dichotomy of salty and sweet on her tongue. "I think Stephen acted very bravely today. He's far more courageous than he believes. If only he understood that, he would have certainly dealt with Robbie long ago."

"That isn't quite what I meant." Tamiko leaned in closer and lowered her voice even further. Her cheeks had turned pink again, making Kisaki wonder if there was some temperature differential that she was unable to sense. When her friend spoke again, it was in Japanese. "I meant, do you think he's cute?"

"Why have you switched languages?"

"Because I don't want him overhearing us, that's why."

"Who?"

"Stephen, of course. Now what do you think of him? Cute or not?"

"Cute? As in like a small furry animal?"

"As in handsome."

"Ah!" Kisaki brightened as she'd found herself considering the same thing. She remembered how her father looked in the photos and in the vision she had of him. There was something appealing about his appearance. He had a brave, rugged manner about him, not unlike the warriors she used to enjoy reading about. He would not have looked out of place wearing armor and wielding a sword.

Though she would never dare pretend to understand her mother's thoughts on such a matter, she could understand how one could have fallen for such a man. Stephen was different, yet not in a bad way. Though he shared some of his great-grandfather's features, they were softer on him, less severe. He looked more the scholar than a warrior, although Kisaki had seen the fire in his eyes when he'd wielded his shotgun.

Despite her fascination with warriors of the past, she found that combination – his gentle nature mixed with his bravery – surprisingly appealing.

"I have given that some thought, and I do believe he is handsome indeed. Mind you, I have little to base that on since the vast majority of my interactions over the course of my life have been with either my mother or Shitoro. However, I cannot help but look at him and feel an odd warmth inside me."

"In a sisterly way, though, right?"

"Sisterly? He's not my sister and I am not his. I do not have a sister, so far as I'm aware, so I don't know how I might feel toward one."

"Well, then maybe how you feel about your mother?"

Kisaki considered that. She had always respected her mother, but beneath that respect had been an unpleasant veneer that she tried not to dwell upon. But the last few days had been an awakening for her, one which had forced her to expand her horizons considerably. She now understood those feelings for what they had been: resentment. She had felt like a caged animal, one that was now free. However, that resentment had since been tempered by what Shitoro had told her.

She'd thought her mother's actions to be … cruel wasn't the word. After all, Kisaki had wanted for nothing. Mystifying, infuriating perhaps? All of it added up to a cornucopia of feelings. But she now knew these things had been done to keep her safe.

She just wished that she'd been told a long time ago. If so, things might have turned out differently. She might not be sitting here eating French fries while the town around her dealt with the fallout from a deadly battle.

But then, she would have never met Tamiko and Stephen either. She might not have ever realized there was more to her than long hours of boring study. She might never have learned about her father.

"Cat got your tongue?" Tamiko asked.

"Hmm? No. Shitoro is still elsewhere, presumably bathing."

"It's an American phrase, I think. It means you were being quiet."

"My apologies. I was lost in thought. There's been so many new developments in my life and so quickly that it's a bit overwhelming."

"Believe me, I understand." Tamiko took a long pull on her soda. "I figured today would be spent doing more paperwork for my dad. I definitely didn't imagine I'd be taking an unexpected holiday to fight monsters in Pennsylvania."

Kisaki nodded. She understood, especially since she was the cause for Tamiko's unexpected travels. "To answer your question, no. I do not consider him to be like my mother. In fact, I believe it is quite different."

"You don't like him, do you?"

"Of course I like him."

"I mean *like* him." Kisaki shrugged, not understanding, so Tamiko clarified. "I mean, like a boyfriend."

"You mean as a mate?"

"Um, maybe not quite that far, but yeah, sort of."

Kisaki considered this for a few moments, mindful that their companions would most likely be returning shortly. She suddenly realized she didn't want them overhearing this conversation either, especially Stephen. She didn't fully understand why but suspected it might have to do with what Tamiko was asking her. Finally, she said, "He does appear to have several desirable qualities."

"Gross!"

"You find him gross?"

"No. I mean, you guys. You're his great-aunt."

"So?"

"So that would almost be like you marrying your brother."

"But he is not my brother," Kisaki pointed out. "Besides, such pairings are quite common among youkai. Divine blood mixes best with blood of a similar caliber, or so I have been taught in my studies."

"That's just ... wrong."

"Why?"

"Because it's weird."

"So you're saying you do not find Stephen desirable as a mate?"

"No! I… it's just…" Tamiko's face turned bright red as she tried to sputter out an answer.

Kisaki was new to this, but some instinct told her that her friend did indeed find Stephen desirable as a mate, or *boyfriend*, as she put it. She didn't expect to feel anything negative at this revelation but was surprised when she did. It wasn't entirely dissimilar to how she'd felt when she saw her servants free to come and go while she was not.

It was an unwelcome feeling. After all, Tamiko was her friend. But it was a feeling that persisted nevertheless, despite being unwelcome. That Tamiko had stopped talking made her wonder if she was feeling the same thing.

After several tense moments of silence, Tamiko said, "This is silly."

"Yes," Kisaki replied with a smile. "Definitely silly."

"I mean, we just met him. I have to get back to Ishigachi and you need to … oh, I'm sorry." She shrugged, looking uncomfortable. "I forgot what's waiting for you."

"It's all right. You are correct." She turned and looked out the window. The street beyond was quiet, this section of town being relatively untouched by the battle. "My outing to Earth has caused far more chaos than I ever intended, but it has also given me memories which I will always cherish." She reached over and took Tamiko's hand.

"Me too."

"Hey, what are you guys talking about?" Stephen asked, walking back. He took a seat next to Tamiko. Kisaki felt a quick stab of jealousy but pushed it back down. "Not talking about me, are you?"

"What?!" Tamiko replied, quickly switching back to English. "I mean, of course not. No, we weren't talking about you, were we, Kisaki?"

"But you said … ow!" Tamiko kicked her under the table. She was about to question why, but then she saw the pleading look on her friend's face and understood. "I meant, no. You are not a topic worthy of conversation."

"Okay then," Stephen replied, looking confused for a moment before reaching for his own drink.

"Where's Shitoro?"

Stephen shook his head. "Your cat is a moron."

"He's not my cat. And why would you say that?"

"You'll see." Stephen would say no more on the subject, instead digging into his cheeseburger.

After several more minutes, they heard the padding of small feet and turned to see Shitoro returning to join them. He'd earlier changed back into his tiger form so as to attract as little attention as possible, although Stephen had argued there wasn't much point since he kept talking.

Kisaki noted that his fur was wet.

"Ah, much better. So refreshing after being ignobly tossed into refuse." He climbed up onto the seat next to Kisaki and began pawing at a plate of chicken that had been left for him. "I simply do not understand why you gave me such grief in there, human. My hygiene is no concern of yours."

"It's because that was a urinal, not a shower stall, idiot."

Kisaki didn't know what a urinal was, but Tamiko immediately broke down into laughter. "He did not!"

"Oh yeah. He did," Stephen confirmed. "You can't make this shit up."

Kisaki looked down at the youkai. "Shitoro?"

"I, for one, do not see what the fuss is about," he replied. "It was perfectly sized for me and, though it cannot compare to the opulent baths of the celestial palace, the cascade of water upon my fur was quite enjoyable, as was the pleasant smelling cylindrical object at the bottom. Tell me, was that some sort of bath oil?"

"Not quite," Stephen replied, barely holding in his own laughter.

Tamiko, for her part, had lost it. Tears streamed down her face.

Kisaki looked at the two of them. "Is there something here I don't understand?"

"Don't ask," Stephen said. Then, after a moment, added, "I'll tell you all about men's rooms later."

"Oh, that should be fun," Tamiko replied, still snickering. "Until then, you might want to avoid petting him."

"I am not a cat," Shitoro snapped, spearing another piece of chicken with a claw. "I require no petting, grooming, or scratching beneath my chin … although that latter can be enjoyable under the correct circumstances."

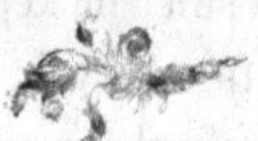

Once Stephen and Tamiko got themselves back under control, the discussion turned to the battle they'd just fought and its consequences.

"What do you think they'll do with Crag?"

"Depends who gets him," Stephen said. "If it's scientists, they'll dissect him. If it's rednecks, they'll throw him in a freezer and charge people ten bucks to look at him."

"A most inglorious fate for a dishonorable foe," Shitoro replied bitterly. "However, there is potential for complications."

"How so?" Tamiko asked.

"The world has changed considerably, and not just in the years since the edict against travel here was laid down," Shitoro explained. "The last time the daimao were active in the world of man was approximately three hundred of your years ago. At that point, the world was just beginning to change, although we did not suspect how much. Youkai and humans still lived side by side, though. It was not uncommon for them to encounter one another."

Tamiko nodded. "My father used to read me stories about feudal Japan when I was a little girl. It seemed like running into demons was about as common as walking to the local noodle shop."

"An oversimplification, but not entirely incorrect," Shitoro replied. "I'm willing to speculate that those stories are probably based more on fact than you know. But that changed. While the daimao slept, the world evolved even more, far more so than those of us tending to the day-to-day matters of the celestial palace realized."

"But before the edict, weren't you free to travel to Earth as you pleased?" Kisaki asked.

"Yes, but that did not mean many of us did. Earth has always been a savage place. Some of demonkind revel in that, but many of us want nothing more than a quiet existence. Not all of us are warriors, nor do we aspire to be. You tell me. If given the choice between safety, fine food, and a comfortable life versus willingly stepping foot onto a world where you could be hunted by anything – human or not – which would you choose?"

"Makes sense," Stephen said after a beat.

"I should say it does."

"But this Crag guy was a warrior, right?"

"A butcher is a better term for it, but yes. A beast such as him was born for the chaos of a world such as this. He was built to thrive in adversity."

"He was built, all right." Stephen blew out a whistle. "When I drove that police cruiser into him, it was like hitting a brick wall."

"Agreed," Tamiko said. "He barely budged."

Stephen looked over at Kisaki. "Which makes it all the more impressive that you threw him like a ragdoll. I still have no idea how you pulled that one off."

"I'm only beginning to understand it myself," Kisaki said. "But that particular move, I learned from my father."

The rest of the table became quiet as her words sank in and she realized what she had just admitted.

"How so?" Tamiko asked. "I thought you never met him?"

Kisaki realized there was nothing to gain by remaining silent, especially to friends loyal enough to stand by her side against a beast such as Crag. "I have not, but just before the battle began…"

"Go on," Shitoro prodded.

"Just as the fighting started, I had another of those visions I had mentioned, except this one was much clearer as to who and what they were about. The first clue was that man in my father's photos, the smiling one. He was there."

"You saw him in your vision?" Stephen asked.

"Yes. At first, I wasn't sure if he was a friend or enemy. The truth is, I am still not certain. But I did realize one thing from this last vision."

"What?"

"That I was seeing it all from behind my father's eyes."

"How do you know this?" Shitoro asked, the food in front of him seemingly forgotten.

"The visions. At first, I thought they acted like those crystals, that I had been sent elsewhere. Except they were different. There's no sound at all and I have no control over my body. Each time it's happened, I've found myself being attacked. The first was by the smiling man. The next was by soldiers, with the smiling man fighting alongside me. The last was again of the smiling man. I spied a mirror in that one and realized the face looking back at me was my father's."

"You were in your father's body?" Tamiko asked.

"It's hard to explain. Yes and no. It was like I was…"

"Reliving his memories," Shitoro replied, his mouth hanging agape.

"Is that possible?" she asked, but the youkai appeared deep in thought.

Finally, he turned toward Stephen. "The man in the photos with your great-grandfather. You said he was his friend, yes?"

"Yeah, from what I understand. Grandpop used to talk about him all the time. His name was … oh man, I actually don't remember."

"His name is not important," Shitoro snapped. "What was his relationship to your father?"

"Oh. Um, well, I think they grew up together. They were friends before the war. They served together, then they worked together as partners for a while afterwards until his friend moved away."

"Partners in what?"

"Everything, I think. From what I heard, my great-grandfather started off as a boxer. He worked the amateur circuit for a while before turning to wrestling. After a while, he and his friend earned enough to open their own gym together. This was just before the war started, if I recall correctly."

Shitoro turned to Kisaki. "Your mother said your father had the spirit of a warrior."

"Yeah, fighting was his thing," Stephen continued. "He and his buddy picked up stuff where they could from whoever would teach them. Before he died, we'd sometimes watch UFC matches on TV. He used to joke that he was ahead of his time with mixed martial arts. If he'd only been born fifty years later, he could have made a fortune."

Shitoro sat back, his tail twitching. "I see."

"What is it?" Kisaki asked.

"You only realized your own fighting potential after these visions started, yes?"

Kisaki nodded. "Before then, I had no idea I could even move like that. It was jarring to discover, but not in an entirely unpleasant manner. Do you know what's happening?"

Shitoro shook his head. "I'm not certain."

"But you just said…"

"Yes, yes, I know what I said. Allow me to explain. Blood contains memories. There are spells that can divine what another being has seen. Usually traumatic experiences, such as death, create the strongest imprints. Nevertheless, reading another's blood is powerful magic, beyond me, but…"

"But what?" Kisaki asked.

"But I have never seen nor even heard of someone inheriting blood memories."

"Maybe it's like instinct," Stephen offered. "I mean, dogs are born knowing certain behaviors. Same with ca…"

"Do not say it," Shitoro warned, a flash of yellow power in his eyes. "But I know what you mean. However, this is completely different. A dog knowing to use scent to get around doesn't equate to it remembering and recognizing its ancestors' masters. Yet that is what Kisaki seems to be doing. Minus the master part, of course. If what she is saying is true, she is reliving portions of her father's life through his eyes. More importantly, she is somehow remembering her father's fighting skills. What he knew, she seems to know, at least when it comes to combat."

"How?" she asked.

"Have you not been listening, child? I don't know. This is unprecedented so far as I am aware. I can't even begin to fathom how deep this connection runs."

"What about her freaky strength?" Stephen asked.

"Kisaki is a hanyou. Her mother's blood flows through her veins as well," he replied dismissively, then fell silent.

"All things considered," Tamiko said after a few moments, "I guess it's a lot more useful than if your great-granddad had been a gardener instead."

Stephen laughed. "Yeah. I doubt Crag would have settled for having his lawn mowed and tulips planted."

Kisaki herself was lost in thought. She didn't know how to trigger these visions, or if they would ever even happen again.

But knowing what they were now did give her an unexpected measure of peace.

When she'd first learned who Stephen was, she'd despaired at the news that her father had died before she could meet him. But now, she realized, that wasn't entirely true. Some of his essence lived on inside of her. She'd experienced a small portion of his life through his eyes. So, in a sense, she *had* met him, and in a way that ran much deeper than a simple handshake or hug.

But she also realized it wasn't enough. She wanted more. What Shitoro said resonated within her. And she hoped that her connection to him indeed went further than combat. If so, then she could potentially meet him again and again, get to know the real him.

Such a thing wouldn't bring him back, but it would answer so many questions and help fill the hole in her heart that, for seventy years, she didn't even realize was there.

The question now was how to control it. His combat expertise was now hers, triggered by the onset of battle and kick-started again with every subsequent fight, seeming to become stronger each time. Perhaps a similar trigger was needed to activate other memories from his life. The only question was how?

Kisaki was about to ask Shitoro this but found him seemingly deep in his own thoughts. "Shitoro?"

"Hmm? Yes, mistress?"

"What is it? Are you okay?"

"Me? Oh yes. It's just that … I was thinking."

"About what?"

"It's probably not important. Just mulling something over in my head. Nothing to concern yourself with. Did you have need of me?"

Kisaki opened his mouth to answer but, before the words could form, the building rocked around them, sending her and the tiger youkai tumbling out of the booth.

"I can't be the only one who felt that," Stephen said as dust from the ceiling drifted down around them.

"Alas, even you are not that delusional, human." Shitoro stood and transformed into his humanoid form, dusting himself off. "We should go out and see…"

The owner of the diner came racing out from the kitchen. "Holy Mary, Son of God. What in hell is going on? You kids stay put, while I…" The words died on his lips as he laid eyes upon Shitoro in his true form. "What in the name of the Holy Trinity is that?"

Before anyone could answer, the diner shook violently again. About half of the windows shattered from the force of whatever was going on.

That seemed to snap the owner back to reality, though his eyes were still transfixed on the little tiger demon. "All of you stay put while I see what's going on. Your … gremlin, too."

The man trudged to the front door, unlocked it, and stepped out while Shitoro fumed. "Gremlin? What is it with you humans and your insults?"

"What we lack in magic we make up for in wit," Stephen replied dryly before turning to the rest. "You two thinking what I am?"

"That there's no way we're sitting in here waiting?" Tamiko asked.

He nodded. "Let's blow this pop stand."

THIRTY-SEVEN

KISAKI HAD BEEN wondering whether the youkai under Crag's command would regroup and counterattack. It seemed unlikely after his defeat. None of them compared in power to him, even the ursines.

Now, she began to wonder if she'd been wrong. What else could have caused the building to violently shake like that?

Stepping outside, though, she realized it was far worse than she'd ever imagined. A furrow of destruction, perhaps fifteen meters wide, had been carved through the town, missing the diner by only two buildings. It had seemingly pulverized everything in its path down to three meters below the surface. Broken concrete, splintered wood, and shattered asphalt were all that remained.

But what could have caused it? Crag's spell, as impressive as it had been, hadn't come close to this. So what…

"Merciful elder gods save us," Shitoro muttered.

"What are you…?" Kisaki turned to follow his gaze. At the far end of the blackened gouge in the Earth, floating perhaps ten meters off the ground, was a figure. It was clad in black armor covered in wicked spikey protrusions. In one hand, it held a blade seemingly made of black fire. Several stunted and disfigured horns sat atop a cruel visage, which appeared to gaze down upon the world beneath it with barely concealed contempt.

"Come out, little hanyou!" the figure said in a voice loud enough to be heard all over town. It echoed among the streets for several seconds.

"What did it say?" Tamiko asked, holding her hands over her ears.

At first, Kisaki didn't understand why she would ask such a thing, but then she realized the creature was speaking neither English nor Japanese. It had asked its question in the divine tongue, the language of the celestial palace.

She narrowed her eyes. Another mazoku, perhaps? "Who is that?"

Shitoro grabbed her hand and looked up at her with panic clearly etched upon his face.

"Ichitiro."

A chill ran down Kisaki's spine. They were facing a daimao, like her mother. No, not like her. Her mother was beautiful, a goddess inside and out. Beneath her cold sense of authority, there was kindness. She would never have done what this ugly beast had. Who knew how many he'd killed in one fell swoop?

What was he even doing here? The edict against traveling to Earth. Shitoro had been certain that none of the daimao would break it. Her own mother hadn't even dared to come looking for her. Had it somehow been lifted?

"Are you sure it's him?" Kisaki asked.

"As surely as I draw breath," Shitoro replied. "And we most likely won't be drawing it for long if he's here looking for us."

She could see the fear in her friend's face. Sadly, that feeling did not seem to resonate to the other friends who also stood beside her.

"Whoa," Tamiko said.

"Let's kick his ass," Stephen added. "Team Midnight Girl rides again."

"Midnight Girl?"

"Long story," he replied with a grin.

Kisaki regarded him incredulously. He had no idea what he was saying. Such a thing was impossible. Ichitiro was a daimao, one of the lords of the multiverse. One did not fight them. One could only run and hope to find shelter to weather the storm.

Sadly, it appeared that ignorant bravery was not uncommon among the humans. A few blocks away, she could see several of the news vans racing in Ichitiro's direction.

Gunshots began to ring out. From where, she couldn't tell, but she had little doubt as to their target.

If they were shooting at Ichitiro, though, he paid it no heed, continuing to hover in the air, looking around … no doubt searching for them.

"I've had enough of freaks tearing my town apart," Stephen said. "Let's go get him."

Kisaki felt heat bloom in her heart at his words. He'd indeed inherited some of her father's warrior spirit. Perhaps not as she had, but it was there nevertheless. Sadly, that spirit would be snuffed out in an instant against a foe like this.

She wouldn't allow that.

Kisaki reached into the pocket of her shorts. *Please let it still be there.*

It was. Her hand closed upon the last of the stolen crystals, the red one. She didn't know who it belonged to, nor did she care. All she knew was what it could do for her friends.

"Your father," she said, turning toward Tamiko.

"What?"

"Your father," Kisaki repeated. "You love him, yes?"

"Of course I do."

"And you miss him?"

"We've only been gone for a day and…"

"Do you miss him?"

"Yes, I guess I do."

"Then I need you to think of him, and of your home. I need you to think of it and how much you wish to see it all again."

"I don't understand why…"

"Please, Tamiko! Do it. For me."

Tamiko inclined her head, but then sighed. "Fine. For you, although I'm not sure why."

"What are you doing, mistress?"

"Come out now, hanyou, and I might consider showing these insects mercy!"

The group turned to view Ichitiro, only to see him let loose a wave of destructive force. It cut a swath of destruction perpendicular to the one he'd already made, utterly annihilating anything in its path as if it had been hit by an invisible tsunami.

"No!" Kisaki cried, but there was nothing she could do save watch as the wall of force cut through at least three of the news vans, flattening them into scrap, presumably with their occupants still inside.

"All those people," Tamiko gasped.

Yes, Kisaki considered with grim determination. All of those people and most likely many more before this devil was finished. So much power, and all of it seemingly directed toward malice. The multiverse was indeed an unfair place if a being such as him lorded over it as judge, jury, and executioner.

There was no time left. She couldn't save those reporters, but she could save her friends. "Give me your hand."

"Why?" Tamiko asked.

"Just do it!"

She complied and Kisaki passed the crystal, which she'd palmed to keep from Shitoro's sight, into her friend's hand, closing her fist over it.

Tamiko looked down, confused for a moment, but Kisaki simply nodded – a silent hope for her to hold her tongue a moment longer.

"Close your eyes and think of your father, think of your love for him, of your love of your home, of how much you want to be there again."

Kisaki released Tamiko, then, quick as a snake, grabbed both Shitoro and Stephen by their wrists.

"What are you doing?" Stephen asked.

"Mistress, I do not know what you have planned, but I would advise…"

Kisaki ignored them both, addressing Tamiko again. "Concentrate on your father's face."

"I'm doing it. I can see him, his smile. I'm … what the?!"

Kisaki knew from her expression that the crystal had begun to pulse. "Do *not* drop it!"

"Drop what?" Stephen asked.

Kisaki, as way of response, dragged him and Shitoro closer in, forcing their hands onto Tamiko's and holding them there.

I need to time this right.

Light began to shine from between the fingers of her friend's closed fist.

Now!

She let go and flung herself backward just as a cascade of energy was released from the crystal. A brilliant flash of reddish light enveloped her friends and, a moment later, they were gone, hopefully sent to the relative safety of Tamiko's home. Stephen would be a fish out of water on Ishigachi, but he'd be a live fish. That was good enough for her. Kisaki trusted that Tamiko and her father would take good care of him until such time as it was safe to send him home.

As for Shitoro, she could only hope he wouldn't be too cross with her for sending him back to…

That thought scattered to the wind as she blinked, cleared the spots from her eyes, and saw his diminutive form standing in front of her.

"You have a lot of explaining to do, young lady!"

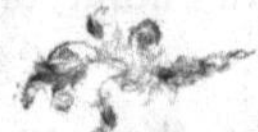

"Shitoro? How?"

"Do you think I was born this century?" the tiger youkai asked contemptuously. "Need I also remind you that felines have exceptional reflexes?"

"You were supposed to go with them, to be safe."

"And you were not supposed to have any more sending crystals upon you. Am I correct in assuming you had it this entire time?"

Kisaki nodded guiltily.

"Why didn't you tell me?"

"I … I didn't want to go back."

"You didn't want to go back. How noble of you. And now, because of your actions, look what has been wrought."

"You think I don't know that?" she snapped, causing him to flinch. "Why do you think I was trying to send you away? It was to make up for my selfishness. To make sure my friends didn't suffer because of me."

Shitoro sighed, but then his expression softened ever so slightly. "Very well. What's done is done. Please tell me that was not your last one."

Kisaki's silence was all the answer he apparently needed.

"Of course it was. Why would the multiverse make any-thing easy? So be it. We shall have to do what the humans apparently do not have the sense to – run."

Unfortunately for them both, just as Shitoro spoke the words, a shadow fell over them.

"Ah, Shitoro," Ichitiro said from above their heads. "You of all youkai should know the futility of even trying."

"L-lord Ichitiro," Shitoro sputtered as the daimao slowly descended to Earth.

The great demon stopped mere inches above the ground, hovering as if he considered touching any part of the Earth to be beneath his contempt. "I had wondered what became of you these last few decades. I so have missed driving home the point that one such as you cannot bar entrance to one such as me. I'd thought perhaps my sister had finally found her back-bone and had you flayed to make up for the ridiculous insult of your existence, but I see now that she had a crueler fate in mind for you – cursed to spend your days as a nursemaid. You should thank me. Once I am finished here, perhaps you can return to your previous duties."

Kisaki could tell the little youkai was frightened, terrified even. He barely kept himself from shaking as he stepped in front of her. "Serving Lady Kisaki has been a blessing, a duty which I am proud my mistress entrusted me with."

Ichitiro grinned as if amused. "So that is how you refer to this creature? *Lady* Kisaki." He turned toward her as if seeing her for the first time. "A noble title for one born so low, fated to accomplish nothing save dying."

Kisaki considered her options. Begging for her life seemed the smartest plan of action, but from her few seconds of acquaintance with this demon, she got the impression that mercy was a concept alien to his way of thinking. Surrender was likely to produce the same outcome. Giving him what he wanted – the Taiyosori, no doubt – was unthinkable. Sad as it made her, Kisaki couldn't see any way out of this that didn't result in her death.

Rather than the fear she expected, though, that cool logic from before began to take hold, pushing everything else away. She might be fated to die, but she would do so with dignity and maybe even in a way this arrogant godling would not soon forget.

She lifted her head to meet his eyes. "If you have come to bore me to death, Ichitiro, then I dare say you are making excellent progress."

THIRTY-EIGHT

ICHITIRO WAS TAKEN aback for perhaps a fraction of a second by what the hanyou said.

He was unused to being addressed in such a manner save from perhaps his siblings, and even they seldom dared.

Had any of his servants attempted to speak even a word in the same tone, he would have made their suffering last for years, perhaps longer. As a result, it wasn't a great surprise to him that his first reaction was to strike down this creature, reduce it to the base atoms that were unfortunate enough to be chosen by the multiverse to make up this bastard offspring.

Energy gathered around him for a moment, but then he dismissed it as another thought took hold. He should have been angry beyond belief. If anything, his dislike for Midnite had turned to outright loathing at knowing she'd sired this, the lowest of the low. But instead, he found himself strangely amused.

And why shouldn't he be?

This hanyou, a creature who couldn't even aspire to being a human ape, had spoken to him in a tone of challenge. This suggested an ignorance that even the most dimwitted of his servants couldn't hope to match.

Besides, he knew this insect somehow held the Taiyosori, confounding the weapon by virtue of its tainted bloodline. His victory was so near that he could taste it with his pointed teeth. If this half-breed wished to challenge him, so be it. Destroying it would fulfill one of the tenets for obtaining the Taiyosori. For the hanyou to initiate the battle would ensure that none of the weapon's bothersome defenses might be inadvertently engaged. He could not have asked for a better scenario.

Ichitiro considered the youkai standing alongside the girl. It would be no effort at all to destroy him. There was nothing to stop him. If anything, Shitoro was in direct violation of the edict.

Not that Ichitiro cared either way. Once the Taiyosori was his, the edicts, wishes, or pleas of the council would be meaningless to his ears.

He decided to allow Shitoro to survive. Someone should bear witness to his ascension. That it would allow the youkai a chance to tell Midnite the tale of her offspring's demise would simply be an added bonus to make his victory all the more sweet.

He smiled, baring his double row of teeth to the two insignificant creatures before him.

"Is that a challenge I hear, little hanyou?"

Ichitiro's response seemed to cause the world to once again slow down around Kisaki. She now knew what it meant, though, and in that knowing came anticipation. She was about to step into her father's shoes once again, draw strength from his experience, which would, in turn, further empower her. Best yet, it might give her some insight into him. He was a part of her, and knowing she could truly experience a small part of him gave her comfort.

The world greyed out around her, replaced by another life through other eyes. This time, however, it was different. She'd sensed the visions had been growing more powerful, feeling more real each time they happened … perhaps a result of her mind gradually adapting to them. That seemed to be the case, for this time, she not only saw the sights from those days, but she began to hear the sounds as well. They were faint, almost as if listening to them from over a great distance, but she could just make them out.

She wasn't in a battle this time, but a classroom of sorts. She sat at a desk, not entirely dissimilar to those she partook her lessons at. She was surrounded by others, men in uniform, also seated. There was a man standing at the head of the class saying something. Kisaki strove to listen, looking down as her father took notes on a sheet of paper.

"No matter how outgunned you are, no matter how badly the enemy has outmaneuvered you, never forget that half the battle is fought up here." The man giving the lecture raised a finger to his temple. "Win this war and you can overcome nearly any advantage the enemy might have over you."

The scene abruptly changed, something else new to this vision, and she found herself standing on a scarred and pitted beach.

"Hey! What are you two doing?"

The voice was deep, filled with authority – something the two men, soldiers in uniform, who appeared in front of her did not seem to possess. It was with some delight that she realized the voice had come from her … or the body she possessed anyway.

Beyond the two men was another figure, a woman dressed in a simple kimono who…

Kisaki gasped, or would have had she any control over her father's body. Save for the hair and complexion, the woman's face was the same she'd seen staring back at her in the mirror for nearly her entire life. For a moment, she was confused, but then realization hit.

There could only be one explanation, for there was only one other face like hers that she was aware of.

She was looking at her mother, in the guise of a human.

Her father seemingly had a similar reaction, for she could feel his intake of breath as he gazed upon her.

The scene continued to play out, more words being spoken, as she took this all in. The two other men had weapons trained upon her mother, not knowing how foolish a move they were making. Her mother, however, had taken no action against them, seemingly as transfixed by her father as he was of her.

"Your buddy ain't here," she … her father snapped. "I am and I don't like what I was hearing."

The discourse continued, her father's tone becoming heated. Despite the two men before her being armed, she could see the indecision in their eyes as he spoke.

With some amusement, she realized her mother noticed it, too.

"Get your asses back to your squad before I have them handed to you."

One of the two soldiers seemingly looked to challenge her father. "With all due respect, sir, you army grunts can't just…"

"Do you want to test that, soldier? Because, if so, I will look forward to seeing your ass in irons before the day is out."

She stared hard at the other man and, within seconds, he lowered his gaze and shook his head. Her father had won despite their superior numbers.

"What was that?" she asked in her father's voice.

"I said no, sir."

"That's what I thought. Now double time it and maybe I'll forget what you two look like."

The two men left in a hurry, leaving Kisaki's father alone with her mother.

With no small amount of panic, she wondered how long this vision would last and exactly how much of their fateful meeting she would witness, but then, just as quickly as it appeared, it faded around her and she once again found herself staring up at Ichitiro.

It seemed that nearly no time at all had passed. He was just closing his mouth after asking his question. Incredible! No matter how often it happened, Kisaki doubted she'd ever get used to it.

"I know who you are," she replied in a calm voice, "and I know *what* you are, Lord Ichitiro. Yet, despite that, it is I who will offer you a chance to leave this place in peace. Scoff if you will, but know that I promise only one thing: whatever outcome this day holds, you will not soon forget it."

Shitoro turned to stare up at her, the look on his face suggesting he thought she'd gone insane. She remained calm, though, allowing that cold logic to suffuse her being, taking stock of her opponent despite knowing he possessed powers beyond her ability to understand.

Kisaki felt a pulse at her side. The quill. She'd heard it speak to her, acknowledge her as its master. She couldn't know if that was true, nor whether it would make a difference against this creature, but she refused to allow that doubt to show on her face.

After a moment, Ichitiro spoke. "You have the fire of a daimao, even if your blood is thin and tainted. I shall give you that, but no more." He held out his hand. "One chance for a painless death, only one. Give me the Taiyosori."

"Kisaki," Shitoro warned, but both would-be combatants ignored him as if he were not a factor in these matters.

"I shall not gift you the sword," she replied, holding the great demon's gaze. "Nor can you inherit it. Therefore, if you want it, you must win it. My challenge stands, but *only* if you give your word to leave this planet in peace at the conclusion of our battle."

Whatever amusement the daimao had seemingly felt toward her evaporated. He stood up to his full height, not quite Crag's size, but towering over her nevertheless. "You would dare offer me conditions. I could rip the Taiyosori from your corpse in an instant."

Kisaki, however, thought she could sense doubt in his eyes. He knew the conditions for winning the blade, perhaps far better than she, and he desperately wanted it. That much was obvious. He could almost certainly make good on his threat, but if she refused to battle him, there was a chance, however slight, the blade might not accept him as its master. The lust in his eyes told her he would not risk that happening.

"I could do that and more," Ichitiro continued after a beat. "But I will accept your conditions. Consider it deference toward my dear sister, your mother, so that she might know you died with at least a modicum of honor."

"Shitoro?" She looked down upon him questioningly. "The daimao, they are honorable when giving their word, yes?"

Shitoro shrugged, but then apparently noticed how Ichitiro bared his teeth at him. "Of course, my lady. A daimao's word is law."

It wasn't much to go on, Kisaki noted with a silent sigh, but it would have to do. "So be it."

"Yes," the great demon replied with a predatory grin. "So be it, indeed."

THIRTY-NINE

THE CHALLENGE ACCEPTED, Ichitiro raised his own blade, a construct seemingly made of solid black flame, and brought it down in her direction.

Kisaki just barely managed to grab hold of Shitoro and dive out of the way. She rolled with the little youkai as Ichitiro's weapon sliced a blackened gouge in the spot where she'd stood just a moment before.

The blow appeared to be little more than a lazy effort on his part, one she'd just barely managed to dodge. It said a lot to her about how this battle might go. Nevertheless, she refused to back down.

"Run!" she commanded Shitoro, her voice again sounding much like her mother's.

To her surprise, though, the little youkai's loyalty proved stronger than her tone of authority. "I will not, my lady. Though we die today, I will take some small comfort in knowing it is together."

Kisaki was tempted to chide him for his pessimistic attitude, but since he was probably right, she decided to let it go. Besides, his fierce dedication touched her. She had little doubt

Tamiko and Stephen would have done the same if they were here. She wished that were so, but at the same time was glad they weren't. If she had any regrets, it was that Shitoro hadn't gone with them.

"Very well," she said with a smile, rolling to her feet, "but try not to get underfoot."

She turned and focused on Ichitiro, studying him. There was little chance of victory, but any she had would depend on her ability to capitalize on whatever mistakes he made – assuming that was, a war god, old as time itself, would make a mistake against an insignificant foe such as herself.

Perhaps that was key, though. Had he considered her a worthy adversary, this battle would have most likely been over already. He'd already proven himself capable of leveling the town if he wanted to. By dismissing her as nothing, he was perhaps already making a crucial error.

If so, maybe it was time to use that against him.

She ran at him, her fist raised in a sloppy attack. He made no move against her and she was able to connect with a pulled punch to his jaw. As expected, it had no effect whatsoever on him. It wasn't nearly all Kisaki had to offer, but the utter lack of give from him made her wonder if her best shot would've had much more effect.

At the very least, she'd proven her theory. He was toying with her, acting as if she was beneath contempt. No doubt his plan was to spar with her for a few moments, perhaps give her hope that she had a chance, only to then strike her down. Knowing that didn't necessarily increase her odds of survival, but it didn't hurt them either.

It was a start.

It was almost a finish, too, because again he swung his blade at her. Casual as it looked, she again just barely managed to dodge, parrying with a block to his arm.

"Is that all you have to offer, hanyou?" Ichitiro asked, sounding bored. "I had hoped that perhaps you'd inherited something of amusement from your mother's blood, but I have killed human cubs who have put up more fight than you."

Kisaki didn't doubt his words for a moment. This foul creature seemed just the type to abuse his power against those weaker than him: warrior, woman, or child. It wouldn't matter to one such as him, drunk on his own power and having never tasted the sting of defeat.

A plan began to form in Kisaki's mind. A psychological edge, something her father had used against those other men. To intimidate a daimao was next to impossible for anything less than a god. But intimidation was only one possible advantage. Anything that threw the enemy off was a factor in one's favor. That could be fear, sorrow, laughter, or…

Ichitiro swiped a clawed hand at Kisaki, just barely missing her. She countered with some jabs that did nothing but make him laugh. "Draw your sword so that you might at least make some sport of it," he commanded.

"My sword?" she asked, making it a point to sound surprised. "To what purpose? So as to make this battle even more unfair than it already is?"

Ichitiro let out a grunt of annoyance and swung his blade, faster this time. That was the ticket. Insult his ego and keep chipping away at him … assuming she could keep dodging.

She did, though, and this time followed through with a kick that brought her heel into contact with his wrist, nearly dislodging his weapon.

Sadly, nearly wasn't enough.

"This kitten has fangs, I see," Ichitiro replied. "Let us see how sharp."

"Sharp enough!" Shitoro cried from somewhere behind her. "Kisaki!"

He didn't need to finish saying her name, for she was already on the move when the torrent of water poured down from the sky onto the daimao. Steam erupted from where it hit his sword, sending up a blinding cloud of vapor around them.

Ichitiro growled in annoyance, his voice giving Kisaki a clear target to focus on. She came in low, spinning, then kicking out, hitting him in the back of his knees.

With a roar of anger, Ichitiro's legs flew out from beneath him and he landed on his backside upon the ruined pavement.

The time for holding back was over. He sat up almost immediately, only to catch Kisaki's knee square in his face.

Ichitiro was blindingly fast, swinging his weapon even as she felt the satisfying crunch of his nose. She'd anticipated it, though, and leapt over the attack to land behind him and launch an elbow into the side of his head.

Angered, the daimao slammed a fist into the ground, shattering the pavement around them and causing Kisaki to stumble back as pieces of asphalt rained down upon her.

By the time she looked up again, he was back on his feet.

"You would dare?"

"You thought yourself too good to set foot upon this world," she snapped back. "But I have proven otherwise. You're just another pig, worthy of the mud you wallow in, nothing more."

Any amusement that still remained in her foe's eyes was erased in a second. Kisaki's hunch had been right. Ichitiro acted little better than a spoiled child. When denied his toys, the only thing he knew how to do was throw a tantrum. Ancient he might be, immeasurably more experienced he was, but all of that training and discipline went right out the window when someone managed to get him good and angry.

He was still perhaps the most dangerous entity to ever set foot upon this world, but his snarling rage could potentially cause him to act foolishly.

Now she needed to make sure she didn't do the same.

Power began to collect around Ichitiro, a dark grey miasma more like a storm cloud than anything. As if to confirm this, swirls of lightning could be seen flashing inside of it. "I will destroy this settlement and all in it, including you. Then I will pluck the Taiyosori from your charred bones. There will be nothing left for your mother to mourn save ashes, and those will be irrevocably mixed with the pathetic humans you share blood with."

"Mistress, I suggest we…"

"I had considered sparing you, youkai," Ichitiro continued, pointing a clawed finger at Shitoro. "But you are testing my patience, choosing this garbage over your rightful masters."

"So this is the true Ichitiro, then?" Kisaki replied, leaning casually against the wall of a building as he continued to draw in power. It was an effort to not run, an even greater effort to not shake as she spoke, but she held fast. "You cannot defeat one lone hanyou in fair combat, so you raze the entire countryside instead? Your bravery astounds. I can see why my mother chose a human warrior over you. All the power in the multiverse cannot hide your true nature."

No amount of magic could shield an ego the size of Ichitiro's. She was well aware that he could finish this battle with but a single devastating show of power. But even if he claimed the Taiyosori in doing so, he would always know that he didn't wrest it from her directly. She was counting on that being a sticking point.

Amazingly, it seemed she might be right for he reined in the miasma around him, raising his sword instead. "So be it, hanyou," he growled. "Know the wrath of Ichitiro."

Just as the last of the miasma dissipated, one of the fingers of lightning struck out. Kisaki was prepared to dodge, but it hadn't been aimed at her. Instead it struck Shitoro, sending him flying back through the air until he hit the side of the diner they'd been hiding in. He slid down the wall and lay on the sidewalk unmoving.

"Shitoro!"

She'd been hoping to use the daimao's pride against him but now realized her small victories had only served to inflate her own sense of self-worth. Ichitiro might be no better than a child drunk on his own power, but he was old beyond comprehension and apparently knew how to play this game as well.

It was a sobering realization as she turned back to find that her foe had closed the distance between them with frightening speed and was even now preparing to hack her in two with his blade of black flame.

Kisaki was quick, even quicker than she realized, but it was still only barely enough. She managed to sidestep the awful black flames by only the barest of margins. The tips of her hair caught fire and her arm was singed as she stumbled out of the way.

She began to realize there was no way she could win this with her skills alone.

The throbbing of heat by her side seemed to confirm this.

That was nothing, though, compared to the heat from her midsection as Ichitiro followed up with a slash from his free hand, tearing four shallow gashes across her abdomen. Kisaki cried out and lost her footing, falling on her backside in front of the war god.

"Now you get your wish. Die by my hand like the filth you are!"

As he brought the sword down, Kisaki reached inside her jacket and grabbed hold of the quill inside.

Please change, please change.

She held it up to deflect the blow, but then could only stare wide-eyed as she found herself trying to fend off a fatal sword stroke with a meager feather.

I'm sorry, Mother. Please forgive me.

She closed her eyes and waited for the pain of the killing blow, hoping his aim was true.

Instead, all she felt was a jarring impact within her arm as if a tremendous weight had fallen upon it. When she opened her eyes again, she was amazed to see the feather actually holding back the blazing hot blade of Ichitiro's weapon.

He was seemingly no less surprised. "What trickery is this?"

Even with her back to the ground, she was finding it difficult to keep his weapon from descending further. He was frighteningly strong. She grabbed hold of the quill with both hands, the delicate feather somehow uncut by the cruel weapon being wielded by her enemy.

Amazed as she was to still be alive, she was equally frustrated that the Taiyosori was still a feather. Unbreakable though it might seem, it was still not much use against a weapon that looked capable of slicing clean through a building.

What am I doing wrong?

It was a particularly poor moment for introspection. Yet, as Kisaki barely held off the killing blow, she was forced to consider what had allowed her to use the sword against Crag.

She'd thought the quill useless. Had almost given up using it, but then it had burned the mazoku badly. It was in that instant she realized how much power the sword actually had. It was in that moment she believed in it.

I believe in you.

I believe in you!

Still, it remained a quill, and she remained inches away from being bisected by a would-be god.

"Now die!"

"No!" a voice cried out just as multiple bolts of yellow magic exploded in front of Ichitiro's eyes.

"Shitoro!" He was alive.

Ichitiro snarled and raised a hand to cover his face, momentarily taking the pressure off his attack.

That gave Kisaki a chance to roll to the side and regain her feet, sidestepping her temporarily blinded foe.

There has to be something else! She racked her mind, continuing to stare in frustration at the writing implement in her hands.

It had seemed hopeless, her battle with Crag, albeit not as hopeless as this fight. At least she'd been able to injure him. Ichitiro might as well be made of solid rock for all the good her attacks had done.

She ran over it again in her mind. The Taiyosori had changed back to its natural form, accepted her as its master. It had even told her so. So then what had caused it to…?

Kisaki could have smacked herself. *Its master.* She was the sword's rightful master now.

I command you to change form!

Nothing happened.

It was almost enough to make her want to throw the damnable thing to the ground and let her foe take it. If it caused him as much frustration as it seemed intent on causing her, then surely the multiverse would survive.

She knew that was the poorest of ideas, though. Ichitiro wasn't some pretender to the throne like she was. He was a full-fledged daimao, a creature worthy of the blade's power. His blood was pure, unlike…

Realization hit in the space of an instant. There had been one more thing she'd done before the Taiyosori had changed into a sword. She'd plunged the tip through Crag's eye.

The weapon had tasted blood.

FORTY

KISAKI WASN'T CERTAIN it would work. In fact, she was mostly convinced it wouldn't. But she also realized she was unlikely to get another chance like this.

Ichitiro was still blinded from Shitoro's attack, but that was likely to buy her no more than another few seconds.

Pushing hesitation to the side, she lifted the quill and drove it into the daimao's wide back, saying a silent prayer to whatever deities protected the vastly outclassed.

The tip of the quill somehow punctured Ichitiro's thick armor and his equally tough flesh. It wasn't a fatal wound by any means, barely a pinprick, but he threw his head back and roared as if she'd stabbed him directly in his black heart.

Kisaki sensed the counterattack a moment before it happened. She yanked the quill out of Ichitiro's back and leapt out of the way as he blindly swung his sword at her. The blade itself missed, but the black flames caught her jacket and it ignited.

She barely had time to note the greasy black blood dripping from the tip of the quill when she was forced to strip off her jacket and toss it to the side before the rapidly growing flames consumed her.

Her arm got stuck in one of the sleeves, and when she tried to yank it out, the fabric parted easily as a translucent blade emerged through the cloth, freeing her. Gone was the quill, and in its place was the blade of heaven.

Impossible!

Ichitiro had been wounded before, as had any number of his brethren. It was part of who they were as a warrior race. Most injuries were inconsequential. It was one of the daimao's great strengths. Their flesh was tough, strong, more than enough to deflect a sword or spear, and Ichitiro's was thicker than most.

On the rare occasion something did manage to penetrate, the damage would mend itself almost immediately. Indeed, he'd fought many a battle in which he'd let a foe deliver a blow simply to watch the triumph in their eyes turn to despair as his wounds closed up before their very eyes.

It had been eons since he'd suffered an injury which refused to instantly heal, but that was exactly what had been somehow dealt to him.

The girl's unarmed strikes had been formidable, almost respectful in their speed and power, but they were nothing that would have felled a being such as him. A momentary amusement at best.

But now he could feel the small trickle of blood continue to run down his back. It wasn't debilitating or even particularly painful, but that wasn't the point. This creature, a hanyou of all things, had actually injured him.

It had to have been a fluke, some bizarre side effect of her mother's blood – a momentary spark of power before being snuffed out forever. Or perhaps a hallucination, a foul miasma of the hanyou's own that he hadn't thought to counter.

That had to be it. First there was that feather, a fragile thing, yet seemingly able to deflect his own weapon, the Kaokatta.

He'd forged it himself in the heart of a black flame volcano upon a dying world, had used it to cleave mountains in two. So to see it bested by a swan's quill was madness itself.

Then there was the treachery of that accursed youkai, allowing the hanyou to stab him in the back like a coward.

Nothing more than tricks.

They'd picked the wrong entity to toy with. If they hoped their cleverness would save them, they were wrong, so very wrong.

Ichitiro shook his head to clear the sparks from his vision, then turned to face where he sensed his foe to be. He was intent on finishing this. Let her try to fend off his full wrath with a mere feather.

Instead, he found the girl holding that which he both desired and feared most, the Taiyosori. Its glasslike blade was leveled at him, the point upon it so sharp it seemed to almost disappear.

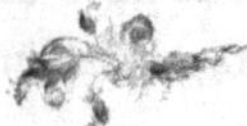

The look of surprise on Ichitiro's face echoed that on Kisaki's, though she tried her best to cover it up. She didn't know what the other daimao knew of the Taiyosori's powers, but he seemed shocked to find it in her hands.

This was what Kisaki had hoped for, something to throw him off his game. She still wasn't certain what advantage, if any, that gave her in the long run, but at the moment, she was counting every extra minute of life as a small victory.

She prepared to rush the daimao and test exactly how sharp the blade of heaven was, but then the roar of engines caught her ears.

Both combatants turned to see humans headed their way in news vans, police cars, and more, but that wasn't all. Other vehicles, larger than this first wave, were closing in on them from off in the distance, a deep rumbling emanating from them that she could already feel beneath her feet.

Airships could be seen on the horizon as well – helicopters, Tamiko had called them – although whether to attack or observe, she didn't know. If the former, she prayed they realized Ichitiro was the enemy here. She didn't favor coming as far as she had only to be felled by misguided hands.

Ichitiro glanced back to her and smiled, his sharp teeth glinting black in the midday sun. "So it seems I have other witnesses to behold my victory. I have no further need for your kitten."

Kisaki's eyes opened wide at the implication. "Shitoro, run!"

Ichitiro held out his palm toward where the tiger demon stood, power gathering in and around his hand. "Now, youkai, learn the price of daring to annoy your betters."

Kisaki didn't think. There was no time. She just acted.

In the moment before Ichitiro unleashed his attack, she was on the move, throwing herself in front of him and trying to shield her friend.

"Two for the price of one?" he asked, bemused. "Very well."

He let loose with a shimmering torrent of power.

A wave of pure force, the same he'd used to devastate nearly half the town, issued forth from Ichitiro's outstretched hand. It was as if one combined the power of a tsunami and an avalanche into one invisible wall of energy.

The street in front of the daimao exploded as the concussive blast tore through it, heading toward Kisaki and her companion.

"Mistress, save yourself! Get out of the…" The rest of Shitoro's warning was lost in the cacophony of destruction that barreled toward them.

Kisaki's first instinct was to grab up the little youkai, shield him with her body as best she could as the end came for them. However, the Taiyosori pulsed in her hand, seeming to disagree with that course of action. Though Kisaki was certain it was madness to attribute opinions to an object, she also realized her plan was good for only one thing: dying in a most painful manner.

She turned toward the attack, said a silent prayer, and held out the weapon before her. The outermost edge of the spell reached her, nearly sweeping her from her feet. It felt almost solid, an irresistible force against…

Solid! Maybe that was it, what the sword was hinting at.

Kisaki did the only thing she could think of. She lifted the Taiyosori and slashed down with it at the onrushing attack.

She expected it to be futile, for the power to plow into her with the same force with which it had leveled buildings, pulverizing her bones to dust in the process. What she didn't expect was for Ichitiro's spell to part before her.

It was as if there were a raging river hurtling past on either side, while she stood unmolested on an island in the middle. The power from the spell whipped past her, causing her hair and clothes to buffet as if she were standing outside in a hurricane, but that was the worst of it. Buildings on either side of her were pulverized, but she herself was left unharmed.

"Unbelievable," Shitoro said from immediately behind her.

She dared a glance over her shoulder and found him a little disheveled, but otherwise okay.

"No, quite the opposite," she replied. "I think it is time I started to believe."

There wasn't a chance to say more, for Ichitiro raced forward, his face contorted in a mix of rage and disbelief. He was upon her in a heartbeat, even faster than his spell had been. He swung his sword and she barely countered in time, the impact so powerful it jarred her to her very bones.

He followed up with a punch that she wasn't able to fully block. It was a glancing blow, but it felt as if her ribs had been struck by a sledgehammer.

Ichitiro spun, bringing his blade to bear once more, and she just barely managed to parry. Another, and again she only blocked it in the barest nick of time.

There was no talk, just swift and savage action, slowly driving her back, blow by blow. Soon her back would be against the wall, quite literally – the remains of the diner she and her friends had taken refuge in. Once that happened, she'd have nowhere else to retreat.

Her spirit was willing, but the flesh was weak, or weaker than her opponent's anyway. That wasn't all. Though she wielded the superior weapon, her foe was by far the more experienced swordsman. That in itself was almost a bad joke. Kisaki's experience was limited to stealing the Taiyosori and a lucky shot upon Crag. Aside from that, she'd never used a weapon before.

She could feel the cold logic in her head trying to dictate her actions, her father's fighting skills helping her stay alive. His knowledge kept her arms and legs moving, dodging, and swinging. Unfortunately, she sensed he'd been more a hand-to-hand expert. Where the sword was concerned, she found her movements much more unsure, choppy, as if she was figuring it out as she went.

Her opponent suffered from no such handicap. His blade moved as if it were an extension of his arm, striking and slicing as if he'd done so a thousand times before.

It was slow, methodical on his part now. Gone was his earlier arrogance, his presumption to end this in one blow. She'd done her part a little too well. He was taking her seriously now, forcing her back and chipping away at her defenses little by little.

A blow here, a kick there, a slice from his claws, all while his own sword continued to hammer away at her resistance.

Shitoro sent a continual wave of spells, both offensive and distracting, flying Ichitiro's way, but the element of surprise was lost. The daimao countered them all expertly, each attack fizzling before it could touch him.

Within short order, Kisaki found herself faltering. Her arms felt like rubber and her body was covered in bruises and cuts, none of them fatal by themselves, but gradually adding up.

Eventually, she felt the crumbled wall of the diner looming behind her. There came another thunderous blow from Ichitiro and she nearly lost her grip on the Taiyosori. Though the blade of heaven itself appeared to be in perfect condition, her arms were a mass of contusions from the pummeling they'd taken.

Shaking from the exertion, she dropped to one knee, her defenses all but breached, but still unwilling to yield.

The great demon paused in his attack to look down upon her. "Impressive, but ultimately futile. Know that Ichitiro shows no respect to his enemies, only disdain, but you have come the closest in many years to earning that which I do not offer."

Kisaki smiled tiredly and then echoed something she'd heard Stephen say earlier. "Bite me, bitch."

"I would not dirty my tongue." He raised his sword above his head, miasma gathering once more, a miniature storm forming around him. He meant to end this farce.

She'd done what she could. There was no shame in having lost to a superior foe. She'd saved her friends, done her best to stop him. She could only hope her mother and the other daimao would succeed where she had failed, and that her mother would one day forgive her for what she'd done.

Ichitiro backed up a step, gathering lightning around his blade.

"Get behind me, Shitoro," she said weakly.

"Mistress, I..."

"Do as you're told," she commanded.

If she was going to die, it would be as one of her station, heir to her mother, Lady Midnite.

The little youkai stepped between her and the wall of the diner. Meager protection at best, but it was all she could do for him. She hoped it would be enough.

Power crackled all around Ichitiro as he prepared to bring down his blade. He began to swing the wicked weapon, the air ablaze with the smell of ozone.

Kisaki braced herself best as she could, and then the world seemingly exploded around her in a hail of thunder and fire.

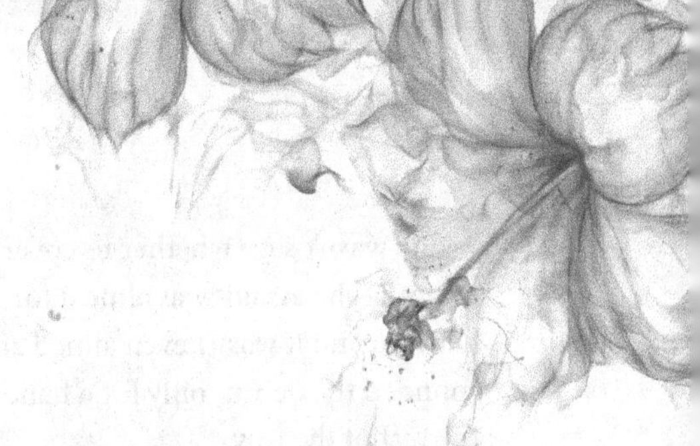

FORTY-ONE

KISAKI WAS THROWN back by the concussive wave that ensued, hitting the wall with her top half and something small and furry with her bottom.

After a moment, she was amazed to find herself still alive. Had Ichitiro's attack faltered?

The sound of thunder continued and she realized it wasn't coming from him. Ichitiro had never released his attack. Instead, he was being pummeled by one.

It was one of the helicopters she'd seen. Black in color and with strange markings on its side, it was firing its guns at him, but they were much larger and obviously more potent than the ones the police had used against Crag. Ichitiro was being peppered with it, slowly driven back under the assault.

"Midnight Girl! This way!" a voice called to her, just barely audible in the conflagration.

Kisaki saw a figure beckoning to her from behind a pile of rubble that had been a building only a short while ago. Shaking the cobwebs from her head, she stumbled in that direction as the fires of Hell were seemingly unleashed around her.

She wasn't sure whether to cover her ears, shield her eyes, or both. The assault was almost too intense for her to stay on her feet, and it wasn't even aimed at her. She stumbled as she rounded the debris, only for a hand to grab her and drag her the rest of the way.

It was Beth Billingsly, along with her cameraman. He was still filming, despite everything going on.

"What are you doing here?" she asked the reporter.

"My job," Beth replied brightly. "We got lucky and that monster missed us when he started blowing stuff up."

"Our van wasn't so lucky," the cameraman replied.

"The station will be able to afford another after this is all finished and done with. Now are we rolling or not?"

He gave a quick nod. "Go!"

Beth stepped in front of Kisaki and immediately took on a more serious persona. "This is Beth Billingsly reporting live from what was once the peaceful town of Cartersville, Pennsylvania. This marks the second time this community has suffered a devastating attack, all in the space of less than a day."

"Third," Kisaki said from over her shoulder.

"What?" Beth asked.

"Third time," Kisaki repeated. "Earlier it was wolves and bears."

"Um, okay. If you say so." She turned back to the camera. "I'm here with Midnight Girl, the self-appointed savior of this town. She has been defending its frightened citizens against the ... alien incursion that has apparently taken place here, proving once and for all that life exists else..."

"Daimao."

"Excuse me?"

"They are not aliens. That is Ichitiro. He is a daimao, a greater demon charged with maintaining the order of the multiverse."

Beth lowered her microphone. "Nobody is going to believe that."

"It's the truth."

"We'll just go with aliens. Trust me on this."

"Let me guess, we'll edit that out?" the cameraman asked.

"You know me too well, Chuck." She made a motion with her hand for them to keep going. "But it seems that even Midnight Girl and her magic sword might not be enough. Fortunately, the local sheriff's office was able to notify the National Guard just as this latest threat arrived. As you can see behind me, they are currently engaging this alien terror."

"Not terror. Ichitiro." Kisaki turned. "Shitoro, please help me explain … Shitoro? *Shitoro!*"

The little youkai wasn't behind her. *Oh no!*

"Who are you calling for?"

"Shitoro. He's a tiger youkai."

"What is that? Like your sidekick or something?"

Kisaki didn't know what a sidekick was, nor did she particularly care. She'd thought her friend was right behind her while Ichitiro was being pounded by the human weaponry. But if not, then where was he?

The helicopters continued to blast the daimao from all sides, along with soldiers now on the ground. Those large vehicles she'd seen earlier, trucks, were now pulling into position. More soldiers poured from their backs, many of them carrying what she hoped was more weaponry.

In mere moments, even more pressure would be put upon the daimao. Hopefully enough to turn the tide. She glanced back toward him and her eyes caught movement low to the ground.

What the…?!

Shitoro was back in his tiger form, prowling toward Ichitiro and using the scattered debris as cover. Kisaki wondered what he was doing. He couldn't possibly be insane enough to attack, especially now.

But the little youkai was apparently in a mood to prove her wrong. He waited for a momentary lull in the rain of death engulfing Ichitiro, then raced forward, faster than Kisaki had ever seen him move. He struck the mighty daimao in the side, barely even budging him. Then, just as quickly, he ran away, heading toward her.

As she waved him on, confused but grateful to see him alive, she noticed something hanging from his mouth. He hadn't been attacking Ichitiro after all. He'd stolen something, but what?

"This is what you were worried about?" Beth asked. "Your cat?"

"He is not a cat. He is a tiger."

"He looks like a..." Her voice trailed off as Shitoro dove behind the same cover they were using, simultaneously transforming into his bipedal youkai form.

"What the hell is that?!"

"It is as I said. He is a tiger youkai." Kisaki bent down to Shitoro, despite her own injuries, and hugged him hard. Then, after a moment, she pulled back. "A tiger youkai I am quite cross with. What were you thinking?"

He shrugged. "I was thinking you could use all the help you can get."

"It talks, too?!" Beth screeched.

"Of course I talk, human. Now kindly stop asking irrelevant questions. Can you not see the threat that is here before you? The twilight of your species is at hand."

Right then, Kisaki couldn't bring herself to disagree. The human soldiers were buying them time, but she feared it would be a few minutes at best. She'd given Ichitiro everything she had and it hadn't been nearly enough.

Beth turned back to her cameraman, holding her microphone up again and quickly composing herself. "You heard it here first on Excitement News. Aliens, warrior princesses, and now talking tiger gnomes. In the space of a day, the world has seemingly gone mad. What we believed to be reality has been shattered by knowledge that the creatures we thought confined to late night movies are actually real."

Kisaki spared her a momentary glance of confusion. *Such a strange woman.* Then she turned to Shitoro. "That was foolish. Why do such a thing?"

"For this." He held up a water skin made of some sort of black leathery material. Shitoro pulled the stopper out with his teeth, then took a small sip of what was inside. "Yes! Just as I suspected." He held it out to Kisaki. "Quickly, drink this."

"Why?"

"Now, young lady!" It was the same tone Shitoro used when he was particularly annoyed with her, usually during her lessons. Force of habit took hold and she did as commanded, drinking deeply from the skin. The liquid sloshed around her mouth for a moment until she recognized the cool crisp taste and the tingling it left behind. "Water from the celestial palace?"

"Yes. Now keep drinking!"

"Why? I have had it many times."

"True, but never when you've been injured. The divine waters contain healing properties that will greatly augment your body's natural ability to recover. It is common for all those traveling forth from the palace to carry a skin of it with them, daimao included."

"But you didn't."

He smiled sheepishly. "I did when I first came looking for you, but I used it after a run-in with a pack of dogs. Vicious beasts. Now hurry!"

Kisaki did as told, draining the water skin. At first, all it did was quench the thirst she'd built up from the battle, but then she realized she was actually beginning to feel better.

When she looked down again, the bruises on her arms were rapidly fading. The cuts she'd suffered had scabbed over and were already peeling to reveal fresh skin.

"Better?" he asked.

"Much, thank you."

"'Tis my pleasure, my lady."

Kisaki glanced at the sword in her hand, still gleaming and now feeling as light as the feather it had once been. She stepped over to Beth, who was still speaking to the camera about an alien apocalypse, whatever that was, and tapped her on the shoulder. "Excuse me."

"Yes, Midnight Girl?"

Kisaki wasn't sure why she kept referring to her as that, but she didn't find the mistake to be entirely unpleasant sounding. Besides, this wasn't the time to debate it. "Can you contact those soldiers?"

"Contact them? Why? Do you have a plan?"

"Perhaps."

Beth turned to the camera. "You heard it here first. Midnight Girl, the world's very first superhero, has a plan to…"

"We don't have time for this," Kisaki snapped. "Yes or no?"

Something in the tone of her voice seemed to get through to Beth. She stopped in the middle of her speech and waved her cameraman forward. "Chuck?"

"I have my cell. No telling if there's any towers still standing, though."

Beth nodded, then said to Kisaki, "We'll try our best."

"That is all I can ask of you."

"Lady Kisaki," Shitoro said. "I have been thinking."

"If you are going to tell me to be careful, Shitoro, I am well aware of the sentiment. Unfortunately, I cannot promise to do so."

"Not that, I…"

"What do you need me to tell them?" Chuck asked.

Kisaki turned away from the tiger demon. "For starters, please ask them to do their best to not fire upon me. I don't believe I would be able to recover from such an assault quite as easily as Ichitiro." That was an understatement. She was certain what they were currently doing to him would easily kill her. However, she kept that to herself, as what she was planning would almost certainly get her killed anyway. "Secondly, it would be most agreeable if they would time their attacks in direct contradiction to mine."

"Not following," Chuck said.

"I am," Beth replied. "You want them to hold off when you attack, then open fire when you fall back. Give you both a chance to regroup while he's kept under constant pressure."

"Yes, I believe that is our best chance at…"

"Killing him?"

"Dissuading him from further hostilities." Kisaki wasn't a fool. She had no delusions about her chances and saw no need to give these humans false hope.

Beth nodded. "Be careful out there, especially once those mortars start firing." She pointed toward a group of soldiers setting up what Kisaki presumed to be more weaponry.

Kisaki bowed to them both, then turned away as Chuck tried to multitask using his phone and keeping the camera steady on Beth. Shitoro was there waiting for her. He opened his mouth to speak, but she held up a hand.

"Brave Shitoro, I could ask for no finer tutor or guardian. You have more than proven your mettle this day, but I can ask no more. Please leave this place."

"But…"

"Find a way back to the celestial palace. Tell Mother I am truly sorry. I acted out of ignorance and brought this down upon myself. But also tell her that I love her and understand what she has done to protect me. If I am to die this day, let her know that I did so on my feet, as one who has both warrior blood in her veins as well as that of the daimao."

Shitoro tried to speak again, probably to protest her decision, but he was drowned out by a booming voice.

"Enough!"

Kisaki looked past him to where Ichitiro was just barely visible amidst the constant assault. He'd managed to gather his miasma back around him and now struck out with it. Bolts of lightning flew skyward toward the helicopters continuing to strafe him. He hit one and it exploded in a fireball, raining flaming debris upon the already devastated town.

Next, he swung his sword and a lance of black flame shot out. Kisaki couldn't see his intended target amidst the chaos, but she had to assume it was the human warriors.

They stood no chance against him alone, especially once he managed to fully go on the offensive.

She stepped past the still protesting Shitoro and prepared to once more engage her foe, when there came three thunderous reports from nearby. They were so loud and sudden, they caused her to flinch in fear.

Fortunately, she hadn't been their target.

Multiple explosions erupted near Ichitiro. It must have been those weapons. Mortars, as Beth had called them. A strong name worthy of the death they spewed.

Ichitiro was knocked off his feet. He landed in a crumpled heap, and for a moment, Kisaki hoped that the humans didn't need her after all. But it was only for a moment. The explosions had apparently caught him by surprise, managing to tear sections of his armor asunder.

Even from where she stood, she could tell he wasn't gravely injured, though. If anything, he looked far more angry. He turned toward the line of trucks and the soldiers lined up in front of them, his eyes glowing red with rage. He lifted his sword above his head and charged toward them.

She had little doubt he would cut through their ranks like paper, showing no mercy to those brave souls standing against him.

She had dallied long enough.

With a battle cry, Kisaki raced forward, her own sword ready for the attack. She intended to hit his flank before he could reach his targets and once more bring the battle to him.

"Kisaki!" Shitoro called after her. "Blasted willful child!"

She allowed herself the ghost of a smile. Now if only he would do as he'd been told, she could engage this devil without having to worry about him.

If so, then she could fully concentrate her attention elsewhere, such as worrying about her own odds against this monster.

FORTY-TWO

THE MORTARS FIRED another volley at Ichitiro, but he was moving too fast, and their shots all fell wide of the target, exploding behind him and throwing up clouds of debris.

The remaining helicopters had better luck, peppering him with fire from above and causing him to stumble slightly.

It wasn't much, but it was enough for her to catch up to him.

Now to hope that Beth and Chuck had gotten through to the soldiers, because if not, she was likely to be cut down the second she stepped into the fray.

There was no time for second guessing, only savage action – seemingly the only communication this Ichitiro understood – so she hoped for the best and took a leap of faith.

Once more, the cool logic of battle descended upon her and she found herself considering possible strategies. There! Ichitiro's path was going to take him past a pile of rubble.

Kisaki put on as much speed as she was able to in the debris-strewn street. Thankfully, Ichitiro's focus still seemed to be on the soldiers. They'd apparently done more to injure him than anyone else.

It was time to remedy that.

She ran up atop the pile of rubble just as Ichitiro was passing it, using it to shield her from his view, then leapt off of it, sword held high and a cry of rage upon her lips.

Amazingly enough, the humans picked that moment to disengage. Either lucky coincidence or the others had been successful.

Now it was her turn.

Ichitiro was frighteningly quick for his size, however. In the moments it took her to descend upon him, he turned, saw her, and brought up his own sword to parry the blow.

She brought the blade of heaven down with everything she had, envisioning herself cleaving this monster in two just as he'd tried to do to her.

The strange blade of the Taiyosori met the burning ferocity of Ichitiro's weapon. There came a squeal of metal followed by a flash of light and then Kisaki once more found herself airborne, being flung back as if by another explosion.

She managed to roll with the blow, slamming the tip of the Taiyosori into the ground so as to slow herself down. She skidded to a halt, pulled the sword free, and bounced back to her feet without further injury. Even she was half amazed at what she'd managed to do.

However, the look on her face was nothing compared to the shock on Ichitiro's. He still held the grip of his sword, but only about three inches of burning blade remained. She'd missed in her gambit to cut him down but was willing to settle for having destroyed his weapon.

This cannot be!

Not only was the wretched hanyou still alive, but she'd somehow managed to destroy his own sword, the Kaokatta.

Ichitiro had no delusions about the Taiyosori being the superior weapon. It was, after all, why he'd lusted after it. But for such a low creature to not only wield it, but somehow find the strength to cleave his own blade in twain, was unthinkable.

Everything about this scenario had seemed so ideal, almost down to the last detail. The hanyou, Midnite's offspring, had stolen the Taiyosori and come to Earth. It was a perfect opportunity for him to step in and pluck it from her corpse. Yet the blasted creature had not only refused to die, but had somehow continued to fight back, even managing to wound him.

This hanyou was nothing more than an insect, but even insects, it seemed, could sting.

Now the humans were getting involved. He didn't know if they'd purposely helped the hanyou or not, but that had been the result. All of the talk his siblings had wasted in the council chambers had been true. The weapons the humans now wielded were far more powerful than in eons past. Arrows, crossbows, spears, even catapults; those had been nothing. Child's playthings to one such as he. But these new armaments were capable of hurting him. And he knew for a fact this was far from the worst they were now capable of.

His siblings would surely be aware of his absence by now, but he trusted in their fear and Reiden's insufferable sense of bureaucracy to hold them at bay. That was a must, because he now understood that this battle wasn't as easily won as he'd originally presumed. He was going to have to draw upon more power than he had counted on, enough for the other daimao to sense his location if they turned their eyes toward Earth.

It was a risk, but easily worth it once the Taiyosori was in his hands.

The time had come to remind the humans why they once bowed down to the daimao as gods.

Bolstered by what she'd managed to do, Kisaki again sprang forward to engage her enemy. As hoped, the humans brought their weapons of war to bear again the moment she had disengaged. She allowed herself a second to be amazed. The weaponry on display was like nothing she'd read about in her studies. If anything, it seemed the humans had been paying attention to the destructive magic wielded by some demons and had been successful in harvesting it in their own way.

It made her heart proud, because it told her that this race, *her people*, were now capable of defending themselves against divine threats.

More explosions rocked Ichitiro, knocking him down again. It was the perfect opportunity, but she was forced to shield her eyes from the debris thrown up. The smoke from the shellfire was thick, and she found herself nearly doubled over from coughing after she inhaled a lungful of the acrid discharge.

She forced herself to continue, though. If they could knock Ichitiro down, stun him for even a few moments, she could do the impossible … use the Taiyosori to end this.

Unfortunately, her hopes turned out to be little more than fantasy.

The smoke instantly cleared as Ichitiro threw out another wall of force, gouging the very earth in front of him and slamming into two of the trucks, sending them flying as if they were mere toys. They landed dozens of yards away with terrible squeals of rent metal. Both vehicles exploded, tearing them apart and setting the nearby buildings on fire.

Kisaki had only a moment to rue the war she'd brought to this quiet town. Soon it would be less a community and more a burning graveyard. She said a quick prayer in the hopes most of the people here had been lucky enough to flee after Ichitiro's first attack.

Her moment abruptly ended, however, when tongues of lightning flared up around Ichitiro, a dozen or more tendrils each possessed of the deadliest of kisses. The energy whipped around him, simultaneously fending off more gunfire while lashing out at those who'd attacked him.

One bolt flared out at her, but she managed to bring the Taiyosori up to fend it off, deflecting it with the powerful weapon. Sadly, she wasn't nearly so lucky with a second bolt. It got past her defenses and struck her on the leg.

She was thrown from her feet, scorched from thigh to knees. The only reason she didn't immediately lose her grip on her sword was that it was as if all of her muscles seized up at once. She couldn't have dropped it even if she wanted to.

Kisaki hit the ground hard and lay there twitching as Ichitiro continued to mount a defense against the humans.

Thank goodness for them, because otherwise, he could have simply strolled up and plucked the sword from her fingers. Kisaki said a silent curse. It seemed every time there came a shred of hope in their battle, he would do something to cut that hope to ribbons and scatter it to the wind.

After several more moments, she began to regain control of her muscles. She forced herself back to her feet, then almost fell again before catching herself, using the blade of heaven as if it were a mere walking stick.

I'd best not think that too hard. Otherwise, it might turn into one.

She chuckled to herself. It helped to distract from the injuries once again being inflicted upon her. Fortunately, though the pain from her leg was pretty bad, it was still able to hold her weight.

Kisaki steeled herself to rejoin the battle. With Ichitiro's weapon destroyed, she needed to get in close so as to bring the fight directly to him, put him on the defensive. Only then would she have a chance of walking away from this.

Unfortunately, she saw that where she was focused on remaining upright, Ichitiro had set his aspirations much higher.

Before she could so much as take a single step, he rose from the ground. Smoky miasma gathered around him and the fingers of lightning seemed to carry him toward the sky and out of her reach.

From the air, he could rain death down upon them all, and there wouldn't be much she could do other than accept her fate.

FORTY-THREE

ICHITIRO ROSE TO about fifteen meters off the ground, hovering as if daring his attackers to come to him.

They did.

Death was unleashed at him from all directions. The ground troops opened fire skyward, but it was the two remaining helicopters that were the real threat. They had larger weapons to bring to bear and, now that Ichitiro was airborne, they did so without hesitation. An explosion to rival the mortar fire hit Ichitiro from the backside, sending him careening through the air.

For a moment, Kisaki held out hope that he would be sent tumbling back to the ground, but he managed to right himself, his miasma almost acting like massive wings of smoke. The helicopter who'd hit him flew past, no doubt meaning to come around for another pass, but the daimao was ready for it.

He held out his palm and a ball of white-hot flame erupted from it. It slammed into the helicopter, vaporizing it midair. As its remains fell to the beleaguered town below, the lightning from Ichitiro's miasma began to form a protective cage of energy around him.

Kisaki's heart dropped as she watched it seemingly fend off all other attacks against him, flaring and crackling as more weapons were discharged in his direction. Nothing seemed to make it through. More fingers of lightning flared out around him, striking the last helicopter even as it sped toward the demon. The discharge hit its tail rotor, sending it in a dizzying spin toward the Earth.

Kisaki noted, with no small amount of panic, that the fatally wounded air ship was headed straight toward her.

Kisaki ran as quickly as her injured leg could carry her. About a dozen meters away, she could see Beth and Chuck, still filming despite everything. They were truly dedicated to their craft. It was admirable, if somewhat insane.

They wouldn't be anything, though, if they stayed where they were.

"Get down!" she screamed a moment before the helicopter slammed into the ground somewhere behind her.

She followed her own advice and threw herself in a desperate dive roll, hearing the whistle as shards of flaming shrapnel flew over her at lethal velocity.

A moment later, there came an explosion, and Kisaki felt a sting of fire as something hard and hot slammed into the small of her back. She reached around and felt a ragged hole in her shirt, hot blood, and the sting as her fingertips touched ragged metal. She'd been hit, but how badly, she did not know.

If she didn't get moving quickly, though, she was certain it was going to get much worse. She tried to push herself up, but the pain from her injury was making it difficult.

"Stay down, you stupid girl, I'm coming!"

Kisaki looked up to find Shitoro sprinting her way, his four-legged form allowing him to circumnavigate the minefield of debris with ease. She wasn't sure whether to be grateful or furious with him for disobeying her command, but decided to settle on the former as he changed and began to examine her.

"I swear, you are helpless without me," he said.

"I told you to run."

"And I promptly ignored you. Do not forget, I was charged with being your guardian, not the other way around."

"It's for your own … ow!"

"Hold still," he ordered. "It's not a big piece, but it's lodged in there. Almost … got it…"

Kisaki screamed as the jagged shard was torn from her, feeling as if her flesh were being ripped apart from the inside out.

"Oh, do stop whining," he said once she got herself under control again. "You have no idea how lucky you are."

"L-lucky?"

"Yes. The metal was quite hot. It cauterized the wound from the inside."

"I shall have to thank the fates once this day is done," she replied, gasping.

Shitoro gently eased her over onto her back. "You should. The very fact that you have lasted this long against Ichitiro is nothing short of amazing."

Sadly, she couldn't share in his enthusiasm. What she saw from this new angle was not encouraging.

Ichitiro continued to rain fireballs at his attackers on the ground, all while his storm miasma protected him from further harm. A nearby police cruiser resembled a heap of burning slag. The few combat vehicles that remained were backing up as quickly as they could. Multiple fires burned throughout the town. Whatever Ichitiro hadn't leveled yet looked as if it were in danger of being consumed by flames.

With a wince of pain, she sat up. So far, Ichitiro hadn't turned his full wrath against her, but she was certain it was only a matter of time. Once that happened, she would be helpless to stop him. Up close, she was barely able to hold her own. At range, she could do nothing save run. "It's over."

"We're still breathing and he doesn't have the Taiyosori yet," Shitoro replied.

Kisaki looked at him, surprised by his sudden show of optimism. If anything, he'd been the one advocating running ever since the moment Ichitiro's name had been mentioned. Since then, he'd been mostly doom and gloom about their chances. Perhaps the battle had driven him mad. Then again, she'd seemingly switched opinions with him. Now she was the one who was failing to see any hope.

Maybe it had driven them both mad.

"He's untouchable up there," she said. "All he has to do is stay in the sky and eventually he'll win. My father's skills, they're impressive, but I don't think they're enough."

"Then don't rely solely on his."

She inclined her head toward him. "What do you mean?"

"I shouldn't have to explain this, child, but you have two parents."

"As I am aware. But what does that have to do with…"

"It's what I was trying to tell you earlier while you were insisting on throwing yourself back into the fray. As a student, you still leave much to be desired."

"I'm not following, Shitoro. My mother isn't here."

"Yes she is." He pointed a finger at her heart. "She is always with you, as is your father."

"I do not understand."

"Nor do I," he said, "but I have been trying my best to consider the possibilities ever since you told me you were seeing visions of your father. Tell me, did it happen again when Ich-itiro attacked?"

From the sporadic sound of the gunfire, it didn't seem like the daimao would be distracted for much longer. She nodded once. "Yes. Before the fight began, I saw him, clearer than ever. If anything, the visions seem to be growing stronger."

Shitoro nodded as if this wasn't unexpected. "What happened?"

"It was a lesson on winning the war of the mind, using that to defeat your enemy."

"Wise of him."

Kisaki nodded. "What does that have to do with my mother?"

"You seem to have inherited an unprecedented gift, a quirk of your unique heritage. You have somehow retained your father's blood memory. But it is not only your father's blood that you have running through your veins. Your mother's does, too, and hers is far more potent."

"But the only visions I've had are of my father." She paused for a moment, remembering them. "Except this last one."

"Lady Midnite was in it?"

"Yes, but only incidentally. I saw her through my father's eyes, their first meeting. It was still his memory, not hers."

"I've been thinking about that and I have a theory as to why. You have been consumed by the thought of him ever since you learned of his existence. It would stand to reason that these visions, his knowledge, are appearing to you during times of need, but I believe you are the one calling out to them."

"Not consciously."

He waved a hand dismissively. "The hows are unimport-ant. That it happened is what matters, even if your waking self wasn't aware of it. However, I see no reason why you cannot do the same for your mother's memories. After all, hers is the divine blood from which this power almost certainly descends."

"But how?"

"I don't know. Only you can answer that."

"And how will that help us even if I can?"

"Think about it, child," Shitoro replied, once again talking to her as a tutor to a pupil. "Your father was a human warrior and, from what I have seen of you in action, he was a formidable one at that. But his experience was limited, both by years and the fact that the only foes he ever faced were human. As such, there is a limit to how much his skills can help you against otherworldly beings. Consider this. You performed admirably against Crag but, if not for the Taiyosori, he very well might have won."

She nodded ruefully.

"But therein lies the key, I believe. Your mother is a daimao. Her experience is far richer. I do not know if it can help us against Ichitiro, but if you can tap into her memories as well, then perhaps you will find something there of use."

"But how do I do that?"

"As I said, I don't know. Perhaps you need a longing for her as deep as that for your father. Or maybe it's something else entirely. Whatever it is, you need to dig down deep inside of you and try to find it." She made to protest, but he held up a paw. "I fear it might be our only chance."

Kisaki considered his words. They made sense, in theory anyway. She had no way of knowing if she was actually capable of it. Then again, barely a day ago she would have sworn she didn't know how to fight at all. Who was to say what revelations the future held for her?

She looked up, seeing Ichitiro raining death upon this town, upon a people who did not deserve it. She owed it to them to at least try.

Perhaps it was time to let go of the doubt. She'd needed to stop doubting in the Taiyosori for it to work for her. Maybe it was time for her to stop doubting in herself as well. She was the daughter of two beings she should be proud of – one a human warrior, the other an ageless divinity.

It was time to live up to her heritage.

"I will try my best," she said, pulling herself to her feet. "But on one condition."

"Yes, my lady?" he asked in a tone that suggested he knew what was coming.

"Run. Find shelter. I cannot do this if I know you are in danger, too."

Shitoro nodded once, then transformed back into his tiger form. "Very well. But know that I will not be far."

She smiled after him. "You never are."

"Ichitiro! You have no quarrel with the people of this world."

The daimao ceased raining fireballs down onto the humans and turned to look upon Kisaki, a malevolent grin on his face visible even from behind the curtain of power around him. "They are ants beneath my boot. Who dares tell me I should not crush them?"

"I do."

"So the gnat seeks to defend the ants? How quaint."

"I am no gnat. And I seek only to protect my people against a coward who knows no honor."

The grin faltered. "Hanyou filth. You would question me about honor? Dare question one who has faced the entropic chaos?! Without me, there would be no mudball of a planet for you to *defend*. I have faced enemies that would paralyze you with but a glance. I have…"

"And yet here you are *bravely* stepping on ants. Spare me your words. They fall upon deaf ears."

"Deaf … and soon to be dead," he growled, flinging a fire-ball her way.

Mother, if you are listening, I need your help.

The ball of flame loomed large before her, as if Ichitiro had thrown the very sun her way.

I forgive you for everything. I know now you were only protecting me.

She held the Taiyosori up in front of her, hoping it was as good at fending off fire as it had been his force blast.

Know that I love you. I always have – love you and miss you dearly.

The giant ball of flame slammed into her. For a moment, she felt terrible heat, enough to char her skin, but then it passed as the mighty blade of the Taiyosori parted the flames as if it were a solid thing to be cut in two.

Kisaki was still alive, if somewhat singed around the edges. Nothing else happened, though, no revelation, no vision … nothing.

"Die!" Ichitiro threw another at her, this one larger than the first.

Again, she just barely managed to parry it but, despite the mighty Taiyosori deflecting the spell, the air was beginning to heat up around her. She was already breathing hard, sweat running down her face.

Ichitiro saw this and laughed. He raised both hands and began to rain fire down upon her, blast after blast. Kisaki understood what he was doing and realized she could not survive such an onslaught for long.

Shitoro was wrong about her powers, her visions. Sadly, there was nothing within them to help her now.

The first of the many gouts of flame hit her, and still she stood true with the blade of heaven, doing all she could. At the very least, her sacrifice would allow any human warriors still remaining to retreat to safety. It was a consolation, however small, that she could save a few lives even as hers was snuffed out one painful breath at a time.

Another blast hit and Kisaki cried out in pain, feeling her arms blister.

Fear began to take hold. She didn't want to die. She was sorry for everything she had done, everything she'd brought upon herself, her friends, and this world. If she could only take it all back, she would have.

Fire surrounded her on all sides. The smell of burning hair, asphalt, and clothing assaulted her nose.

She wished she could go back, but she couldn't. If only her mother were here, she'd drop to her knees before her and beg forgiveness.

I am so sorry, Mother. I just wish I could see you one more time to tell you that!

Time abruptly slowed down around her, each wisp of flame easily visible as it flickered and sputtered.

What the?!

Before, when her visions came, the world greyed out around her, the vision superimposing itself over reality. This time, though, reality simply winked out as if someone had flipped a light switch.

Kisaki was assaulted on all sides by color, sound, and sensation. She was in space, but also somehow outside of it. She watched wide-eyed as galaxies were born, aged, and then died … billions of years seeming to pass within moments. Stars exploded, black holes formed, and then the cycle would begin anew.

The scene before her was both marvelous and terrible to behold, making her realize just how very small she was.

It seemed to go on for hours, the very universe changing before her, but then it ended and she was whisked away to somewhere else. She found herself on a battlefield, but like none she'd ever seen. Triple moons shone in the sky and alien creatures several meters tall raged around her.

Again the scene shifted, and now she beheld a battle between youkai and human wizards, fierce magic flying between them as they attempted to wipe one another out.

Kisaki was confused. Whatever was happening to her, it seemed to make no sense whatsoever. It was as if she'd been transported to a world of chaos, one in which she didn't even seem to have a body. *Where is this? What is going on?*

"Midnite."

The voice whispered at her, faintly as if from nowhere, yet from everywhere at once.

"Midnite."

Louder this time, more insistent.

"MIDNITE!"

The chaos around her ceased and she found herself floating formless in a grey void.

Was she dead? Was this the afterlife?

"Midnite, favored daughter of the cosmos. Stop dreaming and come to me."

Dreaming?!

"Who calls me?" The voice that answered wasn't hers, but it was as familiar as her own. Her mother's.

All at once, she realized she had a body again, albeit one that was still floating in a grey void. She looked down at herself and saw graceful hands clad in flawless porcelain skin.

"Come to me, child."

The voice beckoned again, strong, insistent, undeniable. After a moment, she felt as if she were being drawn somewhere. No, that was too easy of a word. She was being quite literally pulled toward it and, all at once, Kisaki understood.

This was another vision, but she'd arrived as her mother was asleep and dreaming. Shitoro had told her that the daimao spent eons doing such, slumbering as time moved ever onward in the unending celestial cycle.

It had worked! Just as the faithful tiger had predicted, but different all the same.

Someone was now calling to her, but something was off. The voice that rang out in her mind wasn't that of a servant, but of a master. She wasn't being gently shaken awake by some minor youkai. She was being summoned by a power far greater than her own.

But who would dare summon a daimao?

That feeling of being pulled increased to an almost mind-boggling speed but then, just as abruptly, it stopped.

She was in space again, floating above a massive seething ball of energy. Not a star, but something that felt almost alive.

And then that something winked at her.

No, it can't be.

The ball pulled back. How far, it was impossible to say, but as it did, she realized it was actually an eye. Another joined it upon an impossibly large face. Soon, whatever it was towered over her – a massive humanoid figure draped in darkness, visible more by the void it caused against the stars behind it than anything else.

Kisaki suddenly felt very small. Even more amazing, she got that same sense from her mother, whose body, or astral form anyway, she seemed to be inhabiting. If anything, her mother was feeling much the same way as she herself felt when facing off against Ichitiro. Before her was a power that dwarfed her own and against which victory was surely an impossibility.

"Welcome, child."

Kisaki was at an utter loss of words. Her mother, however, seemed to take things in stride. She bowed deeply. "I thank you for the honor."

"*You know who I am?*"

"You are one of the elder gods, those who sleep eternal under our care."

"*Oh?*" The voice seemed surprised to be recognized, although Kisaki thought that was silly. Who *else* would be talking down to a daimao?

"We have not heard your voices in many eons," her mother continued, "but some of us still remember."

"*I am pleased to hear that, child. We, too, do not forget. Though we sleep so as to protect the reality we fought so hard to birth, we see all through our dreams, such as that where you are now.*"

"I am in your dream?"

"*Yes, as I am within yours. It is how one such as I might converse with thee without wreaking havoc throughout the cosmos.*"

"To what do I owe such an honor?" her mother asked.

"*Midnite, you stand unique among your brethren. Powerful, yet not overly proud. Fearsome when called to action, yet never seeking combat. Kind to those beneath you, despite needing not ever fear their hand.*"

"I thank you."

"*There is no need, for I merely state fact, not flattery.*"

"Nevertheless."

"*It is because of these unique traits that I have chosen you to be the bearer of a great gift.*"

Before her mother could question what that was, something appeared in the giant's hands. It was a great blade, a sword hundreds of feet tall, dark as the giant, but with a gleaming hilt of pure white energy.

"The Taiyosori," Midnite said simultaneously as Kisaki thought it.

Images flashed in her, *their* mind. They saw the elder god in the flesh battling horrific monsters, nightmare creatures that made even the ugliest of oni seem palatable by comparison. Though the god was vastly outnumbered, the blade kept the abominations at bay, power flashing out from it that cut them to ribbons both near and far. Many more battles were then shown, all of them appearing at the speed of thought, far too quickly for Kisaki to take note of, yet somehow leaving an impression upon her, albeit one she didn't quite understand.

"You are showing me the blade of heaven, a deciding factor in the defeat of the entropic chaos," Midnite said, as if reciting a historical fact.

"Yes, and it is now yours."

"What?!"

Kisaki had never seen her mother lose her composure as she did just then. Though she had no control over the body she was currently in, she found herself attempting to smile nevertheless. Somehow, that one word ... *humanized* her mother.

"You find this amusing, do you not?"

If Kisaki could have jumped, she would have. It was almost as if the elder god were speaking to her. But then her mother responded, "Amused? Never, my lord. I am merely surprised. I am not worthy of such a gift. It belongs to the gods."

"The gods sleep forevermore. The blade is a force for order in the multiverse. It should not slumber alongside us."

"Another of my brothers perhaps..."

"No. You."

"But why?"

"Because it is my will."

Her mother bowed her head in subservience, but the god wasn't finished.

"It is because you will not misuse its power. It is because others shall lust after it, but you will keep them at bay. And it is because of what is yet to come."

"I do not understand."

"There will come a time when the Taiyosori is once again needed, needed by hands far different from my own. The unworthiest of the unworthy shall rise above their station, and the blade of a thousand cuts will once again be brought forth to battle. Alas, we cannot see all. To protect or to destroy, it is still to be seen what fate holds for the sword. All we know is that it will all depend upon the strength of your blood."

"My blood?" Midnite asked, confusion evident in her voice. "I cannot accept such a thing, it is…"

"Enough! *It is done.*"

Kisaki's eyes popped opened and she realized her mother had just woken up. She recognized her bed chambers. Multiple servant youkai raced in at that moment. Some asked if she were okay, others immediately began preparing her robes for her. However, after a moment, they all stopped what they were doing and stared wide-eyed at her.

She looked down and saw why.

Though Kisaki hadn't been inhabiting her mother's body when she fell asleep, she was willing to bet the Taiyosori hadn't been by her side at that moment. But it was now.

Midnite reached a tentative hand down to the weapon then, seeing the youkai watching her, took more decisive action and grasped hold of it. Kisaki could sense her mother's amazement at holding the weapon, being accepted by it, but accompanying that was also a strange feeling that took Kisaki a moment to recognize.

Her mother was feeling relief, relief tinged with nervousness.

Midnite, one of the daimao, amongst the most influential beings in the multiverse, actually feared the blade's power.

FORTY-FOUR

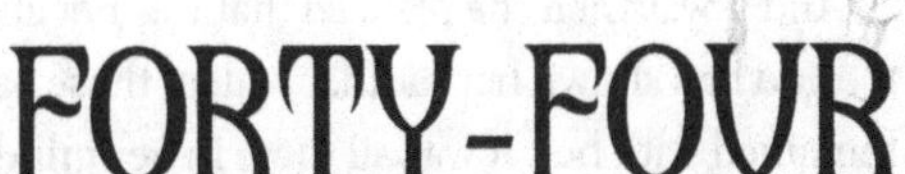

THE VISION DISSOLVED as quickly as it had over-taken her, and Kisaki once again found herself surrounded by flames.

The world was still moving in slow motion, though, giving her an added moment to regain her bearings, but it didn't look good. She'd witnessed the moment her mother had been gifted the blade. It was awe inspiring, both to be inside her dream and then to actually witness the essence of an elder god. Yet, she wasn't sure how that was supposed to help her.

Had Shitoro been wrong after all? Perhaps her mother didn't have any insight that could help her. The history of knowing how she had acquired the weapon was interesting – fascinating, even – but it would all be useless in the next few minutes if Kisaki was burned alive.

Ichitiro, for his part, seemed intent on just that. She could hear his laughter above the roar of the flames being just barely kept at bay by the Taiyosori. Should it falter, she would be instantly cooked.

But in that same instant, she also realized it would not.

It seemed insane. To think that this sword, wicked and sharp though it might be, was the same massive weapon she'd seen in the hands of the god. It was hard to believe.

Yet it was true. She felt it, *knew* it in her bones.

And it was then she realized that was not all she knew. What the god had shown her mother – all of those battles – somehow remained with her. It was all there in her mind. She was able to recall every detail, despite it being shown to her at the speed of thought itself. It was as if an encyclopedia of alien knowledge had been deposited inside her. She couldn't hope to decipher it all, especially not now, but she was able to understand enough of it.

It will all depend upon the strength of your blood.

The words of the elder god rang out loudly in her mind, almost deafeningly so, and she sensed that it was no mere memory this time. Whatever had happened in her mother's past, the god had somehow known she was there watching.

Known she would one day wield the Taiyosori.

It was almost too much for her to handle at once. Her mind felt full, almost to bursting. She needed a way to let it out, to vent before she exploded.

Kisaki screamed, a battle cry that seemed to echo around her. She focused her attention onto the sword – visions of past battles continuing to play out in her head – and then, without quite knowing why, she twisted the blade and sliced it horizontally through the air.

Almost at once, the fire from Ichitiro's attack was snuffed out around her. She was wounded, bloodied, and covered in blisters from the flames, but she felt better almost immediately upon taking a breath and inhaling the much cooler air that followed.

"What is this?" Ichitiro asked from far above her. Amusement tinged his voice. He no doubt seemed to think that perhaps this was some sort of fluke … one he was apparently resolved to correct.

He threw another ball of flame at her and Kisaki again used the Taiyosori to counter the spell, extinguishing it in its entirety before it could touch her.

She looked up at him and, insane as it might have been, actually smiled. "Is that the best you have, godling?"

Ichitiro bared his teeth at her. "Oh, it is not. Not at all."

The lightning flaring around him in his miasma lashed out at her with a half dozen of its electric tendrils.

For one small moment, Kisaki felt fear, but that cool logic descended upon her once more, more powerful than ever. When she swung the sword to deflect the attacks, gone were the clumsy swings she had used earlier. Now she had a fluid grace about her, moving as if the weapon were a part of her being, an extension of her arms.

Not a single bolt touched her.

The mask of anger on Ichitiro's face turned to one of confusion. However, it only lasted a moment. With a roar of rage, he drew power around himself, then unleashed hell upon her.

Spell upon spell. Fire, lightning, force, and much more rained down from the sky. The ground around her was pummeled into ruinous craters, but nothing harmed her. Again and again, she deflected the spells with the sword, cutting through them and dissipating their lethal energy.

Sadly, she realized it was a losing strategy. She had Ichitiro at a stalemate, but it was one that wouldn't last. He was eternal, whereas she would eventually tire. He also had an incredible amount of power at his disposal, which only now was he truly beginning to tap. It was only a matter of time before he hit her with something that even the Taiyosori might not be able to block.

Even if that failed, he would almost certainly turn his rage against the rest of the town. Enough people had already suffered at his hands. As it was, it would probably take them years to recover from the damage, and that wasn't even beginning to count the many shattered lives he left behind.

Ichitiro unleashed another volley of spells at her, sending them faster.

She'd succeeded in the psychological warfare she'd set out to wage against him. He was growing increasingly angry at her refusal to die, and his attacks were showing it. They were a frenzy of destructive power, but with little strategy behind it and absolutely zero restraint. He'd even dropped the protective shield of lightning around himself to concentrate entirely on offense.

If only she had a way of reaching him, of attacking back. She could...

Visions of the elder god fighting flashed through her mind again. She remembered him being swarmed by enemies, but they were nothing. They fell before his sword strokes, both near and far.

Far! The sword was able to...

The blade of a thousand cuts.

The voice rang out clear in her head, and this time there was no doubt something was reaching out to her from across time and space. The words which had confused her mother suddenly became clear to her.

The unworthiest of the unworthy shall rise above their station and the blade of a thousand cuts will once again be brought forth to battle.

It wasn't a warning, but a prophecy.

The Taiyosori; it had always been meant for her hand.

She was its master now, and it was time to use it to bring order from this chaos, to protect this world and the people in it.

Kisaki waited for the latest volley of spells to peter out, then she spun and swung the blade, picturing Ichitiro standing directly in its path. Words formed in her mind, spoken once by a god and now meant for her. Almost as if it had a will all its own, her mouth opened and she screamed out, "SENSURU!"

The sword pulsed once in her hands and then it was as if all the stars shining within its translucent blade leapt forth from the weapon and flew toward Ichitiro, becoming blades in their own right as they homed in on him.

Dozens … hundreds of them. No, Kisaki realized with a twinge of both shock and amusement, a full thousand – the blade's namesake.

Kisaki's eyes opened wide as the attack closed in on her foe, but not as wide as the daimao's. His miasma formed around him, quick as thought, just as the first of the magical blades reached him.

A few were deflected, but most cut through his defenses like butter.

Ichitiro screamed, the sound nearly deafening. Gone was the rage, the surprise. This was a cry of pure pain.

I hope there's enough there for every person you've hurt today!

Lightning crackled and more of the miasma formed, blocking Ichitiro from view as he continued to be assaulted by the Taiyosori's power. But still the screaming continued, the high-pitched keening wail of one who was used to dealing out pain but was a mere novice at experiencing it.

There came a massive burst of light and a crack of thunder as the last of the Taiyosori's attacks hit home. When it cleared, gone was the miasma. Left in its place was an unmoving figure wearing the cracked remains of celestial armor. Ichitiro floated where he was for a moment longer, then he plummeted to Earth.

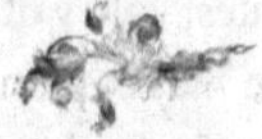

Kisaki wasted no time. She ran to where the daimao had fallen. A dust cloud rose as if he weighed a lot more than his size belied.

She dodged piles of rubble, burning debris, and leapt over craters left in the scarred Earth. She didn't allow herself the luxury of thinking him defeated, that the impossible had been done. The daimao were awesomely powerful and they recovered quickly.

Amazingly, Ichitiro was rising again even as she approached, although he appeared far less formidable than when he'd first arrived. His horns were a broken mess and a gash ran horizontal across one cheek, making it look as if he were grinning at her. Black blood leaked from a dozen or more wounds in his body, and his armor was in tatters. But he was still alive, and that meant he was dangerous.

Kisaki realized she was smart to be wary, for he struck out at her as she neared him, slashing with the razor sharp claws on his hands. It was an ugly attack, ungainly and with little grace to it, but it was backed by a frightening amount of strength. Kisaki dodged out of the way and the daimao struck a pile of rubble next to her, utterly pulverizing rock and sending a shower of dust falling onto them both.

He struck again with his other hand, catching her on the thigh and almost knocking her down.

She was beginning to breathe hard again. All of the power of the Taiyosori, all of the blood memories, they couldn't make up for the fact that Kisaki's body only had a finite amount of resources at her command, resources which she realized she was beginning to reach the limit of.

No matter which way it ended, this battle was nearing its conclusion.

Both combatants seemed to sense this. They engaged in heated combat, each attacking and alternately parrying in a dizzying array of moves. Ichitiro brought strength and speed to the fight, slashing, clawing, and grabbing, while Kisaki moved with deftness and grace, using skill to offset the advantage in raw power that he had over her.

It wasn't enough, though. Gradually, he began to force her back, put her on the defensive. One claw would strike out and she'd deflect it, only for the other to follow before she could mount a proper offense.

"Lady Kisaki!"

It was Shitoro, coming to her aid again, from the sound of things. If anything, she didn't mind the help this time. If the little youkai could do anything to distract her foe it would…

Sadly, it was she who was distracted. Whether by the sound of his voice or her allowing herself the momentary luxury of hope, Ichitiro took advantage of it. He swung at her and she moved to block, but it was a feint on his part. She hit nothing with the blade, the momentum pulling her off balance, allowing Ichitiro to slash her across the midsection.

This was no mere scratch. His claws went deep, digging four furrows across her stomach.

The pain was immediate and intense, as if he'd shredded her innards. She dropped to one knee and put a hand over her wounds, desperately hoping to keep her guts from spilling out onto the ground.

Kisaki heard Shitoro cry her name again, but it sounded muted, far away as if coming from the other end of a tunnel. She could only watch as Ichitiro threw a fireball past her. There came an explosion from outside her line of sight. She tried to turn to see what had happened to her faithful friend, but pain racked her body at the movement and she crumpled to the ground.

Ichitiro, injured as he was, stood above her triumphant. He stared down at her, then at the Taiyosori still in her hand. He bent to reach for it, greed showing plainly in his eyes, but then stopped short with a laugh.

"No, I think not," he said. "But do not fret, little hanyou. I shall claim it before your body has even begun to cool."

Kisaki let out a scream as he grabbed her by the hair and yanked her to her feet, forcing her to face him and exposing her throat. She gasped as he pulled back with his free hand and prepared to end this fight.

"You fought well but are nothing compared to the daimao. Go to your grave knowing this, and pray it is a lesson you learn for your next life."

Kisaki ignored his words as best as she could. She desperately tried to reach deep inside of herself, tried to force the world to slow down – hoping that either her mother or father had some wisdom to share that might help her in this, her most dire moment.

Sadly, they remained silent in her head. Perhaps they had no further insight to give her, or maybe it was their way of telling her that she'd failed them. Either way, she realized she had no one but herself to rely on.

Ichitiro began to bring his claws down, looking to take her head off with one swing.

In that moment, her eyes opened wide. However, it wasn't with fear, but realization.

Perhaps that *was* their final lesson. That there would be times when she could rely on nobody but herself. And if so, then her survival was entirely in her own hands.

Her hands. One was still covering her wounds, but in the other...

Time seemed to slow down ever so slightly, but no vision accompanied it. Only Ichitiro remained, his eyes shining with naked avarice as he moved to behead her and claim the prize he would no doubt use to set the heavens ablaze.

There was no time to think, only to act. Kisaki dropped, pulling with everything she had. She gritted her teeth, feeling as if she were about to be scalped, then threw back her arm and swung the sword above her.

It was a sloppy, desperate move, with almost no force behind it, but it wasn't meant to stop her vastly more powerful foe.

She sliced through her own hair just as his claws closed on her – freeing herself from his grasp. Her reward was a swoosh of air from above that told her time had resumed its normal pace. More importantly, Ichitiro had missed. So mighty had been his swing that he actually knocked himself off balance for a moment.

Fighting the crippling pain in her midsection, forcing it down for one final moment of defiance, Kisaki rolled and came up behind Ichitiro. He turned toward her a second too slow. She lifted the Taiyosori above her head with both hands, feeling her life's blood pouring out of her body and then, nearly blinded by pain, she brought it down with everything she had left, severing the daimao's right arm cleanly at the shoulder.

Steaming black blood sprayed from the wound, scalding hot against Kisaki's skin, but she barely felt it.

She and Ichitiro stared at each other silently for several more seconds, and then both toppled over.

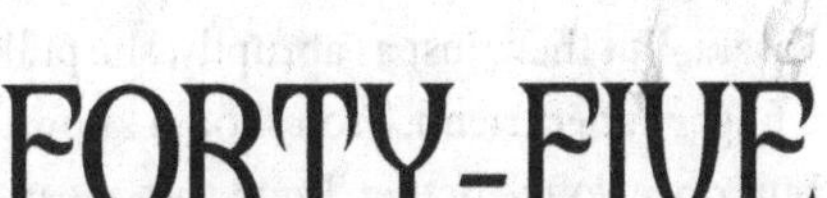

FORTY-FIVE

"**L**ADY KISAKI, DRINK this. Quickly, please."

"Is she going to be all right?"

"Step away from her, youkai. She must not be allowed to…"

"Oh, just shut the fuck up already."

"You would dare?"

"I agree with the human. We will have a reckoning once she is awake, but for now, do shut up. Shitoro, please continue."

Shitoro?!

Kisaki became aware of her head being lifted and something being poured down her throat. She choked, tried to cough it out, but the one administering it was persistent. "Stop fighting me, child, and do as you are told for once."

She obeyed, swallowing several large sips of a clean, sweet liquid. It was more of the water from the celestial palace, but how? She winced as her guts contracted but could feel the healing waters doing their job. After a few minutes, she felt strong enough to open her eyes.

Shitoro's smiling face was there to greet her.

"Are we dead?" she whispered.

"Hardly. I'll have you know, we tigers are quite nimble when it comes to dodging spells."

The little youkai wasn't alone, though, not by a long shot.

"She's awake!" Stephen cried, stepping into her field of vision along with another very familiar face.

"Thank goodness!" Tamiko dropped to her knees and hugged Kisaki. But then, just as abruptly, she pulled back and pointed a finger at her friend. "You should know that I'm kicking your butt once you're better. That was a mean trick you pulled."

"Needed … to save you," Kisaki replied, feeling stronger by the moment. It was going to be some time before her stomach stopped aching, but she felt much better than she had when she'd lopped off…

"Ichitiro!" She sat up with a start, grabbing hold of her midsection as the tiger youkai tried to steady her.

"Taken back to the celestial palace, my daughter, where he will be looked after and mended."

Kisaki recognized the voice at once. It was one she'd heard often, most recently from her own mouth. She glanced up again to find her mother standing over her. She was flanked by two other beings Kisaki had never seen before, but she instinctively recognized what they were if not who. Their regal, divine bearing gave them away – more of the daimao.

The pain of her wounds momentarily forgotten, Kisaki staggered back to her feet despite Shitoro's protests. "Mother."

"Greetings, my child," Midnite replied, her tone and expression both unreadable.

Kisaki did a double take between her mother, the other daimao, and her friends. "How?"

"It was your doing, hanyou," one of the daimao replied. He wore an exquisite layering of horns upon his head, curving around each other to almost form a crown of sorts. A long beard hung from his face, atop which red eyes glared out at her. They matched the long flowing robes he wore.

Wait … red? "That was … your crystal?"

The daimao's eyes narrowed at her, but her mother replied, "Yes. You managed to take one of Reiden's crystals when you fled the palace."

"I sensed it while we were in session," he said to Midnite, as if not quite willing to lower himself to talk to Kisaki directly. "A most rude interruption, but not as rude as the revelations brought to light shortly thereafter."

Midnite sighed at the rebuke but didn't seem overly bothered by it as she turned to face Kisaki again. "The … *circumstances* warranted I finally tell my siblings of your existence and what I suspected you might have taken."

"Thief," the other daimao hissed. She looked almost identical to Kisaki's mother save for her white hair and light-colored robes.

"I beg to differ, dear Hinode," Midnite replied. "We all know the Taiyosori cannot be stolen."

"Speaking of which," Stephen interrupted, pointing toward the ground nearby. "I think you dropped something."

"Do not touch that, human," Reiden commanded. "It would…"

"I know, destroy me."

"Your impudence grows tiresome, boy."

"As does your attitude toward my friend," Kisaki said before she could contain herself. Even she was surprised at the fire of her words.

Before the others could say anything, she half walked, half limped over to where the Taiyosori lay. She gestured toward it. "This is what you really came here for, is it not? This is why you broke your own edict."

"That is not true," Midnite replied, but Reiden pushed past her.

"I would certainly not have done so for the sake of one mere hanyou, an impurity at that."

"Take it, then," Kisaki said, meeting his gaze. Shitoro stepped forward to say something, but she raised a hand and stayed him. "You've come all this way for the Taiyosori. So claim it."

Reiden looked down upon the weapon for several long seconds but did not move.

"You can't, can you? But I can." Kisaki reached down and picked it up. She pointed it his way for a moment, causing him to flinch ever so slightly, but then she smiled and lowered the sword. The moment she did, it flashed brightly and turned back into a quill in her hand. Kisaki let out a small laugh once she saw what it had become.

We are definitely going to have to work on your timing.

After a moment, she grew serious again. "My mother is correct. The Taiyosori cannot be stolen, but it can be inherited. By virtue of my mother's blood running through my veins, I was able to take it." She turned to Midnite and held out the quill. "I am very sorry, Mother. I hope one day you can forgive me."

"There will be no forgiveness this day, hanyou," Reiden said before either could make a move. "If you know my edict, then perhaps you also know the crime your mother committed in bearing you. She is my sister and one with the celestial cycle. You are not. Thus, her crime becomes yours to bear, and the sentence for such a transgression is death."

Kisaki and Reiden locked eyes again. She could feel a similar disgust radiating from the other daimao, Hinode. Only her mother appeared to think differently, her expression still unreadable.

As the tension from their impasse grew, another voice answered them.

"Kick his ass, Midnight Girl!"

A moment later, others joined in.

"Yeah! Do it!"

"We've got your back!"

"Send those goddamned aliens back to wherever they came from."

She looked around and saw the citizens of the town, impossibly still alive, step out from hiding and approach them. Police, soldiers, and regular folks alike, all of them cheering for her. She barely concealed a smile when she noted Beth and Chuck among them, still recording on their camera.

Kisaki felt myriad emotions as they cheered her on. There was shame, because she knew she'd been responsible for bringing this destruction down upon them. However, mixed in it was pride for mankind. For an eternity, the human race had been looked down upon by demonkind. The daimao themselves considered them little more than pests. What happened here today was an eventuality that would have come to pass one day regardless of whether she'd come or not.

And with that realization came another. If she hadn't been here to stop him, Ichitiro almost surely would not have confined his destruction to this one small town. Many more would have felt his wrath. And, judging by the attitudes of the other daimao, his siblings would have done little to curb his efforts.

But that had all changed. As odd as she found them, thanks to Beth and the other reporters who had descended upon this town, word of the existence of youkai, mazoku, and daimao would spread and humanity would once more be made aware of them. That was only half of it, though. The people of this world would also know that they were not helpless in the face of such threats.

Kisaki smiled as she realized she'd become what she'd always admired. She was now a warrior, here to help those in need. These people needed her and, glancing at Tamiko and Stephen, she realized she needed them, too.

She faced Reiden and pointed the quill at him, causing him to take a measured step back. "My life is not yours to judge, daimao. Nor are theirs. You may think yourself superior to me in every way, but know that this day, a hanyou laid low a daimao on the field of battle. Word of this will spread. If you wish to punish me for that or for the transgression of being born of a human warrior, then realize his blood, too, flows in my veins. I do not pretend to think that I can defeat even one of you, much less all, but if you choose this path, then know that I stand before you until my dying breath."

There was a tense moment in which Kisaki became certain she'd soon be fighting not one, but three daimao, including her mother, but no attack came. Neither of the two who had come with Midnite seemed to have the spark of battle among them that Ichitiro did. As for her mother, Kisaki noted she had raised one eyebrow but was otherwise still unreadable.

She had a sinking feeling she'd just consigned herself to an eternity of study, but realized perhaps it didn't need to be that way. She'd started something and now she needed to finish it.

Kisaki lowered the quill and said, "Go. Return to the celestial palace. Put your edict back in place. Do as you must, but leave this planet alone. The people here are no longer your playthings. They have grown strong and are capable of defending themselves. And now they have me standing by their side. Tell the others that the Earth is now under the protection of Midnight Girl."

Kisaki felt a flush rise to her cheeks even as she said it. She hadn't meant to call herself that. It had just slipped out and, once it had, she realized how ridiculous it sounded. No laughter followed, though. Reiden and Hinode continued to glare at her. Stephen and Tamiko, however, both wore big grins on their faces as they moved to stand next to her.

After several more tense moments, Reiden turned to the others. "So be it. We shall tend to our brother and then," he glared at Midnite, "we shall discuss these matters at length."

"As you wish, brother," Midnite replied.

The two other daimao moved to stand together, but Midnite remained where she was.

"Are you coming, sister?" Reiden asked.

"In a moment."

"Very well, but only a moment, no more. The edict for this planet and its inhabitants still remains." He said that last with a sidelong glance, and not a friendly one either, at Kisaki.

Then, in a flash of brilliant red light, the two daimao disappeared, leaving Kisaki, her friends, and her mother. The crowd around them let out a loud cheer and began chanting "Midnight Girl!" over and over again.

Midnite turned to Kisaki's two human friends, her voice audible despite the cheers of the crowd. "Would you mind giving me a moment with my daughter?"

"Go right ahead," Stephen said.

Tamiko nodded, too, and they both stepped back.

All at once, the cheering abruptly ceased. In fact, Kisaki noted, it seemed all sound had. She looked around and found her friends, as well as all the humans present, unmoving as if they'd been frozen in place. Only she, her mother, and Shitoro appeared unaffected.

"Did you…?"

"Of course," Midnite replied. "But I can only do so for a few moments, at least before my siblings realize what is happening and no doubt return to investigate."

"You can freeze time?"

"All of the daimao are powerful, but each has unique gifts as well," Shitoro said proudly. "This is your mother's."

Kisaki laughed as the realization hit. Time seemed to slow for her whenever a vision struck. She'd thought it a trick of her mind but now had to wonder whether it was yet another gift she'd inherited.

"What is so humorous, child?"

"Nothing, Mother. My apologies." After a beat, she added, "For a great many things. I regret my actions and that they have brought dishonor to you."

Her mother stepped forward, her face a mask of neutrality. For a moment, Kisaki wondered if she meant to strike her. If so, she deserved it. But instead, her mother pulled her into a hug.

"You are safe. That is all that matters to me. As for your so-called transgressions, I believe it is fair that we share the blame. Had I not been so overzealous in my need to protect you, perhaps you would not have sought to leave in the manner you did."

"But I stole…"

Midnite held up a finger to her daughter's lips. "You forged your own path, as is your right." The corners of her mouth raised in a smile. "And you did it spectacularly."

"You're not mad?"

"I was never angry. I was merely worried for your safety."

"But the daimao, Ichitiro…"

"My brother will recover in time." Midnite looked away for a moment. "I will not lie. He is not one to let such a defeat go unchallenged. However, he will also have to answer to the divine court for his actions. I do not think he will find it so easy to convince us to dismiss what he has done. Attempting to take the Taiyosori by force, knowing that it was here without telling the rest of us, defying the edict. All of these must be answered to the satisfaction of the council."

"But if he does…"

"Reiden loves his ceremony, so I have little doubt these matters will keep us busy for some time to come. But I urge caution nevertheless. Do not think the others will forget about you or what has been said here today."

Kisaki nodded her head solemnly.

"Before this day, my brethren considered Earth to be a threat to us. Now they will fear it more than ever. I wish I could tell you there was no danger, but I cannot. You have disrupted the celestial cycle." She put a hand on her daughter's shoulder. "Mind you, perhaps it was in need of disruption. Alas, I cannot promise I'll be able to convince my siblings of that. Fortunately for the people here, the Earth now has a mighty protector, well-armed for the task."

That reminded Kisaki of what she'd meant to do. She held out the quill to her mother. "It's yours. I took it without permission and beg forgiveness."

To her surprise, though, Midnite laughed and waved her off. "The Taiyosori belongs to you now. Much to the amazement of all, including myself, it has chosen you as its new master. And, judging from the outcome of the battle, it chose well."

"But … I stole it."

"Inherited it," her mother corrected. "You are my heir, something you have proven time and again this day. The Taiyosori knew this. Otherwise, it would have rejected you. But if it makes you feel better, then I gift it willingly to you before the ever-seeing eyes of the elder gods."

Kisaki wasn't sure what to say for a moment, but after several seconds, she simply smiled and stuffed the quill into her belt.

"An interesting disguise for it," Midnite remarked. "Your doing?"

Kisaki shrugged. "It was the first thing I thought of when I took it."

Now it was Midnite's turn to nod. "It's funny."

"What is, Mother?"

"For a long time, I wondered why it was bequeathed to me by its former master, but now I think I understand."

"Oh?"

"He told me the fate of the sword would depend upon the strength of my blood. I cannot be certain, but I think perhaps it was always meant for you. Use it wisely, my child. Protect this world and your friends." She stepped in and hugged her daughter again. "I dare say, they will need it."

Midnite backed up a step and Shitoro moved to her side before addressing Kisaki. "It has been an honor, my lady."

"And it will continue to be," Midnite said with a grin.

The tiger demon looked up at her. "Excuse me, mistress?"

"You are staying here, Shitoro."

"*What?!*"

"You are my daughter's guardian, are you not?"

"Well, yes, my lady. But..."

"And I do not recall excusing you from that duty. Do you?"

"No, my lady."

Midnite placed a hand upon his head. "There you have it, then. My daughter needs to protect this world, but I need someone to protect her. I can think of no one better suited for the task."

Shitoro let out a sigh but said, "I will do my best."

"I know you will. Take these." She bent down and handed a few black crystals to the youkai. "Use them wisely ... and sparingly."

"I will endeavor to keep them safe."

Midnite nodded, then turned away from them both. Light began to gather around her. Right before disappearing, she glanced over her shoulder toward her daughter.

"Midnight Girl. I think I like that. Quite fitting."

Time resumed its normal flow just as quickly as it had stopped, leaving Kisaki's friends a little dumbfounded.

"Um, where did your mom go?" Stephen asked.

"Home," she replied before turning to Tamiko. "Speaking of which, I sent you to yours. Why are you not there?"

"You mean you tricked us there," Tamiko said. "That wasn't nice."

"I'm sorry, but, as I said, I wanted you to be safe."

"Well, you ended up sending us right to the middle of the lobby. Let's just say I had a bit of explaining to do with Dad about where I'd been and why I appeared out of thin air with a strange boy."

"He didn't seem all that pleased to meet me," Stephen added.

"What happened then?"

"What happened?" Tamiko echoed. "Your mom and her friends zapped in a short while after that. Dad had his hands full trying to explain to the guests that it was all part of an improvised show."

"I think they bought it," Stephen said.

"He isn't the resort manager for nothing." Tamiko turned back to Kisaki. "Once we realized who they were, there was no way I was letting them leave without bringing us."

Stephen nodded. "I'm pretty sure the scary one in red wanted to blast us, but your mom was cool, especially after we told her we were friends of yours."

"Yes, I think she is cool, too," Kisaki replied with a smile. "But what of your father, Tamiko?"

"I think he understood that we kind of needed to get back to your side. Although he did mention that he was going to add international minutes to my phone plan, which means he's going to bug me nonstop about staying safe. But for now, here I am."

"I'm glad."

"Me too," Tamiko replied. "But you'd better not try that again. I mean it."

"Yeah," Stephen added. "That was total BS."

Kisaki held up her hands in a placating manner, glad to have made such fierce friends. "I was wrong to send you away. I beg your forgiveness."

After a moment, Tamiko glanced at Stephen and they both smiled. "Well, maybe this one time."

"This is all fine and well," Shitoro said with a sniff. "But what now?"

"I guess we go back to my place," Stephen said. "Hopefully, it's still there. That guy really did a job on this town."

Kisaki nodded ruefully and surveyed the area. The destruction was terrible indeed, but at least the battle was over. Even now, she saw people helping each other to make sense of it all. "Whatever is needed to be done, I will help. It's the least I can do."

"I have a feeling it's gonna take quite a while."

"Earth is my home now," Kisaki said. "I believe I have quite a while. And if anything else attempts mischief here in the meantime, I'll deal with it."

"Spoken like a true superhero," Stephen replied.

"Does that make us her sidekicks?" Tamiko asked with a laugh.

"I am no sidekick," Shitoro said, crossing his arms in front of him. "I am Kisaki's guardian, but I, too, will do what I can."

"Awesome." Stephen bent down and clapped him on the shoulder. "And maybe my mom will even let you stay with us … once we get you a flea collar."

"How many times must I say it? I am not a cat!"

Kisaki and her friends laughed. After a few moments, Shitoro joined them.

It was well deserved.

They'd survived the impossible and, in doing so, set in motion events that would potentially change the world. Within a few days at most, Kisaki suspected, word would spread and mankind would realize they weren't alone in this vast multiverse.

It would be a time of uncertainty for this planet and its inhabitants. There was no telling what the future held – whether more monsters would emerge from the forests or whether the daimao would return seeking revenge.

But whatever happened, Kisaki vowed the brave people of this world would also know that it had a defender to protect it – Midnight Girl – and she would do everything in her power to keep her new home safe.

ABOUT THE AUTHOR

RICK GUALTIERI lives alone in central New Jersey with only his wife, three kids, and countless pets to both keep him company and constantly plot against him. When he's not busy monkey-clicking out words, he can typically be found jealously guarding his collection of vintage Transformers from all who would seek to defile them.

Defilers beware!

RICK GUALTIERI IS THE AUTHOR OF:

Bill The Vampire (The Tome of Bill – 1)
Night Stalker: A Tale From The Tome Of Bill
Scary Dead Things (The Tome of Bill – 2)
The Mourning Woods (The Tome of Bill – 3)
Holier Than Thou (The Tome of Bill – 4)
Sunset Strip: A Tale From The Tome Of Bill
Goddamned Freaky Monsters (The Tome of Bill – 5)
Half A Prayer (The Tome of Bill – 6)
The Wicked Dead (The Tome of Bill – 7)
Shining Fury: A Tale From The Tome Of Bill
The Last Coven (The Tome of Bill – 8)
Bigfoot Hunters

GLOSSARY

A COMPILATION of notable terms with pronunciations and descriptions

Daimao (*die-mou*) – Demons representing the second tier of divinity. Second in power only to the elder gods, they primarily reside within the realm of the celestial palace. They are considered the custodians of the multiverse, ruling in the place of the Elder Gods. The thirteen most powerful make up a ruling body known as the celestial court.

Mazoku (mah-zoh-koo) – Demons representing the third tier of divinity. Less powerful than the daimao, but often far more powerful than youkai. They often serve as generals and field commanders to the daimao.

Oni (oh-knee) – Troll-like demons, roughly equal in power to the mazoku. They favor strength and stamina over intelligence or use of magic.

Youkai (*yoh-kigh*) – Demons representing the lowest acknowledged level of divinity. They are the most numerous of demonkind, appearing in all shapes and forms, but are considered the weakest.

Hanyou (han-yoh) – Hanyou can mean a mixing of demon castes, for example the offspring of a mazoku and a youkai. More commonly, it is a derogatory term for the mixed offspring of demons and mortal species such as humans.

Midnite (midnight) – One of the daimao and a member of the celestial court. Midnite stands out from her peers by having been gifted the legendary Taiyosori by the elder gods. She appears as a beautiful woman of Asian descent with long black hair and dark eyes. A delicate row of horns upon her head is the only outward indication of her demonic heritage.

Taiyosori (tie-oh-sore-ee) – The legendary blade of heaven, also known as the sword of a thousand cuts. Most of what is known about this weapon is lost to myth and legend, but it is very old and powerful. It appears as a broad sword with a gleaming white handle and a smoky translucent blade seemingly filled with miniature stars.

Ichitiro (ee-chi-tier-oh) – One of the daimao. Ichitiro most closely resembles the western concept of classic demons and devils. He is considered the closest analogy to a war god among the daimao.

Kisaki (kiss-ah-key) – The half-human offspring of the daimao Midnite. Kisaki is approximately seventy years old, but has the appearance and mannerisms of a teenaged human female of mixed descent. Her birth and existence has been kept a secret from the other daimao … until now.

Shitoro (she-tour-oh) – A small youkai who takes the form of a bipedal albino tiger. A faithful servant to Midnite, Shitoro is over two thousand years old and skilled in a variety of subjects and magical disciplines.

Tamiko (tah-me-koh) – Tamiko Yoshida is the only child of Hiroto Yoshida, current manager of the Kabira Bay Resort located on the island of Ishigachi. She's 15 years old, and possesses an outgoing personality, a result of her time spent living and working in the resort.

Reiden (ray-den) – The oldest of the daimao and current proctor of the celestial court. Reiden appears as an old man clothed in regal red robes. He has red eyes and an outcropping of intertwined horns atop his head that resembles a crown.

Hinode (hin-noh-day) – Twin sister of Midnite, daimao, and member of the celestial court. Hinode appears as almost a mirror opposite of Midnite, possessing stark white hair and preferring to dress in light colors.

Ito (ee-toh) – A ferret youkai who serves Ichitiro. Ito is disliked among the other servants of the celestial palace due to his penchant for stealing objects that don't belong to him.

Tanaki (tah-nah-key) – A badger youkai in the service of Midnite. What she lacks in humor, she more than makes up for in efficiency.

Rokusan (roh-koo-sahn) – One of the daimao and a member of the celestial court.

Kaokatta (kay-oh-kah-tah) – A sword forged and wielded by Ichitiro. The Kaokatta resembles a large notched scimitar seemingly made of black flame. It burns hot enough to melt through most metals like butter.

Sensuru (sen-sue-rue) – One of the most feared of the Taiyosori's powers. When activated, the thousand "stars" visible within the Taiyosori's blade leap forth and form projectiles made of pure divine energy.

Ishigachi (ee-she-ga-chee) – Also known as Ishigaki. A Japanese island west of Okinawa. Considered by the daimao to be one of the "blessed isles".

Sata Andagi (sah-tah an-dah-ghee) – Sweet deep fried buns of dough, native to the island of Okinawa.

BONUS CHAPTER
MIDNITE'S LEGACY

K ISAKI CONCENTRATED WITH everything she had left, putting every ounce of her remaining focus to work. Deep down, though, she knew it wouldn't be nearly enough. She'd done the impossible, defeated one of the daimao, but she had a feeling the foe before her would not be so easily bested.

"Well, young miss?" Shitoro asked. "I'm waiting."

"Um, the Carnoterians revolted against their Janjanbi masters because … they wished for self-rule and freedom of expression?"

Shitoro narrowed his eyes and began tapping his clawed fingers upon the desk at which Kisaki sat. "Freedom of expression? Need I remind you that the Carnoterians are an insectoid race with a hive mind? They rose up because the Janjanbi accidentally exterminated their queen, a fact you would know if you put your feeble intellect to work studying instead of staring out the window."

Kisaki threw her arms up in frustration. "I know, and I'm sorry, Shitoro. It's just that we've been at it for seven hours and I'm bored."

The tiger demon let out a sigh. "Tell me, child, what did you think would happen when your mother left us on this backwater world?"

"That we'd work together to protect the people of this fine planet."

"I see." Shitoro continued to tap on her desk. "And how, may I ask, do you plan to protect anything if you are ignorant of even the most basic facts of the multiverse?"

"Basic facts? Those creatures don't even exist in this dimension!"

"A flimsy excuse if ever I've heard one."

Kisaki leaned back and stretched. The dual nature of her relationship with Shitoro could be maddening at times. On the field of battle she was firmly in charge … mostly anyway. But the moment it came time to stand down, his thoughts immediately turned back to her studies. The situation wasn't helped by the fact that her mother's chief servant, Tanaki, had recently paid them a visit, delivering to Shitoro a small mountain of lesson scrolls.

Wasn't this half the reason she'd fled the palace to begin with? Now, here she was, on Earth, but once more relegated to being a veritable prisoner. Her only solace was that she'd made friends here. If only she could have seen them more often than she was allowed. Speaking of which… "Can I please have my iPad back when we are finished?"

"And what use could you possibly have for that contraption?"

"I want to Facetime Tamiko later. See how she's doing?"

Shitoro raised an eyebrow. "Why you feel the need to view that human's face is beyond me. Personally, I don't see the appeal."

Kisaki blew out a pained breath. Some things never seemed to change.

Following the massive cleanup effort in Cartersville, Tamiko's father had requested that she return home. She had her own studies to get back to and, as he pointed out, technically she was in the United States illegally. He wanted her home to continue her schooling, and also so he could work on ensuring that when next she visited Kisaki she wouldn't necessarily need to use magic to cross the border.

All of this had been confusing at first, but gradually Kisaki had come to learn that the myriad nations of this planet were in many ways like the rooms she'd been confined to in the celestial palace. If one did not possess the proper permission, then one was not permitted to leave. Of course, an entire country was a bit different than a mere wing of a palace. Nevertheless, once the shock of their existence had worn off, others began to bring up that same point regarding Kisaki and Shitoro.

Thankfully, they'd had no shortage of supporters in the days following Ichitiro's defeat. Even now, one of them, a purveyor of the law, was elsewhere fighting for what he called their "God-given rights".

Kisaki wasn't sure which of the elder gods he represented, but she could only hope his battle was more interesting than today's history lesson.

She and the tiger demon locked eyes in a silent test of wills until finally Shitoro appeared to relent. "Very well."

"Yes!"

"We will continue for only three more hours today, then you may have a small break."

"Three hours?!"

"Yes, unless you would prefer I send a communique to your mother asking her opinion on the matter." Kisaki's crestfallen face was apparently all the answer he needed. "Oh, do stop pouting, child. Once we are finished, you are free to converse with your pet human. See if she has learned any new tricks."

It was better than nothing.

Kisaki had just resigned herself to a slow death by boredom when the door to the small apartment flew open and her friend Stephen stepped in.

Shitoro glared at him, no doubt annoyed that his lesson was being interrupted, but Stephen ignored him. He walked past them both, to the window looking down onto the street below, closed the blinds, then opened them again a crack to peek out.

"We have discussed this before, human. Kisaki's lessons are not to be disturbed."

"Shh," Stephen hissed. He looked out again, then turned back to them. "Okay. I don't think he followed me."

"Who?" Kisaki stood up from her desk, grateful that he was there. "What's wrong?"

Stephen paused for a moment, as if considering what to say, then replied, "I don't know. I'm probably just being stupid."

"If you're expecting me to be surprised by that confession, you're in for disappointment," Shitoro muttered.

Kisaki approached her friend and looked out the window, too, seeing nothing but an empty street.

Stephen inclined his head and shrugged. "Like I said, probably me just being paranoid. You remember how there were tons of reporters converging on this place after you kicked that Ichitiro guy's ass?"

"They made the cleanup effort more difficult than it needed to be."

"Exactly," he replied. "Well, we still get them on occasion. Usually they'll snoop around, see if they can find anyone who's willing to talk about you, and then leave once they get bored."

Kisaki nodded. "Captain Coulson has been most generous in keeping us from being overly inundated."

"Yeah, well, usually they're easy to spot. But today some guy approached me who I hadn't seen before. At first, I thought maybe he was from my high school, someone I just didn't recognize, but he immediately started in on me."

"How so?" Shitoro asked, having apparently accepted that his lesson was over for now.

"He walked right up to me and said, 'I saw you on the news. You know where to find her.'"

Shitoro made a dismissive sound. "Probably another one of those … what did you call them … ah yes, fanboys."

Stephen shook his head. "That's what I thought at first. So I played dumb." He noticed the way Shitoro was smirking. "Don't start with me, fleabag. I told him I didn't know who he was talking about, so he said and I quote, 'tell me where I can find the hanyou called Midnight Girl.'"

Kisaki perked up at that. It wasn't a term she'd heard many humans use. "He said that word, hanyou?"

"Yep. And that's not all. Maybe it's just me, but there was something off about him. It's weird, he looked like a regular guy, nothing intimidating about him, but he was putting off this vibe that was making the hairs on the back of my neck stand up."

"So what did you do?"

"Told him again that I didn't know what he was talking about, then I walked away. Waited until he was out of sight, then I hightailed it back here. Cut across a bunch of lawns and hopped a few fences to make sure he didn't follow me."

"And yet you still managed to do a piss poor job of it," a voice coolly replied from just outside the apartment door.

All eyes turned that way as a teenaged boy, roughly Stephen's age in appearance stepped uninvited through the doorway. By all appearances he was dressed rather unremarkably – wearing jeans, a button down shirt, and a light jacket. Short black hair sat atop a tanned face. Then Kisaki saw his eyes. They had a slight cant to them, hinting at perhaps a mixed heritage, but it was both their color and intensity which froze her in her tracks. Appearing a muddy brown in the shadow of the doorway, once he stepped inside into the light, the dark red color of his irises became evident. They reminded Kisaki of the color of blood.

Whatever hold his gaze had over her apparently didn't affect Shitoro. He stepped right up and pointed a clawed finger at the stranger. "I will warn you, human, crossing our threshold unbidden can result in nothing save your immediate…"

"Step aside, youkai. My business is not with you."

Yellow sparks of energy began to gather around Shitoro, his attempt at being intimidating. "You arrogant lout, I will…" His words trailed off as Kisaki watched his nose working. "What the? You…"

"Are not your concern." He placed a hand atop Shitoro's head, ignoring the magical energy crackling off the little youkai's body, and pushed him to the side.

Stephen balled his fist and made to step in front of Kisaki, but she put out a hand to stay him. "You say you have business with me. Speak it now."

The newcomer stared into Kisaki's eyes and simply stated, "You're the hanyou they call Midnight Girl."

"My name is Kisaki."

The stranger's neutral expression instantly changed into a grin. "Thank goodness, because that other name … no offence, but it's pretty fucking bad."

Kisaki wasn't sure what to think. This wasn't how a foe typically acted, but his blunt nature didn't exactly suggest friend either. "It was not a title of my choosing."

He nodded. "I know how that is. I've been saddled with my fair share of stupid nicknames over the years. Amazing what people will come up with, isn't it? Well, that's neither here nor there. What matters is you've managed to become quite famous in a very short time, Kisaki."

"Also not my choice."

"Hey, pal," Stephen said, "if you're looking for an autograph you could have just asked."

"You mistake my motivation, child, I … I would not do that if I were you." He pointed a finger toward Shitoro who was preparing another spell. "This jacket is aniline leather and I would much prefer to not get it wet."

Shitoro glanced toward Kisaki and she gave him a single nod of her head. She had no idea what this person wanted, but she preferred they not be the ones to initiate hostilities.

"Thank you," the teen said to her. "As I was saying, I'm not here for an autograph or a picture. If anything, I'm already quite famous enough myself."

"Really?" Stephen asked with a quick laugh. "Sorry, but I'm pretty sure I've never heard of you."

"Haven't you? I had thought the Bible was quite popular in this area of the world. It makes prominent mention of me and the unfortunate fate met by my brother, albeit it greatly bastardized the details."

"Are you shitting us?"

"What's a Bible?" Shitoro asked. "And what has it got to do with you, hanyou?"

Kisaki turned to him, eyes wide. "He's a hanyou, too?"

"I could smell it on him, my lady."

The teen ignored Shitoro as he took a step closer to Kisaki. "I'm not just any hanyou. They call me Cain – the forever cursed, the marked, the first son of man. I have walked this Earth for over four-thousand years, tasked with but one duty by my father – to hunt down and exterminate others like me."

MIDNITE'S LEGACY

COMING SOON

www.ingramcontent.com/pod-product-compliance
Lightning Source LLC
Chambersburg PA
CBHW011203190726
48286CB00009B/2892